4

BLOOD BARGAIN

"Maria Lima captures the essence of urban fantasy, mystery, and romantic elements in *Blood Bargain*."

—SF Site

"A real pager-turner. . . . Ms. Lima has created a wonderful blend of paranormal, mystery and romance. She has a real knack for building characters you get to know and care about, and the setting she paints seems so real. She is also darn good at building suspense and keeping you guessing."

—Bitten By Books (5 stars)

"Lima uses well-known tropes of the fantasy genre, yet gives them enough of a spin to make them recognizable to readers but keep them wondering if things will play out as expected."

—SF Revu

"Urban fantasy fans are going to love this—especially the Kelly clan, an extended family of supernaturals living within human society. . . . A strong tale that fans of Kelly Armstrong and Kim Harrison will want to read."

—Worlds of Wonder

"I couldn't put it down. Maria Lima's second Blood Lines novel is even better than the first, a fun and sometimes poignant paranormal treat." —Fantasy Literature

"Grabs you from the start and keeps you turning pages until you solve the mystery. . . . I certainly will be watching for more books by Maria Lima." —Fresh Fiction

"Ms. Lima spins a suspenseful tale and packs it with paranormal elements that will hold the reader's attention to the end . . . fast-moving." —Darque Reviews

MATTERS OF THE BLOOD

"Dark, seductive, and bitingly humorous. . . ."

—Heartstring

"Fast paced, take no prisoners action . . . grabs you by the throat from the go and doesn't release its grip until you're done." —Preternatural Reviews (4 stars)

"An absolutely spectacular addition to the paranormal landscape. . . . A classy, teasing tale riddled with intrigue and paranormal bliss." —BookFetish

"A complex plot with the requisite twists and turns of a mystery, the passion of a paranormal romance, and the unearthly elements of urban fantasy." —SF Site

"A great page-turner. . . ." —The Bookshelf Reviews

"An excellent book, readable and gripping with varied characters. . . ." —Curled Up With a Good Book (5 stars)

"A brilliant tale of supernatural power, revenge, and the excitement of newfound love." —Darque Reviews

"Refreshing . . . I loved the story's vividly drawn rural-Texas setting." —FantasyLiterature (4 stars)

"Another kick-ass heroine enters the paranormal arena in Lima's bloodthirsty whodunit. Feisty Keira narrates with a biting sense of humor. . . ." —*Romantic Times* (4 stars)

"A superb paranormal whodunit with a touch of romance and with plenty of interwoven subplots . . . but the center holding this superb tale together is the likable Keira, who makes the abnormal seem so normal."

—Alternative Worlds

**Don't miss the three previous adventures in the
Blood Lines series by Maria Lima!**

Matters of the Blood
Blood Bargain
Blood Kin

BLOOD HEAT

MARIA LIMA

POCKET BOOKS
New York London Toronto Sydney

Pocket Books
A Division of Simon & Schuster, Inc.
1230 Avenue of the Americas
New York, NY 10020

This book is a work of fiction. Names, characters, places, and incidents either are products of the author's imagination or are used fictitiously. Any resemblance to actual events or locales or persons, living or dead, is entirely coincidental.

First Juno Books/Pocket Books paperback edition November 2010

JUNO BOOKS and colophon are trademarks of Wildside Press LLC used under license by Simon & Schuster, Inc., the publisher of this work.

POCKET and colophon are registered trademarks of Simon & Schuster, Inc.

For information about special discounts for bulk purchases, please contact Simon & Schuster Special Sales at 1-866-506-1949 or business@simonandschuster.com.

The Simon & Schuster Speakers Bureau can bring authors to your live event. For more information or to book an event contact the Simon & Schuster Speakers Bureau at 1-866-248-3049 or visit our website at www.simonspeakers.com.

Designed by Julie Adams
Cover design by Laywan Kwan

Manufactured in the United States of America

10 9 8 7 6 5 4 3 2 1

ISBN 978-1-4391-6777-9
ISBN 978-1-4391-6778-6 (ebook)

*This one is for librarians everywhere,
especially to my sister and her lovely
colleagues at the Rita and Truett Smith Public
Library in Wylie, Texas.
You-all rock!*

ACKNOWLEDGMENTS

As always, a very special thanks and shout-out to my beta readers, Carla Coupe and Tanya Kennedy Luminati. Though time was tight, you guys gave me some great feedback!

To my brilliant editor, Paula Guran, who keeps me sane, kicks my ass when needed, and generally makes me write better. You are a Goddess!

To friend and colleague Janna Marks for football data plus her patient support of my craziness . . . and thanks for the use of your maiden name and of your husband's name. I hope he likes being a Texas Ranger.

Thanks to Adrian Turner for details about hip pads, girdles, butt pads, and all those lovely masculine parts of a football uniform.

This book would have been much less if it hadn't been for my sister, Laura Condit, for her tirelessness in making sure I got to go to a Texas high school football stadium and refresh my memories of umpteen years ago. Her patience and careful planning for my Dallas trip ensured I really got to re-immerse myself in Texas.

Thanks again to Amber Chalmers for her assistance with the Welsh language. *Diolch yn fawr!*

To Charlie Higginbotham from the International Association of Chiefs of Police for information about deputy sheriffs and their conference. Unfortunately, I wasn't able to use most of the data, but it was greatly appreciated.

To Jessica Parsley, for allowing me to use her as a vampire.

To Jane Miller, who donated to Doorways for Women and Families and became a character in the book.

A very special thanks to Mark and Nick Ashkar, owners of the Plaza Deli in Arlington, Virginia, who aren't werewolves . . . at least as far as I know. They do, however, make a mean milkshake and killer sandwiches. Sorry, Nick, that your name was too close to one of my ongoing characters, so I renamed you "Lev."

I borrowed the name of Hills and Dales, a great place for a good brew. The real roadhouse is in San Antonio, right off 1604 and near UTSA. Years ago, before La Cantera existed, we'd drive out to the then boonies to find beers you couldn't get anywhere else.

Note: the Brotherhood of the White Rock in this book is entirely fictional and has no connections to the Christian group The White Rock Fund, or any other actual group.

I can do you blood and love without the rhetoric, and I can do you blood and rhetoric without the love, and I can do you all three concurrent or consecutive, but I can't do you love and rhetoric without the blood. Blood is compulsory—they're all blood, you see.

—Tom Stoppard, *Rosencrantz and Guildenstern Are Dead*

The past is never dead. It's not even past.

—William Faulkner, *Requiem for a Nun*

Paid â chodi pais ar ôl piso.

—Welsh proverb (Literal translation: *Don't lift a petticoat after pissing;* English translation: *Don't close the barn door after the horses are gone*)

There's tempting fate, then there's giving it a lap dance.

—Tom Bodett on *Wait Wait, Don't Tell Me*

Mais, hélas! qui ne sait que ces loups doucereux De tous les loups sont les plus dangereux?

—Charles Perrault, "Le Petit Chaperon Rouge"

PROLOGUE

Old Joe

No one ever really knew where old Joe came from. Sometimes, he doesn't really remember himself. He's always just been around.

Joe's Trash, proclaims the meticulously hand-lettered sign on the side of the ancient black Ford pickup. Worn wooden slats—once painted white, but now a soft charcoal—cage the truck bed, making a place to hold the stuff he collects. Trash, not garbage. He doesn't take food, organic stuff. Most of the folks who hire his service use that for composting anyhow.

He's been doing this since he can recall, making the rounds every morning and every afternoon. To Leonora's Beauty Shoppe, where the second "p" on the sign is a little crooked because Leo's husband, Ray, got into an argument with her during the painting of it, telling her that plain ole "shop" was good enough for his ma and gran. How come it weren't good enough for his wife? They ain't never got round to fixing it and sometimes, if you squint at it at just the right angle, the sloppy "p" looks like one of them computer emoti-things that Ernie's kids tried to explain to him one time. Like a scrunched-up face sticking its tongue out at you. No matter, though. The white paint on the sign is flaking and the red letters fading after years of scorching in the Texas sun. Ray keeps promising Leonora that he'll fix the sign, touch it up, but since he's been saying that for the past eight years, Joe reckons it's just one of those things married couples say to each other; a conversation more habit than heard.

Joe picks up old towels, empty plastic squeeze bottles, and all sorts of trash from Miz Leo's. Even old plastic capes and used-up hair rollers and such.

Next door to the beauty shop is the package store; just an eighteen-by-twenty hole-in-the-wall with a liquor license. Manny Hernandez owns the place and has Joe haul off all the cardboard boxes, packing materials, and other stuff that comes in shipping. Some he can resell, some he just uses to store things in.

After the liquor store and the beauty shop, Joe goes around to several different houses, some in the subdivisions. Then it's out to some of the outlying ranches. Those, he only hits about once a week or so. Ranchers are the best at separating out the trash from the garbage. Sir Andrew (who wasn't really a "sir" but came from England, so the name stuck) and his wife, Carla, of the Coupe Ranch are his favorites. They've made up several plastic bins and labeled them: one for scrap metal, one for glass and bottles, one for cardboard and paper, and another for plastics. They're always real careful sorting so Joe doesn't have to.

Joe takes his time going to and coming back from the ranches, stopping at scenic lookout points and wide areas in the road to pick up cans and bottles left by the day-trippers and the passers-through.

At the end of the month, after everything is sorted, he makes his trips into Cedar Springs to the recycling center and drops off everything that can go there. Two days a week he's at his roadside stand: JOE'S TRASH, the sign reads, just like on the truck. From hubcaps to cabling to mysterious boxes of assorted odds and ends, the stand pretty much has something for everyone. He mostly gets tourists in the summer, stopping to ask for directions or to ask where the nearest toilet is. He's got an outhouse out back of the shed, but he doesn't let 'em use it. Makes 'em go next door into Hills and Dales. Man has to have some standards. Tourists usually drive up in monster SUVs, all decked out in multiple coats of shiny paint, screaming to anyone who looks that they've got more money than them crooks at Enron and less taste than a drunk after a bottle of cheap tequila.

If they do stop to buy, the men's gazes just slide right past his ebony face; he can almost hear them thinking "boy" or the word his foster mama taught him never to say. Sometimes if it was dusk, they'd miss him entirely, his deep dark face blending into the shadows, his soft white curls cut tight to the scalp. *Just another shadow,* he'd think to himself. *Like I always been. Just another shadow boy.* Don't know where he come from, don't know who he is. Just been here all along. He watches them peer into the dim shed, then smiles, white teeth flashing, startling each and every one. They'd always buy something then, usually some stupid-ass piece of tourist crap that someone else had already thrown out. Guilt, fright, whatever. Got them every single damned time.

He's old enough to remember Pappy Joe, no relation, sitting in the same rocking chair, making nice to the stuck-up bastards from the city as they tried to cheat him out of a dime or a quarter for some piece of stupid-ass junk as they drove up in their swooping huge Chevys, Fords, and Olds. Pappy Joe would just laugh and laugh after the tourists left, telling the younger Joe that the bigger the car, the smaller the dick. Joe used to get all heated up about it, angry at everyone, but time passed and eventually so did Pappy Joe, then all of a sudden it was just him, on account of Pappy Joe left him the business.

He's mellowed now, decades and decades later, doing what the old man had always done before him: collecting, reusing, refurbishing, and selling. Occasionally finding small treasures among the detritus of other people's lives. Now *he* is the old man, joints creaking almost louder than the door of the truck, tipping an imaginary hat to his lady customers, joking with the local folks. Sometimes just sitting there in the rocking chair, waiting. For what, he isn't sure. But it's certainly coming.

When he finds the tied-up bag at the side of the road, back near Bear Creek, he thinks he's hit it. Jackpot. Some rich bitch tossing out her furs. It isn't until he opens the bag wider that he begins to retch.

CHAPTER ONE

HOME. WHERE THE heart is. Where they have to take you in. Where the prodigal child returns and gets the fatted calf.

My question: What if said prodigal had been a vegetarian? What then? Did they slaughter the fatted soy curd?

Not that I am vegetarian. But I got neither cow nor curd when I was a prodigal returning. No biblical best robe, ring, or sandals, either. It was more *Let's just go on about our business and hope the prodigal can figure out her own damn way, 'cause she is mighty, mighty flighty* than celebratory.

My home *used* to be where my family was—my Clan, my kin, people of my blood—smack in the middle of the Texas Hill Country, in the so-small-it's-not-on-the-map town of Rio Seco. (I didn't live there during my first seven years, but I don't count those years when considering family. Nope, not at all. Like a certain boy wizard from a famous tale, I got rescued from uncaring relatives and found that I had a loving family and magickal powers.) After high school, I left for university in England, came back, traveled, left again due to heartbreak (his, not mine), and then, quicker'n a scalded cat, I scooted home hoping for tea and sympathy or, at the very least, a good talking-to followed by hugs and love.

Instead, I found my family on the verge of moving to Canada.

Stubborn child that I was, I refused to go with them, staying to lick my own damn wounds, thank you very much.

Two and a half years later my cousin and sole responsibility was murdered. This was followed about six months later by the attempted rape/murder of my best friend. Hot on the heels of that tragedy, I was gobsmacked by the revelation that I was heir to the Kelly Clan, and I found myself back in the bosom of aforementioned family in Canada, training my ass off, learning how to be the proper successor to the Clan leadership.

Now, after not quite three months of heir schooling, I was back in Rio Seco, still learning how to be the eventual ruler of a powerful family of immortal supernaturals that mundane humans didn't even realize existed, except in legend and fiction. Our array of Talents range from shapeshifting to weather sense to healing, and as heir, I got them all instead of the usual one or two.

The stubborn child has done some growing. Instead of being the frog I'd always suspected I was, I turned out to be a princess of sorts. I'd even found my Prince Charming.

I've found out *home* is the people you love, your family, no matter where they are.

I've also discovered you—particularly if you are a prince or princess—have to be prepared to fight the Big Bad if it threatens your home, your people.

Only I'm not even acquainted with all my people, and I don't know what or who the Big Bad is—at least, not yet.

CHAPTER TWO

A CRACK OF SOUND TO my left. I whirled on one foot and leaned to the right. That was a close one.

Another crack, closer, heralded a brilliant explosion of light. With the smell of burning magick—a lot like hot air and ozone—searing my nostrils, I whirled again, staff clutched in my hands as a focus. Shields tightened, strengthened as I gathered my own power, trying to turn the situation from defense to offense.

Damn it, I could use some help here. But there was no one to help. No one here but me and three attackers—each at least as powerful as I am, considering my newbie status. They were using weapons. All I was armed with were my own talents.

Not what I'd expected as the Kelly heir, I thought, as I ducked some sort of purplish energy ball that shot out of a colorful gunlike contraption. Damned thing resembled a Super Soaker, but instead of water, it shot spells.

I slid past what looked like a booby trap, something shimmering just beyond normal sensory range. I jumped to one side, wishing I could think of something quippy to say, like Buffy did when she was fighting vampires and demons on TV. Kill them with my wit. Instead, I was muttering "Fuck, fuck, fuck" under my breath as I attempted to avoid getting hit. I'd trained for nearly three months with my darling great-granny's minions. Gigi, a.k.a. Minerva Kelly, had the best in the business. Unfortunately, these guys were even better—and more determined to win. I think I'd rather fight demons. At least they had limits. These guys? None. At least as far as I could tell.

The three threw everything they could at me: fire, freezing, starvation—all spells built into their weapons— any one of which could, at the very least, cause me to break down, fall to my knees, and concede. I ducked, tumbled, rolled, and mumbled words I'd only recently learned, trying both to keep my wits about me and figure out how I was going to reach the door on the other side of the room. I knew it was my only safety. My single means of escape. Fighting three men in an enclosed space: never a good idea. But I'd picked neither the time nor the place for this confrontation. Unprepared as I was, I was slam damn in the middle of a mini-war. It could've been worse. They could've all been targeting just me. Oh wait, they were.

"Damn it," I groused to myself as I jumped over a flash of yellow mage-fire, stumbling on my landing and barely ducking in time to miss the orange sparks shot out of a flame-colored mini-cannon by someone whose lap I used to climb onto as a child. If even *one* of those sparks touched any part of me, my skin would instantly feel as if it were being torn from my body, strip by bloody strip.

"Ouch!" A ball of red mage-fire from the left singed my shoulder as it slipped by. "Was that a warning, Tucker?" I shouted as I returned my concentration to the rest of the action.

"Not a warning, simply . . ." He re-aimed his weapon and shot another fireball at me. This time I was prepared.

"Bad aim, brother?" I said as I tucked back a lock of hair that had escaped my braid. About twenty minutes ago, I'd come to the conclusion that long hair was nothing more than vanity, sheer vanity, and a hell of a lot of useless in a fight. Sure, it was bound back in a tight single braid, but a couple of those witch balls had been the really ugly kind. If even a spark touches any part of you—say, for example, a braid swinging behind you as you execute a defense maneuver—the witch fire grabs hold and starts devouring. The hair would go first, quicker than a Guy Fawkes Night firecracker, then fire would move on to the skin, the soft jelly of the eye. It would get inside you as slick as a flu bug and eat you up . . . literally burning you to death. Huh, maybe that explained some of the cases of spontaneous human combustion. Wonder if anyone had ever investigated things from our side of the fence. In any case, I was absolutely cutting my hair off after this—assuming I was still in one piece.

A movement caught my eye.

"Fuck you and the damned horse you rode in on, Ianto." I angled my staff in my other brother's direction, shooting my own flash of bright light. I slid back, hoping to avoid retaliation, but kept my eye on Ianto.

Ianto's gleeful expression turned into a frown as my own spell reached him: a hybrid flashbang—a stunner combined with an expanding binding. Modeled after a mundane military device, it was a damned useful spell I'd created with the help of one of my brothers. My brother threw himself into a crouch, but he was too late. A wisp of light caught a lock of his hair and, instantly, the light flashed *whitehotblinding*—an actinic flash searing sight—accompanied by an equally stunning *smackcrash* of sound, intended to temporarily cripple. He went down faster than a sack of lead weights, slamming against the floor with a grunt. As the light snaked around my now nearly comatose opponent, binding him more effectively than enchanted rope, I threw two more binding spells toward the remaining two, both stumbling about, eyes watering and ears ringing, their sense of balance temporarily gone. The bindings wrapped around them both and they fell to the floor.

"The shields held, Mr. Scott," I mumbled to myself as I set my staff on the floor and wiped my hands on my thighs, the cotton knit of the yoga pants I wore nearly soaked through with sweat. Surveying the damage, I nodded in relief. It could've been much worse. Three seasoned opponents—each of them older than me by, at minimum, a couple of centuries—sending their best damage spells against one extreme newbie. I'd brought the spell weapons, invented by one of my clever Clan cousins, back with me from the family compound in British Columbia. Here in Rio Seco, they'd become part and parcel of my new arsenal—most of which was otherwise made up of my brothers and their natural shapeshifting abilities. Tooth and claw were often more effective than spells—especially when dealing with humans.

I beamed as I caught the reluctantly admiring expression on Ianto's face. Despite the bindings and the flashbang, he'd managed to retain consciousness. "Kudos to you, dear brother," I said in amusement. I walked over to him and patted his face. "You're awake."

He fought the bindings, trying to nod, managing only a squirm.

"Didn't think I'd make it, did you?" I looked at Tucker

and Rhys, each of them blacked out on the floor behind me. "None of you thought I could do this." *For that matter, neither had I,* I thought, and silently blessed the fact that I'd grown up not only with these three but with three other just as formidable older brothers. It didn't hurt that I now lived with a vampire tribe and was partnered to the king of the tribe, Adam Walker, who was, in addition to vampire, Unseelie Sidhe.

These last few months of training had been intensive but well worth it if it meant I could beat out my three most combat-ready brothers, even when they'd ambushed me. The surprise attack was part of my training, but—damn.

"Brava," Ianto grunted as he finally struggled to his feet. "I knew you could do it."

I grabbed the small towel he tossed me and ran it over my face and neck. "Glad you did," I said. "I wasn't as confident."

"In your abilities?" He laughed. "Minerva told me you'd done well, Keira, don't underestimate yourself."

"She did?" I leaned back against the soft padded wall of the brand-new sparring room. "I guess that's why you three ambushed me?" With a smirk, I watched Rhys, Ianto's twin, and Tucker struggle with their invisible bonds. "Ready to say 'uncle' yet?" I asked them both.

Tucker growled. "Yes, damn it."

Rhys said nothing but waggled his eyebrows in amusement and acceptance.

I vanished their bonds with a muttered spell. "Next time, I really would appreciate knowing in advance," I said to Ianto. "I thought I was coming to my new training room to do some yoga, maybe practice a few spell lessons. After all, isn't that why our darling matriarch had this room built?"

Tucker grabbed a towel from the floor and wiped off his own sweaty face. "One reason, yes," he said. "But hell, we couldn't let you see the room without our own brand of fun, could we?"

I tossed my towel at his face. "Thanks ever so," I said sarcastically. "Next time you want to show off one of Gigi's lovely new surprises, seriously, just tell me."

Rhys came to give me a hug. "Welcome home, sis. Glad you're back."

"Me, too," I said, hugging him in return. "Those three months in British Columbia passed fairly quickly in one respect. Gigi kept me damned busy learning things, but I missed having you all there with me." I reached over and pulled Ianto into the hug, too. "You, too, Ianto. Thank you for coming home."

Ianto smiled, his quiet demeanor nearly the opposite of his always-rowdy twin's. "I'm glad, Keira. It's almost like old times to be back in Rio Seco, back in Texas."

With a happy laugh, I motioned Tucker to come over and join in the group hug. He tossed his towel to the floor and did his best to surround us all three with his long arms. "Love you all," he whispered. "I'll echo Keira and be all soppy. Being back here, together, with the twins and my cousin Liz, as part of Keira's retinue, is more than I could've hoped." What he didn't say, and I knew he included, was his being back here with his vampire lover, Niko.

I snuggled into my brothers, soaking in the sentimentality. It could have been way different and a hell of a lot less happy-making. Instead of sending me back with my favorite brothers and Liz—our pilot and the twins' partner—Gigi could've chosen from any among her own court, people whom I knew only by name and not by heart. Instead, she let me choose my Court—and Court these guys were, not just family anymore. No more autonomous Keira Kelly, living off by her lonesome deep in the heart of Texas, away from the notice of Clan and its annoying politics. Instead, I was the Kelly heir . . . well, one of them, to be exact. My distant cousin and former lover, Gideon, was the other, both of us having inherited all the Kelly Talents, from weather sense to spellcasting and everything in between. My brothers, Liz, Niko, and Adam had all returned to Texas before I had. They'd made Adam's Wild Moon Ranch, which was already home to his tribe of vampires, into our hearth and headquarters. Ianto and Liz had overseen the building of the training room, as well as several other additions to the Wild Moon, courtesy of my great-great-granny and with Adam's every approval.

We eventually released one another, every one of us sporting a stupidly happy grin, endorphins and emotion vying for first place in our expressions.

"You did brilliantly, Keira," Tucker said. "I thought three months was too short—not that I didn't want you home."

"Honestly, so did I," I said. "But damn, Gigi packs a hell of a mean training schedule. I was at her side nearly twenty-four, seven."

"I take it you like the room?" Ianto asked, gesturing around.

I turned my attention back to the training room, eerily similar to the one I'd left behind in British Columbia about twenty-four hours ago. This one seemed a little larger, perhaps forty foot square. Padded walls in a muted gray-green surrounded a special soft flooring, just perfect for fight training and/or practice. Unlike the training facility at the Clan enclave in Canada, this room was underground, carved and blasted out of limestone—not with explosives and heavy machinery but with spells. I could still feel the residue of construction magicks. The training room was underneath what had once been a large guesthouse on the Wild Moon property.

"You have a hand in the design?" I asked Ianto, who nodded.

"Did you get a good look at the upstairs?" Tucker teased.

I rolled my eyes at him. "Yeah, throne room, much? Damn thing practically appears like the hall at Edoras, minus a few mountains and a couple hundred Rohirrim. Sometimes I wonder if Minerva whispered hints into John Ronald Reuel Tolkien's ear or maybe she just saw the movies."

My brothers all laughed. "Don't know about Tolkien, but there's a lot of Gigi's influence in that room," Rhys said. "She sent me very detailed decorating instructions."

"And you followed them?" I stared at Rhys as if he'd grown another head. "Unlike you."

"Not exactly," he said. "Her plans called for a lot more bling. I decided that wasn't you."

"Nor Adam," I reminded him. "That room is for *our* reception, not just mine."

"Nor Adam," Rhys agreed. "I worked with Niko and Liz to make it less Minerva and more . . . well . . ." He waved a hand, seemingly at a loss for description. Not surprising. Gigi and I were pretty much two very different sides of a proverbial coin concerning style or anything else.

Anyone seeing the two of us together would immediately pick up on the very obvious fact that I was not my great-great-granny's fashion child. Of course, having spent most of my life in a very rural area meant I was about as far from fashionable as one could get without actually being a throwback. My idea of dressing up was wearing black slacks and a black top with some sort of jacket rounding out the safely monochromatic non-fashion. (Adam, on the other hand, was the epitome of style, in a very pared-down, simple elegance sort of way.) Gigi's dress outfits often cost more than the yearly income of most workers in developing nations . . . and then some. She'd tried to train that part of me over the last few months, but I was having none of it. I gladly succumbed to the rest of the education but completely ignored anything to do with deportment and/or dress.

"You did a good job, Rhys. Thanks."

Tucker cocked his head and frowned a little. "You're not mad," he said.

"At what?"

"This, the remodeling, the fact that Gigi did all this behind your back."

I thought for a moment. As recently as two months ago, anger would probably have been my initial reaction. After all, Tucker and his lover, Niko, Adam's second, were with me in Vancouver when all hells broke loose, with Gigi sitting calmly in the center of the mad web she'd woven. "I think I'm just growing up, Tucker," I finally said. "Choosing my battles, I guess. I could lose my temper at Gigi for interfering, for having the balls to think she could do this without my approval or my knowledge, but you know what? She bloody well can. She's our Clan leader, our ruler. I'm just the heir."

"And Gideon?" Rhys asked quietly. "What of him?"

"Still Below," I answered. "Gigi and Drystan had

some sort of come-to-Jesus meeting, to which my former lover and fellow heir was not invited. She told me his father decided to train him."

"As his successor? I thought Adam—"

"They may share a father, Rhys, but Adam's still Drystan's firstborn son and heir," I said. "Drystan was very clear on that point when I last saw him. Despite Gideon being Adam's half brother and a Kelly heir, too, Drystan isn't budging on that fact."

"He needs a firm hand, Rhys," Tucker said. "Gideon's not one to sit still for Gigi's sort of training. After all, he managed to bamboozle the lot of the Kellys and get himself to Faery and his father."

"That's pretty much the gist of it, Tucker," I said. "Gigi all but said that Drystan can have his sorry ass. She said he'd be 'the whip hand to the boy,' " I quoted.

"Literally?" Tucker snorted a laugh. "That'll be fairly interesting."

"Won't it just?" I laughed. My ex-lover, who I recently discovered was half brother to my partner, Adam Walker, had never done discipline well . . . at least, not on the submissive side. He'd managed to escape confinement here at the enclave and find a way into Faery, to the Unseelie Court, when everyone thought he was in a magickal coma and near death.

"I wish him all the best," I said in my finest sarcastic tone. "Maybe Drystan will knock some sense into him."

CHAPTER THREE

"THERE'S A WEREWOLF here, asking for you." Jess, one of Adam's vampires who'd been assigned as my personal assistant, stood at the foot of the staircase just outside the door to the sparring room.

The four of us turned as one to face the door.

"Shit, it's dark already?" I asked.

"A werewolf?" Tucker said. "Someone we know?"

"I don't know any around these parts," I said. "At least not during my time. You two?"

Ianto and Rhys exchanged a glance and shrugged, almost in tandem. "I'd heard something some years back," Ianto said. "A pack somewhere outside our immediate range, so I never really knew much more. I think Gigi knew."

"So not *important,* then?" I emphasized "important." From my lessons in Kelly politics, anyone not in immediate territory—fifty miles—wasn't anyone I needed to concern myself with. And by anyone, Gigi had meant anyone of supernatural descent. Wers counted, but only if they were within range.

"Guess not," Ianto answered. "He's—or she's—probably here to get a gander at you."

"He," Jess said with an odd twist to her lips as she played with a lock of her hair. Did she have a bit of a crush on the wereguy?

"He, then." Ianto folded his towel and tossed it into a basket. "If you don't want to deal with him, Keira, I can."

"No, I'm good," I said. "Curious mostly. What time is it, anyway, Jess? If you're up and around, it's got to be after dark."

"Only about eight thirty," she answered. "I just got up and John had me go see who was at the gate." John, Adam's day manager, was our equivalent to Renfield, but with a better diet and way more sanity. He and his family cared for the ranch during daytime hours.

"Damn, we've been in here for nearly three hours," I said. "Time flies and all that. Where is this guy, Jess?"

"On the porch," she said. "I didn't think you'd want me to allow him in the building without you knowing."

"You thought correctly. Go on and get him then."

Jess headed up the stairs, her red hair gleaming in the artificial light. She looked all of twenty-five, but who knew with vampires? I might be the Kelly heir with all the Talents inherent to our Clan, but sensing vampire ages wasn't one of them.

"Damnation, it's bloody hot, even down here." I wiped my face as I pulled out a soft bench that had been tucked under a built-in shelf. "This weather sucks even for June. If this lasts, I may be willing to go back to Vancouver for a few weeks and chill out." *Maybe even until fall,* I mused to myself.

"Even the vampires are having issues," Tucker said. "It's been like this for ages. Hottest summer on record; more than thirty days near to and over a hundred degrees."

"The vampires are having problems with the heat?"

I'd never considered that, since, technically, vampires weren't alive—at least, not by human standards. Adam's skin was normally cool to the touch, and I guess I'd gotten used to the thought that he was comfortable no matter what the ambient temperature.

"Yeah, it's bloody hot after dark still. Hunting's rather uncomfortable for them. Us, too, when shifted, all that fur."

"Shit, I hadn't thought about that," I said. "What can I do to help?"

"You've been back all of twenty-four hours, Keira," Rhys butted in. "It's not like we expect you to know everything that's going on right away."

Tucker nodded. "I'm sure Adam would've said something tonight. I imagine you two didn't do much talking when you got home?"

I wasn't about to tell my brothers about my very excellent sex life. I'd arrived at eight last night and—after a brief reunion with my siblings, Liz, and a hug from Niko, who'd just woken—I'd gone straight to Adam's bed, not even letting him wake fully before I pounced. I hadn't seen him in nearly three months.

"Are all the vampire quarters cool enough?" I asked. "Because if not, we can fix this. I'm sure there are plenty of great air-conditioning guys around we can bring in."

"Adam and I have been brainstorming," Ianto answered. "All the homes are fine, the a/c units are working well, but who the hell wants to be cabin-bound twenty-four, seven? It's bad enough that they all have to stay underground for the long summer days."

I thought of eighty-some-odd vampires with cabin fever and shuddered. "Egad. Yeah, not a good thing. I'm sure we'll all figure something out."

How did one cool off vampires anyway? They couldn't exactly have a field trip to the nearest swimming hole. With the drought, most of the natural swimming areas disappeared as the waters receded, and local area pools were private and closed after dark. The oxymoronically named Rio Seco—"dry river" in Spanish—was dammed in the sixties to form the consequently absurdly named Rio Seco Lake. Originally, the name "Rio Seco" was less insane. Without the human intervention, most of this area had been near-desert plains, bordering on unlivable. The river was often "dry." Put in a few man-made lakes, *et voilà*: a fun-in-the-sun resort smack-dab in the middle of Texas. Not that we were copying Lake Travis, Highland Lakes, or anything, nope. I'd often wondered if my dainty-hands-in-many-unknown-pies Clan leader had been involved. Certainly didn't hurt us much, at least for the first four decades or so. Too bad that, eventually, the world found out how absolutely gorgeous it was here and how cheap the land values were.

The sound of descending steps reminded us of the visitor.

I turned to my brothers. "Since when has there been a wolf pack around here, anyway?"

"Since about two months ago, m'lady," a deep voice answered, the sound resonating as its owner followed Jess into the sparring room.

Wow. The appearance certainly matched the voice—only *way* younger than I expected. I swallowed my very inappropriate "holy fuck, you're hot" comment. Bloody hell, this boy was beyond gorgeous . . . and yes, I meant "boy." I wasn't the only one affected. Jess was nearly simpering as she moved to his side. My brothers each looked as if I'd just opened the gates and let a fresh lamb into the wolves' den—our kind of wolves, that is. Tucker was flat-out staring, a quick lip lick his only betrayal; Rhys and Ianto were each giving the kid a once-over, twin looks of approval on both their faces. Whatever this boy had, he had it in spades, and those spades were hitting each and every one of us over the head and dragging us to the secret lair. My mouth went absolutely desert, and I scrabbled for the gallon of iced sports drink on the bench next to me.

At first glance, I pegged him as in his late teens, perhaps early twenties. Technically not jailbait, but still young—far too young for any of us in this room, werewolf or not. After a second glance at his face, I revised my estimate further downward. Definitely jailbait. Smooth, tanned skin holding no trace of age or experience. His lovely cheekbones, which in a few years could be called chiseled, still held a trace of childhood softness. His amazing appearance was only a promise of even more once he reached full maturity. The boy's brown hair was pulled back on the top and sides, divided into two tails sweeping over his wide shoulders to the middle of his very well-developed chest. A soft scent of boy sweat and musk reached me. Four identical throat clearings accompanied my deep gulp of the drink as I again stifled my very inappropriate urges when I met the boy's amber-eyed stare. *There* was the wolf. In those clear, yellow-brown eyes gleaming at me. I could almost see the beast inside him, a puppy, anxious to get out and greet me properly.

He bowed deeply, extending a leg in the most courteous manner, his style belying both his youth and his mundane clothing—a polo shirt and khakis. "My lady, Gregor Ashkarian, at your service. I come representing our Fenrir, Marcus Ashkarian, leader of the Ashkar pack.

He wishes to extend our welcome at your return and invite you to join him at tomorrow night's exhibition game at White Rock."

"You've been here two months? Ashkarian?" My brow furrowed as I searched for a memory that didn't come. "I apologize; I don't recognize the name at all. But then, I've been away."

Gregor nodded, still holding the bow. "A group of us recently came to Rio Seco."

"Do stand up, would you? No need for formality at this point. What brings you to Rio Seco? It's not exactly the hub of the universe . . . or even of the Hill Country."

Gregor stood and held his hands behind him at parade rest, relaxing some but not all the way. I got the feeling he was as uncomfortable with formality as I was, but that his discomfort was less due to the protocol and more to do with getting his message out correctly. "Our pack runs a river rafting and camping ground over near Pedernales Falls. The weather is too . . ." He hunted for a word, then dropped the formality completely. "It's been really sucky. With the falls dried up and no one camping in this heat wave, we needed to find something else to bring in money."

He pronounced the name of the park "Perdinalis." Again, I had to rethink my initial impression. No way was this pack new to the Hill Country: only locals said it that way. The state park and the falls weren't too far from here if mapped directly in a line, but they were a good seventy miles by road.

"How long have y'all been there?" I asked. "Technically, you're at the bounds of our immediate territory, even out that far."

"Your Clan leader knows about us," he said, chest

rising, a bit in challenge mode. His musky scent grew stronger. *Puppy got his pride on,* I thought. Good wolf. Alpha, if I didn't miss my guess. I may be shite at vampire ages, but I certainly understood wolf; after all, with my shapeshifting Talent I could play one pretty damned well. I liked wolf.

"No need to get your hackles up, kid. I'm good with that. I just didn't know. That's why you're here then, the forty-eight-hour rule?"

"Yes," he said. "My Fenrir, our pack leader, is training me—I'm the emissary." With a flash of white teeth, he became all teenager now, and quoted: "All supernatural folk within your immediate area must present themselves within forty-eight hours." He sounded like a high schooler reciting the periodic table for chemistry class. "Though," he added as an aside, "we'll attend the formal reception, too."

"Consider yourselves presented." I left the bench, stepping to him, holding out my hand. "Welcome to Rio Seco."

CHAPTER FOUR

A$_S$ HE TOOK MY HAND, a shiver of energy exuded from his touch. I took it in stride, silently thanking the powers that be for my recent and very intensive training on how not to react visibly. This kid leaked hormones worse than a torn screen door in a rainstorm. Did he have any idea? I doubted it, but I bet all the local girls . . . and some of the boys . . . were sniffing around him in droves.

Gregor gave my hand a firm shake, then stepped back and relaxed. "Thanks. Mark said to make sure to thank Mr. Walker, too, for letting us move here and buy the deli."

The clue light was now shining. This made a *lot* more sense than a random move to Rio Seco. The aforementioned deli had been closed since last year due to the "unfortunate" deaths of its owners, Greta and Boris Nagy, the brother-and-sister team who had murdered my cousin Marty. "Okay, I get it. It's a good place, that shop. It'll be nice to have a local grocery again."

Gregor nodded. "My uncle Mark bought it. He runs the place along with his brother and sister. It's pretty cool, even though I have to work there during the summer." He seemed chagrined at the loss of his freedom. "They've added a soda fountain and ice cream bar along with the grocery section. Spruced up the grill, too."

"Whoa, hold your horses there, kid. Does Bea know about the grill? The owner of the café there in the strip mall," I explained. If the boy's answer was no, I was ready to put some whoop ass on Adam first, for allowing it, then on the wer. I wanted no new business to interfere with Bea's Place. Running it as a deli-*cum*-grocery as it had been was fine, but adding extra food service? With the economy in slow recovery mode, especially with a drought and heat wave, I was sure Bea could use all the business she could get . . . our recent estrangement aside.

"Oh, yeah, totally," he answered. "The brothers met with her first. Mr. Walker said to."

A thousand mental pardons to my partner for doubting his good sense.

"She's good with this?" My eyes narrowed as I studied the boy's face. He seemed without guile, but my exposure to wer of any kind was limited. That, plus the fact I was still utter crap at reading truth in people's demeanor without reaching into their minds made me press the issue. That was one area of Talent that, if graded, I'd have taken a very firm D in. Both aunts and Gigi despaired, but by the hundredth time I'd gotten cues wrong, they'd all thrown up their hands and declared I'd have to deal as is. Funny thing, Talent.

"M'lady Keira." He went back into formal mode and bowed again, this time a short acknowledgment. "We respect your territory greatly and are grateful for your hospitality and welcome here. The brothers would do nothing without Ms. Ruiz's approval."

"Relax, already, Gregor," I said with a gentle smile. He was adorable. "Thanks for letting me know that. You keep calling them 'the brothers,' " I remarked. "Is that some sort of pack designation?"

Gregor laughed. "Just an old joke. Grandpop had so many of the pack boys working for him at his place, he'd lose track of who was who. Mark and Levon were the only blood relatives. Grandpop ended up calling them 'the brothers.' When they grew up and took over the business, they even had it printed on their business cards."

Tucker intervened, putting me back on course. "You said your Fenrir wanted to invite Keira to an exhibition game?"

"Oh yes," Gregor said. "The game starts at nine and he said he'd save a section of the bleachers. He and Lev, his brother, are sponsoring it. He said the invite was for you and yours."

"You mean the entire vampire clan and my family members?" I asked.

He nodded. "Mark said as many as you'd like."

I stared at the boy, wondering what on earth the locals would think of a slew of vampires and several shapeshifters at a local football game. That would certainly be a sight.

Jess sidled closer to me. "Game?" she whispered, not understanding that in this part of Texas, only one game mattered, even in the middle of June: football.

"Later," I whispered back. "I'm going to take a wild guess and assume that Mark of 'the brothers' and Mark the Fenrir are the same person?"

"Yeah, they are," Gregor answered. "Sorry, it's like, I know stuff and I figure you know stuff and well, I forget to explain." He hung his head like a scolded puppy.

"Not to worry." I laughed. The poor kid was doing

his best. "I'm just curious. You said the game's in White Rock. At the high school stadium?"

The boy nodded. "I'll be a junior at White Rock next fall. I play running back."

"So you live in White Rock?"

"With the pack, yes."

"Why would the Fenrir leave his pack and come to Rio Seco?"

"Truth?"

"That would nice. I imagine that some of the officials I'm going to be meeting soon won't be bothered by such niceties, but I really do prefer it. It's much easier to deal with. You said the pack needed money earlier—is the pack broke?"

"No, it's not like that," he said, a bit frustrated but still trying to maintain. "I really don't get all of it, but it's something about cash flow. Mark and Lev are real good cooks. That's why the deli."

"I don't doubt it," I said drily. "Well, then, I suppose this is a conversation I can have with your uncle the Fenrir. Speaking of which . . . Gregor, could you hang tight a sec? I need to ask my brothers a question."

"Absolutely," he said.

"Jess, would you mind? Gregor, just have a seat on the steps, I won't be long." Jess nodded and escorted Gregor out of the room, shutting the door behind him. She stayed inside with us but remained next to the door.

"Can he hear us?" I asked my brothers.

Tucker shook his head. "Doubtful. He's wer, not shapeshifter. Wolves have good hearing, but this door and this room were designed by Kellys. I think even I'd have a problem hearing through it."

"Good enough. About this invitation, then. What do

y'all think? Should I accept? Should we meet Mark Ashkarian before the formal reception? This wasn't something covered by my training."

Tucker shrugged, as did Rhys. "I don't know if it's
kosher or not. Ianto? You're better at this, do you know?"
Rhys asked his twin.

"Depends. That's up to Keira. Sis, you need to start
how you mean to go on," Ianto answered.

"What do you mean?"

"Gigi likes a formal Court, as I'm sure you know. Lots
of protocol. You and Adam can set up your own ambience, your own theme, so to speak—formal, informal,
business casual—whatever you prefer."

"You're telling me we *don't* have to go through all this
reception rigmarole?" Could I really get out of a long,
drawn-out ceremony and all the dress-up and boredom
that came with?

"No," Ianto replied, bursting my short-lived bubble.
"You still need to take the oaths of fealty and we still have
to give you our official blood oaths and bond, but there's
absolutely no need for *all* the pomp and circumstance."

"Don't forget," Jess reminded me. "You and Adam
need to review the list of attendees for the reception."

I waved her off. "I'm sure Lance is probably remind-
ing Adam of the very same thing right now," I said.

"I believe that's right," Jess said. "He was headed toward
the office with the paperwork when I came down here."

"That's fine, then," I said. "Ianto, that's a relief." I
wiped my brow in a melodramatic gesture. "Jess, make it
so. Let Gregor back in."

She opened the door and motioned the boy back in as I
continued. "Guys, I'll totally answer for Adam about the
ambience of the reception: We're going as casual as we

can. Nice duds, but no pomp . . . and most certainly, no circumstance."

"What does 'pomp and circumstance' mean, anyway?" Tucker remarked as he plopped down beside me on the bench.

"Shakespeare." Ianto plopped next to him. "Othello's line. He was talking about the formality that goes with an important event."

"It's also a series of marches for orchestra," Jess piped up. "Composed by Sir Edward Elgar." She got shy again. "Umm, I was kind of a music major before . . ."

"She's right." Ianto smiled at Jess. "Elgar got the title from *Othello.*"

"Well, then, there you have it," I said. "No orchestras, okay?"

"No orchestras," she echoed. "Would an iPod work?"

I laughed, as did my brothers. "Whatever floats your boat, Jess. I'm deferring to Adam on that part. He has tons more experience than I have. In my book, y'all have free rein."

Rhys hopped up from the floor and gave me a huge bear hug. "Oh, most excellent," he said. "I like free rein."

"Within reason, O decorating guru, within reason," I warned. "I said Adam has the final say on this, so don't go all crazy DIY show-decorating with cactus flowers or anything. Simple, got it?"

He bent in an elaborate bow. "I hear and obey, my lady and mistress." I smacked him on the ass with my towel.

Gregor, who'd been patiently waiting at the door, and very much listening with interest, let out a semi-suppressed laugh.

"Sorry, kid," I said. "What I can say? They're my brothers."

"I know what you mean," he said. "I've got my uncles and other pack members . . . not to mention the football team."

"They still haze?" Tucker sounded interested.

"Not much these days, but yeah, there's some. No one gets strung up on a post dressed in their boxers anymore, if that's what you mean."

"That's more or less what I meant," Tucker said. "Keira, didn't some boys over at White Rock get kidnapped, stripped down, and abandoned out at the lake one night?"

"Back in my day, you mean?"

Tucker nodded as he slung his towel over his neck. "When you were a junior, right?"

"I think that's right," I said. "I remember it happening, but not the specifics. That was twenty-some-odd years ago."

"They don't do that kind of thing anymore," Gregor said quickly, as if to prove to us that he wasn't a barbarian. "Church got all hot and bothered over some stupid pranks a couple of years ago, so they laid down the law."

"The church? I thought White Rock was a public school." At least it had been in my day, as Tucker liked to put it. Built around an actual white rock—a large chunk of limestone that protruded from the earth after some prehistoric earthquake—the town of White Rock's foundation was its church, eponymically called The Church of the White Rock. Despite the name, its preacher and members were less of the TV-Holy-Roller persuasion than of the good old-fashioned Sunday school kind of folk. Loads of community service, teen groups, and so forth. I knew very little about the church. Church, any church, wasn't exactly somewhere you'd find a Kelly. We were around before most of these sects, including the big one centered in Rome, were founded.

"It is. It's just that they've got lots of pull in running the school. Board members and all that."

"I don't recall it being quite that pushy," I said. "Tucker, do you? I mean, it's not like we know all that much about how White Rock handles school administration, but word gets around."

Tucker shook his head. "Not really. I think there's a fairly new leadership there. Didn't the old pastor retire?"

"Yeah, about four or five years ago," Gregor said. "Least that's what I seem to remember. We're not really churchgoers." He grinned. "Don't think they'd take too kindly to a bunch of wolves."

"Nor to us," Ianto remarked. "But I do recall that those folks at the church were pretty low-key. Not the usual fire-and-brimstone types."

"Far as I know it's the same," Gregor replied, "but the new pastor seems to be filling up the school board with his folks. Doesn't really matter too much to me. I've got this upcoming year and then I'm trying for a slot at A&M."

"Really? That's a bit surprising," I said. "You don't exactly seem the Aggie type." I pointed to his long hair.

"The hair? Naw, that's just a phase . . . or at least that's what I keep telling Uncle Mark."

Rhys burst out laughing. "You're doing it to piss him off?"

"Pretty much. He's fairly middle-middle, you know. Middle class, middle of the road, middle values. He doesn't like to rock the boat."

"And you're a boat rocker." I looked the boy in the eye, amused at his attitude.

"A little motion is fun," he said. "S'long as I keep up my grades and stuff, I'm good."

We all laughed. "Okay, kid, you're on. We'll be at the game tomorrow night."

"Cool, make sure to watch out for me. Number twenty-two."

CHAPTER FIVE

I FELT THE FENRIR LONG before I laid eyes on him. A
tangle of energy pulsated within a shell of normality,
of blandness. Not angry energy: it wasn't snarled, nor
did it evoke caution so much as complexity. If this were a
science fiction movie, I'd have called it a disturbance in the
Force; in a traditional faery tale it would be a disorder, an
intrusion but, perhaps, not precisely unwelcome.

He tasted of greenery and spring at the back of my
throat, a cool void within the red-orange humidity of the
summer, not unlike the flavor of my own brothers' auras,
their preferred wolf shape part of their particular traits.
This man was true wolf in nature, tooth and claw of animal when changed.

I understood him more than I could possibly have
ever imagined. Having been wolf attuned me to others
of that species. I'd learned this the hard way on a visit
to the Greater Vancouver Zoo a few weeks ago with
one of my trainers. She'd intended that I demonstrate
my enhanced sensory capabilities, learning to sense the
animals, learning to sense humans and differentiate.
Unfortunately, when I'd gotten about two meters from
the wolf den, the howling began. We'd had to leave im-

mediately, as even the other animals had shown signs
of anxiety at my presence. My trainer attributed that to
the fact that I was a Kelly heir, not because of the wolf
shape I liked to use.

"You can shapeshift, Keira, but you're no more a real
wolf than this plastic toy is a true lion." She'd held one of
those injected plastic animals from a machine, a red lion,
still reeking of hot melted wax, its poor head smashed
along one side, a reject. My trainer had wanted to ask for
her money back, but it amused me greatly, so I kept it as a
souvenir. She was right, though, I wasn't an actual wolf.
During a shift, I could play at being whatever animal I
chose to be. I'd done wolf (by far my favorite), dog, leop-
ard, cheetah, panther. Predator rather than prey. Perhaps it
was ingrained in me by my upbringing, as my father and
all six of my brothers were shapeshifters themselves and
nearly always chose wolf form. I'd not done well at the
more domesticated animals such as house cat and cow.
Frankly, I was glad, because beef was dinner, not something whose shape I wanted to take.

No matter which shape, though, as Ianto and I had
discussed, my brain was still human, still the most developed brain of the entire animal kingdom. Even though I
couldn't talk because of the physical restrictions, I could
think, reason, and react as a human. As wolf, I did gather
scents as wolves did and could run as one. Another training session, this time in the Pacific Rim National Park
Reserve, proved that. We'd run across some scat and
found ourselves in the midst of a local wolf pack. After
the requisite submissive behavior, they'd accepted and
then ignored us. Fascinating experience. Part of me wondered if we were actually *Homo sapiens* and not some
other branch of said human family. *Homo kelliius?* Who

the hell knew? There were scientists among our clan members, but none in North America. I'd been given logins and passwords to the entire Clan database and had amused myself one rain-filled day doing some random searching of Clan members and locations. Kind of my own version of geotagging or "Where's Waldo?" A herd of Gigi's pet scientists lived in Switzerland, some others in England and France. No one here, though. It was one of those things that arose in the back of my thoughts when I was studying. The human genome had been mapped, but had ours? Plenty of time to think about that in the coming years. Not a bad project for an heir, either.

As with my experience in the Reserve, I knew the moment we'd stepped close to the stadium that my upcoming meeting with the pack's Fenrir might be more than I'd bargained for. We were just standing in line at the Will Call window when his animal energy roiled through me, calling to my own wolf to come join him. Tucker, a few steps behind me, huffed, nostrils flaring. I didn't have to ask him to know he was just as aware of the energy as I was. Neither of the two vampires seemed at all fazed. I revised my thought as I watched the back of Niko's neck tense. They, too, knew something was up.

Though there seemed to be no challenge, my hackles rose as we drew nearer to the entrance once we'd gotten our tickets. A fairly large crowd tonight, even with the temperature still in the mid-nineties at close to nine p.m. Sitting in a football stadium full of too many humans radiating excitement, leaking it like the Three Mile Island reactor, in this heat was not my idea of fun. But I'd promised, and we were here. My personal shields set to maximum, I'd even gone as far as to deliberately dampen my senses, dulling the possibility of a breach.

"He's up there. Somewhere on the right," I whispered to Adam, who stood next to me in the line waiting to hand over our tickets. "Can't see him but I feel him. Itchy, like crackling."

"You, too?" Tucker was on my right, already naturally flanking me and Adam. Niko was on Adam's left and a little to the back, his sharp gaze sweeping the crowd of nearly two hundred. We'd elected to bring only the two of them, figuring that any more would be flashing fang. Any fewer and we'd expose ourselves to potential danger. Despite my instant like of young Gregor, his Fenrir was an unknown quantity. He might be "middle-middle," as the boy said, but he was the alpha's alpha, leader of a wolf pack. In any book, that meant power and strength and many things not mundane.

This crowd of a couple of hundred didn't add up to a crowd by most city reckonings, but in White Rock, this equaled most of the available adults and children who weren't actually participating in the game or weren't part of the cheerleading squad, the pep squad, marching band, twirlers, flag team, concession stand sellers, or faculty. Compared to Rio Seco, White Rock was a bustling metropolis. It actually *was* large enough to have a football team, unlike my hometown, though not quite large enough for a Dairy Queen.

I narrowed my focus on the wolf's energy and answered my brother. "Yeah. He's somewhere up and to the right. Probably right under the announcer's booth. He's got at least two others with him." I concentrated my focus. "Lots of room around him, though. Like he's not only saving seats for us but created a perimeter. Can't really tell how big."

"How do you both know this?" Niko slid closer, his

hand almost cupping my elbow, wariness in his very stance. "I feel nothing."

"Nor I," said Adam. "Only humans, all around."

"You tensed up earlier," I said to Niko, who nodded.

"Too many people," he said. "However, I feel no wolf."

"It's a pretty big crowd tonight," Tucker agreed. "Fund-raising exhibition game. Besides, not much else going on around these parts unless you want to drive into San Antonio or Austin."

"Yeah, why the hell would the Fenrir of a nearby wolf clan ask us to meet with him tonight? What can't wait until our reception?"

"I'm sure we'll find out, sis," Tucker answered. "Energy doesn't seem antagonistic, by any means, just . . . there. Don't overthink it. We'll have an answer soon enough." He pushed past a couple of women, brightly dressed in shorts and tees, soft drinks in one hand, cigarettes in the other, gossiping madly and blocking the way. They turned to scowl, then saw my brother's extremely handsome face and muscular form. They both began to smile flirtatiously. Tucker never even noticed. "I think I'd best come up closer to you all," he said, taking his place at Adam's side. "It's a hellacious crowd tonight, and I'd rather that Niko and I stick close while we maneuver."

"Exactly," Niko agreed. "If all seems well when we meet the Fenrir, then we can go back to our usual places, before and behind."

I rolled my eyes at the two of them, yet, at the same time, a burst of pride filled me. My Protectors, soon to be Marked as such during the official ceremonies of the reception, acting as our bodyguards—no matter how unlikely anything was going to happen at a high school football game. Pretty damned ridiculous if one thought about it. Archaic, even. But what the hell, it's not like I could give it all back. I'd Changed, inherited all the Kelly Talents and now was heir . . . well, along with Gideon. He was no longer a threat, at least not as long as he remained Below, in the halls of his father's Unseelie Court.

I'd managed to survive finding out that my very attractive and bordering-on-evil distant cousin and former lover was Adam's half brother, a product of my Clan leader's breeding experiment, without too much mental scarring. I'd lived through three months of intensive training at the Kelly enclave. Surely I could get through tonight.

Adam peered into the crowd, his vision blocked by the many bobbing heads and ridiculous football paraphernalia being carried by the crowd. Even though this was only a local exhibition game by the high school—offense vs. defense—too damn many people sported large foam hats, bright yellow cardboard signs proclaiming "We're #1," and various other overpriced gear.

"Is this normal?" Adam asked. "This many people?"

"Depends," I said. "Since White Rock is the only high school in the area large enough to even have a football team, I imagine so. It's a holiday and a special fund-raising game, so there's probably a few more folks tonight than would show up for a regular season game. Of course if they were playing another school, their fans would be here, too. From what I recall, games here are usually fairly well attended. It's been years since I've come this way, though. Since my own high school days. Less populated then."

Tucker let out a laugh. "Yeah, I remember coming along with you, Bea, Carlton, and a couple of others," he said. "I seem to recall you and Bea had some pretty good times here." He looked pointedly at the bleachers. They were the old painted metal and wood kind, with plenty of room underneath to get in shitloads of trouble . . . and many kids had. I can recall at least eight or nine pregnancies in various high schools that I could directly attribute to action beneath the stands. Luckily, neither me nor my particular friends had been that ignorant or incautious. I'd limited my own activities to human boys—absolutely no chance of pregnancy or STDs—and I'd handed out condoms and advice to my human friends, thanks to my wonderful aunts, who'd been happy to give me as many and as much as I wanted. My dalliances with Clan kin required forethought. I'd saved those activities until I'd left high school. Easier that way.

However, I had lost my virginity right here, under these very same bleachers, sometime early in my junior year. Not to anyone I knew. I'd been drinking Coke with a very generous portion of 151, the bottle of over-proof rum acquired by one of Bea's cousins. Bea had poured hers into a thirty-two-ounce mug of Big Red. Less than an hour later, she was puking up pink liquid in the women's bathroom while I had my panties around one ankle, legs wrapped around the waist of one of the most gorgeous boys I'd ever laid eyes on—and considering the beauty of the men in my Clan, that was saying a hell of a lot. He'd had the most beautiful light amber eyes set off by dark, dark lashes and thick dark hair. All I remembered about him, other than his beauty, was that he'd been in town visiting someone and wasn't a resident of White Rock. Was he a senior in Lubbock? Waco? Somewhere not around here. By the time we'd gotten to "hey, where are you from?" I was way too into what we were about to do to pay much attention.

A small shiver of pleasure ran down my spine as I remembered that night two decades ago. Unlike most girls' first experience, mine had been fantastic. He was no virgin, and I was no shy Southern Miss. One thing my Clan taught very well was to enjoy life to its fullest . . . and I'd been a very attentive student.

"Hey, y'all came!" Gregor bounded up to us as we strode down the track, heading for the steps that led up the sides of the bleachers. The boy was barechested, all tail-waggy energy. I swallowed hard, still overwhelmed by his sheer beauty. Next to me, Niko went stock-still, as did Adam. I didn't even have to glance at either of them to know they'd been as bowled over as I had earlier today. Tucker, on the other hand, relaxed and assumed the loose, friendly posture that was more his style.

"Nice uniform you've got there, Gregor." My brother then treated the boy to the full-on Tucker Kelly charm, accompanied by an extremely obvious once-over. Tucker was not the shy one of the family.

The boy blushed, his bare chest turning as rosy as his face. He was wearing only the bottom half of a football uniform—pants, hip pads, socks, and cleats. His jersey and shoulder pads were in his hands, the "22" on the back of the jersey just visible.

I gulped, the combination of Tucker charm and sixteen-year-old wolf pup pheromones nearly overwhelming me. I had to stifle my continued very inappropriate urges as I looked into Gregor's wolf eyes. Damn it, he made *me* feel sixteen again, enamored of a strange boy and aching to go make out under the bleachers. *Get a grip, Keira,* I warned myself. *Gregor is still far too young for you. Besides, you have your own extremely gorgeous man—and he's standing right beside you.*

"I saw y'all walk by, so I came out to say hi." The boy nearly bounced in his excitement.

"Hello, Gregor," Adam said, extending a hand. "Thank you for coming out to greet us."

Gregor dropped his jersey and shoulder pads onto the grass and shook Adam's hand. "Thank you, sir, for coming. My uncle's gonna be really glad you came." He bowed his head at me. "M'lady."

"Gregor," I said. "I told you that I'm not as formal as all that. Please. Just call me Keira."

"Yes, ma'am," he said. "I mean—" He stopped, eyes widening. "Oh shit. I gotta go. Coach'll have my head if I don't finish suiting up."

"Ashkarian, get your pansy ass back into the locker room 'fore I bench you."

"Coach Miller," Gregor wailed. "It's only an exhibition—"

"I could bench you before the season even starts, boy." The harsh words came from a man of medium height dressed like all football coaches I'd ever seen: polo shirt, shorts made from a fabric unknown to nature, a clipboard in one hand, full of vinegar and pure-D assitude. The man wasn't even close to smiling. In fact, from the grim lines around his eyes, this coach wouldn't recognize a pleasant expression if someone carved it into his face. I gritted my teeth against a sarcastic remark. I wasn't here to interfere.

"Yes, Coach, right away, sir." Gregor whirled and took off at a gallop, disappearing into the athletic building, a squat concrete rectangle attached to the left side of the stadium. The coach scowled after him, taking off his cap with one hand and scratching his head. Well, that certainly said a lot, I realized. Should've figured from the man's stance. When he lifted his arm, he exposed a tat-

too on the inside of his right arm: USMC Semper Fi. I
would have known from the haircut alone, high and tight,
showing mostly scalp. A million words of explanation in
two physical traits. Dude was not only former military
but an ex-marine so obviously used to saying frog and
having his minions leap that he didn't even think twice
about barking orders, even in front of strangers. Without
another word, the man put his cap back on his head and
followed Gregor into the building.

The four of us just looked at one another and shook
our heads as we walked into the stadium proper.

CHAPTER SIX

THE STADIUM LIGHTS seared my eyeballs as I searched for the source of the wolf energy, wanting to establish Mark's exact location before we started climbing steps. "Fuck, fuck," I said through gritted teeth as I wiped my tearing eyes. "That was stupid." I berated myself for not thinking ahead.

"Dial it down, Keira," Tucker warned. "You can't go searching for the guy with your usual—"

"I know it, damn it," I said. "I just—"

"Forgot. You're all right?" Adam put a soothing hand on my cheek and tilted my face toward his. His green eyes glowed in the reflection of the nearly fifteen hundred watts on each light pole that surrounded the stadium. Instead of setting up day for night, as filmmakers often did, this was night as day—a night game to lure the parents and community members who worked, the oval area brightened by the massive kilowattage. I felt more than heard the hum of electricity that powered those overbearing lights. I was *very* glad our property was plenty of miles away from here. This kind of glow could be seen farther than one would think in the dark of the Hill Country. No light pollution here, except at this very stadium.

I wondered if nearby residents cared or complained. I knew I would.

Traffic and crowd noise would be a problem, too. During the regular football season, the crowd could easily double in size. This was just a game between the two halves of the same team, so everyone here was family, friends, and community members. Everyone, that is, except for us—and perhaps the werewolves. I still wasn't convinced this was as innocuous a meeting as Adam seemed to think. There was no reason that this Fenrir couldn't have just stopped by the Wild Moon tonight or tomorrow night, for that matter. It's not like we were going anywhere.

"I'm fine, really," I said and gave Adam a quick peck on the lips. "They may not have upgraded the bleachers since I was seventeen, but they've certainly paid dearly for those lights."

He stared at me in puzzlement. "You know this place well?"

"As Tucker said, I came here during high school. Rio Seco was smaller then. Even now, the high school's not big enough to have a football team. A fall Friday night's entertainment back then usually meant hanging out at the lake or driving here to White Rock for a game. Probably still is."

"I thought you didn't like football," Niko said. "You mentioned as much when we were watching that TV show . . . the one about the Texas high school team."

I laughed. Niko was enamored of *Friday Night Lights*—my guess is that he thought the boys on the show were hot; hell, I certainly did—and he'd gotten me to watch with him so I could explain the cultural references. "Yeah, well. I didn't and don't like football—the show's

great, but it's not about the game. Nor were our outings,"
I said. "It was a way to get away. I was a teenager,
remember?"

Niko's head tilt and the expression on his face made it
clear he had no clue. Damn, of course he didn't. He was
born in the sixteenth century. "Okay, Niko, sorry, that totally deserves a facepalm," I said. "Getting away from
our elders is pretty much the modern teen's raison d'être.
In my case, I had a car big enough for at least six of us to
pile in and go elsewhere."

After a moment, Niko seemed to understand. "Freedom," he said. "I believe I understand."

Not something he'd gotten much of, I imagined. A
child prostitute during the first Elizabeth's reign, dead
at seventeen or eighteen of the plague, turned by Adam,
who'd fallen for the beautiful boy. We'd had a rocky start,
Niko and I, his natural cockiness leading to sarcasm and
mistrust as I'd gained Adam's love and attention. Once
Tucker entered his life, he'd mellowed, realizing we were
all family. He was still as much Adam's as I was—without the sex, although at one time in their long mutual history they'd been lovers. Part of the upcoming ceremonies
included an official blood bonding—the renewal of his
oath to Adam—and two new bondings: his to me and he
and Tucker's to each other.

Tucker chuckled at his lover's thoughtful expression.
"We're pretty much old fogies, *cariad*. Little sister here
is not quite thirty-eight. Our teen years are centuries behind us."

Niko flashed a beautiful smile, his light red hair glint-
ing in the bright lights. "That they are, love, that they are.
Still, learning this about your sister is rather fascinating."
He gave me a peck on the cheek, then leaned behind me,

grabbed Tucker's hand, mimed a kiss, and then quickly let go, mindful of our location.

"Memories, only, Niko." I laughed as he returned to my side. "Good ones, but just memories."

Adam, who'd watched this exchange with a knowing expression, took my hand. "And there they shall stay," he said.

A short buzz from my ass morphed into the chorus of "Losing My Religion." I reached into my back pocket and pulled out my phone. Rhys's photo stared at me while I considered whether or not to answer it. Would Rhys be calling me here unless there was a problem? No one else was reaching for his phone, though—a good sign.

With an apologetic shrug at everyone, I pushed the button. "Rhys, what is it?" A note of anxiety accompanied my question.

"Have you seen the latest list?" I rolled my eyes at my brother's full-drama mode.

"Are you calling me about the attendee list? Now? Rhys, we're at the stadium about to meet with the Fenrir. Not a good time."

"Well, damn." He at least had the grace to sound sheepish about the interruption. "Do you at least have a sec to talk?"

"Rhys, my darling, loving, and very capable brother, y'all were given full charge of this event because of your many talents in this arena." He started to say something but stopped when he realized I hadn't finished. "Remember the part where Adam and I gave you carte blanche? We were quite serious. Think of it this way, we're the groom at a traditional American wedding. You and the rest are the mothers of the bride and the wedding planners. Go, plan all the details, and just tell us when to show up and where."

Dead silence on the other side stretched for too many long seconds. "Rhys? Is there an issue that takes precedence over us being here and meeting with a very powerful wolf leader?" As I spoke, the Fenrir's energy continued to pulse around me.

"Maybe."

"Is that a you 'maybe' or a Liz and the others 'maybe'?"

"There's just . . . well, some possibility of conflict with some of the guests on the list."

I laughed and shook my head. "Dear beloved brother, I fully expect to have to do no more than endure the vast majority of this upcoming night and enjoy very little of it."

Adam raised an eyebrow at me as if to remark on my last statement. I shrugged and amended it. "That is, very little except for those parts that remain special to me—when the three of you handfast; when my Protectors take my Mark and give us their blood oath; when Niko, Tucker, Adam, and I renew our blood bonds. Outside of those particular events, Rhys, I'm not expecting much of anything. Just as long as no one arrives planning to cut my throat or that of any of my people, I—and the rest of us—will survive it."

Another pause. "Rhys?"

A bad feeling began to grow in my belly when he spoke again: "Okay, then, I think perhaps this can wait. We'll take care of any issues." With an extremely false "Cheerio," he was gone, not having answered my question—that in itself was an answer.

I pocketed the phone and shook my head. "I think this planning is getting to him," I said to the group.

"Don't you think you might have actually heard him out?" Adam asked gently. "Rhys isn't usually given to overexaggeration, is he?"

Tucker said, "Depends, but I agree with Keira. The

reception is a big deal and Rhys is in full-on worry mode. He wants this to work for you both. No doubt our loving Gigi added some names to the list just to mess with things."

"No doubt," I said. "But I trust fully in Liz's judgment on matters involving high protocol and iffy guests. There's no need for us to get involved in every decision. We've given them direction. I'm sure that Liz will help work it out, or at least come up with a couple of viable seating charts or whatever to present to us later on. I'd really prefer to deal with the matters at hand right now."

I stared up into the bleachers, in the general direction of where the Fenrir's power pulsed, now careful to shield my eyes. That aura of barely leashed energy couldn't be ignored as easily as I could Rhys's call. Unlike Adam and Niko, or any of the Kellys, Marcus Ashkarian hid nothing. While we'd been out in the ticket line, the power was there, obvious yet contained. Now, as we stood at the bottom of the bleachers, he unleashed it, letting it permeate the entire hundred yards of the field and its surrounding stadium seats, ticket booths, concession stands, and athletic building. Like a pulse of heat from a sun flare, it coated me, surrounded me, echoing inside my very bones, tasting of heat, fire, musk—that particular combination that howled "I am Wolf. I am King." Familiar yet strange, its energy caused me to shiver. I wanted to caress it, use it for my own, and give it to Adam, getting it back a thousandfold as we merged together. Whoa, buddy, what the hell was I thinking?

"Fuck, what a rush. It *is* just us who feel it, right?" I said to Adam, my voice pitched so low that even Tucker was leaning in to listen. "You all do feel it now, don't you?" I gave my head a quick shake, trying to focus on the absolute present and not let my emotions run rampant, thoughts of Adam and me, entwined on a dark-sheeted bed, sweaty and glowing with completion. I'd once seen a vision of Tucker and Niko that way, long limbs tangled together in the light of a dozen or more candles, love and lust the same. Not something I really cared to do again, thank you kindly. My own sexual encounters with Adam were more than enough. I had no intention of watching my brother and his lover.

Tucker flashed his teeth at me, as did Niko, the both of them waggling their brows as if to validate my own reaction to the wolf's power. Adam, who also sought out the man at the top of the bleachers, nodded. "I feel it now." He surveyed the crowd, all seemingly ignorant of the sheer power flooding forth. "Yes, I'm sure they do not feel anything."

As with any other sports-going crowd, spectators, families, couples, and gangs of kids milled around, carrying coolers, lining up at the concession stand, munching on popcorn, sausages on a stick, Velveeta-coated nachos. Frankly, the place smelled. Every atom of burned oil and spoiling meat, the godawful smell of *tripas* being fried up in a ginormous pan, was enough to make me spew. I'd never known how people could eat fried intestines. Trying to avoid a very embarrassing incident, I focused on something else for a moment, watching a group of boys in full male display in front of the cheerleaders. Each held a beer, Lone Star for most, Shiner Bock for those more adventurous. Back pockets of their overtight jeans bore the telltale ring of Skoal or Copenhagen cans and rectangular wallet bulges. Unseen, but surely tucked in those wallets, there was a package with a smaller ring in case they got lucky tonight . . . or sometime in the next

couple of months before school started again. Some of
the pep squadders, perched in the stands directly above
the cheerleaders, watched with envy and anger, a mix all
too common in any high school. Like most places, pep
squad was where you ended up when you weren't athletic
and pretty enough to wear the cute short skirt and the blue
sleeveless top embroidered with a bright yellow WRHS,
weren't musical enough for the band, or coordinated
enough for the flag team. Other girls, in their own sort of
uniform, sauntered by, packs of them wearing too much
perfume and overdone hair, cheap jewelry sparkling in
the floodlights, hoping their dreamboat football heroes
would pick them.

The cheerleaders, the highest in this false but very
prevalent hierarchy, weren't very cheery, however. In
fact, they were practically wilting in the heat, their poly-
ester uniforms, designed for ease of cleaning and care,
stuck to their sweaty skin. A couple of them were half-
heartedly practicing cheers, their team spirit fading in the
unforgiving humidity. As I watched, a young family with
two children walked past the group, the parents trying to
find a place to sit, the youngest both sucking on neon-
colored popsicles.

"'Bout time for kickoff. Should find yourselves a
seat."

I turned slightly, just in time to see a dishwater blonde
dressed in full sheriff's gear standing behind us. She nodded toward the seats. "Y'all should go on up." After a
quick once-over, she scowled at us, then turned to walk
away, tension radiating from her with every step.

"Well, that was fucking interesting," Tucker said.
"Wonder what got up her—"

"Lily white ass?" I completed his thought. "Check

around, bro. We're pretty much smack in the middle of good ol' boyville. Even more than in Rio Seco. She probably didn't care for our looks."

We viewed a sea of faces of all ages and sizes, but nearly all of the Caucasian persuasion. Never mind that the four of us were paler than every last one of these white folks, we were neither kith nor kin, and it was bloody well obvious. Somehow, in those few months at the enclave, in my time spent at the Wild Moon, I seemed to have lost a little of my Texanity. Texas now felt like an ill-fitting glove. Though Rio Seco still welcomed me, White Rock, which was probably better representative of small towns in this state, obviously did not.

"I don't belong," I said, my voice flat.

"You belong with us," Adam said, followed by similar declarations from Tucker and Niko. "You're my partner and co-ruler, Keira. You've Changed." Instantly, his energy shimmered, letting me soak in the magicks that made him both vampire and Unseelie Sidhe, kin by distant blood, as all Sidhe are. I was Sidhe as well as Kelly; my mother was of the Seelie Court. Despite disparate Court affiliations, Sidhe were more alike than different. I reveled in the energy, blissful in its acceptance. Belonging.

A sharp stab of power flared, a virtual poke in the side. Adam snapped his shields tight, as did the rest of us.

"The Fenrir seems to be getting anxious to meet us." Niko immediately went on point, while Tucker took our six.

"Indeed," Adam said. "I should imagine this will prove to be quite interesting."

We climbed the steps toward the power signature.

I still couldn't pinpoint his exact location. The glare of the lights and shifting energies of the surrounding crowd masked his physical body, even though I precisely knew what he tasted of, what he smelled of, how he felt beneath my hands, his skin roughened by the out-of-doors, browned by the unforgiving Texas sun. A drop of sweat rolled down my temple.

"Fuck it's hot," I muttered.

"You've said." Tucker teased. "It's been over a hundred for the past thirty days, sis."

"I was trying to concentrate on the fucking alpha wolf up there. If it weren't for him, I could be back in the extremely cool house . . . perfect, cool, and quite comfy."

Adam laughed softly. "I'd have said it was rather hot last night."

I glared at him and poked Niko in the back, since he'd stopped walking. "Go, up the stairs like a good little vampire," I said quietly, so as not to be overheard by the humans. "And you, brother mine, enough with the teasing."

Niko made it up two steps before he had to pause again, to allow a family of redheads, each carrying a stadium seat and some sort of tote bag, sporting bright yellow shirts with the team's Viking logo in blue on the front. There were at least ten of them juggling their gear and trying to force themselves into some semblance of order on the bench.

I glanced past them to the section just to the left and up a few rows. I could only see the top of a dark head, bent down as if to pick something up. "There you are," I whispered.

Adam's hand stroked mine. "Yes," he said.

The last of the redheaded family moved into the row and Niko slid past them. Adam followed with me directly behind him. Tucker placed one hand on my back and walked in step with me.

"Shield with all you have, sis. Even I'm getting dizzy here."

"It's the heat," I said as I took the next three steps at a faster pace, keeping my eyes on the uneven concrete. I may be Talented, but even I wasn't immune to tripping. "What bloody fools decided that the middle of a record heat wave and drought is a good time for a football game?"

"That would be me."

The Fenrir stood directly in front of me. I hadn't felt his power move away from his previous location. Fuck. That could not be a good thing.

CHAPTER SEVEN

As NORMAL LOOKING AS HIS NEPHEW Gregor was drop-dead gorgeous, Marcus Ashkarian stood perhaps six feet tall with close-cropped, dark hair, medium build, and an olive complexion that belonged somewhere other than the landlocked middle of Texas. He was handsome, not homely, but neither was he outstandingly gorgeous. Two men stood on either side of him, both more bodyguards than companions, if I was to hazard a guess. One blond, rangy, sharp featured, longish hair pulled back, and just this side of pretty. The other man's shoulders seemed twice the width of the Fenrir's, his stocky build that of a weight lifter or wrestler. A negative image of the other guard's dark olive skin, dark hair, and square features. Unlike the other guard, this man had hair so short you could see scalp through it, as if he'd once shaved his head but was now allowing it to grow back. All three wore polo shirts in muted colors and tailored khaki shorts. Despite the crowd attending the game, there wasn't a single soul sitting near their small group. This wolf had certainly marked his space.

I waited for the Fenrir to begin the introductions. Wasn't that how it went? The lesser introduced himself or herself to the greater rank? I wondered if I was remembering something I'd read in a novel or if I was recalling actual Court protocol.

"Marcus Ashkarian, my lady." The moment he spoke, I tensed, a growl threatening behind my clenched teeth. Hairs on the back of my neck stood at attention; my skin crawled. My growl increased, magickally echoing throughout the stadium. I couldn't stop it. The Fenrir's voice held raw energy, power beyond his mild appearance. Despite the fact I still shielded to the nines, a wrongness, a bitter, ragged edge jabbed at me. I countered with instincts of my own wolf shape. *This wolf, this alpha, this Fenrir is too close. He trespasses.* I wanted to challenge him, make him submit. The part of me still in control forced the feeling down, chained it. I clenched both jaw and teeth, fighting to keep from doing something I'd regret.

Niko and Tucker jumped to position, in front of me. Adam pushed them aside and placed his hands on my shoulders. "What is it, what's wrong?" He sounded puzzled. I shook my head, trying to clear it. Comments and mutterings from the crowd surrounding us filtered in.

"What was that . . . loudspeakers . . . feedback, probably . . ."

"Keira, what is it?" Adam repeated, his hands tightening on my shoulders. The cool of his energy sank into me, calming my reaction.

"You don't feel it?" I muttered, still holding myself close.

Adam frowned. "I feel nothing else unusual. His power is still the same. Enticing, but just power."

"I think it's a territory thing," Tucker said, stepping behind me. "You and Adam are both rulers of this region, but Rio Seco—the Wild Moon—is your base."

"I don't understand," I said.

"There is much to be said for a physical base. It's part of your power, part of the Earth magicks. Did you never wonder why you chose to stay here, sis?" Tucker asked, his voice lower than a whisper. I had no idea if werewolves could hear as well as we could. Evidently, neither did my brother. What he was saying was for our ears alone, so he kept it subvocal, a trick he'd taught me years ago.

I shook my head slightly, still keeping a steady eye on the wer, who, to his credit, remained silent. At least he knew better than to interfere right now.

"No." My answer was curt, mostly because despite Adam's help, I still fought the instant anger, the feeling of wanting to push out the interloper, banish him and his kind away—far, far away. If another galaxy was available, well then, that might just do.

"There's power at the lake, I've often felt it. I once told Minerva that I thought ley lines intersected under the lake, close to the Wild Moon. Can't prove it, but I'd bet every single one of my twelve-hundred-plus years on it. Sis, you became adult in Rio Seco. Your blood spilled there. Before that, when you were only a child, we—our family—established our own blood ties to the land." Tucker regarded Marcus, who stood stock-still, his expression still friendly. "Gigi did a blood ritual at lakeside, near the old family cabin. Our immediate family, Dad, Rhys, Ianto, and the rest of our brothers marked our territory with our scent and our blood."

"Surely it's gone by now," I said, seemingly as puzzled as the others. "Since none of that was reinforced after y'all left—"

"Ordinarily, I'd say that would be the case," Tucker agreed. "I think what happened this spring cemented the ties." He spoke in vague terms I had no problem deciphering. "You're bound by blood and death, sis. Rio Seco and the immediate area is yours."

Okay, I could live with this. After all, that's what I was bred for—literally. I just hadn't expected it to be quite as . . . whatever. Was I going to feel this challenge with every other group leader I encountered? If that was the case, I was definitely going to call Gigi or my aunts to figure out how to handle this. I couldn't be going all over rabid during the upcoming reception.

I reclenched my fists, having relaxed them a little. Adam's hand closed over mine in support, his other arm coming around my waist, palm flat on my belly. Concentrating with every ounce of determination and pure-ass stubbornness I had, I swallowed hard, forcing my reaction down and back, pushed it until it sat behind a mental solid rock wall. By no stretch of anyone's imagination could it be said that the feeling was gone, just held at bay, its pressure thrumming against my shields like they were an about-to-break dam. Letting go of this now would be worse than levees breaking; wild magick rushing without control in a crowd of humans. *Calm yourself, Keira. Calm.* This is a meeting, nothing more. No threat here. As I relaxed, Adam let go and stepped back down, giving me space.

"Marcus." I started forward, my hand automatically reaching out for the standard "glad to meet you" handshake. With a speed just under that of light (or so it seemed), Tucker grabbed my wrist, his body supporting me from behind as I nearly stumbled.

"Probably not a good idea, sis," he said sotto voce, the warning evident.

Touching the Fenrir, oh yeah, brilliant, Keira. I mentally bitch-slapped myself. A few minutes ago I'd barely stopped myself from launching at the guy to challenge him, and that was my reaction to his energy only. Now I wanted a handshake? Egad. I'd been schooled in the polite human tricks like shaking hands so long, a few months' clan training wasn't going to instantly change my automatic responses.

"Marcus," I repeated as I clasped both hands in front of me and steadied my stance. Tucker stepped back and remained on guard. "Thank you for the invitation." I nodded my head at him, as close as I planned to get to a formal greeting in public.

"M'lady Kelly." The Fenrir echoed my own nod. "Welcome to you and to yours."

"Fenrir." Adam gave his own greeting, vampire neutral and polite.

"M'lord Walker."

"Might I also introduce you to my brother, Levon." Marcus motioned to the stocky man. "He is my Loki, my second." Indicating the other man, he continued, "Jacob, a new addition to our pack."

"Please call me Lev," Levon beamed, his smile lighting up his rather stolid face. The blond wer just nodded, keeping his aura of bodyguard intact.

"My own second, Nicholas." Adam gestured to Niko, then to Tucker. "Keira's brother and second, Tucker Kelly."

Everyone nodded to one another. I held back a guffaw. Here we were at a high school football game: two vampires, three werewolves, two Kellys. A few more of us and we'd have enough for a pickup baseball team. I couldn't help imagining the silliness of this—vampires doing something as mundane as playing sports.

My brother and Niko, now that the formalities were over, stepped aside a bit but remained close.

"You don't resemble much like what I'd pictured," remarked Tucker. "Not much of the Norseman about you." My brother, of all of us, should know, being a Viking himself. Marcus's hair wasn't the only thing that denied a Norse heritage; there have been plenty of dark-haired Vikings. His bone structure and olive skin placed him somewhere within shouting distance of olive groves and sunlit seas, Mediterranean instead of the icy gray waters of the North.

"Not Viking, nor Norseman of any kind, Cousin Wolf. My people came to the U.S. after our own version of the Holocaust drove us out of our homeland—it was the inspiration for the little man who liked to call himself 'Wolf.' " Marcus grimaced, his words angry. "He was no wolf, just a twisted, evil soul that used the slaughter, the genocide of my people to start his own unforgivable bloodbath."

I understood. He wasn't talking about the wolves at this point but this pack's cultural roots. His last name twigged. Why hadn't I caught that earlier?

"Armenian," I said softly.

"Yes. Though we follow the traditions of the North"—he nodded to Tucker—"as is common among our kind." Now he meant werewolf, not his other blood heritage.

"Ashkarian, I should've known," I said.

Marcus shrugged. "A name, taken and used. A distant relative, Diran Ashkar, came to the United States in 1920. We took his name and combined with our Armenian roots, we all became Ashkarian, even those born of other cultures." He studied each of us—me first, a long, slow perusal, empty of sexuality, simply a learning. Adam next, then Tucker and Niko. "Of all of you, the only Irish one, based on appearance alone, is this Viking . . . and I know that is not the case."

I echoed the man's shrug with one of my own. "Kelly is a name. Like yours, taken as a way to unite us. Too long ago to really know why or how or when." I paused a moment, wondering how much information to deliver, what was appropriate. This wasn't Adam's protocol, nor Tucker's. This was for me alone. "Kellys come in all shapes, sizes, and ethnicities," I continued, figuring this was fairly common information among the supernaturals. "My branch, the one that has ruled for many centuries, happens to call the Welsh hills home. The ways of the Celts rubbed off—or, we rubbed off on them. But no matter, Kelly we became and Kelly we are for sake of simplicity."

Marcus didn't bother to hide his own amusement. *"Areithi Cymraeg, 'na?"*

Startled, I laughed in delight and replied, *"Cymraeg yw fy iaith Gyntaf.* You speak Welsh?"

"I like languages," he explained. "Scholar of the spoken word, mostly. Not the dead ones. I used to teach at the University of Texas, San Antonio." That was it, I realized. His looks spoke of scholar, not warrior wolf. I could see him hunched over dusty tomes in a library more easily than hunting in a field. Was that why his power surprised me so much? He was the Fenrir, the alpha of the alphas, the leader of a pack. Everything I knew about wers fit in a large coffee mug, but I knew this: "leader" to them meant highest in power and status—scholar or not.

"You speak well for an 'Englishman.'" I couldn't help but use the Welsh term for outsider, though this man's heritage was as far from Cymru and the Hollow Hills as I was from humanborn.

"As do you," Marcus replied.

"It's my milk language," I explained. "English was my second learning."

The Fenrir's eyebrows raised, his expression turned quizzical. "You really aren't from around here." His voice held a question that I'd never even considered.

Tucker's belly laugh rolled over us. "Oh, Marcus, have you forgotten? Or perhaps you didn't know this of the Kellys? Not a one of us was born here, not even on this continent. For many, this is still the New World."

"But I thought . . ." Marcus's frown clearly indicated that he was puzzled about me.

"I was born in the Welsh hills, Fenrir," I explained gently. "I am both of the Kelly Clan and the Seelie Sidhe Court." Marcus's eyes widened as he began to understand.

"You, also," he said to Adam. "Not just what you seem on the surface, Nightwalker." A statement, not a question.

"Not just," Adam agreed, his tone as bland as plain grits. "But we diverge from our purpose here, talking to you about why you invited us." Adam made the words smooth, without any sort of sting of reprisal. "We are happy to explain that which may be explained," he continued, "however, I do not believe this is the time or the place." With a slight wave, he motioned to the ever-growing crowd, the noise that I hadn't heard in a while. Oh well, hell. I closed my eyes for a second and concentrated, breaking the silence bubble that I'd somehow unconsciously erected. The babble rushed to fill the void, voices chattering, band music playing while the crowd grew ever more excited as the kickoff drew near.

"Umm, oops," I said. "Sorry, still not used to this."

Tucker grinned and poked me in the side. "That's some good subliminal gut reaction, sis. Brava." I poked him back and said nothing.

"Now what?" Tucker turned to Marcus Ashkarian.

"We sit and enjoy the game. My young nephew Gregor is one of the players, you know."

"Number twenty-two," I returned. "Shall we, gentlemen?" I motioned to the bleacher seats just to the left of Marcus, on the same level. I wasn't about to sit with him at my back. He seemed harmless enough, but I still couldn't shake the uneasiness I'd felt at first. There was something hanging around, some sort of underlying tension. Niko and Tucker split, Niko to sit behind us, Tucker in front.

I leaned forward to Tucker as we were moving toward our seats and mentioned it.

"Yeah," he whispered. "I feel it, too. Can't pin it down."

Adam, on my other side, stepped close, his mouth against my ear. "I have no knowledge of the hearing abilities of the Fenrir," he said. "But I can tell you I still feel nothing out of the ordinary."

"Really?" I whispered back as I settled myself on the metal bench and immediately stood up again as the skin on the back of my thighs touched the seat. "Fuck, ouch," I exclaimed. "Damn it, what ever possessed me to forget something to sit on?" It had been years since the last time I'd been in a football stadium, but I could've planned a bit better. Marcus stood and with a small flourish, pulled a thick towel out of a tote bag at his feet.

"M'lady," he said and, with a bow and accompanying grin, spread the towel on the hot metal. "You'd best sit on this."

I nodded my thanks. "Appreciate the gesture, Marcus," I said. "It's been a long time since I've been to a game."

"Yes, it has," he said, and handed a second towel to

Tucker. Niko shook his head as he was offered a third.

I gave Marcus a puzzled look. What would he know about my football-going experiences? He said nothing and just went back to watching the cheerleaders below.

Adam frowned and sat next to me, sharing my towel. "Has he met you before?" he asked me, still keeping his voice very low.

"Not as far as I know," I said. "I'd recognize him. The power signature isn't anything I could forget."

Adam settled and took my hand. I stifled my amused reaction. Possessive much? Oh yeah, and that was just fine by me. I turned my attention to the field below, ready to endure the game.

CHAPTER EIGHT

Nᴏᴛ ᴛᴇɴ ᴍɪɴᴜᴛᴇs ʟᴀᴛᴇʀ, another bout of energy shot through me. This time the feeling was not just disturbing, it was one of utter loathing and absolute hatred. "What the—" Still not a soul near us; at least five or six people-widths between us and the nearest humans on all four sides. What the hell was going on? Who was it coming from? No one could touch me or even get near me. To penetrate the distance and the dense shields I had up would take more than merely solid dislike. This was true, unadulterated, rage-filled hostility. The kind that ended up with a victim dragged behind a pickup truck or stripped naked and bound to a fence to die of exposure. I heard no words, saw no images other than a deep, roiling darkness of anger and misery. I wanted to jump into a hot shower and scrub my mind clean of this sick taint.

"Adam," I whispered, touching him on the arm, hoping to convey my sense of urgency.

"What is it, what's wrong?" He signaled to the boys with a quick tilt of his head. They both began to check out our surroundings. "Who are we looking for?"

"I don't know," I said. "It's weak, I know, but just a moment ago there was this flash of—" I tightened my grip on his hand and projected the emotion in a brief burst, the only way I knew how to describe it. Words weren't adequate.

He recoiled and wiped his hands on his tropical-weight gabardine slacks. "Who was that?"

"That's just it," I said. "I don't know. No one was close enough to me to touch me, not even close enough for me to accidentally catch a scent."

"Human?" Tucker said quietly.

"I think." I rubbed my forehead. A headache threatened. "Didn't feel like one of us."

"How about one of them?" Niko indicated the three wer, all of whom watched us with anxiety written across their faces.

"No, didn't taste of wolf. I'm sure of it."

"Any pattern you might recognize?" Adam asked.

"Nothing, just overwhelming hatred." I checked around once more, trying to determine if anyone was staring at us or even scrutinizing someone else in the crowd or on the field with an other-than-appropriate expression on his or her face. Nothing. I spotted the sheriff strolling behind the cheerleaders, the girls huddled together discussing something. Coach Miller stood on the sidelines, clipboard in hand, studying the lineup. A new play was about to start. A second coach stood a few paces to his right, leaning over one of the helmeted players. A nod and a pat to the boy's back and a quick motion for a switch. The seated player stood, fastened his helmet, and entered the game, passing another boy returning to the bench. Neither seemed angry or upset. After all, this was an exhibition game and all competitiveness aside, it appeared as if the coaches were doing their best to rotate players in and out, probably to study their abilities, their techniques.

The final varsity starting lineup wouldn't be chosen until right before the start of the school year, if memory served me. Not that there were a great many players to choose from. White Rock might have a larger population, but the pickings were still mighty slim for a football team.

I relaxed a little as nothing more turned up. "Maybe I just tuned in to a really bad marriage," I said, trying to keep it light.

"Did you get a sense of the direction, the intended recipient of the hatred?" Adam asked.

"Not really. Just the intensity. I wouldn't want to be the target of that." I shivered a little, as the feeling washed over me again, this time just a clear memory, not the actual emotion itself. "I can't imagine who could elicit that kind of sheer abhorrence."

"I could." Marcus slid closer to Adam and me. "Sorry for eavesdropping, Keira, but I saw your face. I heard what you said."

"No apology necessary, Mark," I replied. "I wasn't trying to hide it from you." His face was grim; no trace of amusement lightened his expression now.

"It's a racial memory thing," he said. "We wolves have a little of it, passed down in tales, in history and emotions from our forebears. Your expression, the hatred you described, we felt in the early part of the last century. Hatred for existing. For being Christian in a Muslim country. Hatred felt by others in a later war for being of another culture . . . and, now, in this land sometimes."

"Here, in White Rock?" Adam frowned. "There are hate crimes here?"

"Of a sort," Marcus replied. "Not the likes of which you'd hear about on the evening news, no Matthew Shepards or lynchings. Just sidelong looks, muttered words said too low to hear, people getting ignored in a restaurant."

"Your people?" I asked.

"Sometimes," he said. "I've heard a few folks think we're some sort of weird religious cult. I think sometimes we disappoint them when our women show up in town and they're not wearing long dresses and aprons. They can't pin us down because we're law-abiding, taxpaying citizens who keep to ourselves and don't stand out."

"Then why the anger?" I asked. "Do you think this was directed at you?"

"Anger comes in many guises," Mark said. "This is why I'm working so hard at having the boys fit in. My nephew Gregor and another boy, Luka, are enrolled in school. They're both stable, even-tempered boys. Having them on the football team goes a long way in gaining acceptance—or at least to being ignored. We're not a long way from Jasper here. I don't want to wake up some night to find crosses burning on our lawns. Most folks think we're just a bunch of Austin-type hippies—white folk who prefer to stick to their own."

"White folk." Tucker nearly spat out the words. "I thought you said you took in wolves from all over."

"We do," Mark insisted. "I just know that it's best to keep those of color closer to home."

I gritted my teeth and clenched my jaw at his words. Adam, who knew my temper and my feelings about this, wrapped an arm around my waist. "Keira, let's go for a short walk. Perhaps you can pinpoint the source of the anger. Tucker, you stay here, please. Niko, if you'll accompany us?"

I kept my mouth shut and my words close until we were completely out of earshot of the wolves and heading out toward the parking lot. We walked past the ticket booth and Will Call window, to the first row of cars, ending up behind a huge SUV of some sort. With a quick focus and burst of a little energy, I threw up a muffling charm that would render my conversation with Adam and Niko unintelligible to any but us three.

I took a deep breath, then another, and then a third. Then I exploded.

"He's fucking as bigoted and discriminatory as the reddest of necks around here. He's only sending the white folks or those who can pass out into town? What right has he—"

Adam cupped my cheeks with his hands, his gaze catching mine. "He has every right, love," he said in his best calm, soothing voice. "He is Fenrir and absolute leader." I started to pull away, still not over my righteous fit, but Adam held tight, as only he could. "Think about it, Keira. You are judging without all the knowledge. You—we—are not in his position. We live in a closed world. Our land is ours, and your town knows you and your family—has known them for decades. You are lucky that Rio Seco was settled by a more diverse group of people. Marcus has not had such luck. His place is here, in White Rock. His children, his pack's children must somehow be assimilated in this human society. Is that not what your father wished for you? for Marty?"

I nodded, unable to say anything that didn't sound petty or annoyingly whiny, especially when he brought up my now-dead cousin. Adam was right, but how could I stand by and see this deliberate discrimination perpetuated by a man whose own family barely escaped mass genocide, not a hundred years ago? This was the twenty-first century, and we were still fighting the same damned battles: being different could get you ostracized . . . or even killed.

I huffed. "Adam, you don't get it. How can someone whose family has experienced this kind of discrimination, even genocide because they were 'different,' do this to his own people?" I turned to Niko to illustrate my point. "Niko, you get it. I hate to be this blunt, but you were a whore, right?" The word fell between us, foul and angry.

Niko remained calm, though, regarding me with a solemn and steady air, his blue eyes deep wells of thought. "I was."

"And how did people treat you?" I pushed a little harder. He didn't even flinch.

"At best, I had patrons who allowed me to sleep indoors, sometimes on a pallet, most times on the floor. At worst . . ." He turned away, staring into the empty air, as if to compose his reply. "At worst," he continued, "I was in the stinking, fetid gutters of the city, praying I could steal enough stale bread to survive just one more day." He turned back to me, just as calmly as before. "Either that, or praying that death would finally come to take me and relieve my suffering." He turned to Adam, his expression softening. "Eventually, it did."

Adam raised his hand and stroked Niko's cheek, a look of love, fondness, and caring directed toward the man who was his second. Their bond comforted me. It had lasted more than four hundred years, first as mentor and student, then lovers, then as family. My own bond with Adam was so new, so fresh, that some days, I wondered if it could last. Seeing him with Niko reminded me that anything was possible.

"Adam," I began gently. "Do you see? You were—

no, are—a prince of the Sidhe, heir to the High King of the Unseelie Court. As vampire, you are ruler in your own right. My story may not be as dramatic as Niko's, but it's close." I moved closer to the two men, wanting nothing more than the comfort of our chosen family tie. "You know that I spent the first seven years of my life captive in Faery, Underhill—the unwanted and uncared for daughter. Then my father rescued me and I came to Texas, to my Kelly family. Even then, I was called names by the local kids. I was different, still am. I had a funny accent, was too pale for this sunny place, didn't have the right cultural references."

I took his hand as he reached to stroke my cheek as he had Niko's. "No, please, let me finish. If it weren't for Bea taking me under her wing, who knows how I would have ended up? I'm no great shakes as it is. I'm fucked up in a lot of ways. I don't trust easily. But one thing I do know—I'd never, ever condemn my people, those of my family, blood or chosen, to live as second-class citizens because of who they are, or who people perceive them to be. I can't . . . and I can't understand why Marcus allows this, how he tolerates it."

"Keira, when I became vampire, it was at the behest of my father," Adam said. "All these ridiculous machinations and plotting—both his and Minerva's—to unite all the kindred, all those of us beyond human. His minions held me down as the vampire chosen to be my maker drained me of all blood, aided by my father, who drained me of magick and my life. They let me fade, starve as we can, depleted of all energy. They held me captive in an empty cave for three days, then, three days later, came to get me as I awoke raging with blood thirst and vengeance." His green eyes held steady on my own gray, his expression hardened. "They set me free from my bonds when we reached Above, right in the middle of a small village of humans. I fed until I was sated."

I reached for him, but as I had, he took my hand and held it back. "Now you must let me finish," he said. "My own people, my Sidhe brethren, became frightened of me. Superstitious lot that they are, they feared that my new state would make them my cattle, my food; that I could drain them just as easily as I'd drained those villagers. My new vampire 'family' . . ." His voice dripped with sarcasm as he said the word. "Let us just say that fear was not the emotion they felt toward me."

"Hate?" I ventured a guess, now beginning to understand another facet of this man I knew so well, yet so little. He nodded his assent.

"Though the youngest of the vampires as they reckon age, I was by far their elder in years, and by far their superior in rank. No one knew what to do with me, so I was given a small tribe of my own straight away, bypassing normal process or procedure."

The three of us stared at one another for a few silent moments. So many differences in our lives, in our making and shaping, yet, at the root, so very similar.

"Well, hell, then, I guess we're all a bunch of sorry-ass loser freaks," I said and burst out laughing. "I concede your point, Adam. I have no clue about the wers' true situation and should trust Marcus."

"Trust him?" Adam raised a sardonic brow. "Oh, love, not as far as he could throw me. Understand that we do not know his agenda, nor his long-range plans and goals. Trusting him is not something I would do quickly."

Yes, this was more like it.

"I don't want them to suffer," I said. "I realize probably better than you two how right-wing this town is, but I thought better of him."

"Because you enjoy his company?" Adam teased lightly.

I gave him a peck on the mouth. "No, fool vampire, because I kind of like the guy. He seems a good sort, and anyone who's watching out for the welfare of those less fortunate, especially when his own core family isn't rolling in dough, rates plenty of gold stars in my book. This was just unexpected."

"Yes, but practical," Niko said.

"Niko and I, and I'm sure your brothers and Liz would agree on this, Keira. Sometimes, one must take the long vision, the slow road. It's much harder to see from your perspective."

"From a relative youngster?"

"If you like." He smiled and kissed me. "It is very difficult for you to be able to fully integrate, to embody the long-range planning, the centuries of perspective as we can. As heir and as a Kelly, you have a much better point of view than most, but one eventually learns that battles must be chosen quite carefully. Plans that seem to be less than fruitful in the shorter term will win out in a much longer one."

"I acquiesce to your great wisdom, O ancient one." I caressed his cheek. "I know I'm impatient and that's something that a few months under Gigi's care isn't going to change immediately. I promise I will try to understand Mark's intentions."

"He's a shrewd one, indeed," Adam said. "Taking this longer road, when perhaps his intentions won't bear fruit in his own lifetime—this is a good leader."

"I'd wondered about their life spans. I've only known

a few wer here and there, during my European days. None well enough to ask personal questions of."

"They are strong, heal quickly, can withstand many injuries that would disable or debilitate a human of similar size. They are also immune to many common human diseases, like colds and flu. Their life spans, however, are just slightly more than average for a human. Eighty, ninety years or so. Unlike us, they can be killed outright." A shadow passed over Adam's face then.

"You've known some?"

"I have," he said. "A story for another time, perhaps, but yes. I once befriended a pack of wolves, some decades back. Many of them died in Prussia, fighting on the side of the Allies."

Niko nudged Adam's arm. "Shall we return?" he suggested quietly.

"Yeah, we'd best," I said. "Someday, when we're settled into this ruling thing, I want to hear stories from the both of you—family stories, history stories. From my brothers and Liz, too. I've lived such a short time, known such a small fraction of life."

Adam tucked my hand into his crooked arm. "Sounds like a lovely way to spend a quiet evening at home. We can be our own bards."

I paled a moment, remembering the bards we'd recently run across in Vancouver, scions of the Unseelie Court, Adam's kin. "Stories, then," I said. "Our own."

CHAPTER NINE

"MY APOLOGIES, MARCUS." I settled into the seat next to him again. "I was way out of line."

He gave me a slow nod, almost a bow. "You have a right to question me," he said. "In the reality of things, you are my liege. I hope, however, that you will come to know why I do what I do."

"Is that why you invited us here tonight?" Adam asked.

"Not exactly," Marcus said. "I truly did wish to get to know you-all, to present myself on behalf of my people. There is one other thing, but that can wait until after—"

"Oh, fuck." The words spilled unnoticed from my mouth as I saw her. She was with someone I didn't know, another woman. The two of them climbed up the stadium stairs, heading in our direction. My breath and my words were trapped inside me as I watched Beatriz Ruiz draw nearer.

Bea looked the same as always, her thick, wavy black hair caught up in a high ponytail to escape the heat. She wore a cute white strappy blouse with denim shorts and a pair of sandals. The woman walking next to her was a knockout. She stood taller than Bea and exuded exotic.

Hell, if I didn't know better, she could be my own sister. As the thought crossed my mind, I quickly muttered a curse on the very idea. Gigi had better not have any more little familial surprises for me.

I couldn't feel any connection, nothing that said Kelly to me. Despite that, even her build resembled mine—sturdy, with some curves. We were both definitely women, not girls, but neither of us were as curvy as Bea, who could give Salma Hayek lessons. The main difference is that this woman was at least four or five inches shorter than me—still, a few inches above Bea's petite height and she was like sex on a stick. Her outfit was very similar to Bea's own. On Bea they were attractive, comfy summer clothes; on this women they were enticing and inviting. The woman walked with a fluid grace, her loose dark hair hiding her face. Who was she?

The two women had their heads together as they approached, chattering away, sharing something I couldn't hear above the pounding in my own chest. Fuck. This is *my* Bea. *My* best friend being all chummy and BFF-ish with some Other Woman. *Whoa, there, Keira,* I thought to myself as I realized my train of thought. *What the fuck's gotten into you?* I swallowed hard and schooled myself to greet Bea. She still hadn't noticed me, deep in conversation with her companion and balancing a cardboard tray holding four Coke cups.

As she got closer, Bea glanced up, as if to get her bearings, then stopped abruptly, the Cokes shimmying in their holder. She grabbed at them with her right hand, saving them from a sure and messy demise on the bleachers. A breath, then two, as the world stopped. I'd heard that phrase before—*the world stopped*—and never really known what it meant. I thought I'd experienced it a few times in my life: when I'd first seen Adam across a crowded room and my primal brain said "I want that, yes, him"; when I met the Kellys for the first time, a crowd of adults of every shape, color, and size, crowding around a too-skinny waif who was still getting used to the sun. But this, *this* was like everything—sight, scent, taste, noise— all vanished as I focused on only one thing: the face of the only person not Kelly who'd known me nearly all my life.

Bea blinked a few times, eyes shining in the reflected light from the stadium. Her mouth opened, closed. No sound emerged. Like me, she seemed incapable of moving, of saying anything. I felt the seconds ticking, as if Captain Hook's infamous crocodile stalker approached, except the tick tocks were in my own head, a metronome measuring the stretch of silence, stretching it thin, stretching beyond its capacity, stretching to its very limits, to its breaking—

A two-second recon on her part as she sussed out who was around her, then she shoved the Coke tray into Tucker's belly, not stopping to see if he'd even grabbed on to them. With a cry of joy and tears rolling down her cheeks, Beatriz Consuela Esperanza Ruiz, sister of my heart, scrambled up and threw her arms around me.

I was truly and finally home.

I crushed her back, my arms immediately closing into a vise grip. This was more than friends, almost more than lovers. This was family lost, now returned. Except who was the prodigal here? Me, I guessed, my brain whirling with words I couldn't even form. My ears and brain weren't capable of translating the noises coming from Bea herself, her face buried in my shoulder.

After a moment, she stepped back and, head tilted to

check out my own teary face, began to scold. "Don't you ever do that again," she said, finger wagging. "Never."

I hugged her again and let go. "I promise, Bea, never ever."

All the men stared at us as if we'd gone bonkers. Adam raised a brow in a silent question. I knew what he wasn't asking. I gave him a slight shake of the head, then turned back to Bea.

"I left because I had to, you know that."

Bea's "never" wasn't about what had happened to Pete Garza, though I knew that was what Adam was thinking. She meant my leaving without talking to her. Ridiculous, yes, because *she'd* been the one refusing to talk to me, but who the hell cared? She was here and I was here and we were making up.

"I know," she blubbered, grabbing a tissue from a pocket and wiping her face. "It was just—"

"I know," I said. "Utter hell, Bea. So much happened."

"I was scared," she began, fingers twisting the sodden tissue, tearing it into bits. "When you . . ." She didn't finish her sentence.

When I deliberately and with great pleasure sentenced her would-be rapist and murderer to death-by-Sidhe, to have his disgusting life drained from him, the body forgotten, lost in the depths of a cave. Pure justice, yet outside the bounds of any human law.

"It's who I am," I ventured, hoping that she'd not chosen to forget my true nature. Even though it could mean the end of a thirty-plus-year friendship, resuming it *had* to be on real terms. I'd come to that realization while I was in Canada—I was Kelly, I was heir, and I was not human, no matter how long I'd been among them. My ethics were not always her ethics, and would never be.

She studied me in quiet defiance, a hand on my arm. "I know exactly who you are, Keira Kelly. I've always known. You, too. All of you." She deliberately stared at Tucker, then Adam, then Niko. "You are what and who you are. And that's that."

I broke out in laughter. That, indeed, was that. The separation was over and we were back to Bea'n'Keira.

"Who's your friend?" Tucker asked Bea, as Marcus took the Cokes from Tucker's hand.

The woman perused him up and down, a slow and steady expression of appreciation beginning to form. Niko, still on my other side, let a small growl escape. The woman laughed, then held her hand out to me. "Dixxi Ashkarian," she said. "I take it you must be our Keira Kelly."

The wolf power was there now that my senses were not saturated with the presence of Bea, who still hung on to me as if I'd vanish again. "I am," I said to her. "Sorry I can't shake, I need to be a little cautious with the, well, you know—" I said as a young couple, wrapped up in each other, seemingly oblivious to whatever "stay away" vibes Marcus was exuding, tried to come sit in the empty area just next to us. With a quick thought and a bit of focus, I sent out a perimeter spell. The couple, who'd been deciding exactly where to sit, quickly scuttled away to the far end of the bleachers. I laughed and nodded at Dixxi. "Consider yourself greeted with the highest politeness possible." Despite my earlier reaction, I liked her. Her aura, her underlying energy soothed me more than bothered me, unlike her Fenrir's, who I suddenly realized was trying to get my attention with a diplomatic throat clearing.

"Yes, Marcus?" I turned to him, patting Bea on the

shoulder, an unspoken promise for a night of catching up, wine, and girl talk implied. "I apologize for having interrupted you earlier, but when I saw Bea . . ."

"I hadn't realized you knew Ms. Ruiz," Marcus said, an odd note in his voice.

"For years," I replied, still grinning at my friend. "She's family."

At that, Dixxi, who'd passed out the drinks and handed over the popcorn and hot dogs to the other men, looked up. "Say what? Family? She's not—"

"No. She's not actually related," I said. "She's family in the way of chosen family everywhere. All but blood."

"Well, this is certainly going to put a crimp into his plans," Dixxi muttered.

Adam's eyebrow raised two seconds before both of mine did. "My apologies," he said, addressing both Marcus and Dixxi. "A crimp?"

"Damn, I forget you people have bat ears," she said. "I, well—shit." She turned to Marcus, eyes pleading. "Mark?"

"What my sister means," Marcus said, having seemed to regain a little more control, "is that once again, we must ask your indulgence and this time, request a boon." He made a gesture of apology, hand open toward us. "This wasn't planned, I swear it," he continued. "But now that we know of your relationship to Ms. Ruiz, we must ask . . . even though it breaks most protocol."

"Protocol, what protocol?" I asked. "I'm not following you, Marcus."

He began to put his hand to his chest and bow, then caught himself as he seemed to realize that we were still in the middle of a high school football game. "Damn. This is going to be awkward."

"Seriously, drop the formality," I said. "We're not much into that . . ." I glanced at Adam and chuckled. "Well, at least I'm not," I added. "What is it you need from us? Land, hunting privileges? Was that why you asked us to come to the game?"

He seemed taken aback. "You're certainly direct, aren't you?"

"Pretty much, yeah," I said.

"Then, I'll be as direct in return. Ms. Ruiz, if I could beg your pardon?"

Bea, who'd been following the conversation enrapt, yet obviously puzzled, smiled at Marcus. "Sure, whatever."

"My brother, Lev, would ask that you allow him to court Ms. Ruiz."

I plunked onto the bleacher bench, at a complete and utter loss for words. Adam sat down much more gracefully. I could tell he was amused. "Court? As in dating?" I asked. Lev seemed about as floored as I was.

"Yes," Marcus said.

"Okay, that's a new one," I said. "I mean why ask me? Bea's right there. If your brother wants to go out with her, all he has to do is ask." Bea beamed at Lev.

"I take it you've actually met him?" I asked her.

"Yeah," she said. "Several times. He, Mark, Dix, and Greg have been spending a lot of time in the café lately. While they get the deli ready. You did hear about that, right?"

"I did." *She's at least not completely turned off by the guy,* I thought. How the hell was I supposed to answer this? Adam wasn't giving me any clues. Neither were Tucker nor Niko. Either they'd not had to deal with this before, or they were letting me row my own boat solo.

"You want to date this guy?" I honestly couldn't care less that the man in question was sitting less than ten feet from me.

She shrugged. "Maybe."

I turned to Marcus, catching Lev's eye as I did. "She says 'maybe.' " For a moment, I felt as if we were playing some ridiculous kid's game. "In my book, that means he can ask."

"Many thanks, m'lady," Marcus replied. "On behalf of my brother, as well."

Lev came out of his stupor at that point. "Yes, thank you very much." He gave Bea a look that was just short of infatuated.

I let my breath out with a *whoosh*. This ruling thing was getting complicated. Evidently, I'd be learning the rules and conventions for groups other than my own odd family. First the vampires, now a wer pack. Tonight was turning out to be more than interesting.

CHAPTER TEN

ABOUT HALFWAY INTO the next quarter of the game, which frankly, I was paying little attention to, Bea leaned over and tugged at my arm. "Hey, could we . . . I just wanted to . . . could we go somewhere else to talk? I'd really rather you and I have a chat that's just a little more private."

What the heck? We'd just buried the proverbial hatchet. "What's up?"

After a sideways glance at Lev, who still held his sappy expression, she whispered, "There're just a couple of things I'd rather say without everyone hearing."

Normally, I'd say yes immediately, but now, things were different. As heir, I had to think of my security and safety, even within such innocuous surroundings as a high school football game, especially this one, considering the wolf pack. I glanced at Tucker, who, with a nod of his head, both indicated that he'd watch out for us and pointed out the small landing at the bottom of the stadium steps. Perfect. Thanks to Marcus's vibes and my little spell, most of the crowd on this side of the stadium had shifted to the center of the stands. The landing was a small oasis, free of anyone who could overhear.

Most people's concentration was on said game, the usual rush, crush, crunch, and whistles occurring without the least of my attention on the actual field. A glance at the scoreboard told me the score was home 6, visitors 0. Since this was only an exhibition game, "home" meant the defensive squad and "visitors" meant the offensive.

"C'mon," I said, "let's go down there. No one's close by and with the game in play, folks'll be focused on that."

"Perfect." Bea took the lead.

As we reached the bottom she turned to face me and gave me a direct gaze. "I just wanted to thank you," she said. "For the house. You didn't have to do that."

I started to protest, but she continued, not letting me speak yet. "I know what it meant for you to do that, so thanks. I like it there." She grinned. "Tio and Tia are happy to see me on my own and not having to watch after them and Noe."

"You took it, you're living there? I was afraid . . ." That she'd shun that offer, that she'd shun everything I offered, including my continued friendship.

Bea laid a hand on my arm, her gaze earnest. "Of course I did. It was what I had left of you, you idiot. I had no clue you were even coming back." Tears welled in her eyes. "You really think I wouldn't have taken it?"

I looked away then, past her to the football field where the boys were completing some play. What could I say without completely breaking down? A blink, then two. Taking a deep breath, I spoke, still staring unseeingly at the field. "When I left for Canada, Bea, I was only sure of one thing—that I was coming back. No matter how long things took, I knew I'd be back."

"Noe told me," she said. "I wanted to believe him, but at the time . . ."

"I know." She'd been hurting, afraid, shocked—all those words that meant that she'd seen deeper into the parts of me that didn't square with her knowledge of who I was. Sadly, what she'd seen was truth. And sometimes, truth is damned brutal . . . and extremely bloody.

"It took me a long time to realize that you were still *you*," she continued. "The worst part? I couldn't talk about it to anyone."

My heart stuttered. Of course not. How could she have? Oh, by the way, Tia, Keira isn't human, and hey, she killed Pete Garza. Well, considering what Garza had done to Bea, her aunt might have celebrated that fact, but Bea outing us? Never. She'd learned who we were years ago, during high school, and swore a secrecy oath to me. Not a blood oath, nor formal, but I knew she'd never break it.

I turned back to her and hugged her. "I'm sorry," I whispered in her ear. "You didn't have anyone to talk to, and I had so many."

"Apology accepted," she murmured and kissed my cheek. "No matter what, Keira Kelly, we are sisters."

I let her go and wiped a tear from my eye as I gave her a wavering smile. *"Por siempre y para siempre, chica."* Sisters, forever and always. An idea struck me. Could I ask her to blood bond? She was human, but even if it was simply symbolic . . . "Bea," I began, then had to step aside as a man carrying a large cardboard tray full of fried *tripas* wanted to squeeze by us. I wrinkled my nose at the smell, still pungent, even away from the hot oil of the pan. *"Chinga,"* I exclaimed. "How can anyone eat— Bea?"

She'd paled under her summer tan, brown skin going ashen as she clapped a hand over her mouth. "Excuse me," she mumbled and stumbled down the final two steps to the ground level. I followed immediately, trying to keep to a run/walk that wasn't out of the ordinary, when every instinct I had made me want to put on my best speed and catch up to her. Either that, or simply will myself there. I'd learned the basics of bending space/distance and could skip ahead up to a mile or more. I reined in my urge—mostly because it would *hurt*—and stayed a couple of paces behind Bea.

She flat out ran into the women's restroom and into the nearest stall, which thankfully was empty. As she slammed the door shut, I saw her fall to her knees. Two women who were primping in the mirror stared at her, then at me. The groaning and choking sounds accompanied by the sour smell of vomit assaulted my senses. Oh, bloody hells.

"Some privacy, please?" I demanded of the two women, who rushed out the door. I wasn't averse to using a bit of a hurry-along charm. After the door closed behind them, I threw a locking charm on the door, followed by a strong aversion charm. There were a couple of portable toilets outside if anyone really had to piss. No way was I letting anyone else in. Bea didn't need the embarrassment of having strangers hear her puking her guts up.

"You okay in there?" I ventured when the sounds paused for a moment.

"Fine," she groaned and then puked again. I closed my senses against the smell. Poor Bea, she must have gotten some bad tacos or something. I hoped she hadn't eaten the *tripas*. I hated them, but most kids brought up in the area grew up eating food like that.

Oh wait, duh, I might be able to lessen her misery. I'd learned a decent number of diagnostic and healing charms. Concentrating, I sent out a tentative feeler in her direction, aiming for her belly. Rumbling and roiling surrounded something else, something not Bea. A regular flutter, so very faint underneath the sounds of her intestines, higher up. What the hell? I searched a bit deeper. There was something there about the size of a tiny pea. Oh, my fucking bloody hells. *Tu est bien fucké, cher,* I thought to myself, reverting to the slang I liked to use when drunk. My best friend Bea was what her Tia Petra euphemistically called "with child": knocked up, *embarasada, pleine,* preggers. Fuck all the gods and goddesses ever worshiped in history. My best friend had a fucking bun in the oven.

"Whose is it?" I asked as she emerged from the stall, wiping her mouth with toilet paper. She flinched and dug in her bag, pulling out a toothbrush and a small travel size tube of Colgate. As she brushed her teeth, I stared at her. For the first time in my admittedly short life, I was completely and utterly speechless around Bea. As hard as it was, I held my words until she'd finished brushing and rinsing.

"Bea?" I prodded.

She tucked her items back into her purse, then with a hand on either side of the white sink, head bowed, she replied, "It's stupid, I know. But damn it, I'm nearly forty; three months ago I was this close to being raped or dead or both, and then, I thought, 'what the hell.' He's *guapo,* and fun, and kind. I figured I'd go for it."

"Who?"

Bea took a deep breath and turned to face me as she leaned against the sink, hands still on either side, resting on the porcelain. "You mean you can't tell? I know you probed me." Her look was a challenge.

" 'Probe' is a pretty sharp word," I said. "But yes, I did examine you. I thought food poisoning, flu, something . . . not that. And no, I don't know who. I didn't get that far." I challenged her back. "Why? Do you want me to go poking around inside you? Really probe? I learned how, you know. To get into your head, see your memories. Even if you're willing, it's not pretty, nor very comfortable unless you're blood bonded. It's the mental equivalent of rape."

Her knuckles paled as her hands gripped tighter. "That was a low blow, Keira Kelly."

"And you assuming I'd go that far was just as low."

She dropped her gaze, staring at her own two feet. "You're right. I'm sorry." After a moment's pause, Bea continued. "I was playing around out there. When Mark asked you if Levon—Lev—could date me. We've already been dating." She raised her head. "Two months' worth. I think I'm about five or six weeks along. It was like this before when . . ."

When she'd miscarried at age eighteen, her pregnancy the consequence of dating the same guy for years, a young romance with a boy who'd eventually come out of the closet. They'd gotten married in a quiet ceremony, then as quickly gotten divorced after the miscarriage. Damn, why on earth did Bea have to have this kind of luck in her relationships? My sympathy turned to anger. She was thirty-eight years old, not eighteen.

"*Now* you pull a Keira Kelly?" I was nearly yelling at her, my voice echoing in the empty women's restroom. "I seem to recall I was the one popping her cherry under these very bleachers outside while you'd only go to second base with Emilio—and you'd been going out since fucking junior high. Hell, you even eventually married the sad bastard. Now you tell me you've been seeing Lev for a couple of months and you're pregnant? Fucking hell, Bea: What's gotten into you? No, wait—don't answer that. I know what got into you, or rather who, but really. This is not you."

"It damn well is, Keira Kelly," she yelled right back. "You ran away. You did what you did, then you fucking ran away from me."

"What the hell was I supposed to do? You wouldn't talk to me and I had to go." Without warning, I burst into tears. "You wouldn't talk to me." My voice shook as I tried to compose myself.

Bea, who'd drawn herself up for another shout, absolutely deflated in the face of my tears. Just like she'd done in the stands, she threw herself against me and wrapped her arms around me. "Shhh, I know, I know," she soothed. "Tucker told me everything when he got back."

I slashed my hand across my eyes and glared at her. "May all the bloody gods damn my interfering brother," I said. "He never said a word to me."

"You've been home what? Twenty-four hours?"

I grabbed her wrist and checked her watch. Nine fifteen. "Just about," I said.

"And you spent the next ten or twelve hours in bed, didn't you?"

I ducked my head and laughed. She knew me too well. "More like twenty," I mumbled. "Hand me a tissue will you?"

With a shake of her head, Bea stepped into a stall and pulled out a wad of paper. "Here. You're never fucking prepared, are you?"

"Never," I said and blew my nose. "Does he know?"

"Lev?" She bit her lip. "Not yet."

I sat back on my heels and studied her face. She did have some of the obvious signs. Her skin seemed a little different. She was right, she could only be five or six weeks along. Not enough to really matter.

"You going to tell him?"

"I have no idea," she said. "I mean, it's not like we're in mad love or anything." She did the air quotes and I laughed.

"No, but he's—" I clapped my hands over my mouth. Oh my bloody stars. Sweet bloody hells. She didn't know. She couldn't. How in all the crazy mixed-up insanities was I going to explain to my best friend, the very human Beatriz Ruiz, that her baby was half wolf?

"He's what—a nice guy, a criminal, what?" Bea eyed me with suspicion. "What do you know that I don't? Does it have to do with all that whatever that was up there?" She waved a hand in the air. "You know what I'm talking about, Keira. You guys were being all weird with that 'permission to court.' You weren't just joking around, were you?"

"Not really." How to put this? Gee, Bea, they're all werewolves and I'm sort of their ruler now.

"Are you planning to have this baby?" I got right to the point.

"Hell of a thing to ask," she said. "How should I know? I only really found out yesterday afternoon. I took one of those at-home tests."

I nodded decisively. "Then what you need right now is data." That was it, I'd introduce it this way.

"I read the pamphlets and the information online at Planned Parenthood," Bea said.

"This century?" I shot back at her.

She didn't meet my gaze.

"Bea?" I cajoled. "Since you found out, have you done anything to research options?"

"I made a doctor's appointment for next week," she said. "I figure I'd discuss it then."

"Cancel it."

"What? Why?"

I took a deep, long breath and let it out as slowly as I could. How to phrase this?

"Remember when last year, you found out that vampires were real?"

Her eyes grew rounder. "You are not saying what I think you're saying—but wait, Lev goes out in the daytime, we went on a picnic last week."

"No, no, he's definitely not a vampire," I said. "He is, however, not as human as he could be." Shit, why was I dragging this out? "Bea, I really don't know how to tell you this, but Mark, Lev, Gregor, Dixxi—they're werewolves."

For a silent half a minute or so, Bea just stared at the bathroom wall. Was she in total shock?

"Nope, this time, you really *are* kidding," she said. "They're part of your family, right? That's why all that 'asking permission' thing."

"We can't breed with humans, Bea. You know that," I reminded her gently. "They really are werewolves."

Bea slumped back against the sink, her hands flying up to cover her eyes. "I thought I was done with the insanity," she whispered. "You people, then vampires, now werewolves? *Chinga!* How could I have gotten knocked up by a fucking wolf?"

"I don't know genetics, Bea. I'm sure they can explain better." I gently pulled her hands away from her eyes and gave her a hug. "I'm here, *chica.* Whatever you do or don't do, you know I'm here for you."

Bea's eyes glittered with the unshed tears. She was doing everything to hold it together. "What the hell am I going to do?"

"Do you want it?"

"I don't know. I thought, well, maybe. I'm almost forty, no kids of my own. This was kind of my last hurrah, you know."

"I know." Did I really? I said the words, but no, I had no freakin' clue. I had decades, hell, centuries of upcoming possible pregnancy years ahead of me. Bea, if her mother was typical for the family, had about eight. "Bea, you don't have to make any decisions for a little while," I said. "I just wanted to make sure you had all the facts before you made them. I'm sorry . . . for whatever that's worth."

She let out a sound halfway between a snort and a sob. "You couldn't have just told me there is such a thing as werewolves?" She began to laugh, the sobs hitching her laughter into something resembling more hysteria than enjoyment, the tears that had threatened now flowing down her face.

I handed her some tissues. "Yeah, well, I could have, but you know, in my defense, I had no idea these guys were around here."

"No, I suppose not," she said, wiping her face. "C'mon, we'd better get back before someone comes."

"You going to be okay?" I peered into her face, trying to look past the tears.

"You're sticking around, right?"

"I'm back for good, Bea. I promise."

"Then yeah, I'll be okay," she said. "I've got you on my side, don't I?"

CHAPTER ELEVEN

WE REJOINED THE others, one of us subdued, the other—me—still chewing this new data in my head. What the fuck was I going to do about this? Bea was family of the heart and I owed it to her to help, but damn it, what could I do? She was the pregnant one. She was the one who was going to have to make a very tough decision. And what would the wolves think about her pregnancy? If they were at all like my own clan, babies tended to belong to the tribe, not the individual. My aunts had been after me for years to give them a child to raise, have a baby for the Kellys. Except their rationale at the time was so that I could possibly produce the next heir. Well, I had, just not in the way they'd imagined. That pressure was off me, but Bea's clock was ticking in a whole different way now.

Maybe I'd ask Tucker to give Bea and me tomorrow night for an impromptu girls' gathering. He could come with me to my former house and hang out outside, and I could totally set this up like one of our once-common nights in. Bad movie, great wine, fabulous munchies, and just hanging with my homegirl. My brother had many more years of experience and was our honorary girl anyway. I'm sure he'd have some advice.

I chose to sit with Bea and Dixxi, instead of next to Adam and Marcus. Adam gave me a questioning look, but I shook my head indicating I'd talk to him later. He acquiesced, but his unspoken words were clear. He'd seen Bea's face, and I knew he could feel my anxiety. He'd just have to wait.

As I navigated past Bea to sit on her right, between her and Dixxi, I noticed a man leaning against the wall at the bottom of the steps. Unlike ninety-nine percent of the crowd, his skin tone was dark as night, his hair cut short, the pure white of old age. He watched me, face nearly as impassive as the vampires when they go all over dead man.

"Who's that?" I asked Dixxi, scootching closer to her so Bea could sit. "That man down there."

She shrugged. "Old Joe. Least that's what they call him around here. He runs a trash collecting truck, goes around to local businesses. Has a roadside junk stand a few miles away. Been over to Rio Seco a couple of times to pick up trash from us. He's probably got the contract to clean up here after the game's over."

"Why's he staring?"

"How the hell would I know? Maybe he's wondering why Bea's got swollen red eyes and tear marks on her face." Dixxi fixed me with a knowing glare.

Fuck.

"I can't tell you here," I whispered. "Plus, it's not really my story to tell."

"Fair enough." Dixxi settled back to watch the game. I could tell she was still checking Bea out from time to time. This woman was no fool.

A half hour later, when Bea excused herself to use the loo for real this time, I realized how much not a fool Dixxi was.

"Our family really is Armenian, you know." She spoke in a low voice, still pretending to watch the game. "Some of us were Ashkenazi Jews who married into the family during the Diaspora. We've got family history of Tay-Sachs and Familial Mediterranean Fever. Problem is, we can't screen in your usual medical facilities because we are also wolf."

I bit my lip and kept my mouth shut. She'd obviously twigged about Bea's condition, but I wanted to hear where she was headed with this.

"One of the reasons I went into genetics is to set up a clinic where our kind could get screened." Dixxi leaned in closer. "It's Lev's, isn't it?"

I nodded.

"Is she planning to keep it?"

I shook my head. "I don't know. She's completely freaked out and she doesn't even know about—"

"Why don't we go for a quick walk," she said. "I don't want my brother to overhear. You're right, this is Bea's issue for now."

I nodded. "Yeah."

"C'mon, let's take a stroll down around the parking lot. Fewer people." I knew she meant her brothers.

"I'll come along," Adam said, throwing me a knowing glance. Good, he'd been listening in. Save some explanations later when I'd allow myself to rant and rave about Bea's stupidity. Not that I really thought she was stupid, but to allow this to happen at her age? Even without the complication of werewolf genes and now all Dixxi was implying. I'd need a good rant and Adam was a great listener.

The three of us excused ourselves. Tucker started to get up, but I shook my head for him and Niko to stay.

Once we passed through the gates, Dixxi continued to

explain about the genes that cause the diseases and how the intermingling of the two communities affected the wolf population, her explanation evolving into concepts that made my head spin. I glanced at Adam, who had his listening face on—attentive, silent, and interested.

"Sorry, I'm not an expert in genetics," I said. Nor was I at all familiar with human genomes and the diseases humans face, other than through reading news items and some basic biology and physiology in school. "Doesn't your other nature somehow negate these bad recessives?" I asked, straining to remember the terms from eighth-grade science and the fruit flies.

"They should," Dixxi said with a snort, "if we weren't part human. Wer are unlike your kind, Keira. You have no human biology. You can't even produce viable human hybrid fetuses. It's like trying to mate a cat with a giraffe. You're another species."

"But wer . . ."

"Wer have always been hybrids. Our origins are lost in the mists of long-ago times. Who knows, maybe there's some truth to the Romulus and Remus stories." She shrugged. "In nearly all the nearby villages in our homeland, there were at least one or two wolf children, according to my great-grandmother's tales. Back then, we were known, we bonded, and the children were fostered out to the pack. We learned to tolerate both worlds. That's how the Tay-Sachs started, actually. A group of Ashkenazi helped save our family groups, slipping us on boats and taking us across the Mediterranean, first to Lebanon, then to Damascus. Eventually we worked our way to Crete and finally took service with some American companies in Greece. By the late fifties, most of our pack was here in the U.S."

"Why Texas? It's not exactly the most multicultural state . . . especially here in White Rock."

"Luck of the draw? My grandfather met an oilman from Dallas in the early 1970s, before the bust. Guy was impressed with Grandpop's cooking and organizing skills. He hired him to come work in his new resort he was building out near the Falls. We've been here since."

Dixxi took a sip of her soft drink. "Gramps started a restaurant after his mentor died and left him a little money. Dad, his son, expanded the business into the river rafting and camping trade. We all grew up working there."

"Thus the deli."

Dixxi grinned. "Yeah, the boys are hella good cooks," she said. "They make mean milkshakes, too." She sobered. "We've had to completely shut down the restaurant, store, and the river rafting up at the lake. Even the camping is too slow. Last of the campers left a couple of days ago."

"The heat?" Adam contributed quietly.

"Yeah, and the drought. River's down to nothing but sludge and rocks in places. If it doesn't rain soon, the deli's gonna be our only source of income."

"How come you're not working at the Health Science Center or one of the med labs around San Antonio or Austin?" I asked. "I mean, you said you were ABD, right? All but dissertation? Don't most folks in your field have research assistant jobs at this point in their career?"

She sounded bitter. "I had to give up my job in town," she said. "I wasn't making enough to warrant the commute and the lack of help at the new deli."

"But what's that going to do to your doctorate—your dissertation?"

A grim chuckle escaped her. "I guess I'll be ABD for

a while longer," she said. "I try not to mind. We've got to make sure we have enough money so the pack can survive."

"Aren't there more adults than you guys who can contribute?"

"A handful. They do what they can. But they all work in White Rock, long hours and such. Someone's got to be there for the kids, especially during summer. We've got summer session home school for most of the ones still needing it. They may not like it, but we've got a ninety-nine percent college degree achievement out of our kids. Most of them go on to advanced degrees."

"And then they leave."

"And then they leave," she agreed. "It's necessary. We need to continuously refresh the gene pool."

"What, you farm out kids to other packs?"

"Pretty much," she said. "We have exchange agreements with other packs throughout the U.S. When they graduate from high school, the kids get first crack at college choices. Often, we'll do a one-year postgrad exchange program just after high school to get a feel for someplace else. Most kids end up going to college at the place they exchanged."

"Might I ask a question?" Adam asked. "Your area of study, genetics. What is your goal, your primary field?"

"Treatments for Tay-Sachs was what started me on this but, as I said, I'd like to be able to do better gene mapping; get some sort of modern gene clinic set up so that all our folks can be screened. I'm not endorsing any weird gene-matching programs for breeding, but there are many things that we can catch early and treat before they become a problem."

"But," Adam pressed, "what if you could screen in

utero, screen potential mates. You could perhaps eradicate those recessives. Clean out the gene pool without having to worry."

Dixxi studied Adam, as did I. Where the hell was he going with this? He was no more a scientist or geneticist than I was.

"I have people who can help," he said simply. "Researchers. They're not local, but they could be. They came up with a blood extract and nutritional substitute for us."

"Which tastes like poop," I said, "and doesn't actually give you all your nutrients. Remember what happened a few months ago. Coma?"

"If I recall correctly—and I do—the coma was caused by your cousin, my love. Not my lack of pure blood intake."

"Yeah, but you can't deny that before you started feeding from me, and participating in the hunts, you were much weaker. Denying our natures usually comes with a price, Adam." I addressed Dixxi. "This all sounds quite noble and good, but I can think of several consequences right off the bat, and I'm not even close to understanding all this."

"I know," she said. "That's why I'm still ABD. Need at least a year or two worth of research to bolster my theories. Problem is, besides the regular research and report writing, I've got to somehow hide the fact that I'm experimenting on werewolves."

"Can't you just spin it as a fairly inbred family group with an idiopathic blood disorder?" I was quoting a line Gigi once pulled on a school doctor who'd been insistent on drawing my blood and testing it for leukemia. He'd thought I was much too pale to be healthy. It had taken all Gigi's clout and some finagling with a Clan member doctor to come up with the diagnosis, which pretty much translated: hey, her blood is different, okay? After that, I had some sort of legal paper in my permanent record that stated that I couldn't be treated by the school nurse and/or local doctors due to religious reasons. I'd nearly laughed myself sick when I found out about that.

"It's a thought," Dixxi said. "I'm just not sure how to pull it off. I've not got any real authority."

"Well, that's at least something we can help with," Adam said. "Let's discuss this soon, yes?"

"I'm sure this isn't why Marcus asked us to come tonight, is it?"

She shook her head. "I doubt it. He's not all that interested in my work. I'm his little sister, you see. Will always be. And I'm damned sure he doesn't know about Bea."

"How about Lev?" I asked. "He's the Loki, the one supposed to be handling the overall day-to-day stuff and keeping Mark in the loop."

"He's even thicker than Mark," Dixxi snorted. "I love my brothers dearly, but they are male wolves. It's all about eat, drink, shit, and shag for the most part. For as much as they are square pegs around here, they're nearly as inculturated as anyone. Die-hard Cowboys fans who think the perfect Sunday evening should be spent grilling steaks, chugging beers, and yelling at the TV screen."

Adam raised a brow. "I'm afraid I didn't catch that last reference."

I motioned around us. "Football—the national sport of Texas. Thank goodness none of our boys were all that interested," I said. "We never watched sports in my house. Mostly, we'd go out and make our own fun. Swimming, hiking, learning to do spells."

Dixxi pulled out her hair tie and retied the ponytail.
"I bet that beats the hell out of a Cowboys/Steelers game
any day."

"Pretty much," I agreed.

"Shall we go on back? Mark looks about ready to pop.
He hates it when he's left out."

"You, my new friend, are so much like me, it's scary."

"Ha!" she exclaimed. "I was just about to say the same
thing about you."

Adam, wiser than the two of us, just rolled his eyes
and remained silent.

CHAPTER TWELVE

WE TOOK OUR TIME walking back, hitting the concession stand for another ice-cold drink. Dixxi and I both ordered Dr Peppers, Adam, a bottled water.

"You can drink that?" Dixxi asked in surprise.

He gave her one of his trademark combination eyebrow-raise/cat-who-ate-the-canary smiles. "I can drink many things," he said.

Dixxi practically spit out her mouthful of ice and soda. "Do not do that," she spluttered. "Warn a girl next time."

I laughed. "Yeah, he's like that," I said and poked Adam in the side. "It's not nice to tease the wildlife, love."

He turned to me with a grin. "We both have teeth, don't we?"

"That we do." I grinned back. Adam took my hand and grinned at Dixxi, who chuckled.

"I like you, too, Adam," she said. "I'm glad you-all aren't what I expected."

"Gigi?" I asked.

"Yeah. Mark was full of stories when he met her a few years ago. Scared the piss out of me."

"I promise I won't do that," I said. "At least, as long as y'all don't do anything to warrant it."

"Fair enough." She walked in tandem with us, a slow stroll back to where we'd been sitting. Bea was back, seeming less worn and more refreshed.

"Hey," I said and plopped down next to her. Adam returned to his seat next to Marcus, and Dixxi sat on Bea's other side.

In front of us, a group of kids wearing T-shirts with FFA logos printed on the back teased and laughed with one another.

"Gods, Future Farmers of America," I said. "I remember them. I guess it's too damned hot for the jackets. When I was in high school, the minute it got cool enough, those damned blue cotton jackets would come out. Then the basketball teams would get out their letter jackets."

"Y'all had a team?" Dixxi asked.

"Yeah, a boys and a girls team. They didn't do too badly, but to be fair, they were playing teams from schools as small as we were—less than three hundred students in the whole junior high and high school." I took a big gulp of my drink. "White Rock was, and still is, enormous in comparison. They've got about nearly six hundred kids in high school now, right?"

Dixxi nodded. "Yeah, enough for several sports, along with cheerleaders, pep squads, pool parties, and subsequent teen pregnancies."

"Sounds like nothing much has changed," I said. "There were always high school girls getting knocked up around here, but we never had many in Rio Seco. As far as I know, there's only been two or three in the last couple of decades."

"White Rock is a hotbed of teen fertility," Dixxi said. "Four cheerleaders pregnant this year. Half that squad out there are alternates. I think, total, White Rock had at least thirty-five pregnancies this past school year, mostly due to ignorance. Their freaking parents don't talk to them about sex and don't let the school teach it."

"Just brilliant." My sarcasm knew no bounds when it came to this sort of ridiculousness. "What century is this again?"

A couple of boys pushed by us and loped down the seats to the fourth row. They and their companions were wearing matching T-shirts, not FFA but some other club. White shirts with some sort of gold logo. Brotherhood of something.

"Hey, Dixxi, what's that group?"

"The shirt says Brotherhood of the White Rock," Adam said from behind me.

"Them," Dixxi spat. "Some stupid macho church group. They tried to get Gregor to join earlier in the year. Thing is, Robert Earl Miller, the assistant coach, helps recruit kids from the team to the cause. That's all we need around here. Football boys with all the testosterone and 'roid rage joining up to some macho gang. I don't like them."

"A macho church group?" Adam asked. "Aren't they supposed to be about community service?"

"Ha, yeah, right," Dixxi said. "They do that, but they're all white kids with attitude. Hardly any black kids around here, not a one in this school, but there are what *they* call 'mescans'—and I haven't yet seen Coach Miller or any of the so-called adult mentors asking them to take part in the group."

"A little prejudiced?"

"Ya think? Soon as Gregor started school, they were all over him about joining. He's not typical of the clean-cut white boy, but he's very handsome. Those girls in school are always all over him, flirting. Cheerleaders, pep squad. Other boys weren't too happy with that, but then the coach asked him to join the Brotherhood . . . I think as a way to keep the team from fighting with him, 'cause mostly, those girls were their girlfriends."

"Did he join?" I asked. I just couldn't see any of the wer attending religious services. I didn't know much about the church, but it was probably fairly typical for the region: a small-town conservative Christian place, preaching against the different.

"Ha, not even. He's pretty indifferent to them all. They're not pack. See that girl down there?" Dixxi points out a cute blonde in a cheerleader uniform leading a section of the stands in a cheer. "That's Coach Miller's one and only," she said.

"He's cheating on his wife with her? No way. She's all of what? Fifteen?"

Dixxi laughed as she heard the horrified tone in my voice. "No, you fool. His daughter. Only child and spoiled rotten. She had the most ridiculous crush on Gregor last semester. Then, when he wouldn't go out with her, she totally and completely went gaga over Luka." Dixxi then pointed out one of the players. "See there, number fifty, on the bench?"

My eyes practically bugged out of my head. The boy was turned toward the stands, waving at us. If Gregor was drop-dead gorgeous, this one jumped right over "gorgeous" and landed squarely in too-beautiful-to-believe territory. He could be at least a year older than Gregor, his features fully adult. Long blond hair braided tightly down the back of his head in order to fit into the helmet. I couldn't see his eye color from here, but his pale skin definitely spoke of the traditional Nordic roots for wer.

"One of yours, I gather," I said.

"You can tell?" Bea asked as she scooted up to us and sat. "Marcus adopted him last year." She frowned. "Though I suppose that means something else?"

"You told her," Dixxi said, her expression a mix of surprise and acceptance.

"I had to."

"Fair enough." She nodded.

I answered Bea's question. "I can tell a lot of things now. Besides the hair and the amazing looks, he feels like a predator—the good kind."

Bea shook her head and gave me a weak chuckle. "Only you."

"You doing okay there, *chica*?" I asked.

"Yeah, best as I can be," she answered. "Dixxi, I take it you know?"

Dixxi shrugged and leaned over me to pat her on the knee. "I kind of figured it out," she said.

"Yeah, okay then." Bea turned her attention back to the boy on the bench. "Tell us about him," she said, changing the subject.

"He's from Canada," Dixxi said. "Distant family. He was only fourteen when he got here."

"He's fourteen?" I stared at Dixxi in astonishment.

"Fifteen now," she said. "Doesn't look it, does he?"

I waved my hand in front of my face, miming a fan. "Damnation, woman, your, uhm, family turns out very lovely boys . . . and girls." I grinned at her.

"They are gorgeous," she laughed. "A definite perk." She checked behind her at Tucker, Niko, and Adam. "Yours aren't so bad, either."

I laughed. "That they aren't."

Dixxi, Bea, and I enjoyed watching the boy as he, in

turn, watched the pep squad cheer them on. The cheer-leaders were over on the other side of the stadium, in charge of leading the spirit for the offense.

"Her daddy's way unhappy at his little girl's interest in our new brother," Dixxi said. "She's got an iron will, that one. She's determined to date Luka and since she's Daddy's princess, he's putting up with it."

"They're dating? Isn't he a little young for that?"

"Oh, she only wishes they were dating," Dixxi clarified. "He thinks she's pretty enough, but like Gregor, he's absolutely not interested."

"They like boys?" I ventured.

At this, both Bea and Dixxi burst out into peals of laughter.

"What?" I asked. "Is that so impossible?"

"Honey," Bea said, "this isn't your family or our town. Even if they did like boys they'd never admit to it."

"Why?"

Dixxi glanced around to see who was close by before she spoke in a low voice. "This is White Rock, home of the Church and the Brotherhood. Practically everyone in town belongs to that church. Christian family values only. Hell, Dr. James Dobson would feel right at home here."

"Merciful goddess," I said. "Rio Seco may be small-town Texas, but this is something out of the fifties."

"Or earlier," Bea said. "I know a couple of boys used their school vouchers to transfer to Rio Seco because of harassment."

"That's a hell of a commute," I said.

"Better a long commute than getting hate-crimed to death," Dixxi said. "That's part of why we homeschool. A lot of our kids aren't bog-standard middle-class white kids; we adopt all races, kids from all over. Some people have trouble with that."

"They're out of potential danger," Bea said. "I like that idea. Lev told me that y'all homeschooled. I just thought it was for religious reasons."

Dixxi laughed. "I could see why you thought that. In this part of Texas, that's usually the case. No, we mostly just want our kids to get a more well-rounded view of the world than the local schools offer. White Rock may be a picturesque place, but the morals of this town set my teeth on edge." She turned to answer my previous question. "Gregor and Luka are straight," Dixxi said. "Not that we care one way or another. We've just asked them to keep a low profile in school. They're there to learn, not to misbehave."

"I bet they get plenty of chances to do that." I was sure that temptation was everywhere for those boys, recently out of homeschooling and into adolescent hormone high.

"Half the girls in school follow them around," Dixxi admitted. "I know it's pissed off some of the other boys."

"Too bad for them," I grinned. "Hell, if I were still their age, I'd probably be sniffing around them, too."

"You did," Dixxi chuckled. "I remember you from when you were in high school. I'd tag along to the football games with Mark and Lev. They hated bringing me because I was such a brat child."

"Really?" Huh, that was fairly awkward. "You knew me back then? I don't remember you at all."

Dixxi shrugged. "I knew who you were—a Kelly. We all did. My grandpop was still alive then and still Fenrir. He'd come out to the games on occasion because he'd grown to like the sport. The Falls aren't all that far away for a drive. I'd come with him." She grinned. "I may have been young, but I do remember seeing you and Mark sneak off underneath the bleachers."

I stood up, spilling my drink all over Tucker, who

along with Niko had come to sit in front of me, guarding point since Adam was now at my back.

"Fuck me and the horse I just rode in on," I exclaimed, too surprised to watch my language. Tucker stood, cursing at me as Niko wiped off the sticky soda with one of the towels Mark had loaned us. "I only did that one time. Once. Ever. That could *not* have been your brother," I said. "I'd remember."

Bea clapped a hand over her mouth. "Shit." Her eyes grew round and she let out a giggle as she stared at me, then at Mark, who until this moment had been completely oblivious to what we were talking about. "Oh my god, Keira, she's right. That's him."

I slowly turned to watch Mark, who was no longer paying attention to the football game. Instead, he stared at me. Adam, on his other side, watched us, a frown on his face. I studied Mark's features. Dark hair: check. Smoldering eyes: check. But Mark's eyes were brown, not— As I stared, his eyes lightened in color, fading from a nondescript brown to an amazing light amber-gold. His average facial structure changed just slightly, cheekbones becoming more prominent, eye shape more elongated, lips fuller.

Fuck. Me. It *was* him.

CHAPTER THIRTEEN

"W HY DIDN'T YOU say something?" I demanded.

Mark only smiled. Then, with a small shake of his head, his features returned to their previous nondescript appearance. "I didn't think you cared to remember."

"You told me you'd only been here five years or so."

"I have only been here that long. I spent some time here as a child, but Grandpop sent me to study with another pack when I was twelve. I was visiting here, and Gramps decided he wanted to come to a football game. I figured I'd come along."

"May I inquire as to the nature of your . . . discussion?" Adam's voice, smoother than melted chocolate and oh, so very amused, interrupted. Most boyfriends/ partners would have started demanding to know what we were talking about. Not Adam, king of vampires and of extreme coolth. I fought the urge to stick my tongue out at both him and Marcus. I caught a glimpse of Bea's face, which had turned redder than what was left of her soft drink.

"Marcus here has been doing a little hiding," I griped. "Seems he and I had a bit of an encounter once upon a time."

"Your first, if I recall?" Mark gave me a shit-eating grin.

"And if it was? Since when can you people do glamours?"

"Not a glamour, just some judicious control over metamorphosis." Mark smirked.

"The moon isn't near full," I said. "Plus, I didn't know you could do that."

"Full moon only means I must," he explained. "Plus, I am who I am . . . and I don't know half the things you can do."

"Nor should you," I retorted.

"Ditto," he said, still smirking.

Adam was about as close to bursting out in laughter as I'd ever seen. Bea, on the other hand, just kept getting redder and redder, ducking her head. Her embarrassment was enough for all of us put together. "I think I'll just . . ." She turned and fled down the stairs. This time, I didn't follow, knowing it was just a matter of her being in the middle of a situation that reeked of possible jealous reactions.

"I think I'll go check on Bea," Dixxi said with a grin. "Y'all just"—she waved a hand—"figure it out among yourselves."

Damn it. I knew Adam wouldn't have an issue with this. After all, I'd been what, seventeen? Besides, none of us really worried all that much about our previous relationships. When your life span can be measured in centuries, that's not really a subject of great importance.

"You weren't honest with me," I said to Mark.

"I was completely honest," he returned. "I just chose not to bring that particular situation up. It's irrelevant at this point in time. Besides, I had no idea how Adam would react."

"Please, Mark," I snorted. "Adam and I are blood bonded, but that doesn't mean neither of us have a past."

Several whistles screeched from the field below, and both groups of players began to return to the benches.

Oh good, halftime. The best part of the football game—basically, the part where there is no football. No, wait, that wasn't the halftime whistle. I glanced at the clock, which showed almost two minutes left to play before halftime. Gee, time flies when you're not having fun. Marcus, whose attention seemed riveted on the field, suddenly stood.

"Gregor," he whispered, voice choked in his throat.

Tucker and Niko were flying down the stairs before either Lev or Jacob could even make it to the railing.

"He can't be really hurt," Marcus said, still staring at the commotion below. "He's one of us. More than likely, he's had to fake something."

"Fake?" I asked, keeping my voice low.

"Probably," he said. "To keep things under the radar. He likely got hit in a way that would have injured a human boy. We've taught him how to exaggerate so that it wouldn't appear odd to the others."

"I don't understand why you let him play, then."

"To fit in," he said curtly.

Okay, that I could buy. "C'mon," I said and grabbed Adam's hand. "Let's go."

THE TEAM surrounded Gregor, who lay on his back moaning. The team trainer, a small man, had Gregor's knee in his hand, palpating it. Marcus leaned into the crowd, pushing the boys away.

"Let me through, damn it," he said. "That's my nephew."

"C'mon, boys." A man who wasn't Coach Miller but was wearing a coach's uniform shooed the boys away from Gregor. "Go on back to the bench." With his play-book in one hand, the man walked away, herding the boys as he went. "Robert Earl, you take care of this. I'll talk to the rest of the team." Coach Miller, who was crouched down by Gregor, nodded. "Will do, Coach Kennedy." Luka, who trailed behind the other boys, pleaded silently with Mark, who shook his head. Dejected, the boy turned and rejoined the team now gathered around Coach Kennedy.

"Greg, how's the knee feel?" The trainer spoke in a calm voice, his hands still supporting Gregor's leg.

"Like hell," Gregor growled as the trainer pushed against the patella. "Andy, damn it, that hurts."

Hurts? How the fuck can a werewolf be injured in a football game? Even I could tell the boy wasn't faking. His olive skin was ashen, his mouth tight against what was obvious pain.

"What the fuck?" Marcus yelled. "What happened to my nephew?"

The assistant coach stood from his crouch, a hand extended. "Mr. Ashkarian, Robert Earl Miller," he said. "I'm sorry—"

"Sorry?" Marcus's eyes began to change color. I stepped on his insole and he yelped, whirling at me. "What the fuck, Keira?"

"Marcus, I'm sure the coach here has an explanation," I said in a soothing voice and blinked my eyes at him. He started, then flinched.

"Shit, yeah, okay." He turned to Coach Miller. "Sorry, Coach," he said. "I was out of line."

"I know, I know." The coach chuckled. "Your boy got hurt and all your instincts came out."

That's not the half of it, I thought. Adam moved over

beside me and put a hand on my shoulder. "Will he be all right?" he asked the trainer.

"Looks like he got cleated real good on the knee," the trainer said. "I'm Andy Dobbs, by the way. Y'all relatives?"

"Of a sort," Adam said in an absent way. "Mark, shall we take Gregor home then?"

Dixxi and Bea had come out of the restroom by this time. Dixxi pushed in front of me and squatted near Gregor's head, holding a whispered conversation with the boy. I did my best to avoid listening as Marcus and Adam made arrangements to get Gregor to our van, probably the most comfortable car.

"That makes the most sense," Marcus said. "I'm in my pickup. It was just me and the boys."

"I brought Dixxi in my car," Bea said. "It's not really big enough for more than three."

"The van it is," I said. "Niko, could you bring the van around?"

"Of course," Niko said and headed out.

"Are you sure you don't want us to have the ambulance take him to the clinic?" Andy Dobbs asked. "It's no problem. It's a ways, but they're open twenty-four, seven and are used to dealing with sports injuries."

Dixxi sidled up to Andy, flashing a huge grin, her arms crossed underneath her rather impressive breasts. "Oh, don't worry about that, Mr. Dobbs," she purred. "Our aunt is a nurse and we've got everything we need at home. I'm sure he just needs to rest up and elevate the knee."

The trainer, still dubious but entranced by Dixxi, agreed. "Yeah, have him take some anti-inflammatories and keep the knee up and iced. He should be okay by morning. But"—he turned to the assistant coach—"no more football at least until regular practices start in August. I want that knee to heal by school start."

"What's going on, everything okay here?" The blond sheriff sauntered up. This time I got a good look at her ID badge: Miller. She was followed by Luka, who'd evidently changed his mind about obediently staying on the sidelines.

"Is he okay?" the sheriff asked. "Do we need to get the ambulance over here?"

Coach Miller nodded his head to Luka and then addressed the sheriff. "He's fine, Jane, just banged up a bit. He's going on home."

"Rob, is that smart? Shouldn't he go to the ER? What if—" She frowned and came closer as if to talk privately to the assistant coach. Miller and Miller: husband and wife? Probably, as they both wore matching wedding bands. "Rob, I'm in charge here tonight—"

"Janey, nothing to worry about." Miller hushed his wife and pulled her aside, far enough away that even my extra-sensitive hearing couldn't pick up their words through the crowd noise. I watched them closely. Something seemed more than a little off. Her face began to get red as he spoke, her lips tight and her arms crossed in front of her. *Extreme body language of anger,* I thought. She seemed ready to haul off and hit him.

"Wonder what's up there?" I asked out loud, hoping that Adam could hear something, or that the trainer could give me a clue. Hands flew on both the Millers' sides as he leaned into her, face turning red. Instead of backing away, she very deliberately put her hands on her hips and whispered even more furiously than before. What the hell was such a big deal? Kids got hurt in football all the time.

Adam glanced over at the couple. "She's upset about

something, but he's facing away from me. I can't quite make out the words. Something about 'handling it,' perhaps?"

"Huh, why would she care that we're taking Gregor with us? I'd think they'd be happy that we're not having to involve the hospital or anything."

"You got me," Marcus said as he came up next to us. "I've told Luka to go on home with Lev and Bea. I'll ride with you in the van and send someone back for my truck tomorrow."

"Shall we take you back to the Falls?" I asked.

"No, that's too far. We can go back to our place in Rio Seco. Lev, Dixxi, and I are living in those apartments near the Rio Seco Lodge," Mark said.

"All three of you? Seriously?"

"Well, five of us, actually," Mark said. "Gregor and Luka are with us for the summer while we get the deli in shape."

"Last time I was there, the biggest apartment was a teeny two-bedroom, barely big enough for two skinny people and a goldfish. Unless they've done some massive remodeling—"

"They haven't," Dixxi said. "We take turns on the floor." She'd left Gregor's side and joined us. "Let's go, we're holding up the game."

A student trainer knelt at Gregor's side, placing an ice pack and wrapping the boy's knee. I frowned as I watched Gregor's face. It wasn't his knee that he was holding, his hand moving toward his side, then away quickly, as though he didn't want anyone to notice.

"We're happy to drive you," I heard Adam saying to Dixxi.

"No, damn it, that's just . . ." I threw up my hands. "That's not good enough. Gregor's really hurt and dumping you off there would be more than cruel." Cruel, yes, but what I really wanted was to find out how a werewolf in the prime of life could be hurt in a human football game. I gave Adam a meaningful look, inclining my head to the boy and back again. Adam's brow lowered, eyes narrowed as he caught my drift.

The student trainer and another boy helped Gregor to his feet, the cheers of the crowd accompanying the action.

"You're welcome to come to the Wild Moon," Adam offered. "My ranch. We have more than enough room at the inn." He smiled at Dixxi and Mark.

"It makes sense," I added. "Stuffing you all into a small apartment when Gregor's hurt . . ." I let my words trail off.

Mark frowned and seemed to consider the offer. "I appreciate it, but—"

"But what?" I said. "You don't like vampires?" I dropped my voice at the last word, as the two boys helping Gregor were passing. Gregor continued to do a fabulous acting job, favoring his knee as he limped slowly off the field. We all walked with him, still talking.

Mark hesitated. "It's not that exactly," he said. "I'd just rather . . ."

"Be on your own turf," Adam said.

I goggled at his use of the slang. "Turf?"

He smiled. "I've been around you a while now."

"They can come to my—your—house." Bea's voice came from behind me. "There's plenty of room there, too."

"That's a good idea," I said. "Thanks, Bea."

"No hay de que." She smiled at me. Her smile didn't quite reach her eyes. I knew I'd laid way the hell too

much on her tonight—learning about her pregnancy, then having to tell her about the wers. The last fucking thing she needed was a hurt kid and a crowd around, but she'd offered, and if Mark wasn't willing to go to the Wild Moon . . .

"My old house it is." I motioned to Mark and Dixxi, who took over helping Gregor. Mark thanked the boys and they both left, back to the game. The crowd was still applauding, shouts of "Go twenty-two!" mixed in with the happy applause, everyone glad to see an injured player walk off the field under his own power.

The van, thanks to Niko, waited for us just outside the gate. I slid open the side door. "Why don't y'all get in the far back?" I asked Niko and Adam, both of whom complied. "Tucker, can you help Mark get Gregor inside? I think he'll be more comfortable if he lies down across the bench seat in the middle. Dixxi, why don't you and Mark help support him?"

With help from Mark and Tucker, Gregor, though wincing and hissing around whatever actual injury he had, climbed slowly inside. Dixxi had already situated herself on the seat directly behind the driver's seat. Gregor leaned into her, practically in her lap, as he stretched out his leg. Mark quickly climbed in and slid under Gregor's foot, holding on to the boy.

"There, that'll do," I said. "We've got a ways to go, but I think this'll work. Gregor, how are you doing?"

"Okay, I guess," he muttered, shifting a little as he tried to find a comfortable angle.

"Sorry, kid," I said. "I know it's not the greatest way to travel right now, but it beats putting you in the back of a pickup in this heat."

Gregor chuckled. "It does."

Bea waved at us and headed toward her own car as I shut the van door and climbed into my own seat next to Tucker.

"Allons-y," I said and motioned with a hand. "Shall we?"

CHAPTER FOURTEEN

H E'S STILL SEARCHING for her even after the game starts up again.

She's something, something special. Needs to talk to her and those whitest white boys she hanging with. Never seen them before, but somehow they're not strangers. The lady reminds him of that other one so many years back. Came up just 'bout midday. Big shiny car backing up like it meant to keep going but someone stopped it. Tiny lady got out, all spiffed up like a Junior Leaguer, suited up in style. She stared at him for several minutes, saying nothing, sharp eyes boring into his. He just stared back; being a sight for white folk never bothered him much. 'Cept this time, two minutes in, he shook just a little. Felt something like—well, like something he ain't never felt before nor since—until now.

Joe explores both sides of the stadium back behind the bleachers, over to the snack bar and drink stand.

Ain't no sign of any of them, like they vanished. Damnation. He needs to talk to her. Pappy Joe, rest his soul, once said if he ever ran across another one like that lady, that they good people. "They different," the old man had mumbled. "Live over to Rio Seco way, but t'ain't all.

They not like us, but they good folk, mostly. You get into something over your head, you go on down there somehow, go talk to 'em. They helpers."

"Angels?" the then seven-year-old asked in wonder. "They guardian angels?" Young Joe had scrunched up his face, puzzled. "Angels got wings, though, don't they?"

Pappy Joe had laughed and laughed, his face all crinkly. "Naw, boy, t'ain't no angels, least none I know of. They something different. But they be helping folks like us out." Then he'd stared at the boy, direct in the eye just like that lady done. "One day, Joe, they be helping *you* out."

He knows he has to find them, tell them about the bag, somehow share the burden.

Knows better now. Knows angels are only a fairy tale told by men in black robes wanting to scare little children into behaving. If there are angels, they're likely more like that one picture he saw once. Tall and shining, sword in hand and war in mind. This world didn't have no fluffy, cuddly angels like them stupid little statues some of the church ladies collected. They just fooling themselves. Ain't no one 'round here lived in the trees enough, on the land enough. There are *things* out there.

A cheer from the crowd distracts him from his gloomy thoughts. With a sigh, he heads into the stands, intending to go up where they'd been sitting, see if anyone knew where—

"You need something?" The woman's voice stops his progress as easily as if it'd raised a rock wall.

He turns, keeping his movements slow, his attitude shifting from searching to submissive. He knows this game.

"Sheriff, ma'am," he says in his best deferential voice,

dropping into the speech rhythms she expected. "I'se going up to see if I could find someone."

Sheriff Miller puts her hands on her hips, settled on her Sam Browne in that pose meant to be intimidating, but on her it was only pathetic. Didn't she know she just seemed the fool? No need to do that when talking to folk. "Who you looking for? Aren't you supposed to be collecting the trash?"

For a brief second, Joe contemplates challenging her, letting her see his true self, that part of him he knew was inside but always hid, especially in this town. Then reason wins out over insanity and he lets himself remain humble.

"I be looking for them folk from Rio Seco," he says. "They were up there." He motioned to the now empty seats. "Did you see them go, Sheriff?"

With a grimace, she turns her head and spits on the ground, clear spit, not the ugly brown of chew. Even so, Joe can't help but flinch a little. She may be sheriff, but she ain't much of a lady.

"Why you need to talk to them for?" Sheriff Miller demands. "You bothering people now?"

He hangs his head and shakes it in the negative. "No, ma'am, just needed a word."

She harrumphs, a sour, angry sound. Why was she always angry? She never smiled no more.

Before she could say anything else, the other one—her husband—comes over off the field, his face near as tight as hers.

Yeah, he angry all the time, too. Joe knows they don't like black folk, never have, but so long as he keeps playing the game with them, playing up to them, they don't mind him so much. He just a trash man. But he watches them, despite that. All of them from that high and mighty church of theirs bear watching. Pastor seemed an okay fellow, somewhat, still—but he hiding something.

Ignoring her husband's questioning glances, Sheriff Miller addresses Joe. "Those folks left a while ago. That kid of theirs got hurt and they hustled him away." Before Joe could ask, she continued, "Don't know where they went off to. Said something about home." She studies him a moment, then turns and walks away with her husband, the two of them seeming even less like a couple than before. They walk with that indefinable space between them—not close enough to be together but too close to be strangers. Each of them held their shoulders in tight, muscles too tense to relax, arms too stiff to swing naturally. No sense of togetherness there at all.

Joe watches for a while as they walk around the track. Halftime activities still going on in the middle of the field, band starts up some new tune that is vaguely familiar. He checks his big watch, a prize from the best Dumpster dive of his life. He'd scored a coupla boxes of DVDs, a handful of real nice costume jewelry, and this watch.

Maybe should just go on out to Rio Seco, check for them there. Get in the truck and drive on over there, though finding them without even knowing their names is like trying to find an honest man down in Huntsville. Maybe just drive on over, nap in the truck till morning, and then go see Miz Leo at the salon when she opens up. She knows everything and everybody around, beauticians always do. Miz Leo'd tell him where to find the lady and her menfolk.

Then maybe he could finally tell the story, release this burden.

CHAPTER FIFTEEN

"I T WASN'T AN ACCIDENT," Gregor mumbled as soon as Tucker pulled out of the parking lot. Tucker preferred to drive. Even though Niko had become an excellent driver since we'd begun living with the vampires, we were on Hill Country roads and they could be deceptively treacherous. One very tame-appearing curve near Rio Seco had been christened "Dead Man's Curve," simply because the pitch was too steep. From either direction, it seemed innocuous, but hit it doing more than the prescribed twenty-five miles an hour, especially in a boxy van or car, and you could find yourself ass over teakettle in five seconds flat. I know. Been there, done that, got reamed out by my aunts. Lucky I hadn't broken anything except my pride.

"What do you mean 'not an accident'?" Mark's voice dropped in pitch, almost an entire octave.

"Kyle, Coach Miller's nephew. He doesn't like me or Luka. I think because of our hair and our last name."

"How exactly are you hurt?" I asked. "I saw you holding your side back there. I'm guessing it's not your knee?"

"I'm not—" the boy protested, trying to sit up straighter, then slumping back onto Dixxi and clutching his side. "They ganged up on me. Planned it out. I was running my play, then before I know it, Kyle Chandler trips me and then, when I fell, he stomped on my side and one of the others cleated me in the knee. When I looked up, two of his buddies were with him, all grinning and stuff. I know Kyle and those other kids from the church planned it. They fucking—"

"Language, Greg," Dixxi warned. "We may be animals, but damn it, we'll be polite."

Gregor subsided with a stubborn expression on his face. "They did," he said and crossed his arms over his chest, his shoulder pads vibrating with the action.

Mark studied Gregor's face with a puzzled gaze on his own. "Gregor, whether or not they ganged up on you, Keira's right. What did they do that hurt your knee so badly? I didn't want to ask out on the field because I honestly thought you were just a good actor." He leaned over and quickly unwrapped the Ace bandage, letting the ice pack fall into his hand.

"It's not my knee, Mark. And it really hurts." Gregor winced as he tried to pull up his shirt. "See?"

Mark pushed the ice pack and unwrapped bandage under the seat, leaned over, and peered at the boy's side. "Turn on the light," he said. I reached up and switched on the center overhead. "Damn it, boy. How the hell—?"

"Tell him, Gregor." Dixxi's voice brooked no argument.

"Dixx . . ." Gregor's voice was just short of a whine, that annoying teenage "but I don't wanna" tone that every single kid between eleven and eighteen perfects.

"Spill the beans, kid, or I will."

"Beans, what beans?" Mark was obviously puzzled.

"He was already hurt, Mark," she said. "Before the game."

"Hurt how? Why didn't I know of this?" Mark demanded. "I'm his Fenrir, his uncle, I—"

"Because you'd just go off, like now," Gregor said. "It's nothing, Mark, really. I was out in the new acreage yesterday . . ." He let his voice trail off and then gave a pleading look to Mark. "You know what I was doing out there and why. Use your head. You'll know what kind of hurt."

"You were doing what where?" Mark's tone became a roar. "What the hell did I tell you about that!"

Gregor bit his lip. "To not go there without permission or supervision—"

"Exactly," Mark cut him off. "Damn it, Gregor, you could have—" He stopped suddenly and glanced around the van. Every single one of us, except Tucker, who was still watching the road while driving, had our eyes glued on Mark and Gregor. "You know what," Mark finished in a rather lame way.

"Oh no," I said. "You are not starting this topic of conversation, then not completing it. What the hell is going on, Mark Ashkarian?"

"It's private," he said. "Pack business."

"My ass." I scowled at him. "If it's pack business, then it is our business," I stated. "Mine and Adam's. I don't want to pull the 'I am your leader' card, but damn it, what on earth could hurt a wer as young and as strong as Gregor? Hurt him so badly that a football injury brings him down?"

Adam, who'd started to clear his throat in some sort of warning to me, gave up as I finished speaking. Something was definitely not adding up here, pack business or not.

"Damn it, Keira," Mark said. "It's private, and I'm not sure I can say."

"Mark," I said. "I know what it's like to keep things inside the tribe. We do that all the time. But you're the one who asked us to come to the game tonight. Was it just to meet us ahead of the reception, or did you have another motive? I'm beginning to think door number two is the answer here. What's going on?"

Dixxi leaned over in front of Gregor and smacked Mark upside the head. "You may be Fenrir," she said, "but you're still my brother. Keira's right. You asked them here to scope them out. Scoping done and now they need to know the real reason. I trust her . . . and Adam." She watched Tucker, who was studiously concentrating on driving but very much listening to every word. "I trust all of them."

Adam gave Dixxi a regal nod and a smile.

"We've got wolves missing," Mark said bluntly. "At least two, perhaps three."

"Missing how?" I asked, needing clarification. "Did they vanish from your homestead or what?"

"We added some new land to our holdings," he said. "Mostly for us to hunt, but also to allow new pack members to have more room to build out—houses and such. In the last few years, the pack's been expanding. We're trying to incorporate the lone wolves in the area into our pack. We offer them protection and safety in exchange for them tithing to the pack. The place used to lease out for dove and javelina hunting but went into receivership."

"So you bought this land. I thought you had to close your camping and boating business in the Falls due to the drought," I said.

"I did, but the land was a steal. The rent from the wer living there will more than cover the land and property taxes. But things have been pretty tough for us these past few months, so I'm waiving payments for pack members who just don't have it. There's plenty of feral hogs and javelina on the Falls property as well as the new plot. As long as we get plenty of fresh meat, we're fine. Still have to pay taxes, though, and they don't take meat for that. Frankly, cash is damned tight."

"Is bringing in new wolves something unusual?" Adam asked. "My apologies for the question, but I'm not at all familiar with werewolf pack etiquette."

"In the past decade or so, it's become more common," Mark said. "It's harder and harder to survive in a more modern world by yourself, so packs like ours that have been around for a long time have extended an open call to loners and couples. We've added about twenty new wolves in the past three years."

"When did these folks go missing?" I asked. "Is it two or three?"

"At least one couple," he answered. "Newbies from New York City . . . Manhattan. They jumped at the chance to have land and hunting privileges. I sent a guide with them that first day. You know city folk, not too keen on the raw land thing. Tame wild, here in the Hill Country, but still full of snakes, brown recluse spiders, things that can be fatal, even to wolves. We're strong but not immortal. The guide's a wolf, just joined the pack about a month ago—from outside the Houston area. He's mostly country-bred, owned a small farm outside Katy until the area got too citified. I figured he'd be good to show them around, find a place to build their cabin."

"They didn't come back?" Niko asked.

"Not a sign of them," Dixxi answered. "They went out a couple of days ago and never showed back up at the lake. No one really noticed right away, because everyone

was out working and/or just doing their own thing. Without Mark and Levon over at the lake, sometimes things
slip through the cracks—"

"Slip through the cracks?" I interrupted. "That's a hell
of a way to put it." I didn't know how to take her comment.

"Sorry," she said, "But no one's really in charge up
there, because the three most senior wolves are here—in
Rio Seco, that is. Didn't really think that anything would
happen. It isn't hunting season, and it's our own land."

"That's the weird part," Mark said. "There's no sign of
them on the land at all. It's a big parcel, about a hundred
and fifty acres of unimproved land, but several wolves
went out to scope it out." He looked at his nephew. "Even
those that weren't supposed to be there, evidently."

"Have you reported this to the sheriff's office?" Adam
asked.

"And say what? I've got some folks missing that
might be wolves?"

"Why would you need to say that?" Niko asked, obviously puzzled. "Your people are human most times, correct?"

Mark shrugged. "They like being in wolf shape in the
country."

"Are you telling me they were out there in broad daylight in wolf shape?" My jaw dropped. "You aren't really
saying that, are you?"

"Why not?"

I rolled my eyes. "Mark, in case it's totally escaped
your attention, most of the land around there is either
state park or pretty open—no fencing, no way of keeping
trespassers off. Was the land posted at least?"

He shook his head. "Not yet, we just signed the papers
right before we came to Rio Seco."

"Anyone could've gone joyriding around there. And—wait. Greg, you never did say how you got injured. So, 'fess up, what do we not know yet?"

Gregor, Mark, and Dixxi exchanged silent glances. Mark nodded. "Tell them."

"I was shot," Gregor said.

CHAPTER SIXTEEN

Tucker, Niko, and I spoke simultaneously. "Shot?"

"As in bang-bang rifle kind of shot?" I continued. "How, I mean—wait, we saw you before the game without a shirt, I didn't see any bandages."

Gregor twisted in his seat and pulled out his left hip pad as best he could. I leaned over to see a dirty gauze bandage, taped tightly just above his left hip. Niko leaned over the back of the seat, nostrils flaring. Even I could smell the fresh blood as Gregor's ill-timed movement broke open the wound.

Niko nodded at me, trying to communicate something. I shook my head a little, not understanding.

Gregor hissed as he let the pad go back to its normal position. "I was stupid, that's all."

"Getting shot isn't being stupid," I retorted. "That's some idiot's criminal behavior. Did you see who shot you?"

"A machine."

"Yeah, right, a Cylon robo-hunter shot you." I didn't hold back the sarcasm at all. But damn, I was already tired of people keeping information from me. I mostly understood political caution and the fact that they didn't know us well, but hell, we were smack in the middle of this now and frankly, I wanted answers.

"Not exactly," Mark said. "But Gregor's not lying." He took a huge breath and let it out slowly. "I think I'd better come clean."

"You do that." I met his gaze square on. "Talk, wolf."

"Five years ago, when I became Fenrir, I presented myself to your leader. To Minerva." He hesitated. "I got the invitation to the reception a month ago. I really wanted to just chuck it in the trash bin, but Lev had a cooler head."

"I take it you and Minerva didn't hit it off." Niko's voice held a note of empathy. "She's not the most likable sort."

Mark shook his head. "I don't think I'd use 'likable' to describe her. Sorry, Keira, Tucker."

"No apology necessary, Mark," I said. "We all know Minerva's more than intimidating."

Mark closed his eyes and took a deep breath. "You could say that. She took my oath and gave me the traditional greeting and then pretty much implied to go on and get the hell back to my territory."

I waited to hear the rest. So far, I hadn't heard anything unusual. What had he expected? Sunshine and roses and a feast? I didn't cotton to Gigi's brusque attitudes, but a "hey, we're here" acknowledgment was pretty much just that. Nothing special, just, I see you and okay, we know you're there.

"Yes, well, I asked you to the game to check you out." A note of defiance crept into Mark's voice.

"To see if we were trustworthy," Adam said.

"Not really, more to see what kind of people you were. Minerva Kelly is trustworthy—"

I snorted. "Trustworthy, yeah, right." Tucker shot me a look. I had no problem interpreting. He was telling me to keep my opinions concerning Minerva's Machiavellian machinations to myself. Family matters within family.

"In any case," Mark continued, ignoring my aside, "I wanted to ask for help. To find out what's happened to our missing wolves, but I was afraid you might be like her."

Me, too, I thought and caught Adam's soft smile. I'd unburdened myself to him in Vancouver and that exact same fear had kept me in a state of anxiety. Now, I knew I could forge my own path as heir. I wondered what Mark thought of Gigi other than trustworthy. I noticed he hadn't actually said. "Uncaring" was the immediate word that came to my mind. Well, perhaps more intimidating than uncaring. She'd have probably helped the wolves, but with a price. Neither Adam nor I would put a price on a rescue, if that was what this was.

"I knew you were with the vampire and were part Sidhe," Mark continued. "I don't—didn't—trust either of those two. You're different."

"You think so?" Adam asked, and gave a full-on vampire stare at Mark, who cringed visibly.

"Stop it, Adam," I said. "Mark, what Adam's trying to get at is that we're not really that different. You have to trust us and let us help anyway, even though we are vampire, Sidhe, Kelly. You're probably still seeing me as that drunk seventeen-year-old girl who threw herself at you at a football game." Tucker's outright laugh reverberated throughout the van. "Enough from the peanut gallery," I warned. "Mark, I'm not her anymore. I'm the Kelly heir and heir to a lesser Seelie Court, niece of the current May Queen. I'm also your ruler alongside Adam. He's—" I stopped, then continued as Adam gave me a silent go-ahead. "He's king of the vampire tribe here as well as heir to the Unseelie Court."

Mark, Gregor, and Dixxi all three seemed stunned.

"I suppose that was a bit much to lay on you at once?"

"I'll say," said Dixxi. "Y'all aren't kidding around, are you." There was no question in her statement, her tone as flat as Kansas.

"Nope. That's why I said we are who we are . . . but that also means I'm the Keira Kelly who grew up in Rio Seco, in Texas. Among humans, as well as my Clan. I . . . all of us, will help you."

"My thanks, m'lady." Mark placed a hand over his heart and gave me as much of a bow as could be accomplished inside a moving vehicle.

"So, a robot hunter?" I prompted.

"You sure about that, Gregor?" Mark asked.

The boy shrugged, then hissed and put a hand to his side. "What else could it be? It's not hunting season."

Mark explained. "A few years ago, some jerk set up remote hunts on the Internet. He'd rigged some blinds with all sorts of controls and such. Set out feeders for deer. Last year or so, a law finally passed to make those illegal. He went bankrupt, all his property went into receivership, and we were able to buy it really cheap."

"But there were still remote hunting setups?"

"Yeah, we found out the hard way. One of my guys went out about three weeks ago and accidentally set off a trip wire. Bullet grazed his side. Lev went out to check it out and found several blinds still set up, still with bullets. The guy had really made the blinds weatherproof."

"Would have to," I said. "What the hell did you do?"

"I sent out a group from the pack as humans in protec-

tive gear and a couple of wolves to sniff out the metal.
We dismantled four blinds and some camera guns, too.
Looks like some trespassers have been there—a couple
of the blinds seemed like they'd been used for last year's
season."

"So you think you tripped another blind?" I directed
my question at Gregor.

"I thought so, yeah."

"Would you be able to tell us where you were when
you were shot?" Adam asked.

"Yeah, pretty close, anyway," he said. "I was marking
territory, left a spray can of paint behind."

"Marking with paint? I thought you-all did that the
old-fashioned way," I said. Did these wolves spray paint
instead of urine? Even my brothers marked territory with
their scent.

"We do," Mark answered. "But last weekend, I also
asked a couple of guys to go out and mark the edges of
the property with orange paint. You know, get a rock to
mark boundaries."

"Ah, gotcha," I said. "So you can put up the No Trespassing signs."

"Yeah, but then I got stuck at the deli with a late delivery and some officious county idiot delaying my final
inspection, so we never got back out there." He glared at
Gregor. "Some people weren't supposed to go with the
others."

Dixxi growled a little. "Leave him be, Mark. He's hurt
and he's young. I'm sure you did stupider things at his
age."

"I know I did," I said, and stared directly at Mark, who
blushed.

"You think it was stupid?" He seemed taken aback
and not a little embarrassed.

"More just thoughtless," I explained. "I didn't know you and frankly, I was thinking with my hormones. I may not be human, but at the time, I had about as much power as a newborn kitten, compared to what I have now. If you'd been a rapist or mean, you could've hurt me."

"But I didn't."

"No, you didn't, and Gregor will heal. We'll get him to Bea's and patch him up. I can do some light healing spells—just need a little space and time to concentrate. He'll probably need to sleep for at least eight or nine hours afterward."

"Thank you," Dixxi said. "We truly appreciate this."

"It is part of my duty," I said. "To take care of you."

"That said," Adam put in, "we need to check this property of yours. Perhaps Niko and I can do a quick reconnaissance tonight?"

"It's not close," Mark answered. "It's back over to White Rock, kind of off the beaten path."

"Then tomorrow night?"

"I think I should take the boys and go in the daytime first," I said. "Then perhaps Niko and one or two others can come back in the night after we debrief."

"Good thought," Adam said.

"Could just be poachers." Mark appeared thoughtful. "I was planning to lease out for dove and javelina when the season opened to make a little extra cash . . . that is, if I didn't have any wolves who wanted to settle there. Margery and Stephen really wanted a place far away from the towns. They'd grown up in Manhattan. Stephen was bitten nearly ten years ago and managed somehow to survive in the city. He was the one that contacted me. Margery—she's fresh, brand-new. Bitten by a rogue and had no guidance until Stephen found her. They needed some place away from people. So that's why I sent them to the back end of that property. It's close enough to the county utilities so that hooking up a double-wide while they build a house won't be an issue."

"Any chance they just ran off ?" I asked, just to hear their answer. Me, I didn't have much of a doubt.

"They might be newbies," Dixxi answered, "but Maki, the guy we sent out with them, is an old country hand. He was born and raised on a ranch in Colorado, lived there until he was thirty, then came to buy his place in Katy, then here. He's been with us only a few weeks, but he's been great."

"Not run off, doubtful they were kidnapped, so . . ."

"Yeah, so," Mark said. "Whatever 'so' turns out to be. I want to know."

"We'll find out, Mark. We promise."

CHAPTER SEVENTEEN

"Fɪʀsт, ᴡᴇ ɴᴇᴇᴅ ᴛᴏ get Gregor to Bea's and comfortable," Tucker said. "We'll work out how to help you-all in the morning."

"Speaking of . . . is there a twenty-four-hour convenience store or anything on the way to Bea's place?" Dixxi asked.

"Not a thing," I said. "The store in Rio Seco is only open until ten and it's long past that. What do you need?"

"I think that even with a light healing, we should make sure we've got ice packs, extra gauze bandages, first aid tape, and such. Probably some ibuprofen or other pain reliever, unless Bea's got stuff at her place."

"Bea's probably got aspirin or something," I said, "but I don't know about any of the other stuff. We could call her."

"You know," Niko said, "there's a Walmart store over near White Rock that is open twenty-four hours."

"Is there? How do you know about a Walmart, anyhow?"

"I told him," Tucker said. "We had an idea on how to help the vampires in the heat. Bloodsicles."

"Okay," I said, with disbelief. "If you say so."

"No, really." Niko took up the explanation. "We read somewhere that the San Diego Zoo does that during especially hot weather—freezes blood and water for the big cats. Don't see why it would be any different for us. We thought we'd get those Popsicle mold things."

When I got over the idea of a 400-plus-year-old vampire and a 1,200-plus-year-old Viking Berserker wanting to go to Walmart and buy Popsicle molds, I responded. "Not a bad idea, I suppose, but we're totally driving in the wrong direction."

"You know, that is rather brilliant," Dixxi said. "We've been having a hell of a time staying indoors in the cool. Our nature is to be outdoors, to run. Hunting's been rough on us recently. Wolves dropping like flies in the heat."

"Well, if you guys really want to go, I'm good. Tucker, why don't you watch out for a good spot to pull over and turn around. If you stop for a few minutes, I can at least do some minor healing on Gregor before we drive any farther." I didn't want to alarm the boy, but I'd finally clued in to Niko's silent message. It didn't take a rocket scientist to figure out that he was bleeding pretty steadily under that bandage . . . which is another reason the trip to Walmart sounded better and better.

"You said minor healing, what does that mean exactly?" Dixxi asked.

"I'm still fairly new at this," I explained. "I don't think I can fully heal Gregor, not without a veteran healer beside me to help. Unfortunately, none of those folks came back with us. I can at least help with some of the pain, maybe help with the bleeding a little. When we get to Rio Seco, I can get my cousin Liz to help. She's not a full healer, but an extra pair of hands wouldn't hurt."

"He'll be good as new?" Mark asked.

"No." I wasn't going to get Mark's hopes up. "Liz can help, but healing's a minor secondary talent that she kept. We'll supplement with the painkillers and bandages so he can continue to heal." I mentally crossed my fingers. Between the two of us, Liz and I could maybe come up with a way to help this kid out. Ibuprofen wasn't going to cut it, at least from what I'd seen so far. That kid was in a world of hurt, even though he was doing his best to hide it. With his youth, his wer nature, and his overall physical fitness level, he shouldn't be this badly off. I had a feeling his "flesh wound" went a great deal deeper than he was letting on. I didn't want to scare him, or out his secret. I'd been sixteen once, with secrets that I kept from my family.

"Walmart, it is," Tucker said and pulled to the side of the road. "You want to do your mojo now, sis?"

"No, really, I'm good," Gregor said before I could approach him. "You don't need to do any healing right now, let's just get to the store and get the stuff you guys need. Then we can go home . . . or to Bea's or whatever."

I studied the boy's face for a sign that he was playing the macho card, but saw nothing there but exhaustion and the desire to get on with it.

"Fine, let's go to the store," I decided. "Anyone know how to get there from here?"

"Sort of," Dixxi said. "I'll see if I can find the address on my phone."

I reached into the glove box to grab the GPS Tucker kept there. "Let me know when you've got it and I'll plug it in here. Adam, could you give Bea a call and let her know the change of plan?"

"I will."

"You mean you don't have some sort of magickal

radar?" Mark teased. "I thought all you Kellys could do that kind of stuff."

I resisted the urge to stick out my tongue at him. "I'm utter crap at directions and maps," I said. "Still am, even after the Change. Geolocation isn't one of our talents. That's why there are lovely things like this GPS and smartphones with Internet service."

Adam only smiled at the exchange.

"SERIOUSLY?" I gritted my teeth. "There's six adults in here with better than human senses and yet we still managed to waste more than an hour getting lost?"

"I thought you relied on the GPS," Tucker teased. "You were the one who said to ignore it."

"Yeah, because it was trying to take us on a road that's not yet completed," I reminded him. "Pull in the damned lot, will you. Park close as you can."

Stupid fucking satellite thing. We'd gone well out of our way and had finally admitted we were wrong after the GPS kept whining at us to take the next exit that didn't freaking exist. Luckily, I'd spotted the glow of the giant sign and somehow, we managed to get there without killing one another on the way. Gregor, poor kid, didn't complain once. This delay had to be hard on him.

The vast parking lot was practically empty of cars. Not a surprise, since it was now nearly eleven thirty. A couple of cars parked to one side, a pickup truck near the entrance on the left, and another truck farther down were the only vehicles there other than ours. Employees must park out back, I mused.

I opened the passenger door as Adam slid open the side door. "Niko, why don't you and Tucker go for the popsicle things. Adam and I will head to the pharmacy section and pick up the meds." I turned my head to address the three wer. "You three—stay in here. We won't be long."

Mark began to protest, but a glare from Dixxi shut him up. "We'll stay," he said.

The overbright lights of the store assaulted us, along with the godawful piped-in music. At least there was no artificially friendly greeter. Perhaps they didn't think they needed one at this time of night. Niko looked like a kid arriving at the gates of Disneyland for the first time. His eyes widened, taking in the overwhelming insanity of it all. Though the store was empty of shoppers, the piles upon piles of colorful displays, sale signs, and merchandise were enough to turn anyone off shopping in person. The fluorescents turned both vampires' complexions an odd shade of greenish pale. Tucker and I didn't fare so well, either; our own fair skins were a sickly yellow.

"C'mon, let's do what we need to and get out of here," I said. "I hate stores."

Tucker took Niko's hand and led him off in the direction of the signs proclaiming "Summer is HERE!" in bold red lettering. I glanced around the ceiling signage as I tried to find the pharmacy. "There." I pointed to the far left. "There's where we need to go."

We found the first aid aisle fairly quickly. I'd picked up a handbasket from the end of the aisle and loaded up with gauze, Ace bandages, ibuprofen, first aid tape, and Bactine. As I was studying one of the shelves, Adam wandered down the aisle and picked up a box of alcohol wipes. "These might come in handy."

"Thanks, love."

Two women passed us, both wearing the typical store apron, each carrying a box. They were deep in conversation and didn't even notice us.

"Damn, it was hot today," one of them said. "You get any a/c out at your place yet?"

"Fuckers couldn't come again," the other answered. "I've got three fans going in the living room just to keep the air moving. Was going to send the kids tubing, but they came back right away. That river raft place shut down."

I grabbed Adam's arm and motioned for him to be quiet. They were talking about Mark's place.

"Yeah, I heard about that a couple of days ago. River's too low, on account a no rain."

"Serves 'em right, though," the second woman continued. "Them weird-ass religious cultists got it coming to them."

"Don't know anything 'bout them being weird, Martha, they just homeschool, like lots of folks do now."

"Public school was just fine for my kids, and yours, too, Betty. Why can't they just send kids to school like we did?"

A pause and a grunt. "Hell if I know. C'mon, help me with this shelf. I wanna get done so's we can take our break."

Silently, Adam and I exited the aisle from the other end and walked back toward where we'd last seen Tucker and Niko headed.

"They were talking about Mark's people," I said. "You think that's the impression of the entire community?"

"Perhaps. I've found that places like this tend to reflect the feelings of the community as a whole." He motioned with his hand, indicating a display of tacky religious tchotchkes—Jesus clocks, sappy plaques with the "Footprints in the Sand" poem, gilded picture frames with angel wings tacked on. Next to it, another display touting the upcoming hunting season—three months off, but still "Just Around the Corner."

"Maybe there's someone or someones here who are unhappy that Mark's buying more land," I ventured.

Adam nodded solemnly. "Or they were spotted as wolf, as you said before. This is a land of hunters."

"That it is," I agreed. We'd reached the summer promotion aisles. No sign of Tucker or Niko.

"Where the hell could they have gotten to?" This was one of those superstores, many thousands of square feet of merchandise, including groceries. "Maybe they decided to go buy food? I mean, it's been awhile since we had snacks at the game. I'm a bit peckish, myself."

"Could be. Shall we?" Adam offered me his arm and I took it. How fucking odd, I thought to myself. Wandering the aisles of middle American retail with my vampire.

CHAPTER EIGHTEEN

I HATED THE FACT THAT retail stores arranged their aisles in such a way that a person had to maneuver in and out, rather than in a straightforward direct pattern. Yes, I understood merchandising theory, but right now, I just wanted to find my brother and his purchase-happy sidekick and get out of there.

As we made our way through the linens, Adam stopped. "There are some nice sheets here," he said. Amused, I watched him as he bent to pick up a sheet set, a beautiful dark dusky purple. Intensely, he began to read the label as if this were something fascinating. Perhaps it was. I doubted that Adam did much shopping for himself, though I had wondered who stocked his house—his towels, bedding, etc. They were all the best money could buy.

He stood there in the aisle, head bent and concentrating. The light above shone on his dark hair, his skin so pale against the black of his clothing. A sudden ache in my chest as I caught my breath. How beautiful this man is, I thought. How amazing my need for him. This want inside me that I've never felt before. *This* I must have, and then knowledge that I do have it. It was suddenly overwhelming. The walls and lights of the store faded, and everything in my being concentrated on the person in front of me. Oblivious, he continued to peruse the label, as if thread count and laundering instructions were of supreme importance.

I nearly reached out for him right then and there, the low hum of arousal clenching deep inside me. A breath, then another, to calm, to focus. I was in fucking Walmart, where Ma and Pa Kettle shopped—though not so much at this time of night, but still. This was the home of the "Save money. Live better," not the up-against-the-linens-shelves quickie.

With a slight turn of his head, Adam's gaze fell on me, a ponderous weight that I welcomed. *You own me.* His unspoken words were as loud as if he'd announced it over the store's PA system. I blinked, my eyes unable to take in the intensity. Could I handle this depth of feeling? This knowing? He knew everything I was and everything I could be with him.

I swallowed and steadied my own gaze. *You own me,* I returned, just as silently. An admission I'd made to no one—not even my Clan. They might claim me, but they never owned me. Despite the venue, the godawful green cast of the overhead fluorescents, the funky plastics and floor-wash smell of the store, I could only see Adam, smell his subtle vanilla and nutmeg scent. I reached up a hand and placed it on his cheek, his cool skin balm to my ridiculous agitation. Without a word, he turned his face slightly and leaned into my touch, lips passing softly across my skin. Acknowledgment and equal agreement that what we were becoming was more than either of us had bargained for. Love? He spoke of it often with me. A word I rarely used. I loved him, yes, but until right this second, it was a love like I loved Tucker and was growing to love Niko. Protective, belonging in a group, filial and familiar with the added bonus of lust. Somehow, in this ridiculously incongruous place, surrounded by racks of cheap bed linens, I began to realize the extent of our bond.

"Shall we find the boys, then?" Adam said softly as he took my hand from his cheek and gave it a quick squeeze.

I nodded, still silent, unsure of how my voice would sound.

"HEY, ISN'T that the assistant coach?" I whispered to Adam as we headed up the back aisle, still trying to locate Tucker and Niko. A blond man in shorts stood in front of a display of ammunition, placing several boxes into his shopping cart. "I'm going to go talk to him, hang on a sec?

"Hi there. You're Coach Miller, aren't you?" I greeted him as I approached. "Guess we're all doing a little late-night shopping."

Startled, the man dropped one of the boxes of ammo back onto the shelf. "Umm, yeah, hello," he said. He looked at me, a frown on his face. "Football game, right?"

"Yes, we were with Mark Ashkarian," I reminded him. "Game ended already?"

"Yeah, short one tonight. Last half went by fast." His frown got deeper, and he began to rummage through the boxes in the cart. Something was making this guy very nervous. I smiled at him and released my shields a little, trying to read him. Anxiety, nerves, jittery; an annoying background buzz interfered. I pulled back and nodded my head at him as if to take our leave, realizing the buzz was the sound of the overhead lights, but magnified.

"I saw those guys that were with you at the game. That one pale one and the other long-haired redhead. Back over there." He motioned with his head behind him. "Up by the toys."

"My brother?"

His eyes grew wide, then narrowed. "They your brothers?"

"The 'other long-haired guy' is," I said. "Niko, the first guy, is his partner."

"They in some sort of business?"

"That, too," I said. "They're married."

"Can't do that in Texas." He grunted out as if his mouth found it distasteful.

"You can in Canada," I said. "We're citizens there, too."

He got that expression on his face like we were something on the order of aliens mixed with rotting trash, but he was too polite to say so to our faces. He picked up another box of ammo and dropped it into his already full cart.

I could see at least one item in the cart was a riflescope. Another box had the words "lure" and "urine" prominently highlighted. Ick. Whatever floated his boat. As wolf or other predator shape, I was lucky not to need that sort of equipment to hunt my prey. Then again, hunting by setting up feeders and blinds wasn't my idea of hunting.

"Urine?" I remarked. "What's that for?"

"I'm training dogs," he said. "It's a training tool." He still seemed distinctly uncomfortable with me around. Hell, maybe his wife didn't like the fact he hunted. I had no clue, nor, frankly, did I care at all. What these good ol' boys did in their spare time, as long as it didn't involve me or mine, was beyond my need to explore. "I gotta go," he said suddenly as he checked his watch. "See ya then."

"Nice to see you, too," I muttered as the man scurried away.

I rejoined Adam, who'd wandered over to the camping food section and was reading a dehydrated food package label. "You know these are mostly salt?"

"Yes," I said. "Which is a problem for humans, not us." I took the package from his hand and placed it back on the shelf.

"You read him?"

"Tried to," I said. "Too much interference from the electricity in here. Something's off, though. He seemed awfully nervous."

"He is buying ammunition," Adam said.

"Nothing unusual for around here. Urine for lures, too."

"Lures?"

"He said he was training hunting dogs," I answered. "It's fairly common: lures made of some material are soaked in a scent that dogs are then trained to spot, flush, and retrieve. I've seen it done with bird dogs but don't really know all that much about it. Hunting season's in a few months, so I suppose Mr. Miller wants to have time to train."

"Unusual," Adam said. "I'd not heard of this method of training. I could see where it would work, however."

"Yeah, hunting season may be rather iffy this year, though. If this drought doesn't end soon, we may be euthanizing a lot more game at the ranch."

"Niko's been worried about it, as well," Adam said. "He's having to work through Tucker with the Texas Parks and Wildlife people to help us handle our herds. The exotics are doing well, since they've been under special management, but he tells me the local whitetail herds and other indigenous species are in trouble."

"Yeah, I know deer are coming farther and farther into developments to find water. Maybe Mr. Miller is doing some off-season hunting. Not something he'd want to be found out for, being a coach at the school and married to the sheriff."

"Makes sense. Shopping at this time of night doesn't, however."

"Who knows, maybe he's hiding from his wife. She's a piece of work."

"Definitely a chip on her shoulder," Adam said.

"More like a mountain," I muttered. "C'mon, let's get out of here and get Gregor back to Bea's so he can sleep. I'm sure it's way past his bedtime. Besides, I'd like to get a little sleep sooner than later. I need to go have a chat with Bea in the a.m."

"About what? She knows they are wer, correct?"

"She does, but I don't want her making a decision without all the pertinent facts. Dixxi knows, by the way." I crossed into the toy section and peered down an aisle. No guys.

"Knows what?"

"About Bea's pregnancy. I did interpret that look from you at the game earlier, right? Before you and I went to talk with Dixxi."

"You did," he said. "Then the conversation with Dixxi was not solely theoretical."

"Nope. Dixxi twigged to Bea's condition either at the game or even before. That's the part I need to talk to Bea about. Their family has some really fucked-up genes."

"You are correct," Adam agreed. "Bea needs all the data."

"Best time to catch her is either post breakfast rush or post lunch," I said. "I'd rather do it sooner than later, just in case she comes down with a case of the honests and spills the beans to Lev. He seems to be a nice enough guy, but it's her body, her decision."

Adam nodded. "There's Niko and Tucker," he said, motioning down an aisle.

Niko was bent over the blow-up beach ball bin in the pool/party area, his ass on display as his cotton slacks pulled tight across it. My brother, never one to let an opportunity by, stood behind him, admiring the view. Next to Tucker, a man wearing a tight T-shirt and faded jeans stood, holding a handbasket. The back of his shirt advertised a trucking firm.

"Sure a pretty bahoonkas on your girl there." The guy made a circular motion with both hands, outlining what could only be his interpretation of an ass. He whistled and gave Tucker that "we're all boys here" look, accompanied by a wide grin. Tucker bared his teeth, a growl growing under his breath.

"He sure is pretty," I said and joined my brother as Niko stood up holding a bright purple beach ball and turned around. The trucker guy's face went a deep red as he realized he'd been ogling a man. With a mutter, he quickly left the aisle.

"Pool toys?" I asked as I studied the overflowing shopping cart.

"We got all the popsicle molds they had," Niko said. "Then Tucker got the idea that we could perhaps use the community pool at the Bar-K at night."

"Any way to do that, sis?" he asked. "I know it's usually closed at dusk."

"Possibly." I shook my head at the two of them. "C'mon, let's buy all this crap and get out of here. I can talk to Carlton tomorrow, or you can, Tucker. He's on the board of the community center. I'll tell him something about y'all being allergic to sun and needing the pool for therapy or something."

Adam cocked a brow at me in disbelief.

"What?" I threw up my hands. "Niko's right. A pool would do wonders, since we can't swim in the lake. You could always build one, but that takes time."

"We can always get one of these aboveground things," Tucker remarked. "They sell them here."

"Oh for—let's go before you two buy out the entire store," I said. "We've got an injured boy in the car and too many damned people to deal with. You can order the pool thing online."

CHAPTER NINETEEN

Outside, we passed Coach Miller sitting inside his truck—a brand-new Ford F-250 with the fancy Cabela's trim and fully loaded for bear—or deer, or whatever. He must have spent a fortune on this puppy. The truck was rigged with those obnoxious round hunting lights on top of the cab, a brush grill on the front, and special hunting chairs mounted in the back. Adam, who until now had kept his counsel, whispered to me, "The smaller the penis, the larger the accoutrements." I slapped my hand over my mouth and raced over to our van, avoiding breaking down in pure laughter.

"Huh," I said as we drove by Miller's truck on our way out of the store parking area.

"What?" Tucker asked.

"When we passed Miller earlier, walking, did you see that there was a person sitting in the passenger seat?"

A chorus of "yeses" came back at me.

"And did y'all notice what I just noticed?" I prompted.

"That's it's some guy?" Tucker responded. "Yeah."

"So what is the coach doing at oh, just past midnight, at the local Walmart with someone other than his wife—with their heads close together like they were about to—"

None of my companions answered me right away. Maybe they were waiting for the punch line?

"C'mon, guys, it's not that hard," I said.

"He's cheating on his wife?" Adam ventured.

"Not likely," Tucker chuckled. "You saw his ink at the stadium, right? Semper Fi. Dude's an ex-marine. What are the chances of an ex-jarhead, who lives in this part of Texas, married to a deputy/acting sheriff and still wears it high-and-tight being queer?"

"Yeah, not so likely," I said.

"It's just as likely as anywhere else," Niko countered.

"I didn't get the right vibe," Tucker said.

"So now you're the king of the gaydar?" I couldn't help sounding sarcastic. "I seem to remember a certain time when I was still in high school that—"

"Yeah, well, okay, okay, I was wrong once. That teacher wasn't ogling me so much as you," Tucker responded. "It never occurred to me that a fifty-year-old man would be interested in a fourteen-year-old girl. At least not in the late twentieth century."

"In any case, what the hell does it matter anyway?" I asked. "Rob Miller isn't anyone we're likely to hang out with."

"You were the one who brought it up, sis," Tucker reminded me.

"I was only wondering who the guy was," I said. "It did seem as if they were going to kiss, but Tucker's right, dude's more than likely not gay."

"Ewww," Gregor said. "Coach Miller?"

"Gay bothers you?" I asked.

"No, just Coach Miller and sex. He's my coach," Greg protested.

I laughed. "I see your point. Mark, Dix, any thoughts on the guy?"

"Not really," Mark said. "Don't know him that well He's a fairly typical guy, I'd say."

Dixxi nodded. "Yeah, I know he doesn't like us much. but he doesn't have to."

"He was rather nervous when he saw us in the store," Adam said.

"I know his kind," Niko remarked. "I have no idea whether he's ever thought of a man in a sexual way and don't care, but he's a bigot. Perhaps that's why he was so anxious."

"Come again?" I asked.

"He doesn't like us, either," Niko said. "Despite our living in the general area, we're not what he expected. I've often found that men—or women—like him don't know how to handle people like us."

"I think I get your point," mark said to Niko. "He's a bigoted, redneck former marine who thinks the corps was the be-all and end-all of life. He's stuck here in this small town, assistant coaching a class B football team, and his wife is the one with the authority in general. He can't be overtly rude or mean, since she's the law."

Tucker laughed. "Definitely, Mark. Hell, from the little we saw of her tonight, I've no doubt she calls the shots at home. I bet he's a holy terror over those boys."

"The team?" Gregor ventured. "Yeah, he's kind of tough."

"Yuck," I said. "Enough with the speculation. I don't like to think about the macho-sadistic ritualism of Texas high school football training. It's unpleasant to think about, and we have neither evidence nor say in the matter. Let's talk about something else."

A loud bang sounded and the van skewed to the left, throwing me out of my seat and practically on top of

Mark and Gregor. Tucker fought to control it as I fell to the floor, while Mark tried to hold Gregor in place. Adam and Niko braced against the windows.

"What was that bang?" Dixxi's voice sounded a little shaky.

"Blown tire," Tucker said. "Damn it." He slapped the dash in frustration.

"You are not going to say that you should've gotten the spare tire fixed, are you?" I asked darkly. "I'm not laughing here, ha ha, movie quote, and all that."

Tucker stared at me with a puzzled expression on his face. "No, it's just bloody difficult to change the tires on this vehicle, in the pitch dark, with no actual shoulder on the road, plus we've got an injured werewolf to deal with."

"All right, all right. Keep your shorts on. Adam, could you please help Mark get Gregor out of the van so Tucker can jack it up?" I peered below the seats to check. Yep, there it was. "Dixxi, there's a bag just below your seat with some towels so Greg can lie down on those outside." I opened my car door and stepped down. "Careful, all, there's a bit of a dip down into a shallow ditch."

"I'll go get the emergency kit," Tucker said and pulled the emergency brake on.

"Could I help you by holding the torch?" Niko asked. Tucker nodded and went to the back of the van. "C'mon then."

Dixxi followed as Adam and Mark helped Gregor out of the van. They walked toward the back, placed a couple of towels on the ground and Gregor sat down. Dixxi helped him remove his shoulder pads and jersey.

"Ouch, fuck."

"Language, kid," Dixxi warned again. "It'll just be

a bit, Greg. Mark, there's not much for him to lean on, could you sit behind him?"

"Is he that bad off?" I asked as I pulled a small flashlight out of the glove box. One thing I'll have to say for us Kellys, we were prepared as Girl Scouts when it came to our vehicles. I had similar kits in the back of my Land Rover. Full-on emergency kit in the back with a big Maglite; a smaller Maglite in the glove box along with tissues, wet wipes, and other gear.

Dixxi leaned forward and peered at Gregor's side, squinting in the red glow from the van's taillights. "Hard to tell, it's so dark. But I think the original wound's broken open and is bleeding."

"Adam, here." I handed him the flashlight. "You hang on to this and keep us lit." I grabbed the wipes. "I'll go see if I can do anything to help Gregor."

"Damn, there's a full-on hole in the tire," Tucker said. "Must have picked up a nail or something. It's too big to patch up with that spray can stuff. I'll have to use the spare. Niko, if you don't mind?" As Tucker went around back to unbolt the spare, with a minimum of fuss, Niko loosened the bolts on the flat and jacked up the van.

"I'm impressed," I teased as I squatted down by Gregor. "Vampires changing tires."

Niko snorted. "I may not have been born in this century," he said, "but I do have my uses."

I could picture the expression on Adam's face, even though he was facing away from me.

"That you do, *cariad,* that you do." Tucker's voice floated from the back. I rolled my eyes. Boys, no matter what age, still with the jokes. I leaned closer to Gregor.

"Dixxi, could you help me get this pad thing off his hip? It's in the way." I could smell fresh blood along with the dried. Adam leaned closer, pointing the light more directly at Gregor's hip.

"Oh, dude, no." Gregor squirmed a little, as if to move away from me.

"What?"

"You can't just take the pad out," Dixxi explained. "It's tucked into the girdle thing."

"Girdle?" I peered at Gregor's side. My night vision had improved quite a bit since my Change, but it was still hard to see fine details, even with the flashlight. The white pad covered part of Gregor's hip and seemed to be tucked inside his football pants somehow.

"You are not taking my pants off," Gregor warned. "I'm tough. I can wait." He lifted his pleading face to Mark, who was biting his lip, probably holding back a laugh.

"Sorry, kiddo," Mark said. "If Keira can help you, then let her."

"I'm fine." Gregor moved to place a hand over his hip. With the movement, he cringed and let out a hiss.

"Fine, my ass," Dixxi said. "Hold still, I'll do this."

"We probably should have just let him change before we took off," I said as Mark moved into a better position to support Gregor, who was totally pouting now. I couldn't help but smile. The boy was utterly adorable.

"We could have," Mark said, "but I didn't want those coaches to take a closer look. At that point, I thought Gregor was faking it."

"True," I said. "Plus we had no idea this was going to be a journey of epic length."

Dixxi quickly unlaced the fastenings on the front of the pants and pulled them open enough to reach in and unlace the girdle. Egad, this uniform was worse than a

1950s maiden aunt's gear. Talk about chastity belts . . .

Eventually, enough gear was out of the way so I could place my hand just above the initial wound, about half an inch from his skin, ignoring Gregor's deep embarrassment. I'm sure he was mortified, having a woman my age poking about near his bits.

"Gregor, I'm going to have to pull off this bandage," I said. "Sorry about this. It's liable to—" With a tug, I peeled the tape away, taking more care in lifting the corner of the gauze. "Hang tight, this may hurt." The bandage was stuck; fresh blood welled up and dripped from the wound I'd uncovered.

CHAPTER TWENTY

"Fuck." Gregor whispered between clenched teeth. No one chastised him about his language now.

The scent of old blood and wounded flesh assaulted my nostrils. Concentrating and trying to remember everything my aunts taught me, I focused, letting the rest of the world fall away. The sounds of Niko and Tucker fussing with the tire dimmed; Dixxi's feet crunching gravel as she worked to get a better angle to help me, began to fade away. Red, angry, pulsating heat rose from Gregor's side, disturbing his otherwise calm energy. I moved my hand around, trying to find the exact center of the wound . . .

There it was, deep, raw—much more damage than he let on, just as I thought. Calling on my own energy, I pushed golden light, purple light, healing coolness toward the boy's side. No ritual here, just energy pushing energy, healing visualization taking away the burning, the part that was broken and didn't belong. I focused more intently, the red fading only a little at a time. More energy, more—

"What the hell—? Adam, did you hear something?" Niko looked up from his task, his words breaking my focus.

I fell back onto my ass, my hands automatically down to catch my fall as the world rushed back into my awareness. "Fuck." My palms scraped across the rough surface, breaking skin. "Niko, what—?" Then I heard it, too. Feet scuttling across dry dirt, twigs breaking, rocks disturbed as something crashed through the underbrush.

"Wait here." In a flash, moving as fast as only a vampire can, Adam disappeared into the brush, making no noise. Behind him, my brother stripped off his shirt and shorts and quickly shifted into wolf, following Adam in less than a minute.

"Where the fuck—" Dixxi began.

"Shh, quiet. I could swear . . ." Niko shook his head, then bent to his task and quickly removed the bolts. "Quick, Keira, hand me the spare. Let's get this done and everyone back in the van as fast as possible."

"What?" I whispered as I scrambled over to him and handed him the tire. Picking up the large Maglite where Tucker had dropped it, I pointed it out toward the brush. "I thought you guys would be done already."

"Light, Keira," Niko said. "No, not done. We were trying to figure something out."

I turned and gave him the light he needed. "With the tire?"

"Yes. The hole's pretty big, a gash really, more than I thought a nail would cause. Then I heard—"

"Someone was out there, I heard the brush rattling," I said, keeping my voice low.

Dixxi and Mark still sat on the ground, both with anxious expressions on their faces. Gregor lay slumped against Mark, his fly still open, shirt rucked up. Poor kid, he seemed so vulnerable. I hadn't been able to finish the little healing I could do under these conditions; he was probably wiped at this point. "Dixxi, Mark, get Gregor put back together again and get him up."

"What is it? What's out there?" Mark carefully held Gregor as Dixxi leaned in to refasten everything she'd undone. "Not a deer, I take it?"

"Human. I know I heard footsteps, not hooves," Niko said curtly.

"Your brother, he shifted . . ." Mark said with awe. "Just . . ."

"Flowed," Dixxi said, her voice mirroring Mark's expression. "I've never seen anything so beautiful."

"Our change is a lot harder," Mark explained. "Nothing that seamless."

I didn't know what to say to them. Sorry? I'd not seen werewolves change but had heard it was more work than not. After all, they were hybrids, human and wolf, not naturally magick as we were. I strained my ears to listen for Adam and Tucker. Nothing. But not surprisingly, as they were the best of stalkers. I needed to figure it out, though, had to try *something*. All my instincts wanted me to shift to a predator shape, join Adam and my brother, but I had people here I had to help watch out for. "Keep an eye out?" I asked Niko as I made a decision.

"Done." Niko took the light from my hand and tucked it between his ear and shoulder, head bending to hold it like a phone.

I braced a hand against the side of the van for support and carefully lowered my shields, reaching out my awareness, keeping control as much as I could. Cedar mixed with the distinctive smell of mesquite, arid dusty ground. A whiff of deer scat and musk slid by as I instinctively followed Adam's unique feel. He crouched low to the ground, a finger reaching out to touch some-

thing wet, something—blood, the taste of fresh blood on
the tip of my tongue, its tang making my nostrils flare.
Rank sweat of at least one human male accompanied it.
It was a man's blood, not a lot, just a few drops as if he'd
scratched a hand on a mesquite bush. Adam stood and
listened. I withdrew and returned my awareness to the
van, realizing Niko was touching my hand.

"Step back?" he said quietly. I nodded and complied,
watching him let the jack down. The van settled onto the
dirt and the new tire held. Using his strength and speed,
Niko finished tightening the lug nuts.

"Mark, Dixxi, inside. Now, please." I kept my tone
low and even, but with a touch of urgency.

Mark, to his credit, just stood and helped Gregor to
his feet. The boy put an arm around Mark's shoulder
and with Dixxi on his other side, limped back to the van.
Mark got in first, then helped Gregor. Dixxi climbed back
into her original seat and situated herself so Gregor could
lean against her.

"Where did Adam and Tucker go?" Gregor mumbled.
"Did they leave?"

"I'm right here," Adam said as he climbed in. I took
my own seat as Niko started the engine. Tucker emerged
from the brush a moment later, shifted back into human
shape, and joined us in the van, clutching his clothing in
one hand. As soon as he slid shut the side door, Niko put
the car in gear and with a lurch, he pulled off the soft dirt
and headed back toward Rio Seco.

"We're going to the Wild Moon," Adam said after
a few moments. Tucker swiftly reclothed himself and
climbed around Adam to get to the far back seat.

"Why?" Mark sat up and glared at Adam. "We told
Bea we were going to her place. The Wild Moon—"

"Is the safest place for you right now," Adam said. "That puncture was no accident." He reached into his pocket and pulled out something and handed it to Mark. I smelled the fresh gunpowder, burnt paper, and plastic immediately.

"Fuck," I said to Adam. "Poachers?"

"It's well past midnight," reminded Niko. "This was no poacher."

"There were at least two men," Adam said. "They headed for a truck and before I could get there, they drove off." In Adam's terms, that meant he didn't chase, he didn't catch up to them. No way would a couple of guys in a pickup outrun a vampire at full speed.

"I agree with Adam," Tucker said. "I smelled two, maybe three human men. They had guns. One of them had scratched himself on the brush."

"I smelled the blood," I said. "Hurt badly?"

"No, just a few drops," Tucker said. "Probably enough to identify him again, though."

"Good. We just have to find them."

"Fuck, indeed." Mark dropped the shell back into Adam's hand. "Deliberate."

"This certainly changes things," I said. "I was going to suggest that your missing wolves had gotten themselves lost in a cave or an underground grotto looking for a way out of the heat, maybe passed out and now can't find their way back, but if someone's out here taking potshots . . ."

"We don't know that Mark or his pack were the target," Adam pointed out.

"True," I said. "But we're not the ones missing people."

"We did think that our wolves got lost, but Adam's right. I'm now positive that someone's trespassing.

Maybe we accidentally flushed them out when Margery, Stephen, and Maki went out on the land."

"Yeah, but, Mark, there's been nothing more than wolf sign out at the property," Gregor argued. "Luka and I went everywhere, trying to find scent that isn't wolf. No human scent for acres, just a lot of fresh wolf scent."

"Fresh? Like perhaps another pack?" I asked.

"I'd know if there was another pack in my territory," Mark glowered. "Didn't you sense me?"

At that, I had to smile, because yeah, as soon as I'd gotten within distance, I'd known he was there. "I did, indeed. So this remote hunting, why did it stop?"

"Guy got killed in an accident," Mark said.

"An accident?" I couldn't help but think of another "accident" last year—the one that killed the former deli owners and their two other human victims. The accident I helped arrange.

Marcus met my questioning glance. He'd dropped the semishift, now appearing as breathtaking as I remembered, if somewhat more mature. "Nothing to do with us," he said. "That land wasn't ours then, nor did I have any beef against the man. Hunting by machine is disgusting, yes, but at the time, perfectly legal. He died skiing in Colorado."

I shrugged. "Makes little difference to me. I just figured perhaps someone was connected to him."

"The boys and several others of the pack have been dismantling the blinds and removing weapons as they find them. Usually, they're easy to find—they smell."

"Gun oil and steel," Niko said knowingly.

"Yes."

"Then who shot Gregor?" Adam's steely green gaze caught Mark's amber one. "And who shot out our tire tonight?"

"That is the million-dollar question, my liege."

Adam gave Marcus a lordly nod. "Inasmuch as you are here, you are ours," he said, a regal expression confirming the king he was. "You may be neither of our blood nor yet sworn allegiance, but we will not leave you to handle this alone."

With a confirming nod, Marcus accepted Adam's statement. "Thank you," he said. "My pack and I accept your offer of help." With this, he turned to Gregor and placed a hand on the boy's shoulder. Even in the dark, I could see Gregor's pain. "Hold on, kiddo," Marcus said. "We'll get you home."

"Do you think this has anything to do with us?" I asked Adam, trying to be as quiet as possible.

Adam shook his head. "I doubt it," he said. "We've never come here to this place, and people here don't know us."

"But they do know and dislike Marcus's family," I finished. "Crap and damnation. A hate crime?"

"Could be." Adam remained extremely calm outwardly, but his energy pulsed against me. I took his hand, feeling the raw anger he controlled. "There were some bumper stickers on the truck that made me think that . . . are there those kinds of groups around here? White supremacists?"

"No, not that I know of anyway," I said. "White Rock's a pretty conservative community, but they're pretty low-key. This is a quiet, churchgoing community. You know the kind, bake sales, rummage sales, summer picnics. I don't remember there ever being any of that sort of crime here . . . just the usual."

"The usual?"

"Petty theft, vandalism, domestics. Nothing much that you wouldn't find in any small town."

"Need I remind you of your cousin Marty?" Adam asked, no irony in his tone.

"You needn't," I replied. "But that wasn't a hate crime, even though it was all about hatred." No, Boris and Greta hadn't targeted Marty, Adam, Niko, and me because of our backgrounds, only from some sense of twisted revenge. It was very, very personal.

From what I understood, most hate crimes are the exact opposite. They aren't about the individual but the person as a representative, however reluctant, of a group—gays, feminists, racial, religious, ethnic—whatever the hate group wanted to target at that time. "Gregor's a star player on the team. If someone hurt him deliberately, it's something personal. Something we don't know."

Almost as one, Adam and I turned to look at the three wer.

CHAPTER TWENTY-ONE

"THEY DON'T LIKE ME," Gregor ventured, "but shooting at me? A little harsh, don't you think?"

"He's right, Keira," Mark said. "Not the type of behavior you'd expect from kids. Adam, what about the bumper sticker? Could you see a logo or name of any sort?"

"Somewhat," Adam answered. "The truck was moving and was filthy—covered in mud. Even the license plate numbers were covered. From the part I could see, where the dirt had come off, it resembled something I'd seen on a news item about a white supremacist group . . . a modified swastika, perhaps?"

Oh holy fuck. Not here, please, not here. We had our share of rabid Christians and the like, but they were most likely to try to get you to convert, not shoot at you because you were different.

"The men were wearing caps," Adam continued. "I couldn't tell if their heads were shaven."

"That's not a necessary attribute, as far as I know," I said. "I think that's mainly the skinheads—a particular group. There's tons of different little groups existing. I imagine there could be one in this rather redneck part of the woods, but my family's been around here long enough that we would have heard." I hoped.

"Tucker?" Niko said.

"Not that I know of," Tucker said. "Rio Seco's fairly liberal, and White Rock's always been conservative, but with church types. Not those kind."

"Did you see the bumper sticker?" I asked him.

"No, I was trying to go around the other side, follow the guy with the wounded hand. Sorry, sis."

Niko's expression remained grim, his focus fixed on the road in front of us. Despite that, I could almost taste the rage whirling inside him. Who would dare attack us? Who was their target? Like Niko, I felt the same anger and anxiety, topped off with a definite feeling of "not again." This was my home, damn it. My own turf, and people just kept coming and disturbing it. Yeah, I knew I would be in for politics and more adult responsibilities, but I'd only been home for a couple of days. Couldn't these freaks find somewhere else to cause a fuss?

"Gregor, might I ask you a question?" Adam's tone remained calm and cool. Of the four of us, his demeanor was the least disturbed, yet beneath it, I sensed an equal rage. Whoever these assholes were, even if this had only been some redneck's idea of a stupid prank, they were going to pay in spades.

"You said earlier you felt that the boys from the church group disliked you because of your hair, and that you and Luka were outsiders."

"Yeah," Gregor said around a yawn. "Sorry, I'm really tired right now. They've never really liked me or him. Cracks all the time about longhairs, hippies, and fags."

"Do they have a reason to believe you prefer men?" Adam continued.

"Naw, not really," Gregor said. "Luka might be more

flexible, but I like girls. I asked out one of the cheerleaders one time and got thrown up against a locker." His gaze flickered away. He was lying again, trying to spare us the true nature of the attack. I just knew it. As he looked back at Adam, then me, I nodded my head in acknowledgment. He gave me a weak smile. I'd cover for him in front of his aunt and uncle, but soon as I could get this kid alone, he'd be fessing up everything. Not that I'd intrude on his mind, his private thoughts, but I was pretty sure I could get Tucker to talk to him guy-to-guy. I glanced over at my brother, who nodded. We knew each other so well.

"What? Why didn't you say something?" Mark demanded. He sat up, nearly jostling Gregor to the floor.

"Watch it, Mark," Dixxi said. "Answer him, Greg. What's up with that? You getting hazed at school? You don't have to go there, you know. We can pull you out."

"I managed all last year, didn't I?" Greg retorted. "I'm good, Mark. You told me to fit in, so I'm trying."

"Fitting in doesn't mean putting up with treatment like that." Mark scowled at his nephew. "You should have told me."

"And then what? My uncle comes yelling at the school principal and then I get treated even worse? I can handle it."

"How about Luka?" I ventured. "You said he's been harassed, too?"

Gregor nodded, his eyes closing as he yawned again. "Same kind of shit, pretty much. We talked about it but decided that if we're gonna be part of the team, part of the kids here, we'll just deal. Anyhow, this is a new year. I'll be a junior, Luka will be a sophomore. Maybe things'll ease up."

"Maybe they won't," Dixxi added darkly. "Damn it, boy, you know you can talk to me, right?"

"I know, Aunt Dix," Gregor pleaded. "But I just didn't

want to cause . . ." He voice trailed off. Had he fallen asleep or was he searching for words? His eyes were still shut.

"Cause a problem?" Mark added. "Did you want to keep this from me because I wanted this to work out so much?"

"Uh-huh." With that, Gregor succumbed to sleep, his head slumping onto Dixxi's shoulder.

"Well, fuck," Dixxi said.

"What she said," Mark echoed. He gave a sigh, then kissed the top of Gregor's head. "I never meant for him to be a target."

"School let out, what? A few weeks ago?" I asked.

"Couple of weeks," Dixxi said. "June third. The boys had special practices, though, for this exhibition game. Every day, three thirty until five."

"Sheesh, during the peak heat of the day? Are those coaches insane?"

Dixxi shrugged. "I tried asking about it, but Greg told me that was the way it was. Maybe now I know why he didn't want to rock the boat."

"Do you think these boys he spoke about could have targeted him literally?" Adam asked.

"Rifles and guns?" Mark shook his head vehemently. "These church members are violently opposed to letting kids use guns," he said. "They teach safe hunting classes and all sorts of things to avoid stupid accidents."

"Good thing in a state that allows just about anyone to carry concealed," I muttered.

"How do you know about the church policies?" Niko said. "I thought y'all didn't attend their services."

"They teach at the high school," Mark answered. "Elective classes, but mandatory if you're a church member and want to get a hunting license. They have swearing-in ceremonies and all sorts of rigmarole. I saw a flyer that Gregor brought home one day and asked about it."

"Intrusive, much?" I said. "What happened to separation of church and state? White Rock High School is a state-funded school, right? Public school?"

"It is," Mark agreed. "But everything in White Rock revolves around the church. They're practically in every pie."

Tucker frowned. "That's more than I remember it being," he said. "When did this happen?"

"Don't know, really," Mark said. "The boys have only been going to school here this past year. I wasn't taking too much notice of the setup before that."

"Wow, not kosher at all," I said. "I don't mean that literally, by the way. That's not the way this is supposed to work. Bad enough the damned football games start with a prayer that is one hundred percent Baptist Christian, no room for other faiths or beliefs, having the church up to their white-gloved elbows at the school is beyond not cool. How do you guys put up with this? Can't you write letters to the school board? To the state school board?"

"It is what it is, Keira." Mark sounded resigned to it. "That church provides a lot of much-needed money for extracurricular activities. State funds are at an all-time low. They're deeply involved in all the community service groups."

"That doesn't explain how they got their fingers in that pie," I argued. "That takes time, not just money. They may be running the school board, but that doesn't mean they completely run the school."

"I don't know," Mark said. "It's a small town, a small population. It happens. Hell, they even offered to help with home-school groups in the area—sent out mailers with suggested materials, offers for help with curricula, ways for home-school kids to socialize and the like." He shrugged. "I read it, realized it was all church-oriented, then shredded it."

"If you knew the church was so involved with the school, why did you decide to send the boys there? Experiments in mainstreaming don't always work. My own self excepted."

"You were mainstreamed?" Dixxi said in surprise. "I wouldn't have expected that."

"I went to school in Rio Seco from grade one on," I said. "Graduated from the high school. Mark, surely you realized that when we . . ." Well, "met" wasn't the exact word I could use, more like "saw each other and fucked wildly once." "You knew, didn't you?"

"That you were from the high school? No. Just that you were a Kelly. Not that it really matters now."

"It doesn't. Just that my mainstreaming worked, but our Clan members don't really have much magickal ability until they Change—usually sometime in their fifties or so. Not quite the same as having natural-born werekids in a human school system."

"I had to try, Keira," Mark said. "Until you came back as heir, Kellys had pretty much left this land, and any umbrella of protection for me and my pack was gone. I did the only thing I knew to do—try to blend in and keep safe."

A pang of guilt lanced through me. Did Gigi realize what the Clan's leaving had done? Did this mean other groups were in the same leaky boat? Adam put a hand on my arm and shook his head. He didn't need to say it aloud for me to know this was not the time to start down this thorny path of discussion. I headed in another direction.

"Mark, I get your point—but just because a lot of the students are church members, that doesn't mean there's not a pack of mean kids hazing in their own special way."

"To the point of gunshots? That's taking it above and beyond."

"Explain then why there were two gunmen out in the woods tonight that managed to hit our tire—which, mind you, takes some fucking excellent shooting in the dark."

"Infrared," Adam said. "I caught a glimpse of one of the rifles. Infrared scope mounted on it."

"Still, even though we weren't taking these curves that fast, shooting out a tire is a hell of a lot harder than it seems in the movies." I continued to argue my point.

"Nor did they," Niko said. "Ricochet most likely. Are you trying to imply they are sharpshooters or something?"

I shrugged. "Maybe. Could be a way to track them down?" The last was a question simply because I was grasping at frail straws here.

"I'm not sure that will help," Mark said. "Too many former military around. All those bases in San Antonio means a lot of folk retire here. There are probably dozens of sharpshooters, not to mention hobby hunters who are really, really good."

I conceded the point. "Then we're back to square zero," I said. "Tucker, why don't you and Rhys go out there in the morning? Liz can check out the tire, just in case there's anything there. She's a fair enough mechanic. Maybe she'll see something we wouldn't."

"I thought you said she was a healer," Mark said.

"She can do some healing, yes," I explained. "We Kellys get one major talent and sometimes can do small things."

"So she's a mechanic?"

"She's a pilot by trade. Shapeshifter by talent. Healing

is a residual talent that she does well . . . mostly through years of practice."

"But you're the heir, right?" Mark asked.

"I am. I have all the Talents, if that's what you're getting at, but it's not like insta-knowledge of how to use them. I still need practice and training to be a full-on healer." I grimaced at the realization that perhaps I'd need to bring in more of my Clan. My original plan of action on returning was to get settled, get the reception out of the way, and then work out further training with my brothers and Liz. Since we rarely needed healers once Changed, especially for those of us who weren't danger seekers, I'd figured on saving that for later—maybe taking a few months' vacation back at the enclave and studying with my aunts. Since danger seemed to be seeking us—or at least people we were responsible for—that aspect of my training might just need a swift kick in the prioritization.

Niko slowed and turned left onto a familiar road.

"We're nearly there," I said. "Just a bit until we get to the gate. Adam, the inn?"

"Yes," he said. I pulled out my phone and hit one of my speed dial numbers. When the ranch's operator answered, I had her put me through to the inn's manager and made arrangements for the three of them to stay in one of the guest suites. I then made a quick phone call to let Bea know we'd be staying at the ranch. She was curious but too tired to pursue it.

"I'll talk to you in the morning, *chica,* okay?"

She murmured a sleepy "G'night."

"You'll be comfortable there," Adam was saying as I snapped the phone shut. "You may order from the kitchen at any time."

"I'll send Liz over soon as we get there," I said. "She'll

get Gregor fixed up as best she can. You all need to get a good night's sleep."

"Yes," Adam added. "We'll regroup tomorrow."

"Regroup tomorrow?" Mark spoke directly to Adam. "We'll have to wait until dark?"

"Not necessarily," Adam said blandly. "I can move around in the daytime, just not in direct sunlight. Someone can collect you and we can meet at my house."

"Look, y'all," I said. "Right now, we all need to get some rest so we'll be ready to make more sense of this." I tossed Dixxi my phone. "Plug in your numbers there, Dixxi, if you would. I'll call you at a reasonable hour."

"Thanks, Keira," she said and promptly began programming numbers in.

Mark stroked Gregor's hair. "Yes, thanks, Keira," he said. "I do appreciate all your help."

I acknowledged his thanks with a nod and a yawn. "Sorry, guys. It's not even close to my bedtime, but all this craziness is wearing."

"You did exert your energy somewhat more than usual tonight," Adam reminded me.

Oh yeah, that I had. No wonder.

With a flip of a remote, Niko opened the gate to the back drive of the ranch.

CHAPTER TWENTY-TWO

"I'LL SEND IANTO to stay with Bea," Tucker said.

He, Niko, Adam, and I sat in Adam's living room after settling the Ashkarians.

"Necessary?" I yawned. "Sorry, I'm just tired."

Adam put his arms around my waist and I gladly snuggled into his body. "Seems a sensible precaution," he said. "Never hurts to be safe."

"She was in bed when I called awhile ago," I said.

"I'd rather her lose a little sleep waiting up for him," Adam insisted.

"Okay, you win." I smiled and tossed him the phone. "But you get to call her."

"Indeed." He returned the smile and dialed. I turned back to Tucker as Adam began speaking to Bea in a low voice.

"When I took Liz over to them Mark was calling Lev." Tucker, who was as ensconced with Niko as I was with Adam, took a sip of coffee. Brilliant brother had read my mind and brewed up a pot before we'd gotten there. "He asked him to stay home with Luka and Jacob and keep the doors locked."

"Good idea," I said. "This Jacob guy, either of you get a feel for him? He never really engaged with us."

"Nothing much," Niko answered. "Wolf, youngish, seems fairly dim."

"Dim?" Tucker asked. "As in not too bright, or low power?"

Niko indulgently leaned back, turned his head, and kissed Tucker's jaw. "I have no indications of his intelligence level, love. Dim as in power. He did not impress me."

"Me, either," Tucker agreed. "He's probably strong, or Marcus would never have brought him along as a guard nor chosen him as third. Smart, no doubt, but not powerful."

"Mark hides his power well," I said. "Couldn't Jacob do the same?"

"Why do you ask?" Adam seemed puzzled as he put the phone down. "He is third, chosen by the Fenrir. Do you suspect him of anything? Bea is fine with Ianto coming over, by the way."

"She's not freaked out or anything?"

"I kept it simple. Said that Mark's family had a bit of trouble, so we felt that having someone there made you feel better."

"She bought that?"

Adam gave me a raised brow. "I can be very persuasive."

"Did you glamour her?" I frowned at the thought.

"I did not. She was tired and I told her you'd asked me to do this. She trusts you, Keira."

A flip-floppy feeling ran through me. Bea trusted me. After the whole Pete Garza incident, she really had forgiven me. "Thank you," I whispered to Adam.

He just leaned over and kissed my cheek. "So what was this discussion about Jacob? Do you suspect him of something?"

I shook my head. "Not really. It's just that he's new, per Mark. New equals unknown quantity."

"To us, perhaps, but we're not privy to Marcus's knowledge of his pack. He might have known Jacob previously and only recently invited him to become a part of this pack."

"True. I hadn't thought of that," I said.

"So what's our plan?" Tucker asked.

"I'll check on Bea in the morning." I drained my coffee. "Let Mark drive your van to the deli and we can meet up with them there. He, Lev, and Dixxi have a business to run, despite all this. I figure we can take Lev with us out to the acreage and the others can stay at the deli, business as usual."

"Do you think Mark will go along with this? He's Fenrir."

"Tough tortillas. At this point, we're the boss of them. As far as I'm concerned, we're taking over right now. I don't want any more injuries on my watch."

"Do you think they're still alive? The missing wolves?"

Were they? Could they be? Possible scenarios flew through my brain as I thought. The only real practical Occam's razor–worthy scenario—I shook my head. "Not a chance. That area of land they bought may be unimproved and out a ways, but it's not that much of the back of beyond. It's fairly close to some developed subdivisions. Mark may be book-learned, but he doesn't seem to be the most wolfish of the lot." I stifled another yawn. "He's not what I expected," I admitted.

"What was that?" Adam murmured into my hair. "Did you expect an older version of the boy you met before?"

I elbowed him and he chuckled. "Since I had no idea

that was who we were meeting, no. I did expect someone more in tune with the wolf, though. I guess I expected warrior-predator and got more Bill Nye Science Guy. I mean, what do y'all think? I've met other werewolves before, just not locally. They've all seemed a bit wilder, less—I don't know—civilized?"

A thoughtful expression crossed my brother's face. "Frankly, Keira, I'm inclined to think that this tribe is less wolf than human. Mark seems to have power, but it skews to lust, not predator. When he released power at the stadium, we all got his flavor, and it wasn't at all what I expected, either. I'm at a loss to explain it."

"You've known other packs, right?" I asked.

Tucker nodded. "Several. I do remember Mark's great-grandfather when he arrived in Texas. He was a strong old coot and ran that pack like a well-greased machine. When I met them then, sometime in the early twenties, I think, I had no doubt that these were wolves. Gregor seems more the old flavor of wolf than Mark," Tucker added. "Hard to tell since we've only seen his human form, but he feels more, *more.*"

"The Fenrir's power seemed rather focused more on pheromones than on actual power," Adam ventured. "Perhaps he was nervous and defensive?"

"It's a thought," I said. "He did say he wanted to vet us, make sure we weren't Gigi-like. Which, granted, is perfectly understandable. I think tomorrow, we split groups up and pair theirs with ours. I'd rather at least one of us is there to handle anything unpleasant."

"Wise decision," Niko said. "If Marcus is the most powerful of the pack, then those with you will be less capable."

"Exactly." I took Adam's hand and turned my head a

bit to see his face. "I wish we could do this at night," I said. "I'd feel more comfortable with a couple of vampires—"

"Sneaking around beside you?" Adam smiled.

"You know me well." I grinned at him, then at Niko.

"I'd still like for a couple of us to go there at night," Niko said. "We were shot at and I want to see if these so-called hunters are prowling there after dark."

Adam agreed. "Yes, sound suggestion."

"I'd like to go tonight, back to the place we were shot first."

"Niko, I'd love the help," I said. "Do you really think it's necessary to go out tonight? It's so late already. We've only got a couple of good hours until dawn. You'll never make it in time."

"Damnation." He closed his eyes. "All these 'alarums and excursions' have truly destroyed my time sense."

"You're tired," I said gently. "We'll go out there and see what we can find out tomorrow. Then you can do your night recon, okay?"

"Of course," he said and smiled at me, a brief nod acknowledging my suggestion.

"And even though no one seems to think this could be the work of that kid who deliberately cleated Greg, I'm not scratching him or anyone else off my list just yet. Liz could maybe check him out while we're searching."

"I think Liz should stay with Bea while we go out," Tucker said. "I'd like Ianto and Rhys to come with us."

"Fair enough. Perhaps afterwards, Ianto could check out the church and see if he could track the boy down," Adam suggested. "Use some sort of ruse. I'd like to meet this service group of theirs."

"Ianto could always see about hiring the group to come, I don't know, adopt a road or something for clean-up. He's good at bonding with teens," I said. "That'll leave us Tucker, Rhys, and me to go with Lev and Luka."

"I believe that you and your brothers should meet up with the wolves as early as possible. It's not going to be any cooler tomorrow," Adam reminded me.

"Good point." Tucker gave Niko a swift peck on the cheek, then slid out from behind him. "More coffee?"

"I'm good. Thanks." I watched him as he trotted into the kitchen and emptied the last of the pot into his mug. "Why don't we meet up with Ianto at Bea's around six thirty or seven? Then we can go out to their property before it gets too hot to be outside."

"Sounds good to me. Frankly, I'm pretty beat." With a glint in his eye belying his words, he motioned to Niko, who flowed up into a standing position as if he were boneless. Beautiful grace, my vampires and my lovely brother.

"Goodnight, my lieges." With a flourish and a bow, Niko laughed, then took Tucker's hand and pulled him out the door.

"Those two," I chuckled and nuzzled into Adam's neck. "I'm not so tired as all that," I teased. "I could deal with a lack of sleep tomorrow."

He put a hand on my cheek and turned my face to his, holding my gaze with intensity. "Then I believe I have a means to keep us both occupied for a while."

"Do you?" I murmured just before he captured my mouth in a searing kiss. For the next couple of hours, the only nonhuman on my mind was my vampire.

CHAPTER TWENTY-THREE

SIX O'CLOCK IN THE morning comes way the fuck too early when one is a night bird. Even though I'd planned this and was tired enough to sleep during the night, by the time Adam and I had worn each other out, it was close to six. I showered and readied myself for a long day. Not that I was complaining about my lack of sleep . . . nope, not at all.

As my brothers, Liz, and I drove out of the Wild Moon heading to town, I noticed the van was gone.

"They sure left early," I said as I turned down the farm-to-market road.

"Mark said he needed to be at the deli for an early delivery," Liz said.

"Hope they got some rest. How was Gregor after you left them, Liz?"

"Better," she said. "He still needs to rest, though. He's at the ranch with John's son, Travis, who's keeping an eye on him. I have him on some prescription painkillers John happened to have. Should keep the kid conked out. Forced bed rest." She half-smiled but quickly sobered. "That gunshot wound was pretty bad. Mark reamed him another one after I finished the healing. Couldn't fix the whole thing, though. I'm too rusty."

"Damn that boy, anyway."

"He's a tough one," Tucker agreed. "He's the next Fenrir, you know."

"I thought Lev was the second," Liz said.

"He is, but from what I've seen, he's not Fenrir material," Tucker explained. "Greg, though—in some ways, he seems stronger than Mark already. He just needs more maturity."

"Yeah, we were talking about this last night," I said. "Greg's got more than just the pretty and the pheromones going for him."

"You know, that could put another face on this situation," Liz ventured. "You think the boy is the center of what's going on?"

"Could be," Rhys piped up. "From what you've told me, the boy seems to be a direct target of someone."

"Then why the missing wolves?" Tucker asked. "Doesn't make sense. I agree Greg's got his own set of problems, but I don't see a connection to the rest."

"We've got too many victims and not enough motive for any of it," I agreed. "We'll just have to find something, some way of narrowing this down today." I pulled the car into the parking lot of Rio Seco's one and only shopping area—a small strip mall shaped like an "L," Bea's Place at the west end, the deli making up the short side of the "L" on the east. Tucker's van wasn't visible, but there were signs of life inside the deli.

"I'm going over to say hi to Bea and collect Ianto," I said. "Why don't y'all go on over to the deli and I'll be there in a flash."

I parked the car in front of the deli. The door opened and Gregor limped out, grinning.

"Hey, y'all. Morning. Mark's fired up the grill. Who wants what?"

I rolled my eyes. "Go on in. Tucker, order me some food. Something with lots of meat. I'll be back in a bit."

Tucker, who could never let an opportunity pass, grinned at me. "Lots of meat, eh, little sister? You wear yourself out last night?"

"Shut it, bro," I snapped. "Wasn't like you two weren't doing the same."

"Never said we weren't." With a laugh, the three of them followed a red-faced Gregor into the deli.

I trotted across the lot. As I reached the door, I suddenly realized that something was off. The main lights weren't lit in the dining area, only the regular night lights. Fuck, what was wrong? Bea normally opened at six for breakfast. Was she okay? As I reached into my pocket for my phone, I saw her walk through the kitchen door and behind the counter. She didn't see me. I pulled on the door handle. Locked. The bells on the door jingled a little, though. Bea turned her head. The great lump of anxiety in my belly vanished as she greeted me with a wave and a smile.

"Hang on," she called out and reached under the counter for the keys she normally kept there.

"You're closed." Inane, much?

"Sorry, yeah," she said. "Ianto thought it would be a good idea to take a day off."

Thank you, O smarter than I, brother, I said to myself. With everything she'd learned last night, Bea deserved a day of rest. "You're here, though?" I asked, wondering why she'd chosen to spend a day off at the café.

"Figured it would be a good day to catch up on paperwork—orders, books, etc. Noe's in the back. He's going to help me with reorganizing stock. Ianto's helping him."

"You feeling okay?" I asked as I followed her inside. "You seem a little peaked."

Bea tossed the keys back under the counter and then grabbed a pot of coffee and two mugs. I let her finish pouring, adding cream and sugar to both, then walking back to where I was still standing.

"C'mon, *chica,* let's sit."

Crap. This didn't bode well.

A sip of coffee, then a second, while I waited for her to speak. For once, I was keeping my trap shut, not pushing. Her expression was closed, pinched in a way that spoke of a restless night and little sleep. At least my own lack of sleep had been for a good reason. Damn it. I should have come back to her, left the wolves to everyone else. I was her best friend, and the only one she could talk to about the delicate details of her pregnancy, and I'd once again abandoned her.

"Bea, I'm sorry—" I began.

She shook her head and waved a hand. "No, no, don't. I mean, Greg was hurt, you had to help. What else could you do?"

"Come home with you," I said fiercely. "I'm sorry."

"Hell of a thing, huh?" she said, a wobble in her voice belying her teasing tone. "I mean, you come back all whatever you are, we make up, and then whammy, I'm . . ." She snorted and then suddenly began to laugh— a broken, ridiculous laugh that within moments, dissolved into tears. "Keira, how do I get into these messes? I figured, okay, sure, baby. I could go through with this. Why not? I'm not getting any younger and at this rate, drooling over a hot thirty-year-old is only fantasy. He's not even looking at me."

"I'm sorry— What?" She'd totally lost me there.

"Jacob," she sobbed. "I'm an idiot. I fell for Jacob."

The news hit me like a two-ton pickup. "Bea, I thought— I don't— What about Lev? I thought you liked the guy? You're dating him, after all."

"I don't know," Bea wailed. "He's nice enough, really a good guy. But . . ."

"No spark?"

"A teeny one," she admitted. "Which is why I went out with him in the first place. Long-term? I don't know if I even have it in me to do that. Now . . . with everything else, I'm . . ." She waved her hands around wildly. "What the hell do I do?"

"Damn it, Bea. Why on earth didn't you tell me this last night?"

"I don't know," she said. "It was just that . . ." She threw her hands in the air. "You were already mad about me being pregnant. Throwing this on top of that? And now I have no idea what to do."

"I wish I could help you decide, Bea, but I'm as clueless in this as you are." I patted her on the back. "It doesn't matter that you didn't tell me about Jacob, okay?" I was lying through my nearly clenched teeth. It mattered beyond the telling. Her relationship, whatever it was, with Lev was complicated enough, now she had to go throwing another wolf in the mix? Yes, this was Bea, my best friend, but damn it, this situation had just gone from uncomfortable to Jerry Springerish.

"You have Adam," Bea argued. "You're settled and co-ruler with him. How is that clueless?"

"Permanent relationships isn't our way," I reminded her. "Yes, I could be with Adam for decades, but that's just a drop in the bucket for us . . . for both him and me. He was with Niko for at least a century, perhaps even more. I'm not intending to break our bond anytime soon, but the way we do things is so not the way humans do. As to the wolves, I have no freaking idea." I reached over and squeezed her shoulder. "Bea, you have to tell Lev. Whether you decide to go through with this pregnancy or not, he deserves knowing. This wasn't some random one-night stand. You dated the guy."

"I know, I know," she mumbled. "I just—damn it, Keira, I don't want to have puppies."

I burst out into laughter. "Oh, honey, that's just too . . ."

She gave a weak chuckle. "Yeah, too, *too* . . ." Wiping her eyes with a tissue, she turned to stare out the side window at the deli. "They seem to be doing okay with the place," she said. "They've had some nice activity already this morning. Mostly droppers by, take-out orders. I've been watching."

"They going to take any of your breakfast customers?" I asked, curious to know.

"Not really," she said. "Most folks seem to come out of there with fancy coffees. Mark told me they weren't going to fire up the grill for breakfast hours until there was enough traffic for us both. I did call over there and tell him to go ahead and serve breakfast today, since I wasn't opening."

"Good guy, Mark," I said. "He's decent."

"They both are," she said. "I hadn't really paid attention, but they're in tune, he and Lev work like a machine. I watched them one day as they were stocking. They don't even need to talk to each other. Sometimes they'd trade words back and forth, laughing, but in another language."

"Armenian," I said. "Their great-grandpa came over. He escaped the genocide by hiding in the woods as wolf. Several of their pack came over that way."

"He told you?"

"Of course," I said. "I'm their liege lady."

Bea faced me with wide eyes, her mouth gaping open. "You're what?"

"Their liege lady . . . I thought you knew all this. You said Tucker told you."

"He told me you'd Changed. That you were the Kelly heir, along with Gideon, and that you and Adam had permission to come back to Texas."

"He left a few things out," I remarked drily, ready to smack my not-so-helpful brother. "He left out all the really important stuff."

"Why are you their ruler? Mark's the pack leader, right? What have you got to do with werewolves?" She said the word with a hesitant pause, as if still tasting its validity.

"Bea, Adam and I co-rule the area for real. Representatives of every paranormal group in Texas, Oklahoma, New Mexico, and Louisiana are coming in about a week to pay their respects and swear fealty."

"Say what?"

"I know it sounds medieval, but it's reality. Gigi sent us back to be rulers, not just to come home."

"Where does Gideon fit in?"

Oh that is indeed the gazillion-dollar question. Would that I had an answer. My former lover—and now, I suppose, sort of brother-in-law—may be out of sight, but as long as I didn't have a handle on him, he'd not be out of mind.

"I have no idea what she plans for him, other than leaving him with his father and the Unseelie Court," I said to Bea. "Adam thought it was an appropriate punishment. He said his father, despite his being an ass most of the time, wouldn't take kindly to learning what Gideon did to force the Change—well, and the fact that Gideon pretty much tried to kill me."

Her fixed stare made me realize that she knew absolutely nothing of what had happened in Canada. With a sigh, I told her the whole story, leaving nothing out.

"I don't even know what to say to all that." Bea slumped against the back of the seat. "It's just too . . ."

"Too," I echoed her earlier phrasing. "Enough about me. I'm fine here without Gideon and as long as he's in Faery, he's no threat. What are *you* going to do?"

"Pray?" She said it as a question but then sat up, her face determined. "Yeah, pray. You'll call it meditation, but I'd like a few days to think about this situation, maybe go to church and just sit quietly and pray that I can come to a good decision." She sipped her coffee. "Jacob's been really good to me, you know."

"Jacob? The same hot, thirtyish, bodyguard-type you're lusting over?"

She nodded, both hands wrapped around her mug as if to seek warmth. "He's been around a lot and doesn't have much to do over at the deli. He's spent a lot of time here just hanging out. We've been chatting. He's pretty religious." She shrugged. "You know I still believe in God." She glanced up from her coffee cup and gave me a steady look. "I don't go to church much because of the café, but I do pray. It's hard to not have anyone other than Tia and Tio to talk to. Jacob and I, well . . . we've talked a lot about life and free will versus destiny and God's plans." She gave a short laugh, more rueful than amused. "Funny thing that. Rather ironic, wouldn't you say?"

Every word I owned, every appropriate bit of vocabulary I'd ever learned in any language just failed me. I took a long, deep breath and then let it out. *"Tabernac."* I muttered a joual oath, grimacing at its appropriateness. Most Canadian dialect French curse words were based on the Catholic religion. "Since when are you that interested in religion?" The blunt words slipped out, even as I cursed myself internally for not being more thoughtful.

Bea set her coffee mug down and glared at me. "Since I had no one else to fucking turn to, okay? I couldn't talk to my aunt and uncle about you, about magick and what happened a few months ago. Couldn't breathe a fucking word to my seventeen-year-old nephew. The only people—you and Tucker—who I could bare my soul to were in fucking Canada. Then when Tucker got back, well, he was busy and wasn't all that available. What else was I supposed to do? Jacob was a stranger, sort of, then a friend." She snorted. "Don't worry, I never said anything about your magick or anything." A sip of coffee, then more quietly, "I guess I could have, though, huh?"

I buried my face in my hands. The last time Bea had said "fucking" that many times, she was cursing the death of her brother and sister-in-law at the hands of a drunk driver. She herself had been six sheets to the wind on tequila shots and all of twenty-two, drunk off her ass after the funeral and sobbing into my shoulder. Noe, their infant son, hadn't been in the car with them. They'd left him in their elderly aunt's care for the night, not knowing that the arrangement would end up more or less permanent.

I finally raised my head, no tears in my eyes. I had no idea what to do now. Bloody great leader I was. I could shapeshift, heal, forecast weather, cast all sorts of minor charms and spells, but dealing with a human friend's very valid emotions? I was utter crap.

"What can I say to make this better, Bea?" I spoke as

calmly and quietly as I could. "You're absolutely right. I wasn't here for you, and I'm sorry. All the powers, the Talent I've been granted, can't turn back time, as much as I'd like to go back and be there for you. I can just be here for you now. Be your friend and give you the best advice I can."

Bea burst into tears and slid out of her seat and next to me, burying her face against my shoulder. "I know, I know." She sniffed the words out. "I'm not blaming you, it's just . . ."

"The situation, I know, *chica*," I said as I kissed the top of her head. "It sucks." *Now* how in all the hells was I going to tell her about the possibility of genetic disorders and that she or her child could be at risk? I made up my mind in two seconds. There wasn't a way to broach this subject without completely destroying her right now. She was too vulnerable. I decided to play the chicken card on this one. Leader I might be, but there was no way I was going to slam Bea with another issue right now. I'd let Dixxi know the situation before I took off to the wers' property, and perhaps she could come over and talk to Bea later.

Ianto came out of the kitchen, worry on his face as he took in the view before him. *She okay?* he mouthed.

I shook my head. *Not really,* I mouthed back.

He pointed to the clock and I nodded. We had to go.

"Bea, sweetie," I said. "I'm sorry, I have to go now. Liz is going to come over here and help you today while I'm gone, okay?"

"Where are you going?" Bea raised her head and wiped her eyes.

"Mark's asked us for help," I said. "Some of his pack are missing."

Her eyes grew round and she nodded. "You'll be back later?"

"Yeah, I promise. We'll talk later tonight."

CHAPTER TWENTY-FOUR

O N THE WAY OUT TO the property, which, by road, was a good forty-five minutes to an hour from Rio Seco, we hashed out some strategies for searching. Lev and Luka accompanied Rhys, Ianto, Tucker, and me—a tight fit in my Land Rover, but it was a better car for maneuvering onto undeveloped land than the van.

"Why did you ask Liz to stay with Bea?" Lev asked me as we neared the property. "She's okay, isn't she?"

"Yes," I said. "Since we still don't know why your wolves are missing, nor why someone shot at us last night, I'm not taking chances on anyone's safety."

"Keira, has it occurred to you that some outside group wants revenge on the wer for us meeting with them early?" Ianto asked.

"I don't understand what you mean, Ianto. Those wolves went missing before Mark invited us out to the game." What was he getting at?

"No, I realize that, but I'm talking about the shooting."

I thought about this a moment as I tried to find a good place to pull the car off the shoulder without running over cacti and mesquite. We'd arrived at the property, signified only by a small stake with purple plastic ribbon drooping from the top of it. "Not much for signage, are you?" I said to Lev.

"Didn't really need it," he said.

I addressed my brother as I pulled off the road and parked a few yards onto the nearly barren ground, trying to avoid the patches of prickly pear. "Ianto, we've practically invited everyone who's anyone within the Texas, Oklahoma, Louisiana—hell, the whole fucking Southwest—to come to a party. A party I'd rather not be throwing, mind you. In any case, who's to say somebody hasn't jumped the proverbial gun and shown up early? It could have happened, and yes, it's possible that our early meeting with Mark triggered—no pun intended—someone's jealous streak."

"Why?" Luka asked. "That's kind of dumb."

From the mouths of babes. Dumb, yes, but if my own family was any indication, the rest of the tribes, groups, and packs of the supernatural world could be counted on for the same levels of intrigue and conniving: read as "dumb." Once again, I thanked Lady Luck, who'd finally decided to shine on me and let me return to my beloved home with my own crew, my own well-loved family members, instead of having to remain in the midst of familial machinations and maneuvering. Not that I thought I was getting out of the cesspit of politics entirely, but here, Adam and I were king—so to speak—and we got to call the shots. Yet Ianto had a very good point.

"Who the hell knows," I answered Luka's question. "Minerva, our Clan leader, filled me in on a lot of the overarching goings-on, which frankly, weren't many. Since the Kelly Clan pulled up stakes nearly three years ago, the Southwest region has pretty much just handled things on its own—each group dealing with their own issues. Now, the Kelly leadership is back. Who knows if someone's not here scoping me out? I'm a relative kid. Adam's been here permanently all of nine months and, until now, kept a profile so low he was practically off the map. Then, voilà, bring on the fireworks and the blazing neon signs: Kellys are back and taking over."

"Wow, sis, way to channel Rhys at his most dramatic," Tucker said wryly.

"Hey!" Rhys smacked Tucker's head as he opened the back of the Rover. "Not fair."

I chuckled. "Hardly. The realm of the supernaturals is rife with small fiefdoms, thus Gigi's not-so-little Machiavellian plot to rule the world via her descendants. Right now, I'm a prime target because not only am I Kelly but I am also Seelie Sidhe, the Court of light. Adam's heritage and position takes care of the other Court, and here we are, a coup in the making—heirs to the Kellys and both Sidhe Courts all bundled together." Though, in full truth, I was only heir to my mother's Court, a lesser Sidhe Court, and not to Angharad, Queen of the Seelie Sidhes' own throne. She had her own heir, but that was picking nits. It was enough that Adam and I represented the three largest and most powerful groups in existence.

"We're certainly no threat," Lev argued. "Why shoot at us? Why target our pack? I think you're howling up the wrong tree."

"Maybe." I shrugged. "But what other trees are there? What choice do I have other than to be über precautious? Before I was even heir, my cousin Marty was killed. Then Bea herself became a target. Coincidence? Perhaps. Perhaps not. We need to be vigilant, make sure that no one else gets hurt or goes missing."

Lev eyed me with suspicion. "You think they're dead."

I returned his steady gaze, letting him see the conviction I felt. "I'm sorry, Lev, but yes. Even if they'd run into some trouble, it's hard to believe that no one's come across them. Your own wolves haven't been able to pick up their scent or their trail."

"I was hoping for something less permanent," he said quietly. "I know Mark is, too. He's a bit of an optimist."

"Kidnapping?" Possible, but I couldn't see the angle. The pack's got very little cash and it's really damned difficult to conceive of someone's holding three wer for ransom for land. How would that work? For that matter, if there were some new player in town strong enough to abscond with three grown werewolves, then the problem is larger than I thought. "Lev, I'm trying to be practical," I said. "We've got a good crew here. I think that the six of us are bound to find something, some clue."

I surveyed the property. Typical lots of nothing but mesquite, brush, cactus, and a hell of a lot of parched dirt. "You know, earlier this spring, when we were searching for those missing kids, Tucker?"

"Yeah?" he said and walked up next to me. "What're you thinking?"

"This reminds me too much of that—same kind of landscape. People missing for no apparent reason."

"You think they've run off and are hiding?"

I shook my head. "No, not this time. But it just occurred to me that we've still got the old cemetery on Wild Moon property with a cave that opens up into Faery. By any chance do you think . . . ?"

"That we could have Sidhe company?" Tucker put a hand on my shoulder. "It did occur to me last night," he said. "Ianto and I went out to the cemetery early this morning, just in case. No sign of anyone, wer, Sidhe, or otherwise. Cave's still open but no indication of trespass. I take it you're thinking that someone could have come through?"

"Could be. This property's pretty far away, but stranger things have happened."

Tucker laughed. "Indeed they have, little sister. Indeed they have. Just so you know, the deadfall at the cemetery's all cleaned out, too. Place is a lot like when you were a kid." He smiled at me and gave me a quick hug. "You know there could be another similar place on this property. We definitely should keep an eye out."

"Absolutely," I agreed. "Let's keep the cemetery up, shall we? I feel a certain obligation. Keeping the place cleaned up, I mean."

"Why?"

I shrugged. "My cousin Daffyd, despite his many faults, is my kin," I said. "That cave is still a door into Faery, and I'd like to keep an eye on it. Maybe one day, some of my less objectionable relatives may decide to come back."

"Were there any?"

I laughed. "Less objectionable? Maybe. Who knows? I was seven when Dad came and got me. Daffyd wasn't a bad sort, maybe there are others like him."

"I still have trouble trusting the fey," Rhys chimed in. "They treated you like less than dirt." He dropped his voice. "Keira, when I called you at the game about the guest list: there are some Sidhe on there."

I stumbled over a small rock. "What? I mean, who?"

"Well, one Sidhe specifically. Name of Eamonn, and a couple of his entourage. Jess told me they had sent a present and a request to attend. I didn't know what to do.

Jess and Lance had already sent confirmation. He wrote that he's neutral and only means to honor you."

Crap. Because I'd told them and Rhys to deal with it, they'd confirmed Sidhe presence. I rubbed my eyes. "I don't know this Eamonn," I said with a sigh. "I suppose it's all right. I'd rather not start an interspecies incident over this."

"But—"

"Let it go, Rhys," I said. "I have to, so let's all do." I mentally crossed my fingers and hoped for the best.

"You planning to reach out and touch someone?" Tucker teased. "Make up with your mother?"

I snorted. "Yeah, and the moon's made of Velveeta and Ro*Tel. No, I'm not planning on making up with my mother, but I don't want to cut off my nose to spite my face. I'm about to greet and take oaths from who knows how many clans, tribes, packs, whatevers. How can I do that and, with a clear conscience, completely shut out the Seelie Court? Besides, they've got no interest here anymore. This is Kelly land and Unseelie as well, thanks to Adam."

"Hey, Keira." Luka Ashkarian walked around the side of the Rover. "Where do you want us to start?"

"Where's Lev?"

"Here," Lev answered and came around. "Just trying to find some water."

I nodded. "It's pretty warm already and it's going to get hotter. Rhys, why don't you go ahead and shift. The rest of you, make sure to take a canteen with you."

Luka stuck his head in the back of the Rover and rummaged around the box of snacks we'd stashed there. "These for us?" He took a bite out of an enormous *pan de huevo* and picked up a couple of *polvorónes* in the other.

"Growing boys." I grabbed a canteen. "Tucker, you guys all set?"

"Any food?" Luka mumbled around a mouthful of pastry.

Tucker laughed. "Plenty of other snacks," he said. "It's not like we're going to be out in the wilderness without resources. In this heat, we're lucky to be able to stay out here a couple of hours without some respite."

"Tucker, why don't you, Rhys, and Luka take the right side of the property line." I handed them a copy of the plat map Mark had given me. "Rhys, perhaps a bloodhound? Luka, no wolf, okay? If whoever is out there is targeting you specifically as wolves, I don't want to wave a red flag."

"I don't know, Keira," Rhys said. "Maybe Tucker or I should be wolf and be bait."

"No bait today. This is recon only," I said. "We need to see if we can figure out what happened. Then we can decide what to do."

"She's right," Tucker said. "I'm not comfortable drawing out whatever or whoever until we have more data."

"Good. Lev, you and I will take the right-hand side. Ianto, you have our six?"

Ianto nodded. "I'll stay in the center, be backup."

Lev leaned closer to me and reviewed the map. "That circled area there." He pointed with a finger. "That's where Gregor got shot." He looked me in the eye. "You want you and me to go there instead of the others?"

I nodded. "Yes. My brothers may be crack trackers and hunters, but I have other talents I can use."

He gave me a questioning expression.

"I'm going to see if I can call up a vision," I said. "No guarantees with this, but I can try. I've got a better chance than just with scent and sight."

"But if you don't want them to shift into wolf, how are they going to track?" Lev asked.

"We can scent nearly as well in human shape," explained Tucker. "With Rhys as a hound, we should be covered."

"Wow, that's way cool," Luka said. "As humans, we're pretty much just human. We're stronger and have more stamina than humans, better senses of hearing and smell—but nothing close to our wolf senses."

"Do your best," I said. "Load up, boys."

CHAPTER TWENTY-FIVE

"WAIT, HANG ON," Luka yelled as we began to separate. "I've got to . . . umm." He sent a pleading glance to Lev, who nodded.

"Go on, then."

"In front of everyone?" Luka whispered as he blushed.

"Unless you can think of another way," Lev remarked. "It's okay, Luka, just go on over to that tree."

The boy nodded, then trotted over to a live oak and with his back to us, unzipped his pants.

"Small bladder or too much coffee?" I asked.

"Neither," Lev said. "Urge to mark territory. He's young. Can't ignore as easily as I can."

"How does he know?"

"We marked out this place when we bought it, then renewed last week. I think I should probably do the same as we go along today."

As I waited, I watched the boy, not out of any sense of pervy old lady ogling a beautiful fifteen-year-old, but just curiosity. Luka was extremely well built. Today, he wore a muscle shirt and olive green khakis. The cutaway sleeves of the shirt set off his well-developed shoulders. "You sure he's only fifteen?" I said to Lev, who nodded affirmation. I shook my head. None of the boys in school with me when I was that age looked like that. Of course, none of them had been werewolves, either. An unexpected breeze brought Luka's scent to me, clean, musky, a little sweat and oh, my. My knees nearly buckled as a wave of teenage pheromones washed over me. Tucker and Rhys, who stood next to each other by the Rover, both let out a small whimper. Ianto put a hand on my shoulder to steady me.

"Hormones," he whispered. "That little boy is a mess of hormones, and they're leaking all over the place."

"Holy gods," I whispered back, "Gregor was the same. Is this constant?"

Lev nodded. "Typical of their age," he said quietly.

Something occurred to me. "Lev, do these hormones affect humans?"

He gave me a puzzled glance. "Yeah, probably, why?"

"Don't you get it?" I said. "If those two are leaking these pheromones all over the high school, no wonder those church boys hate them. Anger, territorial fights. They're defending their turf—their girls, their school— from the new guys. I'm sure those boys aren't even aware of what they're doing. This is instinctive behavior."

"You may have a point," Lev said thoughtfully.

Tucker came over. "She does," he said. "I sensed every bit of those. If I weren't my age and this were my turf, I'd be targeting the kid myself. Pack behavior extends to human packs, too."

"I think your mainstreaming experiment is causing more harm than good, Lev," I said. "Let's chat with Mark about this when we get back, yeah?"

Lev nodded. "I'll go get my water and talk to Luka about marking while we search. Be right back."

"Shit," I said to my brothers. "That kid's packing a punch."

"That's not the only thing he's packing," Tucker grinned. "He's going to make some girl very happy."

"Or boy," Rhys said, smiling.

"Oh yeah? Gaydar?"

"More like bi-dar. He was checking you out, Tucker. Me, too, for that matter. Less like *older guy I could emulate* and more like *mmm, tasty.*"

"Egad," I said. "Age gap, much? He's in high school."

"And full of all those adolescent hormonal surges," Tucker said. "I have no interest in boys of his age."

"Nor do I." Rhys placed a palm over his heart. "He's adorable and gorgeous, just like Gregor, but damn, both of them are pups. Maybe in fifteen years or so."

"By that time, they'll be mated." Lev rejoined us, an amused expression on his face.

"Oh, gods and goddesses," I said. "Sorry. You heard?"

"I did, but don't worry. Luka didn't hear anything. He's still embarrassed about having to piss in the company of a lady."

"You're not mad?"

"Why should I be? Y'all are right. He's all full of piss, vinegar, testosterone, and wanting to fuck. It's natural." He eyed my brothers. "Not that I'd let him actually approach any of you. There are several girls and boys closer to his age in the pack who I'm sure will be willing."

"Why isn't he there with them, then? Safer that way. I don't mean sexually but actually. Gregor's already been physically harmed by the boys from that school. Is being a part of this community so important to you-all?"

Lev scowled. "It was, to Mark," he said. "Not as much to me or Dixxi, but he's our brother and our Fenrir. Now, I don't know. I think we've got some thinking to do."

* * *

WE WALKED slowly, Lev and I silent as I reached out mentally, searching for anything that would give me a clue. Smells of mesquite, dirt, and heat floated in the mostly still air, the occasional breeze a tease. Only eight a.m., and already nearly eighty-four degrees. I sent out a quick weather probe, nothing formal or focused, just getting a sense of what we were in store for over the next day or so. The sense of heat and stifling weather washed over me, an endless trail with no moisture, no break in the pattern in sight. I sighed and kept walking. When I got back to the Wild Moon tonight, I needed to do a real weather reading. I'd learned enough to feel out patterns at least three or four days out, but I needed to be able to concentrate. Not that I could do anything about it, but it was good to know so we could continue to take precautions with our people and work with the wildlife to ease their discomfort.

"Lev, may I ask you something?" I stepped around a clump of prickly pear as I walked.

"Anything," he said.

"You talked about Luka and Greg mating soon. I'm curious, how do you-all work this out? Mark's Fenrir, and I'd assume he'd be paired up, but he's mentioned nothing of a mate."

Lev chuckled. "He is mated," he said. "She's traveling right now, visiting her birth pack in Halifax. Sylvia's littermate, Alan, is marrying again. Mark's not there because of the deli."

"Marrying again?"

"You know wolves mate for life, right?"

I nodded. "That works for wer, as well?"

"Yeah. Alan's first wife died in childbirth. Some genetic disorder that she'd inherited. Luckily, her daughter survived. She was raised by pack members. She's seven now. Alan didn't want to remarry for a long time. He was so heartbroken."

My heart sank. "Is that common, then—genetic disorders that can cause death?" I knew what Dixxi had told me at the football game, but here was a chance to hear from someone else.

"Commoner than we'd like," Lev said as he strode beside me. We were still about fifty yards from where Gregor had been shot. "Dixxi says this particular problematic gene is recessive, but an aggressive recessive."

"What does that mean?"

He shrugged. "Something to do with our hybrid nature. The more human chromosomes, the likelier this disease. She thinks it's some sort of mutation. Alan's first wife was half human. We're not likely to mate among the human community much, but her mother got pregnant by a boyfriend when she was in her early twenties. She was too scared to tell her parents and by the time they found out . . ." He shrugged. "Alan's sister and Alan were twins and both fine at birth. Nobody knew anything until Alan married and his wife got pregnant."

"Can you test for it?"

"No," he said. "Evidently, there are markers, but wer packs don't have their own genetics labs. Dixxi's one of the first wer in her field. There's a couple of guys at Guelph, but both are undergrads still. All the packs are trying to raise money for research facilities and to put more of our kids into medical studies. It's tough, though. Homeschooling doesn't really allow for them to learn the harder sciences—no labs or the more specialized teachers. That's another reason why we're trying so hard to mainstream some of the kids."

I kept the rest of the questions to myself. Bea's situation had just become worse.

"I think you still need to post this land," I said, changing the subject.

"I know, but with starting the deli and all, we haven't had much time."

"Couldn't someone else do it? Another pack member?"

"Physically, yes, but they all work during the day, too. It's tough, Keira. We do try to come out here on weekends, but we've only owned the land a little while."

"Okay, then, we'll help. Tomorrow, I'll have someone come over here and do the official surveying and post the property, if that's okay with you. Tucker or one of my other brothers can oversee it."

"I'd appreciate that."

We neared a large clearing, close to the marked area. "Lev, could you walk over to the other side of the clearing. There, to the right. Keep within eyesight range, please. I'd like to sense out this place. You're a bit of a distraction, but I don't want to lose sight of you."

He nodded and walked away. "This okay?" He cupped his hands around his mouth and called back to me. It wasn't all that far, maybe eighty yards or so, but he didn't know about my enhanced hearing.

I waved at him and nodded my head as I crouched down and touched the soil. Focusing on the land itself, I let my senses swirl open, reach out, taking in everything. Dust, dirt, heat, dry leaves and parched bark, acrid smell of urine. Wolf? Yes, old below, fresher above. Two different wolves by the feel. Some scat far left, a bobcat? Old, though, days old. A sharper smell of metal somewhere near. I focused on that, trying to make it out. Was it a bullet? I sank to my knees. No, only a nail, rusted and bent. I reeled in my senses and stood up. Lev rejoined me.

"Anything?"

"Just wolf urine," I said. "Nothing to show there were humans or anything other than wolves here." A tentative expression on Lev's face made me ask, "What? You keep staring at me as if you want to ask something."

"I kind of do."

"But . . ." I encouraged him. This guy may be beta wolf, in charge of security, muscular and square, but his demeanor now seemed more puppyish. As I'd done with Gregor, I revised my age estimate downward. Less forties, probably early thirties. A little young for Bea, but what the hell. Who was I kidding when my own lover/partner was centuries my senior, and vice versa with Tucker and Niko.

"Can you tell the future?" Lev rushed the words out, like a flash flood, breaking through a deadfall.

"As in divination?"

"Yeah. Like on TV, but for real."

I laughed. "Not in the slightest. Part of my heritage is that I have all the abilities, every single Talent that is inherent in the Kelly genes, but divination isn't really one of them. We have some seers, those who are probably more sighted than most, but it's not reliable. Never is. There are always too many variables."

"But, Talentwise, you can do anything?"

"I've got all the possible Talents, yes, but like any ability, one must practice." I said the last in a faux poncy teacher voice. "That little gem of information got explained to me recently." I grinned. "I can shift shapes with very little effort—seems to be dominant in my branch.

Some of the more esoteric things? Not quite yet. It's like any mundane talent—for music or sports or math or whatever—you get better with practice and experience." I scuffed a boot into the cracked earth. "I'm sure they'll all come in handy at some point, like learning more than just basic cooling and heating charms, learning to forecast weather with some decent accuracy, but needs must, I suppose."

"Have you *tried* seeing into the future?" Lev seemed insistent.

"Not really. I've not, if you'll forgive the pun, seen much of a use for it." Barring the visions I'd had in pre-Change, the ones that were real. Visions of the past, visions of the future, visions of present happenings; only those were the rumblings of the dice of Talent, typical of a Changeling, not of an adult, one who'd already Changed. "The one or two relatives I know who were practicing seers always seemed kind of out there—you know, lost in the vastness of branching futures. I think I prefer the good solid now." I watched his expression grow, if not sullen, disappointed.

"Lev, why do you ask? You can be blunt with me, you know. If I don't want to answer something, I'll just tell you."

"I kind of wanted to know if the thing with me and Bea would work out," he said, staring at the dirt as if fascinated by the random cracks and small crevices caused by the lack of rain.

I twitched, remembering my conversation earlier this morning with Bea. Damn it, last thing I needed was to become some sort of Dear Abby figure between my best friend and her baby's dad. "You care about her that much?" I ventured.

"Yeah. She's amazing."

"She is that," I said, "and more." I walked over to a tall, flattish rock and plopped down, trying to ignore the radiant heat on its surface. Good thing the rock was mostly in shade. How to address this? Lev was obviously head over paws in like with Bea, bordering on love. On the other hand, Bea wasn't, yet she was pregnant with Lev's baby—egad, this was a paranormal soap opera waiting to be written.

"Lev, Bea has been my best friend and the closest thing I've ever had to a sister nearly my whole life. She's a wonderful person who's had crap come down in every serious relationship. She'll probably kill me for telling you this, but you deserve some honesty." I took a deep breath. "For a very long time, she only did serial dating. You know, one date for dinner, a second for sex, and then a third for a 'hey, see ya around.' She wanted to have fun, to never let herself get caught up in a real partnership, owing to her past. Just a few months ago, someone from out of that past kidnapped her and was planning to rape, then kill her."

Lev's big hand clamped down on my arm, his eyes wild. "Where is he now, I'm gonna—"

I covered his hand in mine as our eyes met. "Dead. Very, very dead." Without saying another word, I let him see, dropping my guard long enough to leak out the last minutes with Pete Garza.

"Oh." He blinked and stared out at the clearing. "She's pack—family, but human."

"Yes." I patted his hand and then stood up, stretching. "I'm good with this, you know." I waved a hand at him. "You and her. You seem to be a good man, Levon Ashkarian, and good for Bea." I mentally crossed fingers and all sorts of other digits. Maybe something good could come out of this relationship, pregnancy or no, and despite Bea's attraction to Jacob. I blamed the hormones. Of course, I could just be trying to fool myself into wishing a steady relationship for my best friend.

"Do your people believe in a soul bond?"

"What, seriously?" I chuckled, then realized he wasn't joking. "Oh, you really are serious."

His dark eyes stared into mine. "Do you believe in someone being your soul mate, like you and Adam?"

"Wow, that's, umm . . ." I took a few paces forward, then back toward the boulder. Lev now stood, still watching me with that plaintive expression. "It's not something we believe in, no," I answered. "For us, our lives are too long to even contemplate that kind of thing."

"But I see it in you and Adam, in Tucker and Niko. You are connected far more than a normal relationship."

"You see it? How?"

"It's in your scent. I may only have human traits when I'm in this shape," he said, "but I've still got a decent sense of smell. Y'all are pretty intense."

"We are." I had to agree. "Intense" would be the exact word I'd use to describe our two pairings. "Maybe it's the blood bond," I guessed. "Don't know really." Something he hadn't said caught my attention. "So you wolves, what's your life span?" My half-spoken question darkened something in his eyes.

"We live about the same length of time as normal humans, maybe a little bit longer. A good life is probably eighties or nineties. Changing is harsh on us. By the time we're in our late sixties, we tend to spend more time as wolf than not."

As I walked forward, my boot caught on something

and I tripped, falling forward. As I threw out my hands to catch myself, my palm landed on a loose stone, my wrist twisting, and I fell flat on my face, dust billowing into my mouth.

Blood, I tasted blood.

CHAPTER TWENTY-SIX

*S*HE LOVES IT OUT HERE. *Fresh air, clean land. A new beginning, a fresh start: all those tired but perfectly true clichés that meant she'd get to start over. Ahead of her, her new husband, Stephen, disappears into some underbrush. Gods, he's fucking gorgeous, she thinks as she trots along behind him. She just can't believe her luck. How she'd snagged—no, deserved—Stephen. Tall, dark-haired, smoky blue eyes with a permanent twinkle and so freakin' nice on top of everything. She's beyond lucky, bordering on the verge of "pinch me before I wake up."*

How the hell else could she explain it? Here she is, in the middle of a glorious Hill Country outdoors, enjoying the sights, smells, and sounds of nature, just as she was always meant to do. No more steel-and-glass canyons, reeking of old garbage, the stink of unwashed men and women wanting a handout, the acrid burning odor/taste of too many cars, buses, and other vehicles crammed onto an island less than twenty-three miles square. Her father hadn't known what to do with her when he—when they—found out about her condition. As with most situations in her life that didn't fall into his strict plans for his only precious daughter, he ignored it. That is, until it was too late.

After the first incident (that's what he'd called it: an incident . . . not murder, not manslaughter, words he used daily in his position as a defense attorney), he'd spoken to her in that "you're my little girl and I will take care of it" voice that she hated so much. Damn it, she was an adult. Daddy'd offered her the only thing he could think of: a trip around the world. Sixty-three thousand dollars' worth of Daddy's guilt/cover-up. Sure, it was a trip most twenty-two-year-olds would sell their bodies for, but she knew, however tempting it was, there was no way she could take him up on it. What if it happened again, this time in Rome or Paris, or . . . no, she shook her head remembering that fruitless conversation. After the second "incident," just a month later, Daddy began to realize that, despite his money and powerful influence, there was absolutely nothing he could do.

With a sad sigh and a boatload of cash deposited into a special account, he'd let her go, his dreams of a huge society wedding overshadowed and supplanted by a hurried trip to a justice of the peace and then back to their Upper East Side apartment to grab her suitcases. She hadn't cared, too excited about her new life to look back, too exhausted trying to keep up appearances in the city to worry about anything else.

Now, out here where her new home was going to be built, she thanks all the powers that be that everything worked out. Stephen, handsome, stalwart, quiet Stephen started off as simply her guide, her escort to her new life; a stranger she'd married as an escape. By the time they'd reached Oklahoma, a drive of way too many miles, too many roadside Stuckey's stops, and too few clean restrooms, Stephen had become more.

They're still the best of friends. Stephen's quiet

demeanor hides a wicked sense of humor and an unfaltering belief that they are both much more than just a shared "condition." He's lived with it all his life, as have both his parents. They've learned not only to exist but to love who and what they are, to see the potential and the beauty of what she'd been given. When she and Stephen had crossed the Red River and hit Texas, she'd begun to agree with him.

Now, six weeks later, she's as much an advocate as her husband. How quickly her worldview changed. For the better, she thinks, and smiles as she remembers, the new life inside her. She hasn't told him yet—she just figured it out this morning thanks to a home test.

Stephen will be so happy. He told her a couple of days ago that he's always wanted a lot of kids. He's an only child, his mother accidentally killed by a lone hunter when he was just a toddler. His father, raddled with grief, never remarried and remained outside the pack, a loner for the rest of his life. He, too, was killed, another accident victim, climbing a mountain in the north, trying to prove . . . something. Probably trying to forget, she thinks. If Stephen's parents had an iota of the camaraderie, the love she now felt, she could understand his father's grief. If anything ever happened to Stephen . . .

A rank odor assaults her nostrils. Something wrong, very wrong, that can't be . . . a thrill of fearcautiondread rushes through her, a shiver runs up her back, every hair on her body stands on end. A growl escapes her throat as she steps cautiously around a bad patch of prickly pear. Warn them, she thinks, warn—

The first shot skids a hot trail of friction across Margery's spine. She whirls, and in the same fluid movement crouches low to the ground, ears pricking to listen for *the source. A yip and bark behind her tells her that her companions are moving closer. She growls, a low threatening sound, more warning to the others than to the invisible shooter. She has to find him—her?—before he shoots again, before he shoots at the others. Crawling on her belly, she bites back sound as her hind leg brushes against the sharp spines of the same cactus she'd so carefully avoided just moments before.*

The early evening remains quiet as she continues to slink forward, nose attempting to locate the source of the shot. A trap? Could be, that's the only reason she would be smelling— A sudden flash of light blinds her as, too late, she trips a wire of some sort. She freezes, uncertain of her next move. Silence for three breaths, two, one.

The next shot hits her dead-on. Margery Flax Ashkarian, new wife to Stephen, six weeks pregnant with her first child, slumps to the arid Texas ground, her blood sinking into the parched earth. As her last breath escapes, she forces the Change, not wanting to die as a wolf. Her furry body shimmers, bones crack and bend, and wolf begins to change to a small, nude human female, cocoa-colored skin shining in the low-hanging sun, luxuriant curls of dark hair flopping forward to cover the ragged wound in the side of her head. She lies there, silent in her death, her body caught between wolf and human. Neither one nor the other. Both.

When the others reach her, they howl. Two more shots silence them.

CHAPTER TWENTY-SEVEN

I CRINGED AS MY INNER ear heard the howling, then the deadly silence. I pulled my hand out of Lev's, tears running down my face. We'd reached the place where Gregor was shot, and once again, I'd extended my senses.

"They're all dead," I whispered. "All three of them. Murdered."

"Where?" Lev pulled away from me, tearing at his clothes, his anger visible. "Where are they?" He stumbled back several steps, lost his balance, and fell with a thump to the dry ground, a puff of dust raised as his backside contacted the earth. Hands gripped the ground as he fought with himself, struggling, twisting in what could only be agony, howling as loud as he could in human form.

"Lev, get a grip!" I yelled. "This isn't going to help anything." I approached him, cautious in my every move. If he was shifting to wolf, he might not be in his right mind. I'd heard stories, tales of wer so caught up in the body change that they struck out and wounded, even killed.

"Lev!" I put all my command voice into the word, letting the subharmonics and strength carry it to his ears. He whined and whimpered but still writhed on the ground, his feet pushing off his shoes, hands ripping at his shirt and jeans. Crap. "Tucker!" I called physically and mentally with everything I had, then quickly stripped off my own clothes and shifted to my wolf form, a smooth, quick Change, causing me no pain.

Lev continued to howl and twist; by now he'd torn off his T-shirt and jeans, and was on all fours panting and growling, back arching as he raised his head to the sky and howled again. I growled at him, a soothing sound, trying to calm him. He was too lost in his Change to hear me. Keeping my distance, I watched as dark brown-black hairs sprouted from his skin, first along his back, then everywhere, a Chia Pet gone nuclear. His face lengthened into a snout and then suddenly, there was Lev-the-wolf, smaller than I was by about an inch or two at the shoulder, but broader and heavier. He threw up his head once again, sending a howl of grief and anger to the skies. When he dropped it, his expression turned from grief to attack mode.

I growled a deep warning, alpha to beta. In wolf-speak, I'd pretty much just commanded him to yield. He bared his teeth, ignoring me, paws scrabbling at the dusty ground, not yet willing to invoke full challenge.

You dare me, do you? I caught his amber-eyed gaze in my own silver-gray, white wolf to brown wolf, my teeth bared in warning. This was where the shapeshifter met the wer, and it wasn't going to be pretty. Whatever set him off—was it my vision? the scent of old blood? the urine smell?—he'd internalized it as some sort of territorial challenge. This could get pretty damned messy in less than no time, as his pack had not yet sworn fealty to me and mine. To Gigi, yes, but she wasn't here.

With a leap, he was on me, teeth reaching for my throat, paws scrabbling to pin me with his considerable weight. With a lithe twist, I slipped free from him, my human brain and fighting Talent still present, even in wolf shape. I nipped his shoulder as I threw myself against his side in warning. *Don't fuck with me, werewolf,* I said in wolf-speak. *I own you.*

Again, he twisted and leaped, we rolled together, first one of us on top, then the other, as we scrambled for dominance. In the background, I vaguely heard sounds of feet running, human voices calling, but I couldn't lose concentration or Lev would be at my throat. He bit my shoulder, teeth slowed by my thick white fur, still enough to scratch deeply. I yelped and pushed against him harder, twisting my body and angling to get hold of the scruff of his neck, to make him bow down and accept me as alpha. I'd barely gotten leverage when my head hit a rock, hard. Reeling from the blow, I dropped my guard, and Lev managed to gain position again. As I tried to scooch away, pushing against the large rock with my hind legs, I saw Tucker, running naked toward us, leaping into the air and landing as wolf, a cannonball against Lev's side, pushing the brown wolf away from me. Rhys stopped to shift into his wolf form as Ianto came to my side to help me, still in wolfhound shape. Lev and Tucker tussled not two feet from us, the larger, more experienced wolf quickly gaining advantage. Tucker's red wolf quickly subdued Lev, who turned belly up and exposed his throat. As Tucker leaned down, I barked at him in warning.

I stood up and shook my head to clear it, then trotted over to the now cowering Lev. Tucker sat next to him, Rhys on the opposite side. I stared into Lev's eyes long enough to see submission, then bowed my head and took his throat in my jaws. A heartbeat, two, three . . . all the way up to fifteen, just so he understood I meant it. I owned him now. Mark might be his Fenrir, but I was even more powerful—and wasn't afraid to take it all the way, if need be.

Luka stepped forward, after silently asking permission with a look. I nodded. He crouched down next to Lev, who sniffed the boy's hand and rubbed his snout along the skin. Luka bent down farther and whispered into Lev's ear. The wolf whined, skittering a little as if wanting to continue his challenge, but then settled. Luka stood, still staring at his uncle.

I shifted back and got dressed as the boy gathered his thoughts.

"He should be okay now," Luka said. "It's tough, really. We're more animal than human in wolf form. He's used to it, so can maintain a little better."

"What did you say to him?" I asked, my curiosity getting the better of me.

"Nothing really, just nonsense sounds so he could register my voice, focus on me. I think I should let him mark territory, though. If you don't mind, that is. I think it will help." Luka waited until I responded.

"No, sure, that's fine," I said. "We'll move back some, let him do his thing and leave you lots of room. Ianto, why don't you shift back and keep me company, just in case."

Ianto nodded and quickly changed back. He picked up his discarded pants and shirt but didn't bother donning them. "We'll give them a goodly space." The four of us walked away at least forty feet, remaining as much upwind as we could. I wanted to make sure Lev's wolf was comfortable. Luka, smart boy, realized right away that marking territory would give Lev back some face, let him keep some dignity.

After five or so minutes of staring and sniffing, Lev began to growl/howl. This time, no one waited. We all ran toward the wolf, Tucker and Rhys shifting as they ran into human shape. Lev crouched low just left of the spot where we'd begun tussling. "What is it, what's wrong?" I gasped, exhausted from running in the heat.

Luka seemed positively terrified, his eyes wide and mouth open. "I don't know, I don't know how to stop him."

"Lev," I commanded, letting my voice go into command mode, subsonic tones weaving through the sounds. "Stop. Calm."

The wolf struggled against my command, a whine replacing the growl. He shook all over, nosing against the dirt, paws on either side. Another whine and a glance in my direction.

"What is it? Tucker, go, please, look."

My brother shifted again as Luka pulled on Lev's shoulder, attempting to move him away. "Is it blood scent? I know there was some earlier, but so very little."

"No," Ianto said. "It's wolf urine. Just like you told us before. I don't see why—"

Tucker growled/whined and stepped away from the area, shifting back. "Fuck," was the only thing he said. He shook his head. "Luka, can you get your uncle to shift back?"

The boy, though shaking himself, nodded. "I'll do my best." He crouched low again, palm smoothing over Lev's back, soft, slow whisper coaxing.

"What is it, Tucker?" I asked as I watched over Lev, who'd begun to shudder.

"That's not their scent," he said, panting and groaning.

"The urine? Not whose scent?"

"It's not Ashkarian scent markers. They all have them, even the new people," Tucker said. "Something to do with the blood bonding that happens during acceptance into the pack. That urine is from another source."

"I know," Lev croaked out, as his human form took over. He dropped from all fours to his knees and bent his head. "Some other wolf has been here."

Another wolf? "Rhys, what other packs are in Southwest territory that might be on the invite list?"

"Only one," Rhys answered, "but they're in southern Arizona and aren't even coming. They sent word that they're only sending one representative and that she can't get here until the day of the reception. That's still nearly a week away."

"Isn't that too convenient?" I asked. "Can we call this pack's Fenrir? Do you know them?"

My three brothers each nodded. "We all know them from before," Ianto said. "Back in Gigi's day—"

"It still *is* Gigi's day," I reminded them. "She's still our Clan chief and will be for a very long time to come." I prayed to the powers that be that this was the unvarnished truth, as I'd gotten it from that old horse's mouth and very specifically.

"Do you want me to finish, or did you need to spell that out just one more time?" Ianto stood patiently.

I waved a hand for him to continue.

"We all hung out with them some years back. Before you were born. They came visiting when the current Fenrir was new. He's in his seventies now and rather arthritic, which is why he's sending his emissary. Could it be him—the emissary, I mean?"

"He's sending his daughter, Teresa," Rhys said. "I did say 'she'—besides, I've known her a long time and she's a good person."

"And another besides," Tucker said. "If you'd stopped to pay attention, this urine is male wolf. Alpha male."

Thus Lev's reaction, I thought. "Damn it," I said. "Do we have a rogue wolf on our hands?"

"Doesn't feel right," Tucker disagreed. "I don't know why, but . . ." He leaned over and sniffed the ground again. "There's something off about the scent. It's wolf, yes, but stale. Like it's been there for a long time."

"How stale could it be?" I said. "These guys have been marking this place every few days or so. Lev, you'd have noticed, right?"

He nodded. "Absolutely. We made sure to mark the corners and each of the sections where we found deer blinds and tore them down. This was not here three days ago."

"Okay, then what's the answer, O brilliant ones?" I addressed all five men, even Luka. "If it's not a new wolf or a rogue wolf, and the urine is stale—but it wasn't there three days ago." Something pinged in the back of my thoughts: urine. Of course. Stale like one might buy in a box at Walmart. Like Miller had in his shopping cart. Something used as a training tool by hunters. Damn it.

"Lures," I said. "Remember Walmart? Could it be so simple as hunters using this place to train dogs?"

Tucker frowned. "Simple explanation is usually best, but . . ." He turned to survey the area and shook his head. "I don't know. Could they have thought they were wild dogs?"

"The hunters?" I asked. "It's possible. But why would they then shoot the two others? If my vision was correct, Margery shifted to human as she died."

"I'm thinking we should get out of this heat and go back and tell Mark," Ianto said. "Sitting here theorizing won't help us." He leaned down and scraped some of the dirt up. "Keira, do you have a paper napkin or something I could put this in?"

I pulled a clean tissue from my pocket and gave it to him. He wrapped up the dirt and gave it back to me, seeing as how he and Tucker were still starkers. "Thanks. Maybe Mark will have a clue," I said.

"Or you could see what kind of divining you can do once we're in a more secluded area," Tucker suggested.

"Or that, too," I said. "Why don't you two change back, maybe dogs this time? Lev, Luka's got your clothes."

Lev took his pants and shoes from his nephew and put them back on. "I'm extremely disturbed by this, Keira," he said as he laced up his sneakers. "This is creeping me out."

"I know, Lev. I'm sure there's a reasonable explanation," I said. "We'll figure this out, I promise."

"'Fraid the T-shirt's too torn up," Luka said. "I've got another one in the pack, though." He rummaged through it and handed Lev a black shirt with an AC/DC logo on it.

As Lev put on the shirt, Tucker spoke. "That answered the main question, I think," he said. "There's just one more thing." Tucker turned to Lev. "Why the hell did you attack my sister?"

CHAPTER TWENTY-EIGHT

"I HAVE NO IDEA," I answered for Lev. "I had a vision right here." I pointed to the ground and then indicated the surrounding area. "This is the place the three wolves were shot. Right here," I said. "From the direction of what's left of that hunting blind. I tripped and fell down, so when I had the vision, Lev was touching me, helping me up. I think he shared it." I turned my attention to Lev. "He immediately started to howl and Change, then attacked me."

Tucker growled, baring his teeth. It wasn't quite as dangerous as in wolf shape, but still, poor Luka, who'd been standing in the background through all this, shivered.

"Cool it, Tucker," I said. "He's grieving. Get dressed, will you?"

Tucker nodded to Luka, who held a set of clothes in his hands. "Here," Luka said. "I picked them up when you guys shifted." He handed a second set to Rhys, pulling the clothes out of his backpack.

"Thanks, kid," Rhys said. "Appreciate it."

"I've never seen Lev do that before," the boy whispered. "Is he okay?"

"I think so," I said. "Is your Change always this painful?"

"Mostly." Luka stepped forward and handed his uncle a canteen of water. Lev took it and gulped deeply.

"You okay there?" Rhys asked, still not leaving Lev's side—more to guard against him springing at me again, than to help Lev.

Lev nodded and handed the canteen back to Luka.

"Keira, I'm so sorry." Lev hung his head and buried his face in his hands. "I never meant to—"

"It's fine," I said. "What brought your first reaction on?"

When he looked at me, his eyes reflected nothing but sorrow. "I saw, felt, what you were feeling," he said. "Margery, Stephen, Maki—all shot, all dead."

I nodded. "Someone was over there, at that blind." I motioned to a pile of wood planks and debris, not twenty feet from where we were. "Only thing is, I never got the feeling of wolf, outside of Margery and your other two. I'm guessing hunters."

"But it's in pieces," Lev argued as he stood up, now clothed and shod. "There're no guns or machinery left. We took this apart at least three or four weeks ago—at the same time we came around to mark territory the first time."

"You're positive?"

"Absolutely. I was in charge of the teams and I checked each location out afterwards."

"Then how was Gregor shot just two nights ago?" I asked. "He's not fool enough to be out here, see hunters, and let them shoot him. Same goes for the others."

"That's the real question, isn't it?" Lev said quietly, losing steam. "Poachers?"

"Maybe, maybe not," I said, somewhat distracted as I

tried to figure out the scenario. Poachers could be night hunters, like the men who'd shot at us last night. Could they have driven out here, hidden their truck, and somehow avoided discovery by three wolves? It didn't seem likely, but given the fact that two of those three were city-bred and the third was unfamiliar with this place, it wasn't beyond the realm of belief.

I stared at what was left of the blind, some wood, mostly. The wolves really did a number on it. What was once a fairly comfy little shack to sit in while hunting, or to house a remote-hunting setup, was now only broken boards. They'd taken the machined pieces away, to sell at a scrap yard.

"C'mon, we're going in closer," I said. "I want to stand there. Tucker, Rhys, you guys want to keep searching on your side?"

"Not particularly," Tucker said, voice still angry. He barely glanced at Lev. "I think we'll stay right here."

"Suit yourself," I said, not wanting to get in the middle of another fight. He was right; despite what Lev had explained, Tucker and my other brothers would want to stay with me to protect me.

"Then come help me walk over here." The ground, though bare in most spots, was littered with dying cacti and all sorts of brush, most of it sharp and ready to snag. Glad I'd worn my heavier jeans, even with the heat, I stepped carefully over some flattened prickly pear, using Tucker's arm to keep my balance. I slid down the side of a chunk of limestone, grabbing on to Lev as best I could. "Damn it," I exclaimed. "Sorry, didn't mean to clutch so hard. This is fairly tough going."

"Just hang tight," Lev said. "We got over there in wolf form last time."

"In the freaking daylight?" I practically shrieked the words at the man. Tucker growled at him.

"Well, yeah, it's private property," Lev said, trying not to cower.

"For fuck's sake, Lev—I already chewed Mark out about this, but I'm about to tear you a new one, too. This is private property, yes, because y'all bought it. But property lines mean very little out here, especially if the property's not posted or fenced. Neither of which y'all have done. Basically, the rule of the open range still applies: no signs, no fence means you're okay with people wandering through. How long have y'all lived out here again?"

Lev managed to look sheepish. "Years."

"And you didn't know this?"

"Not really," he said. "I mean, we only bought this land earlier in the year, and we're too busy with the finances and stuff like that to really start checking out the place. Our place out at the Falls, where most of us live, is pretty much all fenced in or out."

"In or out?" I asked as Tucker and I finally managed to maneuver our way next to where the blind originally sat, and among the debris. "What does that mean?"

"We fenced in some areas, but didn't need to along certain boundaries on account of the state park is next to us and that's already fenced."

"Ah, I get it. You fenced yourselves in and the park fenced y'all out."

"Yeah."

Tucker scrambled the last few feet, trying to avoid a particularly nasty clump of mesquite.

"Didn't really know we needed to do anything out here," Lev continued.

I turned to face the clearing where I'd seen Margery

get shot. "Nope, I don't get a direct line from this blind,"
I said. "You?"

Tucker stood on the opposite side of the piled-up
boards. "Not really. There's a bunch of branches from
that live oak in the way." He put up his arms as if holding
a shotgun. "Even with a laser scope, it'd be a tricky shot.
No way someone could have gotten all three of them."

Assuming the someone was human, that is . . . which
wasn't yet a given.

"I've never gone hunting," I said to Lev, "at least, not
with a gun or any kind of human weapon, but I'm positive the shot came from over in this general direction.
Margery was facing to our left, which means her right.
The bullet hit her left flank."

Tucker motioned to Rhys, who joined us. Ianto remained at Lev's side. Tucker said, "There's all sorts of
scents here, human most likely. Three-wheeler tracks,
too—these unimproved acres are often a mecca for jeeps,
three-wheelers, kids having fun. Dirt's so cracked from
the drought it's tough to distinguish anything, much less
pinpoint dates or times. Like you said, Keira, this place
isn't fenced off or even posted; who knows who's been
running around here and when?" He shrugged. "I can
shift, do some more sniffing around, but I can't guarantee
that I'll turn up anything."

"Tucker's nose is a thousand times more sensitive
than mine," I explained to Lev. "Besides, he's had centuries of being wolf. I've had all of a few months. I'd rather
he search."

"I can Change again," Lev offered.

"After that last?" I asked. "No thanks."

"I'm not likely to challenge you again," he said quietly.

"It's not that," I said and took a gulp from my own

canteen. "That's over with, done, you submitted. It's the fact that you seemed more animal than man, am I right?"

"Yeah, but wouldn't that help?"

"Not if you can't understand English directions, or take some less-than-verbal cues from me while you're a wolf."

"He can?"

"We all can. I've not yet Marked or blood-oathed my brothers, but we're blood kin, and that connection allows us a certain level of communication when we're in animal form. I don't think I can do that with you."

"Fair enough," Lev conceded.

I scrambled back across the boards to allow my brothers room to work. "Tucker, why don't you guys see if you can sort anything out from the debris?" Tucker nodded and I settled myself in a sort of shady spot, on top of a nearby rock. "I'm really glad we did this so early," I said. "It's not even ten and it's bloody boiling out here."

"This is when I start to really hate Texas," Lev said. "When I wish we'd gone north to Canada and lived somewhere that didn't get hundred-degree summers."

"I know what you mean," I said. "I've half a mind to talk to Adam and relocate our respective asses to Vancouver, or at least up to the family enclave. The weather's a million times better."

"So why don't you?" Lev seemed legitimately puzzled.

"Good question," I replied. "Sometimes, it's because I'm too damned independent for my own good. Others, it's because this is the only real home I've ever known. It's a safe haven for me. Primarily, though, right now, it's because this is my turf; the territory assigned to me and to Adam by my Clan leader. I promised to give it a shot here. So here I stay."

"Do you guys think this has anything to do with last night?" Luka asked. "When you got shot at?"

Rhys and Ianto began to methodically search around the debris as Tucker replied. "We need to be practical," he said. "Two groups taking potshots at the wer? For what reason?"

"I'm not happy with even one group," Lev said with a sad expression on his face. "We've lost three wolves, my nephew got shot. Why?"

A thought crossed my mind as I surveyed the area again, trying to get more of a sense of what had happened. "To that point, where?" I countered and indicated the area. "Where the hell are the bodies?"

"I don't think you want to know the answer to that question," Tucker said.

CHAPTER TWENTY-NINE

R HYS PULLED OFF another board and tossed it to the side, nose wrinkling. "Yeah, you really don't."

I stood and approached the debris. They'd pulled off most of the brush and several of the boards across the top. What was left could be the bottom part of the blind, just a few boards nailed together to form front, back, and sides, no higher than a couple of feet.

"Oh." I turned to Lev. "I think you may want to step back," I said. "Like away from scent distance. You, too, Luka."

"Why?" Lev watched the boys curiously. "What did you find?"

"Lev, please." I turned to him. "I know your sense of smell is lessened as human, but it's been really, really hot out here." I knew what was in the remains of the blind had to be covered in pretty heavy-duty plastic, because I only caught a faint whiff, even with my enhanced senses. We'd definitely found the dead wolves . . . I hoped. The smell was bearable, someone had obviously done a good job in trying to cover it up, but still . . .

Lev did as I asked, taking Luka with him. Tucker and Rhys waited until they got about fifty feet away, then leaned over.

"Heavy-duty lawn and leaf bags, it seems like—at least triple bagged, in fact, or else the odor would be greater. Inside of the pit is coated with lime," Tucker said. "Damn it. We can't burn, it's too dry out here and we're likely to get unwanted sheriff's department attention. We're under brush burn ban."

"I know," I said. "We'll just have to take them with us and dispose of them at the Wild Moon. All three in there?"

"I'll check." Rhys squatted down and felt through the plastic. "Definitely two, maybe three."

"Lev, how big was Margery?" I yelled out to him.

"Smallish, about five two or three," he answered. "Is that them?"

"Don't know for sure. It seems like only two—one in each bag, but I could be wrong. I really don't want to open these out here. Ianto, could you please go get the Rover? We'll just have to load up and check out the insides when we get back. I'm not in the mood for postmortems in the middle of nonposted property in broad daylight."

"On it." Ianto turned and loped away.

"What are you doing?" Lev asked.

I left Rhys and Tucker to maneuver the bag out of the hole and walked over to Lev to explain. "We're taking them back to the Wild Moon," I said. "I want to be sure that it's them and I'd rather not do that here."

As Ianto drove up, Rhys bent down and picked something up off the ground next to the blind. "Hey, I found something."

He climbed back over to me, something shiny in his hand. "Seems to me like this was smashed or run over," I said. "Some kind of pin?" The object was small, about a half inch wide, but scarred and scraped as if someone had run over it with a car. "Maybe some sort of religious pin," I said. "Some initials, maybe?"

Rhys took it from me and held it close. "Looks like a curlicue letter 'B' in the center, a 'W' and 'R' on either side." He flipped it over. " 'Forever,' " he read. "That's about all I can tell, but yeah, this is a pin of some sort. Definitely religious, see the cross symbol?" He pointed to some lines engraved behind the initials. Definitely a cross.

"Oh, great, that's all we need, religious hunters," I joked. "Not that they don't exist, mind you. A good Baptist boy'll go to church on Sunday, then off to hunt during the season. It's expected."

"They're not much for medals, though, are they?" Rhys asked. "Baptists."

"I was making a generic analogy," I said. "I have no idea what Christian group this medal belongs to. It's not a crucifix, so probably not Catholic. Could be any one of these church groups out here. Didn't this used to be a campground or something?"

"Years ago," Tucker said. "Not religious based, but some sort of community group over at White Rock. They lost their funding about twenty years or more back. Somebody bought it for next to nothing back then and eventually couldn't keep up the taxes. It wound up in receivership a year or two ago. Mark probably got this for a pretty good deal. It's not really worth much for the weekend resort folks. Not close enough to the water or to any of the golf courses . . . and all unimproved. Would take a lot of money to make this a subdivision or even a nice weekend ranch."

"Which is great for the pack," I said. "I can see why they wanted it. It's fairly well isolated."

"Could be a gift," I ventured. "Lev, could it be Margery's?"

"Doubt it," Lev answered. "She and Stephen are—were—Jewish. Culturally, but not so religious. None of us are. No established traditional religion has room for our kind." He said the words as if they tasted of ash in his mouth.

"What's up, Lev? You sound, well, bitter. I thought Armenians are Christians, right? It's what led to the genocide, the eventual Diaspora last century. But most Armenians aren't werewolves," I argued. "Or are they?"

"No, they're not."

"Does that stop you from your faith? Your being wer?"

"It shouldn't," Lev answered. "But it has."

"How so?"

"We're an abomination."

Stunned, I studied Lev's face to see if he was in any way being facetious. He stood steady, his face placid and determined.

"You're dead serious," I said in wonder. "You really think that."

His face flushed and he hung his head. "I do," he whispered.

"Lev, your brother is the Fenrir of the pack. You're the Loki, the second: How does this mesh for you?"

"It doesn't," he said. "Mark is my brother, the only blood relative outside of Dixxi that I have left. I will stand by his side as long as he needs me—but, I'm torn. My faith is stronger than Mark's. He's a scholar, a questioner. I'm a fairly simple guy. I believe with everything I have. And I believe that we're cursed. How else do you explain why we get these diseases, why our wolf natures don't burn them out of us?"

How could I answer those questions? This was nothing I'd ever had to face. My family had no disease, nothing like this. We'd never cared for religion, no matter whose traditions. We tended to follow our own pipers and create what we wanted.

"Jacob's pretty religious, though," Luka piped up. "He and Bea were talking about stuff."

Lev's head whipped around as he stared at his nephew. "Jacob was talking to Bea about religion?"

Luka shrugged. "Something. I dunno, I got bored so I went back to the deli to help Mark."

Lev's face fell as he took in the news.

Poor man, he was beta wolf but not at all strong in personality. His looks, though fine for any regular group, were certainly less amazing than Jacob's or even the young boys'. I was sure that part of his attraction to Bea was finding a way of establishing a normal life, a chance at being part of another community. Bea wasn't much for churchgoing, but she did occasionally attend Rio Seco's one and only church—a nondenominational service held Sunday mornings over at the Bar-K ranch. They traded off between priests, preachers, and rabbis.

I began to understand Lev a little, his obvious feeling of being an outsider, even though integral to the pack. After all, his case wasn't dissimilar to mine—at least before I Changed.

"I was hoping Bea and I . . ." He paused for a moment, staring off into the distance. "When I was a kid, I grew up listening to stories from my grandpop. Stories about his great-uncles, our homeland. He'd say things like 'We stay together in adversity. We were Christian in the heart of the Ottoman Empire—strong leaders, strong culture.'" Lev sighed. "You know the rest of the story— the Young Turks came in and everything changed. So many dead; so many slaughtered. No ovens, no camps, just death, and Diaspora. When Grandpop told me these stories, they became kind of my touchstone. I knew I was never going to be Fenrir. Knew I was always second to Mark, but our history, our religion, made me part of something whole."

"Mark doesn't seem to be that embedded into religion," I said softly.

"Mark," he snorted. "Like I said, he's a scholar, a thinker. We've had way too many fights over the years. He's such 'a modern diversity of knowledge' guy." Lev shrugged and walked over to the car. "I think I'd rather sit here while you guys . . ." He motioned toward the plastic bags, now on the ground.

As I watched him walk away, a thought struck me. Could he be the one responsible for this? He wouldn't be the first of a group to resent incomers, but was he resentful enough to kill? This was definitely something I wanted to discuss with my own family as soon as we returned.

Tucker and Rhys hefted the bags, each taking one end at a time, and placed them in the back of the Rover.

"I'm sorry it's so tight back here," I apologized. "My car's an old-style one. Not really meant for a lot of people or cargo. Lev, why don't you ride shotgun? Tucker, you drive and the rest of us can sit back here." With the bodies. Two bags, three bodies. As we got situated, I pulled out the two bags of ice we had in the cooler and placed them across the top of the plastic bags.

Luka nodded and threw me a shy smile. "Thanks," he whispered.

As Tucker threw the car into gear, the unmistakable sound of gunfire and an accompanying ricochet rang out.

"Fuck." Tucker slammed the car back into park and

leaned his head out the window. Being smarter than the average bear or person in a B movie, instead of running toward the gunshots, he yelled, "People here, hold your fire." He then honked the horn and yelled again.

"Go," I said, "let's figure out what the hell is going on."

CHAPTER THIRTY

Two boys, no older than fourteen or fifteen, were reloading their rifles just west of where we'd been. Hidden by a small ridge, we'd have never known they were there, had it not been for the gunshots. Fifty feet away from where they stood, the boys, or someone, had set up beer cans atop some rocks. As soon as I saw them, my tension began to drain. When the Rover topped the ridge and neared them, they turned, eyes wide.

Tucker barely stopped the car before he swung out and went into full parental mode. "You boys know you're on private property? Did you not hear us yelling?"

"I . . . we . . ." The taller of the two boys blinked in the face of a six-foot-four Viking. Cowering behind his companion, the shorter boy mumbled something I couldn't hear.

"What was that?" Tucker demanded.

"We didn't know." The taller boy stood up straight, facing Tucker with not defiance but strength of purpose. "Sorry, dude, but we always come out here to mess around."

I slid out of my seat and approached the group, motioning for the rest of the gang to stay inside the car. "Hi, boys, my brother here was just worried that someone was going to get hurt. This property is now privately owned, and the owners just haven't gotten around to posting it yet." I smiled and held out a hand. "I'm Keira Kelly, a friend of the owners."

The tall boy shook my hand. "Josh Reeves. This is my brother, James." I nodded to James and Josh. "Make sure to tell your friends this land is off-limits, okay? Folks are going to be camping here and I want to be sure no one's shooting."

Josh grinned. "Sure thing, miss," he said. "We'll let 'em know up at the church, too." He pointed northeast.

"The church is over there?" I asked.

"Yeah, just over that ridge is the back end of the church property line. We're not allowed to target practice on their land. Church kids come out here to shoot, so we figured it'd be okay." He shrugged. "Sorry we messed things up for y'all."

I glanced at the other ridge absently. There's no way any vehicle other than a three-wheeler drove over that. Even my Rover would have some trouble. "You boys walk over here?"

James spoke up. "Yeah, we rode our bikes up to the lumber pile and then walked the rest of the way."

Lumber pile? What the hell was he talking about?

"Is there construction on the other side of the ridge?" Tucker asked, his mood mellowed.

"Yeah, Pastor said something about building a new rec center and stuff. Weren't paying much attention."

"You boys seen any hunters hanging around here?" I asked, making a mental note to not only get someone out here with the No TRESPASSING signs but to check out the building and land use permits as soon as possible. I knew there had to be some sort of easement between the church land and the wers' property. I'd seen it marked on the plat map. That ridge was far too close to allow for a utility easement.

"Naw, not this time of year," James said. "Bunch of the old farts come hang out in the back forty, just so they can shoot the shit and drink without their wives catching 'em."

"The back forty?"

He tilted his head in the direction of the ridge. "That's what we call the back end of the property. Nothing's there but some piled-up boards and stuff. It's kind of far off from the main buildings. My dad used to hang there with his buddies."

"Used to?" Tucker asked.

The boy shrugged. "He got deployed to Iraq couple months ago."

On that note, both boys slung their unloaded and open rifles over their arms. "Guess we'll be going," Josh said. "See ya."

"Thanks, boys," I said.

They trudged away from us, flip-flops flapping and kicking up puffs of dust.

As soon as they'd climbed over the ridge and out of most human earshot, I turned to face Tucker.

"I'm going to go over there and check for tracks," he said.

"Three-wheeler?"

"Yeah. Send Rhys out, will you?"

I nodded and returned to the car. "Rhys, go with Tucker, please." I filled the others in on what we'd learned, which, frankly, wasn't much.

Luka studied the plat map and his phone as we all

chatted. "Keira, I hate to tell you this, but it's a good half mile from here to the main road where the church is. That's a hell of a lot of property."

"I thought that map only had your land on it."

He gave me that exasperated expression that only teenagers master. Climbing over to the driver's seat, he shoved the map at me, then showed me his phone. When I clued in, I nearly said the unvoiced "Well, duh" for him.

"GPS," I said. "Of course."

He punched a few more buttons and keys, then showed me the screen again. "Check this out. This is the Google Earth street view," he said. "That's the church building there." He pointed, then scrolled down some. "There's the ridge right there in front of us." He zoomed in a little, and slowly scrolled back to the church. "See, that's all full of live oaks, mesquite, some cottonwoods. Not a lot of empty land."

"Not really conducive to driving a truck in, even if you did walk over the ridge," I murmured. "Back west of the broken-down blind was even worse. No way to get a big vehicle in."

"I suppose they could've walked," Lev said. "We did."

"Three-wheelers," Tucker announced as he and Rhys returned. "Some tracks over the ridge, and beyond, but it's tough to tell how old they are. Ground's too hard, too dry. Saw some oil drips, but that's about it." He motioned for Luka to scoot back and entered the car. Rhys climbed in as well.

"So no incriminating cigarette butts with a unique shade of lipstick, or special aftershave scent?" I teased.

"Hell, even Sherlock himself would have a hard time finding anything unique about those tracks," Rhys said. "We're no closer than we were."

"Could it have just been an accident? They hit one, and then panicked and killed the others?" Lev ventured, a note of hope in his voice.

"Three wolves? I doubt it," Tucker said. "We're fast as wolf and I'm sure you are, too. If they did this by accident, no human has the reflexes to think, point, shoot again, and kill three wolves without at least one of the wolves hurting the human first. No, this was a team effort."

"I'm frightened as hell, Keira," Lev said. "This land was supposed to be for expanding our pack, for peace of mind. Mark needs to know now. I'm going to call—"

"And do what? Get him out here for no reason? There's nothing Mark can do right now that we're not doing."

"He's Fenrir, he needs—"

"To chill and just let us do this," I insisted. "Lev, I'm not dissing your instincts. You're right, Mark is Fenrir, and the pack leader does need to know. We'll tell him when we get back. No need to rush over here." The last thing I needed was to endanger the pack's Fenrir. Until I knew more, I wasn't about to go any further.

"Tucker, let's do a quick drive-around to the church?" I asked. "The map thing Luka has is cool, but I want to see the edges of the property. See what roads or dirt paths lead in and out."

"Your wish is my command."

CHAPTER THIRTY-ONE

A<small>S WE TURNED ONTO</small> the main church road, after more than an hour wandering around property lines and trying to find access, I spotted Old Joe's trash truck turning off the road ahead onto church property.

"Wonder if he saw anything?" I mused out loud. "He seemed to be staring at me with intent the night of the game."

"Intent? What kind of intent?" Tucker asked.

I shot him a dirty look. "If I knew that, I wouldn't have to wonder, would I? There's just something . . . Tucker, go on, I'd like to talk to him."

"Make it quick, okay? We've still got these bodies in here."

It wasn't that I'd forgotten but more that I was determined to figure this out right now. Talking to Old Joe shouldn't take long. "Done, I'll flag him down." I rolled down my window and waved at the truck. The old man slowed the truck and pulled up alongside, his pale eyes steady on my face. Was it a trick of light, or did something flash behind the pale gaze? I blinked, the mid-morning sun too bright. Must have been a reflection.

"G'day, miss, sirs," he said and nodded. "Y'all need Old Joe for something?"

As he spoke, I began to feel something odd, just a creeping-in feeling, as if what made Joe substantial flickered in and out, solidity nothing more than illusion. I rubbed my eyes and eyed him again but saw nothing amiss. A quick reach of my senses as I said the appropriate words. "Joe, could we possibly have a moment of your time?" Nothing, he was solid as the giant white rock jutting from the ground in front of the church's main building. Nothing special about him, nothing special about it other than its size.

"Certainly, miss," he said. "How's about we pull on into the church parking lot so's we don't block traffic?"

Tucker nodded and complied, following the old man. I focused on the truck, trying to get past the metal shell, trying to feel out the weird vibe and define it.

We parked and both Tucker and I got out and approached Joe, who'd alighted from his own vehicle.

"What can I do you for today?" he asked, a genial smile on his face. His face . . . lines out from his eyes, laugh lines, sun lines, otherwise smooth dark skin as if carved from sea-polished ebony driftwood. It held a sense of being, of stillness, of character so deep that one could get lost in his knowledge, his wisdom. It was as if I was staring into the eyes of eternity and its innate serenity. Something in his eyes distracted me for a moment, as if he wanted to say something but politely waited for me to speak first.

"Joe," I began, wanting to ask him of his origins, his birth, but a car drove past us, a man inside glancing at our small group. Instead, I asked him about the land, quickly inventing a cover story, that some campers had heard shots and were afraid of poachers.

His eyes followed the car as I spoke, then he turned back to me as if absorbing my words and trying to find the right ones to answer me with. I still couldn't shake the feeling that something was absolutely odd about him. As the man who'd driven by us parked and opened his car door, Joe spoke. "Can't rightly say, Miz Kelly. I just pick up trash and sort through it. I sell stuff at my road-side stand. Thursday through Saturday, I'm there. Pick up Sunday evenings after church, then Monday and Tuesday morning. Wednesdays, I go on up to the Methodist church in town, spend a day there with a few folks I know."

"You know my name?"

Joe nodded. "You're familiar."

Familiar, huh. I suppose he was right. My family'd been around quite a long time.

"So you go to church here?"

"When I go. Sometimes I like to drive on over to Blanco. There's a nice choir up there I like to listen to. I mostly go for the music."

"But you haven't seen anything weird around here— around this property that's back of the church. Do you ever go round there picking up cans and bottles for re-cycling?"

"I do, but pastor says it's okay for me to." He nodded toward the car that had just parked. "He might be able to tell you more."

"No, that's fine, that's not the problem," I said. "Just trying to find out if you saw anyone suspicious hanging around? Some friends of mine bought this land as an in-vestment, and we just wanted to make sure—"

"Oh my," he says, "friends of yours? Well, I didn't know that."

"Know what?"

He opened his mouth, then got a simple expression on his face, as if he'd suddenly lost a hundred IQ points.

The man might be old but he was in no way stupid. His accent turned into something out of a 1930s blackface talkie. "Now, y'all's friends, they going to like it here, Miz Kelly, yes ma'am. Nice place the church. You tell 'em Old Joe sent you."

A man approached us, the same one who'd parked. He was dressed in a conservative pair of khakis, topped by a short-sleeved, mid-range polo, something from Target or a mid-range department store, not a discount place or a designer shop. Like Gregor had described Mark, this guy was middle-middle, medium brown hair cut into a style out of a right-wing catalog. He greeted us with a smile that was closer to that of Fred Rogers than Pat Robertson. Hell, if it were winter, I totally could imagine this guy in the requisite cardigan and slippers.

"Hey there, folks, welcome. I'm Pastor Calvin Hagen, y'all new around here?" His smile grew larger as he saw my car close up. I could almost see the dollar signs floating around his head and the *ka-ching* sound echoing in his brain. Though not a luxury car by any means, my Land Rover was a collectible car, brought over from England and refitted with left-hand drive for me. It was one of a kind, really, and Pastor Hagen obviously knew trust fund money when he saw it.

"We're just visiting," I said politely. "Nice to meet you, Pastor. We just wanted to stop by and let you know that we found some kids out back, popping shotgun shells at cans. Not really that big a deal, but my friends just bought that property adjacent to yours. It's not posted yet, but we plan on helping them put up the signs tomorrow. Could you please let your parishioners know?"

"Oh, my word, I am so sorry." The pastor seemed put out that someone in his flock could have crossed a boundary. "I'm afraid it's all my fault. You see, I've been letting our boys back there, thinking they could get some practice. We've been planning a father and son deer hunt for fall, you know. It's really popular. I had no idea the property had sold." He patted my arm, in that irritating condescending way some males have toward women. "Now, I'll make sure to take care of it, Miss . . . ?"

"Kelly," I responded. "Keira Kelly."

"So these are your . . ." He motioned toward Tucker and the men in the Rover.

"Brothers," I said. "We've been away for a bit, but we're all back now, in Rio Seco. Just up here checking out my friends' land. We were thinking of a campout but it's too darn hot."

"That it is," Pastor Hagen said. "Wanted to do a pool party with the kids next week, but it's almost too hot to do that, so we're holding a social tomorrow night instead. Y'all churchgoers?"

"Not really, Pastor." Tucker smoothly stepped in front of me. "I'm sorry, I really hate to interrupt, Keira, but we have an appointment."

"Oh my, I'm sorry, Pastor." I smiled at the man, giving him my all-time sweet southern gal impression. "I'm afraid I let the time get away from me. My brother's right, we must be leaving."

"Well, I hope to see you folks in church sometime," he said. "It's not that far of a drive—and you're welcome to come join us for worship or just socialize."

"Thank you for the invitation," I said. "Joe, thanks for helping us out. I was afraid I'd gotten us all lost." There was no way I was going to get Joe into any trouble, just in case. His sudden slide into slaphappy Uncle Tom speak had been a warning I wasn't going to ignore. Joe did not like this pastor person and was reluctant to be himself around him. Until I knew why, I figured we'd best play the game.

Joe nodded solemnly. "Glad I could be of help, Miz Kelly. Now y'all be sure to come visit the shack real soon, all right?"

I nodded back pleasantly, trying to convey *Yes, damn it, soon as possible* with my expression without raising the pastor's suspicions. Joe climbed into his truck and rattled off.

As he pulled out of the drive, the pastor gave us another one of his large smiles. "Y'all sure you don't want to come inside for a cool lemonade," he offered. "It's mighty hot out here and y'all seem plumb tuckered out."

"I'm afraid we don't have time," Tucker said politely. "We do have an appointment and I've got to get my sister back home. Thank you for the offer, though." He shook the pastor's hand. "That's a fine display window you've got there," Tucker said.

I shaded my eyes and looked toward the building. It was pretty far away from where we were parked, but my enhanced sight could tell that there were trophies lined up inside the window, as if it were a hallway display case.

"Trophies?" I asked. "Hard to tell from out here."

"Oh yes." The pastor grinned at us and nodded his head. "We have a vibrant youth group here. They've won numerous awards and competitions."

"That's commendable," I said, trying to keep the sarcasm out of my voice. Wonder what kind of competitions they entered—how many nonbelievers could you convert?

"Well, thanks for your hospitality, Pastor Hagen," Tucker said. "We'll be seeing you."

"I hope so. Y'all have a blessed day!"

We climbed into our car and Tucker drove out of the lot. I didn't wait for long to ask him why he'd pointed out the window.

"Tucker, what was that all about?"

"Did you see what I saw in the display window?"

"The trophies? I wasn't checking all that closely," I said. "Rhys, Ianto?" Both shrugged. Since they'd stayed in the car, it would've been hard to see from how we'd parked.

"There's a logo on each of those trophies," Tucker said. "Seems a hell of a lot like that pin we found."

"Say what?" I twisted in my seat, as if through the back window I could actually see into the display and see what Tucker was talking about.

"I looked," Tucker said. "We were close enough for me to see a couple of the larger trophies. I'm not saying it's exactly the same, but it could be."

"I'm getting a really bad feeling about this," I muttered. "Tucker, should we go back? Talk to the pastor some more? He seemed nice enough, not so smarmy as some."

"We've got two bodies in the car, Keira," Tucker reminded me. "Let's take care of them first, but yes, I'd like to talk to the man."

"Jacob's a member of the church. You can talk to him, too," Lev offered.

"I thought y'all weren't churchgoers," I said. "Mark said as much."

"We're not," Lev agreed. "How do you explain a wer child Changing or howling in the middle of a service because they're tired or cranky? I have faith, I still want to believe, but I don't see that going to a building and listening to some man preach at me is going to make me any more religious."

"Or woman," Rhys said. "One of our former wives was a preacher."

Lev's brow lowered as he turned to Rhys. "Our? I don't understand."

"Ianto and I," Rhys explained with a satisfied grin. "We share."

Luka's eyes widened a bit. Lev nodded slowly as if digesting the data. "Okay, sure. I guess to each their own."

"Indeed," Ianto said. "And that's enough about that. Please go on, Lev. I'd like to hear about your Jacob and his belonging to the Church of the White Rock. You said he was religious, but that doesn't necessarily mean belonging to a church."

"He's young." Lev shrugged as if this explained everything. "Sometimes, you feel like you have to be part of a group outside the pack. He's pretty stable, so Mark didn't see an issue with it."

"So he may know the symbolism of that logo?" I asked.

"I suppose. At least, he's pack and you won't be raising any suspicions if you ask him."

"You have a point." I smiled at Lev and he smiled back. A bump in the road jarred one of the trash bags in back, which started sliding. Ianto and Rhys both leaned over and hefted it back into position. Lev's face crumpled as he watched them. How could this feel to him? Second in the pack, Mark's right-hand guy, and he's the one to find the bodies. My instinct was to comfort him, go to him as his liege and take over, take care, but I couldn't fix this. He had as much right to his sorrow as I had to my own feelings of whatever they were right now. Mostly, I was confused. I'd buy hunters, poachers, someone who'd seen the wolves and planned an attack for pelts. Greed, I totally got. Hateful though it was, I understood the driving force behind it. That perhaps a church member was involved? Well, there're a hell of a lot of Sunday Christians, especially in these small communities. Fornicate and fabricate your lies through Saturday, because on Sunday, here comes Jesus to bail your sinful ass right out.

Bitter? Yeah, a lot. I hadn't the experiences of my much older brothers, but I'd certainly seen and learned about enough hypocrisy in my less than four decades to have an instant distrust of organized religion. Too many of them seemed full of empty promises and easily purchased indulgences—just another way for the rich and powerful to get off easy.

Lev, though, was absolutely entitled to his faith, as was Jacob. How the hell I was going to deal with the whole triangle o'Bea, I had no idea. Bea seemed utterly fascinated with Jacob, but for reasons that escaped me. Frankly yes, he was hot, gorgeous, and yummy, but connection due to religion wasn't my cup of incense. Lev, on the other hand, seemed a perfect match for Bea, despite his being a werewolf. He was kind, considerate, even-tempered. Not drop-dead bloody gorgeous, but who cared? The one thing I needed to make sure of was that neither Lev nor Jacob was the instigator of these kills. Lev might be resentful, but jealousy created more monsters than wer did. It wouldn't be the first time someone threw a wrench in the works because of a woman. In pack structure, because of his newness and his tertiary position, Jacob was lower than Lev, which could mean that if it came down to it, Lev got first dibs. Ridiculous in hu-

man terms, even in Kelly terms, but these people are also
wolves and follow pack structure.

Could this be what was going on? As unreal as it
sounded, I couldn't pass up the possibility.

"I'll go talk to Jacob about the logo," Tucker said,
interrupting my thoughts. "Maybe guy-to-guy he'll give
me more to go on."

"Good idea," I agreed. "Tonight, though, I'd like to
have some vampires out here, at the church property and
on the wers' property, patrolling and eavesdropping on
anything that might be going on there after dark. They
can keep out of sight and report back."

"Recon only?" Tucker asked.

"For now," I said. "Barring self-defense, that is. I want
names, faces, license plates, anything that seems out of
the ordinary."

"I'll come out with Niko," Tucker said. "Him, a couple of the security team. That should take care of things."

"Luka?"

"Yes, Keira?" The boy had been staring out the window. Probably trying to keep his mind off what . . . who
was in the plastic bags in the rear of the Rover. "I'd like
you to do a little Internet research on wolf pelt markets
this afternoon, just in case. And also on this church. Can
you do that?"

"You bet."

"Great, give me a call if you do find anything interesting."

"Should we attend tomorrow night's social?" Rhys
asked. "Wouldn't be a bad idea to mingle with these
folks."

"I think so," I said. "Though I'm leaning toward going
with either you or Ianto instead of Adam."

Rhys nodded. "Because we pass better." He ran a hand through his short-cropped, dark hair, so different from Adam's long black mane. Rhys could definitely pass, especially in light of the fact that this was a small-town church social. Adam would stand out like a Hummer at a Smart car convention—and probably piss the men off while attracting the women. Not a good idea at all. Play it low and keep it quiet was my motto for tonight.

"Yes. Recon tonight with vampires outside. Tomorrow night we go inside and socialize. Maybe Dixxi should come along, too."

"Not a bad idea," Ianto said. "Rhys and I, you and Dixxi. We can gather whatever intel there is to gather. Lev, is Dixxi free tomorrow night?"

"As far as I know."

"Good, Dixxi can come and pretend she's interested in the youth group on behalf of the boys."

"Good point, Ianto." I checked the car's clock. "C'mon, then, let's get back to the ranch, and take care of our . . . cargo."

"I want to give them a proper burial," Lev said.

"We can do that. There's an old cemetery on ranch property. Will that do?"

He bowed his head a moment in thought. "Could we get a priest or a pastor?"

"I'm afraid not, Lev," I said gently. "I know you'd like to do this right, but we can't bring in outsiders."

He sighed. "I know, I just . . ." He turned away from me. "Could we at least say a few words?"

"We will," Tucker assured him.

"We'll hold whatever ceremony you'd like, Lev," I said. "I promise. Besides, Mark will want to be there, too. I'm sure we can find a place at the ranch cold enough to store the bodies until there's time to do this properly."

Lev's eyes brimmed over with tears as he turned back to face me. "Thank you," he whispered.

I nodded brusquely in the face of his emotion. This being a liege thing was becoming far too serious in too short a time.

CHAPTER THIRTY-TWO

A LOUD BUZZING IN MY pocket sounded as I descended the stairs. I fumbled in my pocket, trying to shut it off. "Damn it," I muttered under my breath. I pulled my phone out and flipped it open, just in time for the call to end. A number I didn't recognize showed in the lit display.

"What is it?" Adam mumbled from the bed.

"Sorry, love," I said. "Didn't mean to wake you."

He switched on the bedside lamp. I blinked in the sudden light and smiled at him, all rumpled and sleepy, his hair spread across the pillow. "Who was it?"

I crossed to the bedside, leaned over, and kissed his forehead. "Don't know," I said and tossed the phone on the nightstand as I scooted onto the bed. "Missed the call."

He hooked an arm around my waist. "Care to fill me in on your day?" he murmured. "What time is it, anyway?"

"Still early afternoon," I said, closing my eyes as I snuggled into his embrace. As we lay there, comfortably cozy, I told him everything we'd found, and what the plan was for the evening. "Tucker and Ianto are taking care of the bodies," I said. "We figured keeping them in the spare walk-in cooler over at the inn would work until we could give them a decent burial. It can be kept locked and is nowhere near the food prep area."

"Logical," Adam replied. "Lev and Luka?"

"Rhys is taking them back to town. Lev's going to report in to Mark. Luka's taking care of some research for me."

"Sounds good." He scooted closer, dropping a kiss on my thigh. "Do you have to leave anytime soon?"

I did some quick math. "I think I could spare about an hour."

He grinned back and pulled me in closer. "Good."

"HEY, KEIRA, sorry you're not picking up. Anyway, I think I know where the pin's from, also, found something really hinky on the wolf urine. You totally won't believe this. I'm gonna check it out and call you guys back later, 'kay? Text me if you get this before three."

Luka's voice burbled out of my phone's speaker. He'd been the mystery caller. I could feel guilty about ignoring it for a little fun time with Adam, but I didn't. I'd been home far too short a time and had missed Adam for far too long to let myself fret over an hour's worth of recreation. I'd give Luka a quick ring in a few minutes, but first, I took advantage of Adam showering and called Bea.

I made arrangements to stop by her place on the way out to Joe's. I had to talk to her about the possibility of genetic disorders, whether I wanted to or not. This wasn't an option.

I felt like I had this weird checklist of to-do items for the rest of the day. 1. Tell Bea that her pregnancy might result in a child who is not only part werewolf but could have or carry any of several genetic diseases. 2. Go talk to Joe the trash guy and figure out what the hell was up with him. 3. Have vampires stake out a church and figure out if anyone there is a murderer. 4. Figure out what to do about 1 and 3—or rather, determine where my responsibility ended.

Adam came out of the bathroom, toweling his hair dry. "What is it?"

"What's what?"

"You have that look on your face, the one that says you're thinking deeply about something and don't know what to do."

I sighed. "You know me that well, do you?"

He sat on the bed next to me. "I do. Talk to me."

"How far do I take this?" I asked. "Bea's situation? The wers' situation? What's my—our—responsibility as the co-rulers of this area? Don't get me wrong, I'm not complaining about having to deal with this stuff, I just want to know if it's either my right or my duty or if I'm just stepping in where I don't belong. I want to help. I've been specifically asked for help, but I also can't deny that I'm not sure how far to take this." Leaned into him, despite the fact he was still damp from the shower. "I've never been in charge of anything before. It's just . . . weird."

Adam smiled, his brow creasing as he thought. "No, you've been the somewhat indulged youngest child and only daughter of seven children," he said fondly. "Despite your earlier childhood, this is rather new to you."

"True, and my training months were great, but there's only so much one can learn in such a short time."

He placed a kiss on the top of my head. "Much of this cannot be learned by training, love. There's a great many aspects to ruling that are simply learned 'on the job,' so to speak."

I sat up and turned on the bed to face him. "O great ruling leader, then what's your advice? You've been on this job for centuries. Advise me."

He chuckled and continued to dry his hair. "Talk to Bea, but call Dixxi and have her join you. She's the expert on the genetics of the werewolves. You might want to have one of your brothers along, too. Tucker's a good choice, Bea thinks of him as a friend. You'll want the backup. I've no doubt Bea is strong enough to hear this, but she will be emotional . . . you'll be there for her, but you need someone there for you." He eyed me as if to see whether or not I felt insulted. At one point, time past, I would have, but Changing made a whole hell of a lot of difference.

"Yes, good points, all. Am I going too far in telling her all this?"

He shook his head. "No. You're right, she needs as much information as possible. Until now, Bea had no knowledge of other species that could breed with humans, she only thought she was dealing with an accidental pregnancy. This is a great deal for her to handle, and knowing there's a possibility of genetic issues is more, but she needs to know. Knowledge is power. You're her friend, you've known her for years. It will be easier for her if she knows you're in her corner."

"How about the other stuff?"

"You have good instincts, Keira," Adam reassured me. "Don't doubt yourself. Help Marcus out. If you find nothing tonight, if Tucker and Niko find nothing on their stakeout, then perhaps it's time to let the wer handle the rest of the investigation. I do, however, think that you've nailed it."

"Hunters from the church?"

"More than probable," he said and stood up and walked

into the large closet. "It's a tightly knit, close community. The pastor practically told you that hunting is one of the skills they teach their youngsters. I would not be surprised if this was a result of a group of men accidentally running across the wolves, then coming back to prove something, get pelts, something along those lines. You've made a good decision to have Niko and Tucker go camp out at the land," he said, voice a little muffled. "I believe that they'll find something more concrete."

"Why?"

"Because those men who shot at us did so at night," he said as he emerged attired in a lightweight pair of black linen trousers and a black silk button-down shirt—not as casually dressed as he'd been since my return.

"Official business tonight?" I inquired, indicating the outfit.

"More or less," he said. "I thought I'd ring John, have him drop by for a quick debrief about the bodies. Get him to work with Marcus regarding a funeral ceremony. I figured they'd want this done in the daytime. Later, I'm meeting with a few of my staff, going over security preparations for the reception."

"Thanks, Adam," I said. "I'm sure Marcus will appreciate your help." I remembered what Rhys had said regarding the guest list. "Rhys told me someone named Eamonn was coming," I said. "You know him?"

He nodded. "From my father's court," he said. "I believe Father is sending him as a peace offering."

"Peace offering? You think he feels the need?"

"I am still his first son and heir," Adam replied. "Despite his current tolerance of my half brother and your fellow heir, Father has always been one to observe the formalities."

"Formalities being sending a representative."

"Exactly."

"I thought Lance and Jess were handling things," I said, watching him as he slid his bare feet into a pair of Italian loafers.

"They are handling most of the preparation, along with Rhys and Liz," he answered. "Security, however, I will not leave to them alone." He smiled at me. "Not that I think your brother and his almost-wife cannot handle it." He came over and drew me in close, his green eyes shining as he gave me a long, deep kiss.

"I want no problems and I wish to ensure that your safety is in the best hands possible," he said as he pulled away.

Dropping a light kiss on his lips, I smiled back at him. "Yours, I take it?"

"Mine," he growled and with that, lowered me back onto the bed.

A much too short few moments later, he released me. "Now I believe you must away, love. Duty calls."

I muttered a few curses under my breath, most of which maligned the concept of duty and the lack of time. "Duty sucks, love," I said as I, too, rose, straightening my clothes.

Adam flashed his fangs at me. "Only sometimes."

CHAPTER THIRTY-THREE

Not too long afterward, Tucker and I drove up to Bea's. Another car, a small fuel-efficient generic compact of some sort, was already in the drive.

"Feels a little funny," I said as we pulled in behind the other car.

Tucker nodded. "Yeah, coming here to what used to be your house. You miss it?"

I shook my head as I opened my door. "No, not at all. Home's mostly a place where you feel you belong. This was just a place, because I had to have one. The Wild Moon's home—with my family."

"Thought as much." He tossed me the keys. I'd asked him to drive so I could think and sort out how to approach this discussion while we drove over.

Before I could knock or ring the buzzer, Dixxi opened the door and handed me a glass of wine. "I've told her."

"What? You were supposed to wait for me." I pushed past her to see Bea sitting hunched over in what used to be my comfy chair, where I ended up when I wanted to pout, think, or just play emo-chick.

"Bea, *chica,*" I said as I hurried over. "You okay?"

She turned a tearstained face up to me, her expression saying all the curse words she rarely thought, much less said. I crouched next to her and placed a comforting hand on her back. "I'm sorry," I whispered. "I meant to be here, to tell you myself."

She nodded and sniffed. I handed her a tissue from the box on the side table. "I know. Dixxi said to wait, but I knew something was up and I just—" She blew her nose and hunched over again, sobbing.

"I'm sorry, Keira," Dixxi said. "She just kept insisting."

I nodded. "I know, I know, you got subjected to the sad puppy eyes combined with the Ruiz rant, no doubt. I've known her for thirty-plus years and I'm not immune. I don't blame you for spilling the beans." I kept patting Bea's back, not really knowing what the hell else to do. I was horrible at this. Emotions? I don't do them—or at least, not very well. When Marty was murdered, the most I felt was a vague surprise, then guilt because he'd died on my watch. Tea and sympathy weren't in my repertoire at all. I could say the expected words, but they'd ring hollow and uncaring. Bea deserved better.

Tucker, who by now had entered, came over and squatted on the other side of the chair, his own large hand on Bea's back, soothing up and down as one would a crying child. "Bea, hon, we're here for you."

A shudder ran through my best friend. I put my hand on the back of her head, wracking my brain for some way to calm her down, to make it better. I knew a few calming charms. I sent an inquiring glance to Tucker, who shook his head. He slid his arm around her shoulder and then moved around so he could wrap her in a bear hug. She clung to him, sobbing, words I couldn't make out muffled in the cloth of his shirt.

Dixxi leaned in, her loose, dark hair brushing my face. "Bea, I'm sorry. What can I do?" She paused and repeated, correcting the pronoun. "What can we do to make this better for you?"

Bea shook her head, smearing tears across the light blue cotton of Tucker's shirt, fists still clinging like a lost child. "There, there, sweetheart," he murmured. "It's okay. I promise you, it's okay."

The three of us did the only thing we could—we waited.

Several sodden minutes later, Bea's sobs slowed and became sniffs. She nodded her head, as if having decided something, and let Tucker's shirt go. Tucker, after looking down at her, gave her one huge squeeze and then let her sit on her own. She remained bent over, not facing us, as if gathering thoughts—perhaps courage. If I were in her position, would I even want to be in a room with three other people? Probably not. Then again, I truly could not comprehend being in her position—pregnant by a werewolf with a high possibility of a genetic problem. I could sympathize, say words all I wanted, but she knew and I knew, this wasn't a problem I'd ever have.

I opened my mouth to at least say more words of sympathy but caught Tucker's head shake. Okay, so I should stay quiet. Dixxi, no doubt smarter than me about these things, just sat on the floor and kept her mouth shut. Another couple of minutes and Bea's tear-smeared face examined each of us in turn.

"Thanks," she whispered.

I nodded, still unwilling to say the wrong thing.

"You okay, hon?" Tucker asked.

"As okay as it gets, I guess," Bea said. She shifted, stood, and walked over to the kitchen bar, stared at the refrigerator for a moment. "You know," she said, "it's not that I'm totally against abortion."

My brow furrowed as I wondered why she'd started with that. Then I saw it—a pink flyer from Planned Parenthood stuck to the fridge with a cheery smiley-face magnet. Was this just a weirdly appropriately timed mailing?

"As soon as I began dating Lev, I sent away for information," Bea continued, explaining the flyer. "On account of I've really not needed anything more permanent than a condom for the last several years." She turned to me. "Ways to prevent contraception have changed since we were younger, you know."

I shrugged and tried to appear supportive. Once again, not much of an issue with me. In my twenties, I was mostly dating humans, who couldn't get me pregnant, and if I'd had sex with Clan, we'd used protection. Condoms worked just fine, spells worked better. The pill—not so much.

Bea walked back over to her chair and sat. "When I figured out I was pregnant, I thought, well, why the hell not. I'm healthy, I'm nearly forty, it could work. Then, you threw me a curve. You told me about Lev being a werewolf. Not as simple, but all right, I could handle this. I like Lev."

I started to ask about Jacob, but Bea shushed me before I could get a word out.

"Please. Let me finish?" I nodded at her and she kept talking. "I'm healthy, Lev's healthy. There was no reason that we couldn't work this out."

"Do you love him?" I finally asked. "Enough to risk this?"

"No." She rubbed her eyes, then faced me directly,

her gaze as blunt as mine was. "Maybe I just hung around you-all too long," she finally said. "You Kellys."

"What's that's supposed to mean?"

"The way you handle relationships, children—it's for the good of the Clan, right? My having this baby would be for the good of their pack."

"Well, the children part, yes," Tucker agreed. "All my own children have been fostered to families who wished to raise kids. I'm not that guy. Nor, do I think, is my sister."

"Definitely not," I said. "But since I'm with Adam now, that's not something I need to worry about."

"You could," Dixxi piped up, changing the focus of our discussion to me.

"I'm sorry, what?"

"You could, if you wanted to, I meant."

"Get pregnant, have kids? In case you failed to notice, Dix, Adam's a vampire. For all intents and purposes, he's dead. Dead men can't make babies." I found myself echoing my aunt's line from last year when she'd found out I was with Adam.

"He's Unseelie Sidhe." Her expression was both direct and disconcerting. "They don't die."

I stared at her in a daze. I had no words. She was absolutely right. When we discovered Adam's heritage, it never occurred to me to ask *how* he became vampire. As far as I knew, a person had to die, and three days later after being bitten and drained and sharing blood with the vampire, the person would wake as the living dead, Nosferatu. Niko had died. He'd told me his story. He'd been dying of the plague when Adam found him, turned him.

"How do you know this? That his semen could be viable?" I demanded.

"I don't," she said. "But I'm a geneticist. If Adam never truly died, it's far more likely that his sperm are only dormant. His vampirism probably masks the Sidhe genes. Has anyone ever tested him?"

"What for? I have no intentions of bearing a child," I said. "I just got started with my adult life in the Clan. Even if what you're saying is true, and that something could be done to make little Kelly-Walker progeny, it's not something I care to even consider for at least several decades."

Bea made a small sound, almost a whimper.

"Shit, Bea, I'm sorry," I apologized. "This night is about you, not me." Could I be more self-centered? Though, this time, Dixxi was the one who changed the subject. Distraction, maybe?

"Bea, I'd like to get a blood sample from you, if you wouldn't mind," Dixxi said.

"Why?" Bea seemed worried. "I can't go to my doctor and ask for genetic testing—you were the one who told me that. The werewolf genes and all."

"No, you can't go to your doctor," Dixxi agreed. "I could call in a few markers, though, at the Health Science Center in San Antonio. I might borrow a lab, get a friend to do me a favor or two."

"Whatever you need, Dixxi," I said. "Money, whatever—the Kellys will be glad to help."

"I appreciate it, Keira, but my friends don't really operate that way. It's mostly favors, you know, all us ABD types. We trade."

I pulled my knees up to my chin and wrapped my arms around my legs. "I feel useless here," I said. "I'm not a scientist. I can't help by giving you money. Bea's my best friend. I want to help and all I can do is sit here—"

"I've got an idea," Tucker said. "Dixxi, can you describe to Keira what kinds of things you'd be looking for in the blood? She could perhaps scan Bea, see if she sees anything that way."

"Scan how?"

"Magickally," I said. "Scan her body, her aura, her—"

"Can you get down to genetic level?"

I had no idea. "Probably. It's worth a shot." I crossed my mental fingers. I had to try.

"Okay, then let's plan on that. I'll have to run by the apartment and get some notes off my laptop. I can bring them by later." She paused a moment. "Or maybe tomorrow, if you're busy later on. Lev told me what was going on. That you guys were going to do some detective work up at the church."

"Sort of," I said. "I'm sending some folks to check things out after dark tonight. Tucker and I need to go have a chat with someone else right now. Feel free to come by the ranch, though. We can meet up there. Say six or seven?"

"That'll work. Deli closes at seven and I usually help Mark clean up, but I'm sure I can get out of it . . . considering."

Considering Bea, or the dead wolves? I wondered. No matter, in any case, helping Bea was still a priority.

"Perfect," I said. "Bea, you should rest, hon. We can come by later if you're up for it, or even better, in the morning. You can sleep tonight, close the café again tomorrow, or get Noe, Tia, and Tio to run things while you're out."

"Did I miss something here?" Bea sounded a little more like her usual self. "You're going to play Nancy Drew?"

"Long story, but in a nutshell, we're trying to find out who killed several of the pack's wolves. We think it's poachers, guys from the Church of the White Rock."

Bea shook her head. "I don't even know. I'm not sure I want to ask for details at this point."

"I promise I'll tell you the whole sordid story later," I said. "Pinky swear, okay?"

She wiped her face and let out a tired sigh. "Later then. If it gets too late, call first, okay? I get tired quicker these days."

"Deal."

CHAPTER THIRTY-FOUR

"Y<small>OU HEARD BACK</small> from Luka yet?" Tucker asked as we turned into the drive at Hills and Dales Ice House, just a few miles from Rio Seco's main crossroads. Thankfully, driving there didn't take long. I didn't begrudge Bea the time, but I kept feeling a strong urge to get to Joe's and find out what he knew, what he'd been alluding to earlier.

Next to the ice house sat a tired gray wood shack, hubcaps hung from the storm gutters, all sorts of odds and ends decorating the small yard in front. J<small>OE'S</small> T<small>RASH</small> the sign proclaimed. The old black truck was parked behind the shack, but I could see the tailgate from the road.

"Voice mail," I said. "I've left a couple of messages." I nodded at the shack. "Looks like he's here."

Tucker nodded back. "Good. I wish Luka would call you back, though. That message from him was pretty cryptic."

I parked the car. "He's a kid. Wanting to be mysterious or something."

"No doubt."

We got out of the car and walked up to the shack. Joe exited the small place, a pipe in one hand and a large mug of something in the other. He walked with deliberation to a black wooden rocker on the right side of the tiny porch, sat, then set his mug down on the porch rail. As he began rocking, he tamped his pipe, pulled a Zippo lighter from his overalls pocket, and puffed. Did he not see us or was he just ignoring us?

After a few minutes of us watching him, him ignoring us, I shrugged and began to turn away, figuring the very least I could do was to go inside the ice house next door and get me a cold one.

"Y'all just gonna stand there?" Joe's gravelly voice emerged from around the mouthpiece of the pipe.

"May we ask you a few things?" I ventured.

He motioned to a couple of short stools next to him. "Free country."

Tucker and I approached, each of us pulling up a stool. Great, now I felt as if I were a recalcitrant student preparing to be chastised. My knees nearly reached my chin. Tucker elected to stay standing, one foot on the stool. Stubbornly, I stayed seated. "Joe, when we talked before, we were interrupted."

"We were," he said, and rocked some more.

I suppressed an irritated sigh. "Joe, could you help me out here?" I asked, trying to keep my voice steady and not let it degenerate into a pleading whine.

Joe glanced over at Hills and Dales, watching as a couple of local guys loaded down with twelve-packs and ice got into their pickup and drove off. The lot was empty now, no one out there but the yard dog, an old yellow mutt who started to walk over to us, then slunk away once he got a whiff.

Tucker grinned and whispered too low for Joe to hear. "Too much wolf around here for him."

Joe stopped rocking, his eyes narrowing and the expression on his face changing from old-guy-relaxed to sharp and inquisitive. "Wolves, you say?"

Tucker stood up straight and stared at Joe. "You heard me?"

"I hear lots of things, boy. Just because I'm old don't mean I'm deaf, too."

"Not too many people could have heard my brother," I said, now standing up, too. "Who are you?" Perhaps the right question was more "what" than "who," but I'd start off slowly.

"Can't rightly say, miss." Joe's face became bland again as he answered. "Was a foundling, they tell me."

I put out a hand, palm flat up in the air about two feet from Joe's head. I felt it immediately. Damn it, I should've known—those eyes, those damnable old-as-the-hills eyes. "You're a changeling," I accused. "Part fey."

"Maybe, maybe not. Like I said, don't rightly know."

"What do you know, then?" Tucker demanded.

Joe turned his face from us and stared out into the road. "I know that I found a bag. Out back of the church. They all been up to something, something not good. Lots of money coming in and out of the place, but behind the scenes. They never notice me. Not the old trash man."

"Drugs?"

He shrugged but still wouldn't meet my eyes. "That's what I thought. So I grabbed the trash bag when I saw it. Felt like something soft, heavier than drugs. Didn't open it till I got here." He turned slowly, his inhuman eyes nearly glowing. "First thought it were furs, thought I'd hit on some illegal fur sales. Then I saw below."

In a movement almost too fast for me to see, he grabbed my arm. "*See*—look at what I seen," he whispered, the sounds sibilant and compelling.

Flashes of fur and blood and a dainty hand, mani-
cure still intact but covered in blood. The stench of heat-
ripened dead flesh assaulted my nostrils, raped my mind.
One blue eye rolled toward me in a half-human, half-wolf
face, its perfectly waxed eyebrow incongruous next to the
ravaged remains of her head. I pulled my arm free and
ran, down from the porch, out back to where no one could
see as I puked my guts into the hot Texas dirt. Above my
retching, I could hear Joe explaining to Tucker.

"I thought the wolves ate the lady, but I was wrong.
Once I got my stomach back, I could see . . . was just her.
Part person. Part wolf."

"What did you do with her?" Tucker's voice stayed
steady and calm.

"Buried her out where no one'll find her. She deserved
a Christian burial," he said. "Ain't no marker, but I said
the right words and such." He cocked his head and stared
at me a moment before continuing. "Was going to come
see you. Was told if I ever was to see anyone else who
was like her, that I was to come talk to you." He paused.

I barely heard his words as I wiped my mouth with
the back of my hand and fumbled in my pocket, hoping I
had a breath mint or something. Nothing but my phone.
Damn it. Doing the best I could to spit out the taste of my
own vomit, I wiped my mouth clean again and rejoined
Joe and my brother.

Joe handed me his mug. "Peppermint tea," he said.
"Cold. It'll settle you."

I took it, nodding my thanks, and sipped at the refreshing drink. Tucker patted me on the arm. "I'm okay," I
said. "Go on, Joe, please. Who told you to talk to us?"

He explained about the lady who'd stopped in at his
place. I knew exactly who it had been.

"My great-grandmother," I said, leaving out the extra

"great" for simplicity's sake. "She told you that if you ever saw anyone who was like her, to come talk to them?"

"She did," he said. "I figured she were a harbinger."

"I hope not of doom," I tried to joke. "Sorry," I quickly amended. "Poor taste. Blame it on what I just saw."

He nodded gravely. "No offense taken, Miz Kelly."

"You didn't think of talking to Sheriff Miller?" Tucker asked. "She was at the game. You found the bag in her county."

"Don't like her. Even less than her husband . . . and he's mean to those boys, cruel even."

"Why don't you like her?" I asked.

"There is something deeply wrong with that woman," he said solemnly. "Evil in her being, I know this."

"Do you often feel how people really are?" I asked. "Inside, I mean."

He just watched me, those light eyes boring into me. "All the time," he said. "All the time."

"How about the pastor, then?"

"Pastor Hagen?" Joe seemed to think a moment. "He's not a bad sort at heart. Just weak."

"Weak?"

"He thinks t'other folks know better than him. He's new to this, you see. Just been pastor a couple of years. Don't want to rock the boat."

"What boat might that be?" I urged gently.

"There's pure hatred here, Miz Kelly. Hate that runs hot and deep. Hotter than these temperatures, even."

I pulled back away from him, puzzled. "Hatred how?"

"They don't like outsiders."

"Pretty normal," Tucker said. "This is a small and very insular community."

"They is that," Joe agreed. "But this is more . . ." He

stopped a moment, his gaze turning away from me. "I don't rightly know if I can even say how. I don't know particulars."

"But there are particulars?"

"There are," he said. "What I do know is that group of theirs—the Brotherhood—there's more to them than community service. There's something wrong. I tried to listen one night, heard some of the boys outside the church. But they saw me and went away."

"Are you in any danger?"

"No, ma'am," he snorted. "They just think of me as that ol' nigger man who picks up trash."

I flinched at his bluntness. "Joe, I want to be sure you're safe. If for any reason, you feel uncomfortable, come to the Wild Moon Ranch. You know where it is?"

"I do. It's your people, isn't it?"

"My people?"

"More than me, more than a changeling."

I eyed him carefully. "Yes. And you are someone we can care for."

"I get that," he said solemnly. "I promise, I will come."

With that, I shook his hand and we left.

"I want to go back to the church." I entered the car. "Now, please."

"Done." Tucker, who'd taken my keys, started the car. "Call Luka while we drive there, please? I want to make sure he's okay and hasn't gone gallivanting off to play Sherlock on his own."

"Crap, you think he might have?"

"He's fifteen. He's a werewolf and full of hormones."

"Fuck."

CHAPTER THIRTY-FIVE

L UKA STILL WASN'T answering his cell, so I tried Jacob's number. He answered on the first ring. "Luka's gone to the library. Probably turned his phone off. He said he needed to look something up then was coming back here to the apartment. Why don't you all stop by?"

"Jacob, we're kind of in a hurry, but while I have you on the phone, could I ask a couple of questions?"

"Sure." His voice seemed okay, positive, upbeat, but I couldn't help feeling something else sliding underneath. Something not kosher. I closed my eyes as I spoke to him, trying to picture his energy, his shape, his movement. What was he hiding?

"Bea says you guys have been talking a lot about religion, about the church over in White Rock."

Silence for a second, then a cheerful reply. "Yeah, sure enough," he said. "Since I came here, I was so glad to find the church. Don't know if you know my story, but I was a lone wolf, like a lot of the others. Only, I didn't really know I was a wolf for a long time."

"Really, how so?" I grabbed on to the handle above the car door as Tucker took a turn too fast. He mouthed a quick *sorry* at me and slowed down a bit. I focused on Jacob's voice, trying to ignore my brother's driving.

"Orphaned," he said curtly. "Left on church steps. I guess some kids saw the church as a bad place, but they kind of saved me. I could always come talk to the pastor at my home church even when I was in foster care. First time I Changed, I knew that it was evil, so I ran away. Scared myself and didn't know what to do. Ended up finding a pack that eventually led me to Mark. Church's been good to me over the years."

"Why this one?" I pressed, still feeling something not said. "There are several closer churches." The feeling of unease grew, a staticky, sticky sense behind the crystal clarity of the actual phone speaker.

"I've always been a believer, Keira," he said. "They helped me be part of a community again. I can belong."

Why wasn't I believing him? Was it just that the physical image of the drop-dead gorgeous bodyguard werewolf didn't jibe with the devout born-again Christian he kept insisting he was? "Isn't the pack your community, Jacob?"

"It is," he answered. "Truth is, I need more." He paused a moment. I reached out, focusing on the phone signal, hoping to get a better sense of the person on the other end. Nothing. Though my spidey-sense kept tingling, the words just below his spoken words slid from my awareness like water down a rock face. Swift, flowing, too fast to make out what lay beneath. The hum of tires on asphalt acted as background, white noise.

Jacob continued his thought. "Marcus leads us, but he's too devoted to books, to his history. There's no room in his life for God." The static crackled and poked me, a wave of energy emanating from the phone.

What in all the hells was I supposed to say to that? Religion of any kind never really found a foothold in Kelly minds. We've been around too long, seen too many religions rise, evolve, die off to believe in any one true Word. Hells, I was half-Faery. Adam was full-blood Sidhe plus vampire. The two of us alone defied the so-called natural laws that most Western and a hell of a lot of Eastern religions held sacred. To me and mine, sacred was the family, our people . . . but I had no heart in busting Jacob's chops. If he wished to believe, that was his choice. For now, I had to take him at face value.

"Marcus allows you this?" I asked.

"He does," Jacob said. "As long as I am present when needed and I tithe to the pack, I'm free to pursue my religious beliefs."

"Fair enough. Tell Luka we'll follow up in a few, please."

"I will do so." He ended the call. I flipped my own phone shut and tucked it into my shorts pocket. "I don't like him," I said to Tucker. "Underneath his pretty, pretty words, I felt something unstable, uneasy." I shifted in the car seat. "If I were in the same room with him, I could pin it down, I think."

"Well, let's get this errand over with and then you can interrogate Jacob face-to-face," Tucker said. "We'll talk to the church pastor and then go back to the their apartment."

LESS THAN fifteen minutes later we were back inside the church, thanks to Tucker's insane driving skills. If we'd not been who we were, I'd have worried. Hill Country roads weren't designed for speed.

"Sorry, dears, Pastor Hagen had an appointment this afternoon. He'll be back a little bit later. Y'all coming to our social tomorrow?" The helmet-haired church secretary fit every stereotype in the book. Her kindness, though, seemed utterly genuine.

"We're planning to," I said, pasting on my best cute gal expression. "We're interested in joining the church. A friend of ours, Jacob Ashkarian, just raves about it."

"Oh, he's adorable, that boy, pretty as a picture. He's so helpful with the younger ones . . . as if he's not young himself." She chuckled. "If you want to wander around and read some of the literature and whatnot, feel free. I need to do a couple of things in the office." She motioned with a hand to an open door some twenty feet away. "I'll just be in there if you need me."

"Thanks, Mrs. . . ."

"Miller, Fran Miller."

"Any relation to Coach Miller over at the high school?" I asked, trying to be nonchalant.

"Distant cousins, or something like that," she answered with a smile. "You know Robert Earl?"

"We've met." I tried to smile back as warmly as she.

"His wife, Janey, she's sheriff, you know."

I nodded.

"Guess most folks hereabouts do." She scuttled away, her cotton dress a bright flash of color in this drab hallway. "Now just holler if you need me."

"So, anything you see?"

"I want to check out those trophies again," Tucker said. "Trophy case is over here." The main hallway intersected where we were and led to a more luxuriously appointed reception lobby. Nice carpet, upbeat posters on the walls, an extremely full trophy case, surrounded by a series of eight-by-ten framed photos of groups or individuals, each with a metal plaque below, engraved with data.

"Check this out," Tucker said, pointing to a trophy of a pair of praying hands. "For excellence in Bible study, 1976. Calvin Hagen. Guess Pastor Hagen comes by his calling legitimately." I studied the rest of the trophies. Some for swimming, tennis, golf. Most for some sort of religious study or the like.

"Look at this picture, Tucker," I said. "Pastor Hagen again." The photo was marked as a camping group in the early 1970s led by Pastor J. R. Miller and his wife, Jonetta. Calvin Hagen lounged in the front of a group of teens, a rawboned, skinny, and studious boy, all angles and glasses in too-short black shorts and an oversized T-shirt.

"No, this one." Tucker hauled me over to another picture, much more recently taken. Same composition, but instead of Pastor Hagen, it was Robert Earl Miller and Janey Miller at the side of the boys' group. A few of the boys were wearing pins—just like the one we'd found mangled at the murder site. Tucker dug into his pocket and held it up. A match. Unlike the rest of the photos, this group didn't have an explanatory plaque on it. I recognized a few faces from the football game, including Gregor's rival, Kyle.

"You two getting on okay?" Mrs. Miller walked around the corner, her arms full of some flyers that she dropped onto a table at the end of the lobby.

"Mrs. Miller, what's this photo of?" She walked closer and peered at the wall.

"Oh, that's the Brotherhood group picture from earlier this year. Lord help me, I keep meaning to order that darned plaque." She beamed at Tucker and me. "Aren't they all just handsome as can be? See, there's Robert Earl there and Janey."

"So they sponsor the group?"

"Oh yes, they love working with the boys' club. It's been around, oh, for decades, I think. All tradition and whatnot."

"How about that pin that some of them are wearing?" I ask in my best angelic tone. "They don't all seem to have one."

"It's some sort of service pin," she explained. "The boys have to earn it. Complete some task."

"Hmm, sounds interesting," Tucker mused. "Could we ask what that task is?"

"Oh, lordy," she giggled. "I haven't a clue. It's a boys-only thing—all secret handshakes and exclusive meetings behind locked doors." She giggled again. "Boys will be boys. It's so cute. They think they're being all mysterious and manly. Poor Janey gets all hot and bothered when they leave her out of stuff, but I keep telling her, that's the way it's always been, can't fight tradition." She trotted away.

"Like the KKK?" I said to Tucker in quiet disgust. "Or Freemasons maybe?" But no, these folks aren't quite that mysterious, with all the degrees and such that I never understood. "Naw," I continued, "this is a small-town church, it's probably some stupid-ass Promise Keepers club or a similar kind of thing. Chastity club or whatever. You know, a year without—"

"Someone's coming."

"Oh, hello again." Pastor Hagen rounded the corner, a look of puzzlement on his face as he caught sight of us. "I didn't expect to see you back so soon. Is there something I can do for y'all?"

I beamed at him, plastering "cute and clueless southern gal" back on my face. I tried to avoid looking coy—or gagging. "We happened to still be in town," I said, "and wanted to stop by and get some information about the church before we come back tomorrow night. Mrs. Miller has been quite kind to show us around."

"That's marvelous," he said. "Y'all have any questions?"

"Mrs. Miller answered most of them. But maybe you could help with one thing." I flapped my hand at Tucker, who shrugged and handed over the crushed pin. "We found this on our friends' property earlier and just saw the same pin in that picture there. I wouldn't have said anything, except it wasn't in the target shooting area. I just wanted to be able to return it if it belonged to one of your boys."

Pastor Hagen's face paled to a shade lighter than my own—a feat until now matched only by the vampires at the Wild Moon. *Gotcha!* I thought with glee. He knew who the pin belonged to. Pastor Hagen pasted on a sick smile and took the pin from my hand. "Thank you. I'll return it. Now that I know the property's sold, I can assure you they won't trespass again, I promise."

Forgive us our trespassers. The misquote winged through my mind as I watched him regain his composure. Yeah, fat chance. If any of his people were responsible for those three deaths, I'd be forgiving no one.

As he turned to leave, Tucker stopped him. "I know it's a secret, but how do they achieve a pin?" Tucker turned his charisma on high, sending out the trademarked Tucker Kelly charm.

Even that didn't register as the pastor started the same community service spiel as had the secretary.

"Oh, Pastor Hagen," I drawled and leaned toward him in a flirty pose, stopping short of pushing my boobs in his face. "I'm just so intrigued by all this manly mystery. Surely, you can give me a hint?"

He paled even more, his complexion now the color of curdled milk. "Sorry, if I told you, I'd have to kill you."

For an interminable second, time seemed to slow. The look in the man's eyes didn't reflect his sudden forced chuckle. Before he could say anything more, three boys burst into the hallway, chattering and laughing.

"Hey, Pastor H, we're all done over there at the apartments—" The boys all stopped, and the boy who'd been talking immediately shut up as soon as they saw us. It was Kyle, from the football team. "Umm . . ." he mumbled, grabbed the arms of the other two, and pulled them down into another hallway.

Tucker's brow lowered. In a flash, he excused himself. "My apologies, Pastor, we've taken far too much of your time. Before we go, may I use the facilities? It's a long drive home."

The pastor nodded, not quite focused on us.

I fumbled around for some comment to make as Tucker disappeared, saying something inane about the social, continuing to yammer on about what to wear, bringing a friend, and things that I could barely remember even the moment after I said them.

Pastor Hagen kept smiling and nodding at me, his gaze still focused on the hallway where the boys had disappeared. In just a couple of minutes, Tucker returned and we all mumbled our goodbyes, with a promise to see him the next night.

The moment we were out of earshot, I spoke. "What?"

"Those boys smelled of fertilizer." He broke into a run. I followed, not knowing why, but realizing that something demanded quick action.

"So what?" I asked as we climbed into the car. "They were probably gardening at some apartments, part of that community service."

"They said something about the apartments by the

Rio Seco Lodge, Keira. I was around the corner, but they weren't even talking softly. They were bragging. Teasing one of the kids that he was earning his service pin. Earning *bones*."

"Oh holy fuck." I dug my phone out and dialed Rhys to fill him in. "We're at least twenty minutes or more away, even with Tucker driving," I said. "Where are you?"

"At the ranch," Rhys said. "I'm a good twenty minutes out, too."

Tucker spoke up. "Hit Speaker, Keira." I did. "Rhys, that's not all of it. The boys also smelled of fuel. At first, I thought it was lawn mower fuel. That would go with gardening, earning community service points. Then I put two and two together."

"And got?" I asked.

"Fertilizer bomb."

CHAPTER THIRTY-SIX

THE ENTIRE WAY THERE I tried to get through to anyone who'd pick up. No answer from Mark, Lev, or Jacob. None from either of the two boys. I left frantic messages on each of their cell phones. I even called Bea, but Tia answered and said she was napping and hadn't seen anyone since Dixxi had left. Damn them, where the hell were they all? Dixxi had said they'd be at the deli until seven. Clock was just ticking over to six fifty now.

"Park at the lodge lot," I said to Tucker. "We'll walk over." There were only four small duplex-style apartments in the development and very little in the way of a parking lot. I was still holding my phone to my ear, redialing Luka's number in hopes he'd answer. I got the damned voice mail again.

Tucker complied and found a space along the back side of the lodge—the part that was directly across from the main entrance to the complex. It wasn't far, just across a narrow two-lane road, but it was on the downside of a hill, and cars tended to take it too quick, not necessarily seeing pedestrians.

As we alighted from the Rover, the smell of fertilizer assaulted us. "Gag. I expected a shit smell, but this is worse."

"Chemicals," Tucker said, his nose wrinkling. "Not here, though." He indicated the dried-up verge on our side of the road. "It's definitely coming from the apartments. Were you able to reach Luka?"

"No, just his voice mail again," I said. "He's probably not home."

"Good," Tucker said. "Makes this easier. Let's go see if we can find the damned bomb."

I pulled the neck of my T-shirt over my nose, which did nothing to stifle the stench. As we began to cross the street, a hot wave of air hit us, like the pressure of a thousand plows, slamming into our bodies. We flew backward, only then hearing the crashing boom of the explosion, following by the tinkling shards of glass slamming into the road. Horns blared as nearby car alarms were set off by the concussion. I landed on my back, my elbows grinding into the rough surface of the pockmarked macadam of the lodge's lot as the shock wave pushed me along. Tucker had somehow managed to roll into a ball, arms and legs tucked tight to his body. My own body flipped over, and I landed hard on my face and hands, skin scraping painfully off as gravel ate into it.

A scream from the lodge above us as a woman, dressed only in a T-shirt and panties peeked out of a now-shattered window, her face white and red, scratches from the broken glass shards zigzagging across her cheeks.

"Call 911," Tucker managed to yell out. The woman froze a moment, staring at the apartments, where a gout of flame burst through what once was a doorway. "Now!" Tucker yelled. He fumbled in his own pocket and found his phone. "I'm calling the deli."

I pulled my own phone out and dialed the Rio Seco sheriff's private line.

"Rudy Garza." The voice sounded vaguely familiar, yet distant as if I were hearing him down a well. I was expecting Carlton Larson, the sheriff, to answer himself. Where the hell was Carlton? Didn't matter.

"Explosion, apartments across from the lodge," I yelled into the phone. "Tell Carlton."

"On our way."

I pushed myself to my feet with Tucker's help. He wasn't too badly cut up. I was mostly bruised and scraped, injuries that would heal themselves sooner rather than later.

I started across the street when my brother forcibly pulled me back.

"You can't."

"Someone could be—"

"Or maybe Luka is still at the library and Jacob left, too," Tucker said. "How's your firefighting ability, Keira?"

I sagged into him. "Nonexistent," I mumbled. "That's not one of our Talents."

"I know." He held me tight as we both watched helplessly from across the street. I saw no one emerge from the small four-apartment building. Not even a cat or dog. How many renters were there? I was pretty sure the landlord didn't live on the premises but had the lodge's owner act as super when needed. Normally, these apartments tended to rent to passers-through, summer hires, and the like. Just a small and unassuming place for a budget-conscious weekender to stay.

Less than ten minutes later, which seemed eons, the recognizable whine of the volunteer fire department's truck dopplered in over the top of the hill. The truck skidded to a stop, blocking all access to the road, and firefighters sprang into action. One man ran to the hydrant, which luckily was on the lodge side and seemed undamaged. The others began strategizing.

A tall woman approached Tucker and me as we huddled together. "Captain Pineda. What did you see?"

I shook my head. "Nothing. We'd just parked here at the lodge. Going to visit a friend when 'boom.' " My voice shook. "I don't know if they were home . . ." My voice wobbled a little, my senses raw with shock. Unthinking, I reached across the street with my mind, focusing in on the one place—no, no, just— "They're there, fuck, they're inside."

She got on the radio. "Check inside unit . . ." She paused and looked at me oddly.

"Two," I said, "two people, unit two." Two bodies? Two living bodies? I couldn't tell. The taste of ash and fire overwhelmed me as I reeled back my focus and sagged into Tucker's hold.

"Unit two. Possibly two people," I repeated to her. I'd felt at least two but could tell no more at this point.

"Could be two people," she repeated into the radio. Captain Pineda might wonder how I knew, but she wasn't pausing to question it.

"Ten-four." A disembodied voice crackled through. "Checking now."

Three firefighters approached the blazing flames, skirting the building. I couldn't watch. Tucker pulled me away, closer to my car.

"Keira, focus," he urged. "Can you sense them? Sense anyone in there?"

I stared at him in a daze. "Sense, yes, I did. I just wasn't ready." I turned back to the fire and fixed my attention on the left apartment. Focus, Keira, focus. Flames, heat, burning, flames, light, heat, behind . . . someone coughing, saying something, hand holding cloth over mouth. Who was that? I held on to Tucker's arm as if to ground myself. "There's someone in there bent over, holding a cloth—"

The sound of shattering glass interrupted me, breaking my sensory focus.

"Got one," someone yelled. "No, two."

I slumped against Tucker again, letting my brother take all my weight.

Crackling noises over the radio again. The captain turned her head in our direction, then deliberately stepped away from us a good ten or more feet. She talked quietly into her radio. With a hand motion, she waved down an ambulance that was just arriving. She held up two fingers to the driver, who nodded. In tandem, he hopped out of the driver's seat as another EMT rounded the back of the ambulance, trying to lead two gurneys.

The ambulance driver, Eric something—I'd known him in high school—took the second gurney and the men trotted over, loaded down with gear and gurneys. The fire was nearly out now, a long stream of water curving gracefully over the road and onto the roof, into the building, dousing the death and destruction.

A scream above me—Dixxi was running around the backs of the trucks, avoiding a sheriff's deputy who was trying to stop her. "Keira, Tucker." She fell, scrambled to her feet, and kept running, darting glances across the street. "Who, how?"

"I don't know, Dix," I said. "Two people are inside, though."

She sank to the ground sobbing. "Lev and Luka," she said. "Lev went back to the apartment after talking to Mark. He wasn't feeling up to staying at the deli."

"Luka?" Tucker asked.

"He went with Lev. Wanted to do more Internet research and was getting on Mark's nerves, so he sent him back. We closed the place, just had to wait around for a delivery."

I sent up a silent prayer to the powers that be. They were both wer, both stronger than human. They had to survive this. "I talked to Jacob earlier, he was here, too."

"I don't see his car," she said. "Maybe he left?"

"Where's Mark?" Tucker moved me to the side and helped Dixxi stand, throwing an arm around her shoulders.

"Probably right behind me," she said. "I was walking over to Bea's—to the café—I wanted one of those *polvorón* cookies, when I saw Deputy Garza go running as if hellhounds were after him. I overheard the dispatcher calling all units to come here . . . because of a bomb."

"Fertilizer bomb. Had to be."

"How do you know?"

"When we got here, it smelled like a chemical dump. This wasn't a gas leak or an accident. Someone planted a bomb and set this off knowingly." I quickly explained what we'd overheard at the church. "We tried to call you earlier, no one picked up."

"When?"

"As we left White Rock. You were closer—"

Dixxi sobbed. "We must have been in the back. Mark decided as long as we were closed, we could do inventory. I think it was his way of coping after Lev told us about Stephen and Maki. Lev probably turned his phone off to try to get some sleep. If only—" She began crying harder but quieter as she fought to regain some semblance of control. "I've got to keep it together," she said. "Handle things."

"We have company coming." I nodded in the direction of the hill, where another vehicle had just arrived.

The deputy sheriff's SUV made its way between the ambulance and the fire truck and managed to squeeze by into the lodge's parking area. He pulled in and parked.

"Keira, Tucker." He nodded. "How long you been here?"

"Long enough to see it blow up," I said. I told him about coming to visit Lev and Luka and introduced Dixxi. "Where's Carlton?"

"At an International Chiefs of Police conference in Dallas," he said. "I'm it right now. Got a couple other guys on duty, others who're coming in. You see anything?"

"Other than smelling the fertilizer smell, no," I said. "We'd just gotten here when it blew. Tucker and I, that is. Dixxi just now got here." I held a silent conversation with Tucker, expressions only. I didn't want to tell Rudy what we'd overheard, not just yet. I wanted us to handle it, not the law.

"You live there?" Rudy asked her gently.

"Yeah, with my brothers and our nephews," she said. "We own the deli now."

"Rudy," I interrupted, "we think that one of her brothers and one of her nephews are inside."

Rudy sucked in a breath and hissed. "Oh crap, sorry."

"EMTs went in there a bit ago," I explained.

"I'll go check. You guys stop by the office and give a statement?"

"Yeah, we will," Tucker said. "C'mon, Keira," he urged. "Let's go on. We can take the back way over to the—"

"Stop." I held a hand up as I saw two men emerging from the side of the unit, pulling a gurney. Luka's blond hair was easily visible at one end.

"Luka!" Dixxi yelled and ran across the street.

"Ma'am, stay back!" One of the firefighters grabbed Dixxi and fought with her, trying to keep her on this side of the road. "Ma'am, they're going to take him in the ambulance. Go on up there to the vehicle. No need to get closer to the building."

Tucker and I joined Dixxi and led her up the steep hill, to the waiting vehicle. It seemed like hours before the gurney reached the road and arrived at the back of the ambulance.

Luka was strapped in tight, face and arms burned so deeply I had to turn away. One of the EMTs held up a saline drip on one side of his head. He was unconscious, though seeming to try to waken. "Luka," Dixxi said. "Luka."

His eyes fluttered once, then twice. "Jacob . . ." he whispered through cracked lips, the flesh shiny and tight. Then he lapsed back into unconsciousness.

"Dix, you go with him," I said. "Tucker and I will talk to Mark and wait for . . ."

"Keira." Tucker nudged my side. I turned to see two firefighters pulling another gurney around, only this one had a closed body bag on it. A shudder ran through me as I realized it had to be Lev in it. That body had come out of the same apartment.

Dixxi sobbed out loud. "Lev, oh no, Lev . . ." She clutched at my arm.

"We need to figure out who did this," Tucker whispered, his face close to mine.

"I know." I gave Dixxi a quick hug. "Dix, go with Luka, do what you can." She wiped her face and nodded, knowing what I meant. This was no time to try to persuade the authorities to allow us to take Luka home, as we'd done with Greg the night of the football game. "Where's your car?"

"Up there." She pointed to the small compact skewed across the main road. "Keys are in it."

"Okay. Tucker, park Dixxi's car up on the side road at the lodge and leave it locked. You and I need to go to the deli and tell Mark."

"Mark's coming here," Dixxi reminded me. "And we need to find Jacob."

"No, Mark's not," I said. "We'll stop him." Tucker ran up to Dixxi's car as she entered the ambulance. "What hospital?" I asked the med tech.

"Emergency clinic up on 1577," the EMT answered. "Then, I don't know. Depends on when they can stabilize him. May need to airlift him to Austin or San Antonio."

"Dix, keep in touch." I turned away from the ambulance and climbed to the top of the hill to head off Mark. Rudy or someone had set out flares. A deputy was already out there in trademark orange vest, to wave off traffic.

"Hey, James," I said. "You seen the new deli owner drive up?"

"Nope. No one's come up yet," he said. "How come y'all are here?"

"Happened to be here when it happened."

"Damn."

"Yeah." I tried not to think of that body bag below, but then a thought occurred to me. This was a crime scene, or possible crime scene. "James, one of the guys died in the fire, he was sort of a friend. Where would they take the body?"

"Once the coroner gets here and pronounces, they'll take him on up to the emergency clinic for now," James explained. "Then, depending on the coroner and investigation by the fire marshal, they'll release him or send him over to Bexar County Medical Examiner's."

"Thanks. If Mark, the new deli owner, heads up this way," I said, "he's the guy's brother, okay? So be kind. Tell him I've gone to the deli looking for him."

"Oh man, Keira, really?"

I nodded. "Thanks, James."

"Take care, okay?"

"Sure." I trudged down the hill to meet Tucker at my car. Without a word, he climbed in the driver's seat and took charge.

"No Mark?"

"Not a sign," I said. "James Wood is up there. He was in school a couple of years ahead of me. He's a deputy here now. He's waving traffic off. He'll let Mark know to come to the deli."

"Jacob?"

"Not him, either."

"Have you tried calling Mark?"

I shook my head. "Not sure I can do that just yet."

"Hand me your phone."

I complied. "Speed dial ten," I said.

He dialed and waited a moment. "Mark, where are you? It's Tucker."

I didn't bother to listen in on the rest of the call. Instead, my brain was full of what happened and what needed to be done. What did Luka mean by saying "Jacob"? Was he safe? Where the heck was he?

I grabbed Tucker's arm. "Ask him where Jacob is."

"Is Jacob with you?" Tucker nodded. "Okay, we'll be there in a few. Please hang tight." He hung up and tossed me the phone. "Jacob's at the deli. They'd run out of milk at the apartment, so he drove up to get some. He was just about to leave."

I slumped in my seat, relieved that Jacob was safe, but still wondering . . . had Luka meant Jacob was responsible? Was he really involved in this? Damn it. I should've ridden with Dixxi, told the EMT we were sisters or cousins. We resembled each other enough. Then maybe I could've sensed something from Luka. Maybe I could've helped with some healing, stabilized him. The sight of his burned face haunted me. No, he was going to require more Talent than I knew how to channel yet.

"They're going to cordon off the area with crime scene tape, have a couple of deputies keep an eye on it tonight," Tucker said.

"Rudy?"

"Yeah, he filled me in."

"We need to get in there," I insisted. "It's less than an hour till sunset. Soon as it's dark enough, send Rhys and Ianto here. Have them shift into something nocturnal and do some sniffing about."

"Going to be hard to distinguish scents among all the burned wood and chemical smell," Tucker said.

"Do what you can. Then you and Niko can go out to the Ashkarian land. Maybe Liz can go with Rhys and Ianto—or with you two. I want this to stop."

"Hush, little sister, we'll do the best we can."

"Tucker, this is me calm," I said, my teeth grinding. "I've seen more death and destruction up close and personal in the last twelve months than I have in my entire fucking life. That's not counting the 'I'm thousands of years old and I'd like to die quietly now' kind of death I'm used to. This is balls-to-the-wall full-on vicious murder and sheer bloody brutality and I want this to stop. No one else dies on my fucking watch. Is that clear?"

I wasn't angry at my brother, or at anyone in particular really. Just that now, this was officially my turf, my responsibility, and damn it, no more violence. I didn't plan on becoming a one-woman Carrie Nation crusader, but this had to stop. We'd not even held our official reception and already, another person was dead and another burnt so badly that I could barely stand to remember what his face looked like. Four people dead, a boy shot just days before, and my own group shot at, as well. Whatever it took to make Rio Seco and the surrounding areas safe for my people, I was willing to do it.

CHAPTER THIRTY-SEVEN

"MARK, I'M SO SORRY." I sat next to the sobbing man, my arm around his shoulders. All that wild sexual energy he'd had at the game was now gone, submerged inside his grief. I kissed the top of his head, a gesture from his liege, then stood and nodded to Jacob. "With me, please."

Jacob stepped away from the wall, where he'd been hovering over Marcus.

"Ianto, please go check on the deli," I continued. "Make sure everything's okay there. You and Liz go on over to Bea's. I want to make sure she's home and safe. Anything hinky there, you get Rhys, phone the ranch. and get some backup. If everything's cool there, have Liz stay with Bea and then you twins can go scope out the scene of the fire. Get details from Tucker." I stared out the window at the darkening sky. "Most of the vampires should be awake now. Take Mark with you to the ranch? Keep him safe."

Ianto, who'd met us at the deli, nodded and put a hand on Mark's shoulder. "C'mon, Mark. Let's go. We'll get you to a safe place."

Mark twisted out of Ianto's grip and slid down the

bench seat. "I'm coming with you, Keira," he growled. "They killed my brother, hurt Luka, shot Greg."

I stared at the wolf, his eyes beginning to glow, anger sparking his change. "No." I threw out a hand and concentrated on the binding spell. I'd used it successfully in sparring; now I wanted to bind his wolf, bind his energy. The last thing I needed was an angry Fenrir going all Lon Chaney on us. The spell whispered in my head, energy swirling out of my hand and surrounding Mark, who stiffened and let out an angry howl, but a human one, not wolf.

"What did you do?" He gripped the edge of the table and strained. My energy field tightened around him, prohibiting the wolf from emerging.

Ianto gave him a small smile, recognizing the power and the spell. "Mark, please. Just come with me and we'll handle things."

Jacob stepped forward and spoke quietly but firmly. "Fenrir, you are not a fighter," he said. "Let our new liege and her people handle this, get our justice. Stay alive." Jacob's eyes burned fiercely in the gathering gloom. We'd not turned on any lights in the deli. "I will fight with them."

I started to protest, then caught Tucker's quick head shake. What was he trying to tell me?

Ianto placed his hand on Mark's shoulder again. "Come."

Mark slumped and with a sob, stood and let Ianto lead him away. At the door, he turned. "To the death, yes?"

I met his gaze. "Yes."

"I've called Niko," Tucker said. "He's heading out to the property with a couple of the security staff."

"You're not going with?"

Tucker eyed Jacob, then turned to me. "No, I'd best stay here."

"Fair enough." I flipped the light switch on the wall, illuminating the table area. "Jacob, please sit."

He hesitated but then complied, seating himself at the bench across from where Mark had been sitting. Tucker moved to stand behind him. Jacob didn't even blink at this.

"Third degree?" he asked flatly.

"Whatever you want to call it," I responded in a similar tone. "You tell me. You're the new guy to the pack, involved in this church of hatred. Those boys kill for their pins, don't they?"

Jacob said nothing, his gaze steady on mine. "What do you think?"

"I don't need to think. Tucker heard them talk about making their bones. Unless they're playing at a game they know nothing about, those boys are killers. They set up a fertilizer bomb at the apartment building, hightailed it back to the church. We were there to see them, smell them, hear them laughing at the fact that they'd 'finished.'" I sat across from him, never losing eye contact. What was hiding back there? He never flinched, never shifted his position or his own eye contact with me. No telltale twitches gave anything away. I was going to have to do this the hard way. "Tucker."

My brother heard the unspoken command, moving swiftly to hold Jacob's shoulders. Jacob blinked once, then settled back into the stolid, steady gaze. Who was he that he could be so calm? A fanatic? A True Believer? Somehow, his earlier explanation wore thin in his presence. This wasn't the aura of a religious fanatic nor even one of a rock-steady man of faith. Steely gaze held mine, almost taunting me to find the truth, composed in his knowledge of right but not righteousness.

I closed my eyes and let my senses unfurl, my barriers lower just enough. I reached forward, feeling, touching, hearing, scenting, tasting. Jacob tasted of citrus and oak, cleanliness of purpose and strength of will. The censer smoke of religion just a thin veil over what was behind. A flash of silver bright, a star surrounded by a circle. Jacob, right hand raised as he takes an oath. Oh, holy hells.

Pushing away from him, away from the table, I stood and stared. Tucker, alarmed, tightened his grip. I waved a hand, shaking my head. "No, let him be, Tucker."

"At your service, ma'am," Jacob parodied, tipping a nonexistent Stetson.

"So, Sergeant, how in all the bloody hells does a were-wolf become a Texas Ranger?"

Tucker, startled, knocked over a salt shaker on the counter behind him. He quickly picked up a pinch of salt and tossed it over his left shoulder.

Jacob seemed startled but not surprised at my words. "It's more like how does a Texas Ranger become a were-wolf," he said. "Come, Tucker, sit. Keira, sit, please."

Tucker turned to me for guidance. I sat back down, so he did the same, but to Jacob's right.

"What's with the hair?" I motioned toward his long blond hair, pulled back into a short, stubby ponytail, just like the night of the football game. "Not standard, is it?"

He shook his head. "I was undercover before this—drug gang. They pulled me off to—"

"To come here?" I questioned. "Do the Rangers know something about what's going on around here?" A thought occurred to me. "It's not terrorism, is it?"

"No, then Homeland Security would be involved. It's

good ol' boy bigotry, that's all." He shrugged. "You know the old saying 'One riot, one Ranger'?"

I nodded.

"I'd be the one Ranger . . . well, the one werewolf."

"You knew about the church, didn't you? That's why you came to Marcus."

"I did," Jacob said. "I got sent here to work within Company D, in San Antonio. Normally, I'm farther west—with Janna Matjeka's pack out of Big Bend, Redwolf tribe. I think your folk know them? Workwise, I report to Company E out of Midland. The captain here called for me because he—"

"Knew you were wolf," Tucker interjected.

"Yes."

"How?" I asked. "The Texas Rangers know you're a wolf?" I was trying to make this information fit. Trying to figure out how one of the oldest law enforcement groups in Texas knew about and condoned werewolves.

"It's a deep, dark secret," Jacob replied. "Only three others know. My captain, Company D's captain, and my sometimes partner, Andy Marks. I'd been mauled by a rogue wer while I was out on patrol, nearly died. Andy found me, took me to Janna. He's known her since they were high school age. She nursed me back to health."

"I didn't know a human could become wer."

"If they survive, they can," Tucker explained. "Thing is, wers rarely attack humans and humans who are attacked rarely survive." He watched Jacob carefully, keeping his expression neutral. I could tell most of my brother's moods just by looking at him. Tucker was a little surprised, a little pleased. "It takes a strong person to live after a wer attack."

Jacob simply bowed his head and said nothing for

a moment, as if acknowledging my brother's approval.

"So the church . . . ?" I prompted. Bully for Jacob's strength, but we had an agenda here—at least I did. I needed to know what the hell he knew.

Jacob continued his story. "Captain Hansen, our local guy, had heard stories about this church, but nothing enough to really warrant an investigation. He'd also twigged to the wolves."

"How?"

"One of his officers came to the office one day spouting some story about these wolf-looking dogs out by Canyon Lake."

My heart sank. Marcus and his people were even more oblivious than I'd first imagined. "They were seen?"

"By the lieutenant and his buddies—I know, I know, it was damned stupid of the wolves. I knew Marcus's pack was in the area and that he'd begun to mainstream his older kids. When Captain Hansen called me and I confirmed, he pulled me from the other investigation right away. We didn't want this to become a witch hunt."

Nor did I. If normal humans got wind of a werewolf pack for real, I could only imagine the kind of panic this could engender. "You think church members saw wolves and overreacted?"

Jacob nodded. "I do now. At first, I was just investigating the hazing, the whispered stories that this boys' club was a front. Miller and his gang run things. Have ever since his own father was preacher here."

"Then that Brotherhood is just a front for white supremacists, isn't it," Tucker stated.

I gasped. "That's what—"

"Yes," Jacob said, a low growl in the back of his throat. "I was blind, following a lead about a nonfatal beating of a Mexican kid. They try to keep the town, the church 'pure.' " He rubbed his eyes. "After I got accepted by Mark, I joined the church. Offered to help out with the boys' group. I've been hanging out with them for weeks—and nothing more than pranks happened. They just tried to force people to leave in disgust, in fear." He stared past us, eyes unfocused. "They've never killed before."

"They killed Margery," I said.

"And her husband and Maki." Jacob pushed away from the table and paced up the length of the area. "I wanted to tell Mark at that point—that I was a Ranger, but the captain forbid it. He's scared that anyone else knowing about me is one too many. He's already having to juggle too many reports, physicals, fake bloodwork so I can stay on the job. I even begged Janna as my Fenrir, to allow me to reveal myself to Marcus. She refused. She didn't wish to endanger our pack." His hands flew to his head, then down again, anxiety written in the tense muscles. "I thought—no, I didn't think. I was arrogant, careless. Figured I'd work this out. Figured I could handle it. But now Luka's badly injured, Lev's dead, and I had no fucking clue." He whirled and faced me. "They're good, Keira, good at hiding, good on multiple levels of deceit. I'm a professional, and I never realized they were playing me. I never got to be in any of the secret meetings—only in fake ones." He slapped his hand against the wooden support beam. "Damn it, I could have come to you. I should have—"

"Nothing," Tucker said. "You should have nothing." He stood and joined Jacob, placing a hand on his arm. "You did what you could. No one is infallible. Not even a Ranger."

"Not even a werewolf who's a Ranger," I added, getting up to join them. "Jacob, what's done is done. Perhaps things would have worked out differently if you'd defied your captain and your Fenrir—but you are a wer and a Ranger and you've sworn oaths." I gazed into his eyes, trying to make him see that I understood his agony. "Adam and I are your lieges, as well, Jacob. I forgive you."

He sagged against the support beam, head bowed. "I'm sorry," he whispered. "Truly sorry."

"I know," I said and laid a gentle hand on his head. "C'mon, we need to strategize, let's move forward." He nodded and stood, giving his head a quick shake as if to re-don the mantle of the Texas Ranger. It worked.

"You know that I really was only being a friend to Bea," he said quietly. "I wasn't trying anything, or leading her on. I was just . . ."

"Offering a friendly shoulder?" I ventured.

"Yes. I realized too late that she'd developed a crush, even now that she's pregnant."

"For fuck's sake," I said. "Does everyone know she's pregnant?"

He shrugged. "I'm a wolf, Keira."

"The wolves here don't seem to know . . . except for Dixxi, but she twigged at the game."

Jacob nodded. "Sadly, this pack isn't much of a pack," he said. "Marcus is a good man but not what they need as a leader. They're less wolf than human, I'm afraid."

"We'd discussed that very thing," Tucker said. "So what now? I'm all for storming the castle."

"Ditto," I said. "I don't need any more evidence. Jacob, you in or are you going to be Ranger on this?"

Jacob's eyes slitted as his jaw set. "I'm in—but not as

Ranger. This is pack business." I nodded at him as I took his meaning. He was working outside the Texas law now and within pack law. Good.

"Okay, let's lock up this place and head out. We can meet Niko up at the property and go in the back way."

I CLOSED the front door of the deli, locking it with the keys Jacob gave me. "Damn, this strip center is looking like the last gasp of abandonment," I said, motioning around me. "I mean, check it out—the café's closed and locked up. The deli's closed and locked up. The laundry's under renovation until August. The video store's closed for vacation." I sighed. Hell, even the parking lot lights seemed dimmer, faded somehow against the night sky.

"It's summer, sis," Tucker reminded me gently. "This happens."

"It's just so . . ."

"Sad," Jacob said. "This is a sad place now."

I turned in surprise. "You feel the sadness?"

"There's been a lot of anguish here, death, misery. I can smell it. It lingers."

"You can smell like that in human shape?" I asked. "Lev's abilities were much less sharp when he wasn't wolf."

"With all due respect, Keira," Jacob said, "Like I said, there's too little wolf about that pack. We may not be natural shapeshifters, but my pack is still real wolf."

Tucker nodded in agreement. "Your wolf is much stronger. I've felt it all along." He motioned toward the buildings. "You're right about this place. It does need a huge cleansing."

"I thought I was the only one who felt that way about the center," I muttered and shook my head. "I'm going to call Isabel—not because of what y'all just said, but I want her to go help Luka out. Then perhaps she can help me with the cleansing."

"She's our aunt," explained Tucker as he climbed into my Rover, Jacob getting into the back.

"A healer. That's good. The boy's in bad shape. I took the liberty of sending one of the pack women to the clinic," he said. "To sit with Dixxi and Luka. I called in another favor, too."

"Oh?" I tossed Tucker my keys, gave Jacob back his.

"Lev," he said. "Normally, he'd be autopsied as a crime victim." Crap, I hadn't thought of that. "I called the captain, he's pulling a few strings and taking charge of Lev's body as part of an ongoing need-to-know investigation."

"You can do that?"

"Evidently," he said. "Cap's been in this area for nearly his full twenty. He knows where bodies are buried. He wants to keep this quiet as much as I do."

Logical . . . and practical. One more hurrah for the Rangers being on our side in this. "Let's get going," I said. "I'll call Isabel as we drive."

As I pressed the speed dial button and hit Call, a wave of wrongness washed over me, just like I'd felt at the football game. I turned and Jacob's eyes rolled back as he slumped onto the floorboards, body twisted and twitching. "Jacob," I yelled and turned in my seat. Reaching down, I touched his hand, trying to force calm and serenity into him. Instead, I got a rush of rank energy, dark, rotten, and as twisted as Jacob's body. "Tucker, he's been poisoned. Something—damn it, I can't. Drive, Tucker, get us to the ranch."

I held on to Jacob's hand and the phone with the other.

Isabel's voice had been saying "hello" for at least a minute when I finally heard it.

"Keira, what is it?" She immediately went into action mode. "I'm packing now. The plane's already warming up."

"How?" I babbled.

"Please," she admonished. "You're the heir, dearling. I've been getting ready to come to you since this morning. I had to wait for a plane to get here. Minerva was off somewhere." She didn't volunteer where Gigi had gone, nor did I ask. That wasn't important.

"I've got a young werewolf in an emergency clinic nearly burned to death. He's in desperate need of a master healer, and I've another wolf right here, poisoned by something. How fast can you get here?"

"We'll take off in ten," she said, her voice turning businesslike. "It will still be close to three hours."

"Damn it." Jacob's twitches grew more violent and I held on tighter. "Fast as you can, Aunt." I thumbed the End Call button and tossed the phone on the floor, slipping my body back to the rear of the car. I fell against the left side as Tucker took a turn.

"Only fifteen more minutes," he said. "Fuck."

"What?" I managed to wedge myself onto the floor and hold on to Jacob, one hand holding his jaw. "Fifteen minutes isn't bad."

"No, not that. My phone's buzzing," he said. "In my pocket."

"Ignore it. I'm going to try to see if I can stabilize him. My binding is still on him, so that may be what delayed the poison reaction."

"What do you think—"

"No idea," I said. "I'm shite at poisons. He wasn't

eating or drinking anything at the deli when we got there, but who knows, maybe he'd had something before. Now hush."

I maneuvered my body on top of Jacob's, hands now holding his face as I concentrated on building a stasis, increasing the binding to more of a neutral holding energy. His colors had gone from the clear, sharp citrus to a muddy green-black winding its way through his system. I pressed my lips to his forehead. "Slow," I whispered. *"Mynd yn araf."* I lapsed into Welsh, stronger at spellcasting in my mother tongue. The dark color became sluggish, thick. I forced my energy around it, gold-white light weaving and braiding a cage, stifling its progress. A minute stretched into two, into four, and finally, the invading poison just stopped, held in place. Jacob's eyes fluttered open, then closed again, a soft sigh as his body relaxed into sleep.

My own phone began to buzz against the floorboard. "I've got it," I said and reached over Jacob's still head to grab it. "What?" I muttered into the receiver without checking the caller ID.

"Where are you?" Adam's voice thundered.

Glancing out the window, I took my bearings. "About five minutes away. I've got Jacob here, he's been—"

"Poisoned, I know," Adam said.

Tucker jerked the wheel as he heard Adam's answer, his preternatural hearing just as sharp as ever.

"How?"

"Not now. Get here and I'll explain. Is he stable?"

"Yes. I managed to bind the poison and put him in a sort of stasis. Isabel's on her way."

"So I gathered. She phoned me a few minutes ago wanting to make sure I knew to prep the runway."

I'd forgotten about that. "Thank the bloody stars Gigi saw fit to equip the ranch with a private airstrip," I said. "Did everyone else get there?"

Adam paused so long I thought I'd lost the call. "Hello?"

"I'm here, and yes. I'll explain when you get here." He ended the call.

Explain what? Tucker didn't even bother to talk to me but forced the car to move even faster down the treacherous winding road. Something, indeed, was up.

CHAPTER THIRTY-EIGHT

"H E POISONED JACOB," Adam said as we hustled Jacob into the living room and laid him down on one of the couches.

"He who?" I asked. I arranged Jacob's arms to his side. Crossing them on his chest was just too macabre, though probably more comfortable. "Isabel's on her way," I said as an aside. "I've got him in a temporary stasis. Not sure how long it'll hold."

Adam joined me. He touched Jacob's forehead. "I think he'll be all right," he said. "His blood flows sluggishly. Perhaps that will save him." Adam turned to me. "Marcus did it."

I whirled to face him. "What? How?"

"Wolfsbane." Mark's ragged voice came from behind me. He was sitting in one of the dining room chairs to our left. I'd not noticed him there, his aura suppressed by grief and what? Guilt, perhaps.

"Why on earth?" Words failed me.

"I thought he was behind the murders," he said in a small voice. "He was new, arrogant."

"Not done, Fenrir, not done," I said. "Poison's the weapon of a coward, Mark. It's not elegant, nor was it called for. Jacob's on our side. If you'd suspected him, you should have called him on it, called him out. You're the Fenrir, the leader of the pack." I meant no disrespect in calling up the name of that old tune, but wanted to rub the man's nose in reality.

Mark livened a little, anger slicing through him. I felt the energy change, but just a little. "How? He was seducing Bea right out from under Lev's nose. He's a member of that damned church. He's part of it, I just know."

"You know nothing of the sort." I attacked. "Marcus Ashkarian, you are one poor excuse for a Fenrir. You've let the pack get soft, weak, interbred too much so that you lost the wolf. You're not a fighter or a warrior and have misled yourself by your immersion in books and research. Not that any of those things are inherently bad, but in a werewolf pack, you must be the supreme leader, leading by example and strength. Instead, you've channeled all your energy into other things. There is no backbone to your pack and they are lost. Bringing in new wolves did nothing but lose them even more. And you, deciding to 'man up' and poison a person you suspected—not done, Mark, not done." I repeated my earlier admonishment. This was not the powerful Fenrir I'd felt at the football game. He'd channeled his energy, all his potential power into what? Hatred, jealousy?

He hung his head and refused to look at me.

"Yes, go on, feel shamed. You deserve to." I knew I was brutal and hurtful, and I damn well meant it. "Now get out of here and let us tend to Jacob and to your mess."

"Mess?"

"If you hadn't wanted to fit in so badly to the community at White Rock—which is rotten to the core—no one would be dead. No one would have been a target. I'm not taking you to task now on this, not doing anything more until we finish, but consider yourself on notice, Marcus."

Egad, I was sounding like the bitch from hell, like Gigi, even. I almost retracted my angry words until Adam caught my eye and shook his head. No, I was right, angry and perhaps a little overboard, but right. A leader must lead. If I'd learned anything at Gigi's knee these past few months, it was that. Before my Change, I'd been a child, adult in human years but frankly, left to play, enjoy, whine, and bitch all I wanted. No more. I might not have chosen this path, but thanks to my Clan leader's genetic machinations, I was heir, and I'd be damned if I didn't act it.

"C'mon, Tucker, Adam, I think this calls for the cavalry. We're going to—" Before we could leave the room, Tucker's knees buckled and he fell to the floor. His head rose, mouth falling open in a tormented howl. I felt the agony, destruction, and anguish in the wordless sound, emotion a *bean sidhe* could not match. The hollow, screaming cry surrounded me, swept me up in its desolation. The knowledge slammed into me a second later. Niko. Niko was taken. Adam rushed to me and Tucker and grabbed us both in an embrace, his eyes full of rage and tears. "Niko," I whispered, my own voice echoing the pain in my brother's. Our companion, his partner: hurt, taken somewhere dark. He called to us.

"Go, now," Adam commanded, vampire voice and Sidhe energy entwined, power rushing through us, building, merging, forcing a pressure so strong it crushed the very sound from the air. Our surroundings shimmered and danced as we somehow moved through the In-Between, the spaces belonging to Faery, outside the realm of humanity and their earth. My bones ached with longing and disgust: the part of me that was birthed in Faery needed it like a drug, the part of me that was Kelly rejected it. I held my breath against the alienness as Tucker's howl echoed in the empty infinite, surrounding us and keeping us anchored to him.

Reality popped back in a furious rush of air and sound. We were at the Ashkarian property, in the same area where those boys had been practicing target shooting.

"Nice aim," I said, my voice shaky as I took my bearings, trying to shed the lingering effects of Faery. "Didn't know you could do that."

Adam stood, his movements slightly awkward, not his usual graceful self. "Neither did I," he admitted. "Where are we?"

"Back end of the Ashkarian land." I crouched next to my brother, still hunched in a miserable ball. "Tucker?"

His head tilted up, his eyes red-rimmed, pupils blown large. With a sniff, he announced, "Blood." Tucker stood in one powerful stretch, all six foot four of him alert and alive, hair no longer bound in a neat braid, red tresses waving like a matador's cape in the breeze—my brother, the hunter at the ready. "There," he growled.

We looked where he pointed. Just below the piled rocks and empty beer cans used as targets, two bodies . . . or what was left of them.

"That's—"

"The two security staffers we sent with Niko," Adam finished.

I stepped closer to the bodies, partially burned, cut, and otherwise abused. My fists clenched. I whirled around. "Let's go, let's get those bastards."

"Niko's blood is also here." Adam rose from a crouch, where he'd been examining the ground. "Signs of a struggle. He's still alive. Bound in silver."

"As were they," I said of the two bodies. "Garroted,

the both of them, with silver razor wire and bound in silver chains."

"They know," Adam said, fangs extending.

"They must," I agreed. "They knew what to use. Heads nearly severed."

Tucker no longer listened but paced the ground, sniffing and whimpering behind his low humming howl. I'd never seen it before, but I knew what was coming. I knew what my brother had been, so many centuries ago. "Adam, I'll need your help focusing him."

Adam simply nodded and like me, closed in on Tucker, not touching him. My brother's T-shirt was ripped as if someone had clawed across his chest. He'd taken a strip of the cotton and tied it around his forehead to keep the hair out of his eyes. Those eyes. Normally a clear, amused blue, twinkling with kindness, now dark and vicious, the red no longer just irritation from tears but a sign of warning, crimson glowing in the light of the waning moon. Barefoot, he stalked past the empty beer cans once used as targets, up over the ridge, and into the mesquite and oak-riddled ground that belonged to the church. Up ahead, the lights of the building shone clear in the hot night, no sign of people. No sign of anyone.

We followed, silent in our determination.

"What is he doing?" whispered Adam as Tucker gained ground ahead of us.

"Going Berserk," I answered in equally quiet tones. "I've never seen it, but he's told me about it. He sees nothing and no one now. He's only focused on one thing."

Adam increased his pace as did I. We were nearing the landscaped area of the property, just behind the church buildings. "He wants revenge."

I nodded. "It's not going to be pretty and I'm not planning on stopping him."

"Nor am I."

The eerie quiet wrapped around us, dark corners and shadows in the sporadically illuminated church campus. Niko had to be here, but where?

Sweat dripped down my forehead as the oppressive heat made itself known. I'd ignored it, my concentration on Tucker and saving Niko. Like my brother, I ripped the bottom of my T-shirt and tied the strip around my forehead. My hair was already in a high braid.

Adam arched an eyebrow at me, then motioned to my shirt. "May I?"

I nodded and he tore another strip off the bottom. My shirt now skimmed my waist, an inch or so above my shorts. I'd not come prepared to fight, wasn't wearing my sparring attire, but that no longer mattered. Adam took the torn cloth and twisted it around his hair, tying it back from his face. Vampires didn't sweat, but loose hair in a fight could blind or be grabbed by an enemy.

Tucker stopped in his tracks and dropped down, his fingers brushing the rough concrete of a sidewalk. Head shaking and muscles quivering, he raised one fist, a command for us to stop, breath coming in short huffs. Not completely in Berserker mode yet, I thought. He was still capable of rational action. He bent low to the ground and sniffed around again. With a jerk, he stood and ran.

Adam and I broke into full-out runs, our own more-than-human speeds no match for my brother's. "Why doesn't he shapeshift?" Adam asked as we wove through the buildings, heading straight for the main church.

"No idea," I said as I rounded a corner. "Berserker mode is human, don't know—"

With a howl and scream of rage, Tucker tore off the remains of his shirt and stormed the church's office door. He pulled on the handle and flung it open. If it had been locked he would have torn it off its hinges. He raced into the building, Adam and I close on his heels. I stumbled on entry, Niko's pain reverberating within me. He was close, so close. I grabbed Adam's arm as we ran.

Two corridors later, we turned the corner. Four men faced us, rifles at the ready.

They fired.

CHAPTER THIRTY-NINE

I HIT THE FLOOR, reactions enhanced by fight training and my heritage. Adam leaped over me, reaching at least one of the attackers. Tucker's body shook with the impact of bullets, his enraged howls echoing in the small hallway. I barely made out the sign behind the men, above a set of double doors: BIBLE STUDY ROOM. I laughed at the irony.

With a crack, Tucker snapped the neck of one man as Adam did the same to another. I rolled and pointed with my hand. "Cover!" I shouted as I let loose a flashbang spell. Tucker ignored me, but Adam complied, shutting his eyes and sliding past the last two men to the doorway. Tucker, eyes tearing, tore the weapons from the men's hands, tossing them in my direction. I pushed them away, and as my brother killed one man, I snapped the neck of the other.

We burst through the doors, Tucker tearing one of them off its hinges. Robert Earl Miller, his wife, Janey, and two others, both men, not high school boys. All of them faced Niko, his body tied to a small child's chair, long legs bent awkwardly, ankles fastened to the chair's short legs. He was unconscious. Bruised and a little bloody, but alive.

Tucker led the way, his howls louder now as he could

see his mate, helpless and still bleeding. He pulled out the first man, kneeing him in the crotch, then the face, kicking him to the side before breaking his neck.

"Wait!" Miller yelled, a rifle forced against Niko's head. "The bullet's silver."

I held my position, just inside the door. Adam, who'd grabbed the second man, held him tightly but did not move. Tucker quivered on the verge of pure animal rage, enough of his humanity still present for him to hold.

"I will blow his head to pieces," Miller warned, his demeanor as calm as if he were stating the day's crop prices.

His wife shook next to him, her mouth trembling as if she were ready to cry. "Rob, no," she whispered. "Let him go."

"And then what, Janey?" Miller threw out the words in fury, all his composure disappearing. "They'll just let us go? Do you think I'm that stupid, woman?"

No one uttered a sound. Tucker's muscles still twitched, he was that close to pouncing. His energy held tight only by force of will. I sent out a soothing pulse to him, trying to let him know that no matter what, we'd save Niko and destroy these people.

"We didn't mean for this to go so far, Rob. Please." Janey's pleading voice did nothing to sway her husband.

Miller growled a human wordless sound of disgust at his wife. "Yes, I did. These people are unnatural. They can't live here."

"Even though we're as white as you are?" I taunted. "Niko's heritage is purer than yours, I'd wager."

"We only wanted to make those foreigners leave," Janey tried to explain. "The Ashkarians. Tried to hurt the boys in school . . . then—"

"Then what? You saw wolves on their property and you just thought you'd shoot them? Nice tactics you have there. What the hell did that prove?"

Her husband gave me a brutish grin. "Target practice. Then that one half-turned into human after it was shot. Freaked my boys out. We'd seen some dog-wolves with them folk one day out to the lake. I put two and two together—"

"And came up with murder?" I spat at him. "Did your boys enjoy blowing up the building? Will they sleep well tonight knowing they've killed a man, nearly destroyed a boy? Will they?"

Miller squirmed a little under my gaze but didn't back down.

"They're evil," Janey stated flatly. "Creatures of the devil."

"No more so than you are," I countered. "Evil lives in humans as well as in those not of your species."

Her eyes grew wide. Miller jammed the gun's muzzle deeper into Niko's skin. "I don't know what you people are, but silver hurts you."

Tucker's low growl reverberated throughout the room, its sound almost outside human hearing range. I sent him a wordless plea. No matter how fast he could move, how fast Adam could, Miller's trigger-happy finger could easily jerk, sending a deadly bullet into Niko's skull—something I wasn't capable of fixing.

Behind Miller, a poster of an extremely Caucasian Jesus in bright blue robes caught my eye. The Jesus bent over a sleeping child, some verse or other inscribed below. The words themselves hidden by Miller's head. How could I break this stalemate? I'd fought standoffs before, in sparring, in training only, never when real lives were

on the line. Flashbangs, mage-fire, wizarding spells—al
those I knew and could use, but any of them relied or
noise, light, fire, and could just as easily condemn Nik
as a physical attack from the three of us.

Adam's captive twisted in his grip, a useless struggle
He whispered into the man's ear. "You destroyed those
who were mine. Now, you pay." Adam snapped the man'
neck and let the body drop to the floor.

To my right, Tucker whined, muscles tautening for
spring. "No, brother," I said in a calm voice. "Not yet.'
He wriggled and twitched, all sense of humanity stripped
from his eyes and expression. Was he on the verge o
shifting?

"Well, then, what do we do now?" Miller taunted
"I've got you-all by the short hairs." He chuckled and
traced the gun barrel down Niko's cheek. "He is a pretty
one, if you like that sort of thing."

My own lips drew back into a snarl. "Short hairs, my
ass," I said, perhaps unwisely. "You're not getting out o
here, Miller."

"Neither is your pretty boy," he tossed back at me. "I
I go, he goes."

"Why this far?" I had to ask. "Why take it so bloody
far as killing? I thought you Christians believed in saving
lives, not ending them."

Miller spat on the ground. "Not for your kind," h
said. "You're not even people."

Here we go again, I thought. Why did it always come
down to some sort of ridiculous prejudice, based on noth
ing but assumptions and hatred? No sense in arguing with
a madman—or a fanatic, either description would do.

I scanned the room for some way out of this mess
Tiny child-size chairs, a teacher's scratched wooder

desk. Colorful children's drawings pinned to a bulletin board. Printed Bible verses decorating another wall, interspersed with common child's prayers.

Honor thy father and thy mother . . .

God in heaven hear my prayer,
keep me in thy loving care . . .

Now I lay me down to sleep,
I pray the Lord my soul to keep . . .

One poster showed Jesus, a lamb in one arm, crook in the other, shepherding a flock of sheep. Sheep, that's exactly what these people were, following a dogma of hatred, teaching found nowhere in their New Testament. They disgusted me, these blood purity advocates, caught up in twisted beliefs, fanatics nearing the evil of Hitler, of the Young Turks, of all those who destroy people who are not like them. My own people were no saints free of bloodshed, but our wars tended to be based on true hatreds, revenge, territory—not that any of those reasons mattered more, but they seemed less tenuous than basing hatred on something so very untrue.

Hear my prayer . . .

Indeed. I hoped someone somewhere heard their prayers and could salvage their souls, because they weren't surviving this day.

Now I lay me down to sleep . . .

Then it struck me: a sleep spell. Not one used as offense or defense, simply a way to help enable sleep when it eluded you. How well would it work on humans? No idea, I'd never tried, but no time like the present to try.

Sleep, I thought. *Rest, relax, sleep.* I focused my attention on both the Millers, letting my facial muscles relax, my expression morphing into a less aggressive one. *"Mynd i gysgu,"* I whispered under my breath. "Go to sleep." Adam's brow rose as he recognized the words. Tucker twitched in place, his brows narrowing. I didn't want him to be affected, though in Berserker mode, I doubted he would be. I sent out wave after wave of energy, directing it toward the Millers. Janey's eyelids fluttered. Miller's brow wrinkled, his hold on the rifle tightened. A few breaths more. Silently "pushing" the spell, I kept a sharp eye on Miller's gun and its position. Tucker, to my right, did the same. A heartbeat, two, three, four. Miller swayed, only a brief movement, but the barrel of the gun dipped down, and in the space of half a breath, my brother pounced, becoming wolf as he leaped, mouth closing over the gun barrel and flinging it across the room. Adam went to Niko. I jumped and grabbed Janey Miller's arms, pinning them to her side.

"Surrender, I surrender," she said in a whine. "Leave my husband alone!"

Tucker was on top of Robert Earl Miller, his jaws around the man's throat. He stopped at her plea, eyes glancing once to her and then to me. I blinked and nodded to him. Janey Miller slumped against me. "Thank you," she whispered. Then Tucker tore out her husband's throat.

CHAPTER FORTY

"YOU PROMISED," Janey wailed, sagging in my hold. I let her fall to the floor. Tucker, now shifted back to human, his rage spent, went to Niko's side, tearing away the silver chains binding him. Adam stepped away, allowing Tucker to take over.

"I promised nothing." I kept my words brief as I watched Tucker gently laying Niko on the floor, holding him, whispering words of love, his big hand stroking Niko's hair. I turned my attention to the cowering woman. "You and your group shot and killed three innocent people. You wounded a boy, sixteen years old. You blew up an apartment building killing at least one and maybe more. You kidnapped my brother-in-law. Why? For the sake of your stupid blood purity, your white supremacy? Stupidity, arrogance. You and your kind poison those people in this community who wish only to be kind, true Christians. I have nothing to do with your so-called faith, yet I know its tenets are not to kill, to wound, to hurt. To do unto others as you would have them do unto you. Aren't you supposed to love, despite others' failings?"

Janey Miller crouched by the remains of her spouse and sobbed, her face hidden in her pale hands. "My husband."

"A killer." I turned away from her in disgust. "Is he all right?" I asked Tucker.

Tucker nodded and buried his head in Niko's hair.

"He's still unconscious but will be fine," Adam said. "He'll need to feed, regain his strength."

I surveyed the blood-spattered room, the rich iron tang now making its way into my senses as I came down from battle-ready, the bodies. "What the hell are we going to do with this mess?"

Adam eyed the dead and one living. "Greta and Boris?"

I shrugged. "Good a plan as any." I pulled my phone out of my shorts pocket and dialed my brother Rhys. "Heya," I began, intending to ask him to bring Tucker's van so we could get everyone home.

"We're actually here," Rhys said before I could continue. "Just pulling up now."

"How?"

"You disappeared, Keira," he said. "It didn't take a genius to figure out you somehow located Niko. I phoned home and got one of the seers to help pinpoint you."

"Damn, that was some good thinking, Rhys," I said. "They could do it this far?"

"Gigi helped," he said. "Once you Mark us, we'll be able to find you, too."

That made a buttload of sense. "C'mon then, we're in the back of the main building. Bible study room."

Rhys chuckled. "Only you."

"What can I say," I said. "See if you can find keys to the church van on your way, okay?"

"Done." He ended the call.

I shoved my phone back into my pocket and knelt down next to my brother and Niko. Adam joined us. I placed a hand on Niko's chest, feeling deep inside him, trying to find the spark of what animated him. Magick, not blood, not heartbeat. Adam had let me do this to him last year. I'd felt no heartbeat then, but now I knew that had only been a glamour, as he'd been hiding his Sidhe heritage from me. Niko, though, had once been human, a boy, a teenager, dying of plague during the end of the first Elizabeth's reign, rescued by Adam, who'd been captivated by his beauty. There, the spark. There was little I could do here, but as long as it held steady, he'd be fine.

"Tucker, your wrist? I think it would be best to do this now."

He extended a wrist to Niko, a gesture I'd seen many times, mostly as a Mark of love and belonging, now as a means of feeding for Niko. Though still unconscious, Niko stirred as the familiar scent of his partner reached him. Fangs appeared in his mouth and he latched on, rich blood flowing from my brother's veins into his mouth. Satisfied, I stood and approached Janey Miller, who was still cowering by her husband's bloody and torn body.

"What am I going to do with you?" I mused. "You're sheriff here, not exactly a low-profile person. You can't just disappear."

She whimpered. "Don't kill me. I'll leave, I promise."

"And do what?" I leaned in, pushing my face close to hers. "What will you do, Jane Miller? How will you explain all this?" I indicated the room, the bodies. "I can't let you out in the world knowing about us, about what happened."

She shrank against the wall, eyes terrified. "I don't want to die."

"Did Margery Flax want to die? Did Stephen? Did Maki?" She cringed at my words. "Those were their names, Jane. Those three wolves, also people. Margery and Stephen were newlyweds, looking forward to a new life together. Did you know she was pregnant, Jane?" The erstwhile sheriff burst into tears, once again hiding her face.

"I never knew they were killing," she wailed. "Only thought they were scaring people away."

"Ignorance of the actions of your husband and his men is no excuse, Sheriff. Isn't that what you say about the law? You've broken many laws these past days. More than just human law, but the laws of all sentient kind." I couldn't leash my anger, my resentment that these pitiful assholes used guns and intimidation because they thought they were better than others. Fear and loathing in White Rock. Film at eleven . . . or never, because no one would ever learn about this.

"Hey there, sis," Rhys's voice broke into my diatribe. "Got keys to a twelve-seater van. Ianto is standing guard outside, Liz is keeping Tucker's van running in case we need to leave quickly." He paused a moment, studied the room, and whistled. "Damnation, Keira, what happened?"

"Later," I said. "Load up the bodies in that van, will you?"

"Done." He moved past me and Jane, hefted one body over his shoulder, then snagged Miller's foot and dragged him away, leaving a trail of blood. Jane whimpered.

"Quiet," I warned. "Adam, could you please help Rhys?"

He stood, quietly picked up the body of the man he'd killed, and followed Rhys out the door. Tucker still bent over Niko, who was now awake and still feeding. "Be careful there, brother. You'll need your own strength."

Tucker broke out into a delighted grin. "I know my limits." He pulled his wrist away and helped Niko to a sitting position. Niko blinked and took in the room.

"I suppose I have you to thank?" he asked me.

"All of us," I said. "We'll fill you in later."

"What are you going to do with her?" Tucker nodded to Jane. "She's our only remaining witness."

"Yeah. I know."

Tucker stood and began straightening the room.

I stood and pulled Janey up with me. "You're coming with me," I said. "Tucker, could you hang on to her for a moment?"

"Gladly."

I concentrated on the room and cast a cleaning spell my aunt had taught me. With a whoosh of energy, most of the blood was gone. I cast it again and the rest disappeared.

"Neat trick that," Niko grinned. "You do windows, too?"

"Funny vampire," I shot back. "You good to stand?"

He nodded and slowly stood. "Yes, I'm fine," he said. He gave me an abbreviated bow. "Thank you."

"Anything for family," I said with a smile. I turned to Janey and put my hand on her forehead. She tried to back away from my touch, so I gripped her other arm. Tucker, who'd let her go when I approached, grabbed on to both of her arms again.

"What are you going to do?" she whispered through dry lips.

"Nothing you'll remember," I said. *"Anghofia."* Rumbles of subsonic sound accompanied my command to forget. "Remember nothing and no one." I forced energy through her, envisioning her brain as a jumble of color and sound, the wave of the spell erasing it, muting it. She sagged. Tucker caught her before she could fall. He eased her to the floor just as Adam and Rhys returned to the room.

"We got the bodies in the hall, too. All in the van," Rhys said as Adam began picking up weapons and ammo. "Now what?"

"Drive the van to a good cliff on a curvy road," I said. "Just like before with Boris and Greta Nagy. Crash the van over the side and throw a bit of mage-fire to make sure it burns well and thoroughly. There'll be enough left for the sheriff's department to identify, but not enough to determine cause of death or much of anything else."

Rhys nodded. "No accelerant residue."

"What about her?" Tucker, his oversized body perched on one of the undersized children's chairs, indicated the unconscious Janey on the floor at his feet.

"Damn it." I scrubbed my face with my hands. I didn't want to have to kill her, but what could I do? "Rhys, could you leave her at the accident site? As if she were in the van, too?"

Rhys studied Janey for a moment before answering. "I could, Keira, but frankly, that'd probably raise more questions than not."

I looked at Adam. His face was impassive, but his eyes locked on mine: one ruler to another. I turned away and stared at gentle Jesus and his lamb on the wall.

What choice did I have? The small blond woman lay still on the floor. Her face slack, free of guilt, of conscious decision. Was this what I'd come to? Judge, jury, executioner? For a sick moment, visions of my great-great-grandmother passed before me, a woman who always did whatever it took to keep the Kellys safe. Was that my job now, too? I considered the options. Leaving Janey in her car to be discovered at the accident site might work—but why would she have lost her memory? We could cause another "accident" with her, crashing her car into a tree, a rock, even down the same ravine . . .

No. Too many "accidents" usually involve a greater degree of investigation.

Damn it. Would this never end well? If I wanted no repercussions, no chance of discovery, there was only one answer. I thought of Adam's now truly-dead vampires, the dead wers, and Luka. They were "evil creatures of the devil" and, to her warped mind, didn't deserve to live. She claimed she hadn't known. But if she had, would she have done anything? If we hadn't arrived, Janey Miller would have let her husband destroy Niko right before her eyes and done nothing to stop him. And even with her memory wiped clean, Janey Miller would still be Janey Miller and hate anyone she thought "different" or "unnatural." Old Joe had known: there was something deeply wrong with this woman. Evil in her being.

I straightened my shoulders and faced Rhys. "She goes in the church van," I said.

He nodded. "I'll take care of everything, except you need to do another clean-up job on the hall on the way out. Adam, you might double-check for spent casings out there while she does her Mrs. Clean thing." Adam and I both nodded in acknowledgment. "Then y'all take Tucker's van and get back to the ranch. I'll meet you there after I'm done."

"I'll send a car—" I began.

"No, no need to risk any more exposure," Rhys said. "I'll shift and go cross-country. Won't take me long."

"What about the blood?" Tucker asked. "I can still smell it."

I sniffed. "Yeah, it should dissipate soon. It's good enough for humans."

"Not for Luminol," Rhys said.

"No one will suspect anything happened here," Adam said. "Their cars are in the parking lot. They met here and left. That is all. Why closely inspect anything?"

"Right. There's no reason they'd hire a forensics team to come out here from Austin. These people will have been in a tragic accident." I moved away from Tucker and Janey and surveyed the room. It looked just like we'd found it, sans tied-up vampire and men with guns. A nice, cheery little classroom, ready to teach the next generation about love, Jesus, and hopefully, nothing about white supremacy. I eyed the torn-off door. Three sets of hinges hung from the doorframe, screws still embedded in chunks of wood. No hiding that damage. "Rhys, can you fix this?"

He shrugged. "Can't do anything about the door, but the door frame is fine. I'll just remove the pins from the hinges and take them and the door. It will look like the door was removed for repair or something."

"Excellent. While you're at it, leave a note on the pastor's desk. Say you're taking the van and sign it "Robert Earl Miller.' Leave his car keys there."

"Better yet, I'll add that a little horseplay damaged the door, that I've taken it to repair and will bring it back tomorrow."

"Even more excellent, Rhys, and . . . thanks."

He laughed. "A good brother helps you move . . . a better brother helps you move bodies."

I rolled my eyes. "Let's hope we never have to do this sort of thing again," I said.

"C'mon, guys, let's leave Rhys to his carpentry and get the hell out of here."

CHAPTER FORTY-ONE

L IZ WAS IN THE ranch's van, motor running, as I exited the building after a final check of the corridors for evidence of carnage. Adam sat in the second seat. Tucker and Niko huddled together in the back. "Heya, Keira," she said. "You okay?"

"Well as I can be," I said and climbed aboard to sit next to Adam.

Ianto, who sat next to Liz, eyed me in concern. "This isn't you," he said. "Not the you I'm used to. Adam told me what happened in there."

"Better get used to it, twin. I'm the heir now, no longer a kid. I have to do what has to be done."

"Impressive," Liz piped up. "Kudos to you, cousin. You've learned a lot."

"That I have, Liz," I replied. "Too bad I had to put some of it to actual use." I looked behind me, at our two men, huddled in each other's arms, neither giving in to unconsciousness yet. Niko might have said he was okay, but he was still exhausted, beat. "Boys, sleep," I said. "Isabel should be here in no time. She'll watch over Niko properly."

Tucker groaned, the activities of the past hour finally

getting to him. "Damn," he whispered, cradling Niko's head to him. "I can last, but Niko—" Damn it. Niko had fainted. Stupid vampire, telling me he was all right when he wasn't.

"I can donate—" Ianto began.

"No, wait." I stopped him as he started to crawl over the seat to Tucker's side. "Let me."

"Why you?" Ianto asked. "Either Liz or I could."

"We're fixing to get blood bonded anyway," I said. "Plus, my blood is different from yours."

Adam agreed with me. "Good point, love," he said and squeezed my shoulder.

"Let's go, Liz." Ianto turned back to the front. "Get some miles under us."

"Yup," she said and shuddered as she watched Rhys climb into the church van. "He'll be okay, won't he?"

"Rhys will do just fine, sweetheart," Ianto said. "Won't be his first time at this."

"Better be his last," I muttered. "I hate this."

"Keira?" Tucker whispered. "Niko . . ."

"I'm here," I said quietly as I joined the two of them in the rear seat. "Here, Niko, drink." I extended my bare wrist. Niko's head lolled as he tried to gather strength.

"He's too weak, Keira," Ianto said. "You'll have to—"

"Do it for him, I know." I smiled as I recalled the first and only other time I'd done this. Except last time, Niko had bitten my arm so I could offer the then-dying Adam my blood. "Ianto, switch on the light, please?" He complied. I concentrated a moment, focusing on my mouth, my teeth, moving the cells around, the shape of the incisors lengthening, pointing, honing to needle sharp.

Ianto whistled. "Damn, woman, you're good."

I grinned, my newly sharp fangs prominent over my

bottom lip. "Why yes, my dear brother." I sank my own teeth into my wrist, bracing myself for the pain. "Fuck," I exclaimed. "That hurt. Here, Niko, now." I held out my arm again as I let my teeth shrink back to their natural shape.

Niko sniffed, and with both Tucker and me holding his head, he drank. Energy slammed into me, pleasure, a rush of dizziness accompanied by a near orgasmic sense of well-being. It came across as taste/scent/touch. Niko's aura tasted different from Adam's, smoky and green, like tea or something woodsy. Damn vampire's been around Tucker too long, I thought. After a few minutes, Niko began to truly revive, his energy stronger, his aura lighter, less weighed down.

"Help support Tucker," I said to him. My brother sagged against Niko, his own energy spent. "What the two of you need is rest," I said. "Sleep."

"Thank you, my liege." Niko bowed his head in my direction. "You didn't have to do that."

"Yes, I actually did," I said. "You're as much my responsibility as being my Protector, Nicholas Marlowe. A good leader, a good liege will support her people as they support her."

Tucker gave a wan smile, light-years away from his usual energy-filled, charming grin. "You have grown up, little sister." He groaned as the van took a curve too fast, pressing him into Niko's arm. "Hold tight, Tucker," I said. "Let me try to at least stabilize you."

I put my hands on my brother's face, closed my eyes, and rested my forehead on his. Niko, on his other side, now restored, let Tucker lean against him. "I'll need your help, Niko," I whispered. "Put your hands over mine." He did, and immediately the cool magickal living energy that was vampire flooded me. I wove his energy with mine and pushed. Tucker's shields were down to nothing more than a flimsy, rotted shell, crumbling beneath my beneficial assault. All throughout him lay pools of dull red pulses, torn flesh trying to mend with little energy. I visualized golden light, white around the edges, filling him, restoring him. I didn't think I could give him back the blood he'd lost, but I could probably slow the hurt, reduce the pain. I couldn't dare try to remove any bullets or bullet fragments, or even to heal the torn tissue. This was just a stopgap until Isabel could go further.

I watched almost outside myself as our combined energies, Niko's pale green and my golden-white, mingled and swirled, surrounding the damaged areas, pushing against the intruding metal, reducing the pulsating angry red to a much safer orangey-pink. With a final general sweep of his body, I kissed his forehead, then a light peck on his lips before I, too, sagged back, letting my body rest against the seat arm.

"That should do it," I whispered.

Tucker shuddered and with a surprised glance, swept me into a bear hug. "By all the gods," he whispered. "You fixed me."

I nodded into his shoulder. "Well, not completely. Enough so Isabel can help finish up. She's still going to have to get that metal out of you."

Tucker took my face between both his hands and stared into my eyes. "No, Keira," he said. "No need for Isabel. I'm done."

"What?" I peered into his gaze, letting my consciousness slide behind his eyes again, inside him. Not a single sign of damage remained. He was right. I *had* healed him. No sign of raw angry wounds, no sign of intrusive metal fragments. No torn blood vessels. Just healthy, solid muscles, all the veins and arteries doing their assigned tasks. I sagged back against the car seat, stunned. How the hell had I done this?

"Damn, Keira," Ianto said. "You don't know your own strength."

"Evidently not," I said. "Honestly, all I got taught while I was gone in regards to healing was just simple field spells to hold things together until a real healer could do their magick. I couldn't even heal Gregor from that pesky bullet graze."

"You're a quick study?" Niko ventured.

I snorted. "Doubtful. Maybe it was our relationship?" I was totally guessing.

Tucker looked thoughtful. "Blood will out," he ventured. "Perhaps you are right—it's our connection, our common blood tie."

"That explanation will do for now," I said. "I'll talk to Isabel about it when she gets here. After she fixes Luka up."

"You are the heir," Rhys said. "Could be you're just getting better at these things."

"Not at keeping you from harm," I said to Tucker and Niko. "I am so sorry. I had no—"

"Hush." Tucker crushed me in a hug again. "None of us knew. It was not your fault."

I nodded and let him keep holding on to me.

"We're here," Liz said and turned into Adam's circular drive. I hadn't even noticed we were this close.

"Now for the reckoning," I said.

"Reckoning?" Adam asked.

"Marcus." I stared out the window of the van. "Adam, we can't leave him to lead anymore. Lev's dead, Jacob will most likely be going back to the Redwolf pack, and that leaves Marcus with his sixteen-year-old successor, Gregor. This group is liable to disintegrate even further if we leave things be."

"Your plan?"

"The only thing I can think of is to ask one of the other packs in our territory to take them in, or split them up or something. Until Gregor is old enough to lead his own pack . . ."

"That seems to be a valid solution," Adam agreed.

"It's the only way," Tucker said. "Marcus is no leader."

"Fine. Tucker, you know the packs in the Southwest; when we get inside, could you make a few calls? I'm sure they're each sending a representative or two to the reception."

"Will do."

I started to open the car door when Liz stopped me. "Keira, how about Bea?"

"Damn it." I settled back into the seat. "Does she know about Lev yet?"

Liz nodded. "Dixxi phoned her from the hospital. Bea's here, you know."

"Here? At Adam's?"

"You did want us to bring her to safety," Ianto reminded me.

Oh yeah, that seemed like ages ago instead of only a few hours.

"She's inside, then." I mentally girded my loins and slid open the van door. "Well, here goes nothing."

CHAPTER FORTY-TWO

Bea and Mark were sitting next to each other on one of Adam's couches. Of course it was the one facing the front hallway. I paused in the foyer, taking a deep breath to catch my nerve. I'd just faced down a number of men setting out to kill me, helped kill several of them, and dealt with the consequences, but the thought of having to face my pregnant best friend made me quake. Adam stepped up behind me.

"The others are going over to Niko's for a bit," he said. "Giving us a little time and space."

"Thanks," I whispered back. "Any sign of Isabel?"

"They phoned about half an hour ago, according to my operator. They should be here in another hour or so."

"Once more, into the breach," I joked as I stepped forward into the living room.

Bea's head snapped up at my entry, her face streaked with old tears. She sprang from the couch and launched herself at me, enveloping me in a hug. "You're safe, you're safe," she said, over and over again.

I leaned into the hug and kissed the top of her head. "I'm fine, Bea. I'm really okay. C'mon, let's sit down."

Jessica came in from the kitchen, bearing a tray of

tea and various snacks. "I thought y'all might need some food," she said.

"Jess, you are a lifesaver," I groaned, looking at the laden tray. I'd just donated blood to Niko, lost all sorts of energy in a fight, and now that I was home, I realized I was this close to collapsing . . . which I did, onto the couch opposite Mark. "Bea, sit, eat. Sorry, but I'm pretty beat, I need food." Adam joined me on the couch. "You okay?" I asked him.

"Very well, thank you," he said. "You did the bulk of the work."

I chugged down the tea, grateful for its cold icy flavor. "This is excellent, Jess," I said, snagging a small roll stuffed with roast beef and slathered with dark mustard. "Good," I mumbled around a mouthful of food.

"Bea, if I might ask," Adam said as Bea sat back down. "I know this has been a very hard time for you lately and even harder now. Is there anything we can do?"

She sighed and shook her head, hands fluttering cautiously over her belly. "Thanks, Adam, I— Keira, you've been really tough on me lately, and I—"

"Sorry, I'm so sorry." I put my sandwich down, ready to go over there and hug her again, but she waved me off.

"No, you were right," she said. "I was just too freaked out, too stubborn to realize it." She gave a rueful chuckle. "Kind of stubborn, the two of us, huh?"

I chuckled back. "Yeah, kind of."

"When Dixxi told me about Lev, I nearly lost it. Here was this kind man, someone I'd liked enough to sleep with, get pregnant by, and he was dead. And I never told him."

Mark startled at this. "You're pregnant?"

I shot him an angry glare and he subsided. "Bea, go on," I urged.

"With everything happening, I wasn't sure what to do. So I kept thinking about what we'd discussed." She smiled at me, a tentative smile that didn't quite reach her eyes, but she was trying. "I've decided to have this baby, then let the pack raise it."

Mark's eyes lit up at this, but Bea's next remark deflated him.

"Not your pack, Mark, sorry," she said. "The baby will be fostered out to a strong pack. Jacob promised to help me find the right place."

I sighed in relief. "That's great, Bea," I said. "I'm happy you've found a solution you can live with."

"I can't raise the baby myself," she explained. "Much as I might think I'd like to, I'm not the mom sort. Plus, I have no idea what to do with a half wolf."

"Did you talk to Dixxi about the genetic situation?" Adam asked gently.

"I did," she said. "I'm strong, we've got no reason to believe any of those markers are in my blood, so Dixxi thinks I can chance this. Since your aunt Isabel's coming, she could check things out like you said. Maybe it'll change my mind, but Dixxi thinks my chances are pretty good that things are okay."

"I've offered her a place here," Adam said to my surprise.

"You did?" I asked.

He nodded. "We've got plenty of room here for a lab," he said. "I can bring over some of my own researchers from England and they can work together." I didn't mention the researchers were free because the blood substitute experiment hadn't worked. "She accepted."

Mark let out a growl. "So you've suborned my sister, my brother's dead, and you don't think I'm capable of leading my pack. Now what?"

I exchanged glances with Adam. "Now, I propose that you and your pack find a home with another pack," I said. "I—we—can't have you here, Marcus. You're a danger to all of us in the area."

He stood and paced. "Dangerous? I thought I was just weak?"

I stood to face him as he turned back and paced in my direction. "That's exactly why," I answered. "Your inability to lead your pack, to keep them safe and hidden, endangered my people, my family. I had to kill on your behalf, Marcus Ashkarian. I lay those souls at your feet."

He glared at me, amber eyes darkening, unleashing his energy. It surrounded me, pushed against me. I stood my ground. Now that I knew him, knew his power was only a façade, only sexual in nature and not true strength, I was ready for it. He pushed harder, energy flaring, swirling. I simply stood and let it surround me, failing to faze me. After a few minutes, he subsided and sank back onto the couch. "You're no longer affected."

"No, nor would I have been before had I been smart enough to really analyze the energy," I said. "Accept this, Mark, you'll be happier not leading a pack. Let someone else be the leader. Take Gregor, Luka, the rest of your people and live a happy, safe life under a true Fenrir."

He winced at that last, knowing I was telling nothing but truth. "Where can we go?"

"Tucker is making some calls now," I said. "There are a few options. In the meantime, you can stay here at the inn, along with Gregor. Close up the deli. We'll buy the place from you." I was shooting out ideas as they came into my head. "Give you enough start-up money to go elsewhere and not be beholden to anyone."

Marcus stared at me with enormous eyes, anger warring with resignation. Bea laid a hand on his arm. "Marcus, do this, for me, for Lev. Start over." She spoke in a quiet, calm voice. "There's no point in anger and hatred. That's what led to this." He turned to her, a petite, beautiful woman whose face had settled into serenity. Bea had accepted her fate, had made her decisions. Now it was Mark's turn.

"Well, then," he said, "I suppose I have little choice."

"There's always a choice," Bea said. "Always. Keira is offering you a good one. Take it."

His mouth twisted and slowly, he nodded. "All right, then," he said. "I'll go. But first, Luka needs to be healed. Your healer is coming, right?"

"She is," I said. "What's his condition?"

"Critical," he said. "He's still in the emergency clinic. I wouldn't give them permission to move him."

"Stable?"

"For now. Mary, one of the pack women, is with him."

"And Jacob?"

"Also stable. He's sleeping in the study. Dixxi came back and is sitting with him."

Adam took my hand. "Perhaps you could do the honors, work on Luka first?" he said. "You did heal Tucker."

"Could you?" Mark asked. "The place is only a half hour's drive from here."

"I'll give it my best shot," I said, trying to project assurance. Except I was less than sure. I think Tucker had it right: I'd healed my brother, but he was Kelly, near immortal, used to fighting, wounds, and healing. Luka was a child, a werewolf with many human genes. Mortal. "I'll get started. If Jacob's stable, we can concentrate on Luka. Send Isabel as soon as—"

"There's no need." Dixxi walked into the room from

the direction of the study. Tears flowed down her cheeks.
"Mary just called me. Luka died twenty minutes ago. I
called Jacob's captain to get his body released without
an autopsy. He managed it somehow. Mary's bringing
Luka's body home."

I slumped against Adam and buried my face in his
neck. Luka, that bright, beautiful boy, so much potential,
so much life inside him, snuffed out by hatred.

Dixxi crossed the room and snagged both Bea and
Mark into a hug. Silence reigned for several minutes as
we each grieved in our own ways. Adam stroked my hair,
murmuring soft words. I sank into his comfort, so very
tired now. Tired of fighting, tired of the hatred, tired of
everything that made humans—made anyone—want to
hurt others simply because they were different.

Eventually, Dixxi stood and wiped her face. "John,
your day manager, gave me a house," she told Adam. "A
house."

He nodded. "Yes, it's yours for as long as you wish
to stay. My researchers will be here in a few days, after
our reception, to help you set up a lab. In the meantime,
feel free to order whatever you need in the way of clothing, food, whatever. Just tell John or have him give you
a credit card to order it online." He faced Marcus, giving
him a regal nod. "Fenrir, we will make any arrangements
you may wish for burial. We've a cemetery on our land.
I believe it's for the best not to do this through normal
channels."

Mark said nothing.

"Thank you," Dixxi said simply. "We appreciate your
help." She turned to her brother. "Marcus, come. You'll
stay with me tonight. We'll can talk about the funerals.
Bea, you come along, too. Sleep here and I'll drive you
home in the morning."

The two of them rose and followed Dixxi out. Bea stopped briefly at my side, leaned over, and gave me a kiss on the forehead. "Thanks, *chica*. I'll call you." I nodded and let her go.

"I don't know about you, love," Adam said, "but I could sleep for a week." He glanced at the mantelpiece clock. "It's only ten," he said. "Isabel should be arriving any minute."

I stifled a yawn. "Fine, good." I scrubbed my face with my hands, the exhaustion seeping over me, a heavy blanket sapping my energy. "How stable is Jacob?" I asked.

Adam studied me for a moment. "Stable enough. I'll have Jess take Isabel to him as soon as she arrives."

I nodded and mumbled around a yawn. "Sleep?"

Adam picked up the phone and dialed Jess, who stayed in a small house next door to us. I hadn't seen her leave, but I supposed Adam had. He gave her quick instructions and then hung up.

"Let's off to bed, my love. We've got a reception to attend in a few days."

CHAPTER FORTY-THREE

"STOP, YOU'RE PINCHING ME," I complained. Jess and Liz were helping me with my gown. "I don't know how I let y'all talk me into this. I'm not a gown kind of person."

Liz laughed. "No kidding, tell me another one." She pushed at my shoulder and bent to lace up the side seam. "Hold still, damn it."

"Be nice, you. I'm your liege lady."

"You'll be my very underdressed liege lady unless you hold still," Liz muttered. "Damn it, Keira, let me finish lacing this."

I grumbled and let my hands fall onto Jess's shoulders. Liz quickly did up the side lacings and moved to my other side to do up those. "There, that's done." She stepped back and gave me the once-over. "Gorgeous. What do you think, Jess?"

Jess grinned, showing a bit of fang. "Brilliant," she said. "That color suits you."

"Any color suits you, dear," Isabel piped up. She was sitting in a comfortable armchair next to the mirror, watching me. "You tend to dress in such drab shades. I like this on you."

The dress was a brilliant shade of royal blue-purple,

some sort of heavy silk material sewed in a way that it conformed to and enhanced my body, while still swirling around my thighs, calves, and ankles. Underneath it, I wore a light silk chemise, silk stockings, and slippers, the very epitome of a Faery princess and about as opposite my true self as I could get without going all-out Fifth Avenue. "I don't understand why I just couldn't wear a simple black dress if I needed to wear a dress at all," I grumbled. "Isn't this a little overkill?"

"It's all about presentation," Liz said. "You're about to be presented as the Kelly heir, a Sidhe princess, co-ruler of the Southwest region. A plain black dress, even from Nordstrom or Neiman's, wouldn't have fit the bill."

"Instead, I have to be all medieval Barbie," I grumbled.

"If you say so," Liz said absently as she fiddled with my hair. Instead of the usual neat braid, she'd done something to it that made it curl and twist into a tail, weaving strands of pearls and crystals into it. It was pulled back from my face, emphasizing my widow's peak, then draped over my right shoulder. On my head, she placed a simple coronet made of twisted silver wire, with draped pearls and crystals falling onto my hair from the head-piece. The pendant from the coronet fell to the middle of my forehead; its center a circle with a crescent moon and the outline of Texas in the middle, claw marks slashed through the state's shape. A single ruby hung from the bottom, representing a drop of blood. The coronet's symbol was my own, my Mark, merging the Wild Moon's logo with my own legend, a Mark to be given today to those of my blood, my Protectors. I took a huge breath. For them, for Adam, I would do this. I'd get through this day as best I could, dressed up like a doll, and play the regal heir.

AN HOUR later, I wasn't so sanguine about the whole thing. Rhys, who'd rushed to my side and started babbling about something, I totally ignored, as I was too focused on the ritual I needed to remember. "Later, Rhys," I mumbled, and with that, I took Adam's hand and entered the hall. It was just dusk, the lowering Texas sun red-orange at the horizon, its rays limning the special leaded crystal in the windows. The hall itself was lit with torches and candlelight. Tonight, we kept to the old traditions. What seemed to be hundreds of bodies lined the room, each dressed in their most regal costumes, fit to present themselves before royalty—which, damn it, we were. I'd promised myself to take this as seriously as it needed to be taken and no further.

Adam and I settled into our chairs. Not thrones, exactly, but regal and made comfortable by a handy spell Isabel taught me. At our sides stood Tucker and Niko, behind them, Rhys and Ianto. Liz, Isabel, and Dixxi sat in chairs to our left.

Before we began the meet and greet, we needed to perform two rituals.

I called to Jess and Lance, our assistants, to bring up the cup of bonding. They were both dressed in flowing black, Jess in a dress, Lance in a tunic. I tried to hide my amusement. They were both so careful to keep their solemnity. Jess winked at me as she handed me the silver chalice. Lance, with a bow, presented a small elaborate knife.

"My brothers, my Protectors, please come forth." My voice rang in the room, as if there were no bodies to soak up the sound. Great, someone had cast an acoustics spell.

The four men knelt before me, baring their right forearms. I took the small knife and nicked my wrist, letting four drops of blood fall into the cup. "Drink." I handed the cup to Tucker, who drank. It was wine laced with a few herbs and now a few drops of blood. A symbol and a bonding much less bloody than olden days, when each Protector had to drink a full goblet of the ruler's blood. Not that Niko would mind. I'd nixed that and gone with the lesser option. It still held the same magicks and cost me less plasma.

As Tucker passed the cup to Niko, I grasped my brother's forearm with my right hand, palm to skin. "As you protect me, I shall protect you." The ritual words accompanied a pulse of energy. When I lifted my hand, my Mark appeared on Tucker's skin. Like the silver carved symbol on my coronet, but this one in blood red. Tucker kissed my hand, repeating the words. A rush of energy—so intense it was nearly visible to the naked eye—joined us. I smiled at my brother and turned to Niko, repeating the ritual. He grinned and, as he kissed my hand, licked up a drop of blood that had dripped there. I shook my head ruefully. Niko would always be Niko. Then on to Rhys and Ianto, twins of soul and bonded by their birth; their protection would be almost more to me than the others'.

When we finished, Adam stepped down, took each man's face in his hands, and placed a kiss on each set of lips. "My brothers, my Protectors. As you protect my heart, I shall protect you." The men bowed their heads and Adam stepped back onto the dais.

Tucker and Niko rose and returned to their places, Niko by my side, Tucker by Adam's. Liz then stood up and joined the twins, kneeling in between them. She'd dressed in a deep green frock, similar in cut to my own but much simpler. Her bright red hair was pulled back into a braid, small seed pearls woven into it. The three joined hands, forming a loose circle. As they did so, I took a second cup from Jess's hand, this one containing wine and drops of each of their blood, collected before we entered the hall. "Liz, Rhys, Ianto," I intoned, "brothers of my blood, cousin of my blood, you wish to enter a full blood bond?"

"We do," they answered in unison.

"Then let it be so," I said and handed Rhys the cup. "Drink and share your blood, as your lives will be shared with each other."

The three passed the cup, drank deeply, and when done, returned it to me. I drank the last sip, binding them to me and, through me, to Adam. "Rise, my brothers, my sister."

Rhys and Ianto rose and returned to their positions behind us, Liz to her seat.

Lance stepped forward, the very picture of a courtier, and spoke. "Now we shall greet our peoples." With a bow, he stepped back and they began to come up, one, two, four at a time, representatives from all over the supernatural Southwest.

Three hours later, I was about to tear my hair out with the boredom. Sure, I knew this had to be done, but an ongoing parade of dryads, nymphs, water sprites from cave lakes, a few were Clans—mostly coyotes—from New Mexico, various fey and half fey. Even Old Joe showed up, resplendent in a dark suit.

He approached us, a beautiful crystal bell in his hands. "My lady. My lord." He bowed from his waist, both hands still cradling the bell. "From my people to yours."

"Joe?" I asked, my question both tentative and perplexed.

"Miss Keira," he replied, deep voice full in power and strength. "After you left that day, I got to thinking. I asked around, dug up some records, and discovered where I'd been found."

"A cave?" I ventured.

"Yes," he said. "Near White Rock, near the rock itself, actually. So I went there and sat. When night fell, they came. My people."

Adam looked at me with questions written all over his face. "Later," I murmured.

"You're going with them?"

Joe nodded. "I am. In thanks for finding me, and leading me to them, they sent this. If you ever have need of us, ring it. We will come."

I took the bell from him, holding it in two hands as he had. Power thrummed through it. "We thank you, Joe, you and your people."

The old man nodded and bowed again, then vanished into the crowd. I smiled. *Not bad, Keira,* I thought, reuniting an old changeling with his Clan. Too many of the lesser fey got lost that way in years past, mostly in the old country. Leaving changelings, taking human children in their place. Sometimes, they forgot to retrieve their own.

A young man was next in the rota. Dark hair and light eyes, pale skin placed him as either a lesser fey or Sidhe. I shielded hard as Sidhe energy reached me. Damn it. Adam gripped my hand.

"Eamonn," Adam said, voice neutral.

"Aeddan." The young Sidhe bowed and grinned at Adam, calling him by the Welsh version of his name. "I am here to wish you and your lady well on behalf of our liege, your father."

"Welcome, Eamonn," I recited, the words now automatic, a part of the ceremony. They came, they bowed and sometimes brought gifts. We welcomed them. Some pledged fealty and allegiance, others just acknowledged us. This was an ancient courtly ritual dance of words and action. Eamonn straightened, in preparation to—no, he wasn't leaving. What the . . . ?

He open his arms, a ritual gesture again. "My lord. My lady. I crave a boon."

"Speak then." Adam kept his surprise hidden, but I felt it just the same. I knew he was taken aback by Eamonn's words. These actions were not in the script.

"I bring a request from your father, your family to present themselves."

"Drystan is here?" I said quietly. "Why?"

"My lady, he wishes no harm, no ill will toward you. He and his party only wish to be recognized. M'lord Drystan and his other son wish to rejoice with you on your bonding."

Wait—Gideon was here, too? "No ill will, my ass," I whispered. "Gideon's shown me nothing but that since we broke up."

Adam smiled at me. "My love, there is no reason to ignore them. We can take the high road on this. My father has done nothing ill toward us."

"Well, Gideon can fucking well take the road and keep right on going. Adam, your father is welcome, but his other son is not."

"Keira," Adam said in a low voice so as not to be overheard. "We cannot allow one without the other. Gideon can do nothing to you here. You are surrounded by our Protectors. You have the advantage of home ground."

"Damn it, you always have to be rational."

"Not when it comes to my brother and your former lover," he said. "But we cannot be seen to be childish in front of the Clans."

I gave him a wordless growl, then acquiesced. "So be it then, but if he tries anything . . ."

"Then blast away, my love," Adam said, amused at my ire.

I gave the young Sidhe a nod. He bowed and exited. Less than a minute later Drystan entered, his bearing mighty, his face with a grin the size of the Rio Grande, beaming at me. "Welcome to our family, dearest Keira." He approached me with arms held out wide. "May I?"

I sighed and nodded. I rose and he swept me into an unexpected hug. "Welcome, my dear, indeed."

Before I could resettle myself, my "spideysense" pinged. Gideon. In an echo of his father's pompous entrance, he swept in, dressed to the nines, if your nines equaled what was top of the line Underhill. Dark gray cloak, black tunic embroidered with the finest of silver threads. Too bad his gear could never outshine Adam's simple yet elegant plain black. Adam wore his majesty as comfortably and easily as his own skin, hundreds of years of being the Unseelie prince and heir, then vampire king. Gideon's relatively new royalty fit like a prêt-à-porter suit, well tailored but not truly a part of him.

"My lady, a boon?" His light eyes stared directly at mine, catching my gaze and holding it. I barely paid attention to the various other Sidhe who entered, probably Gideon's retinue.

"What do you want, Gideon?"

"A small request, something you can easily grant." He bowed, a showy formal sweeping bow that only served to reflect his youth. I thought I was carrying this off fairly well; Gideon just seemed to be playacting. "I request to set up my court in the hollow hills of Texas, my home for many years. There is a cave—"

"No fucking way." I stood up, but before I could sweep down the steps, Adam grabbed my arm. "He has no right to this land," I protested. "No right to that cave, nor that entrance to Faery."

"But my dear girl," Gideon said as he bowed deeply, a smirk on his face. "I absolutely do have a right."

"How's that?" I challenged.

"By right of primogeniture, of course."

"Sorry, bud, that just won't fly with me. You may be a few months older than me, but our Clan leader gave me this territory. Gigi's call, not mine . . . and from what she last said of you, I doubt you'll get a clod of dirt from her, much less the caves."

"Oh, you misunderstand, I'm not speaking of Kelly blood but fey blood. The land belongs to Faery, and right to a piece of this should, by law, belong to the eldest."

"Still screwed. Adam is the eldest son and, so far, not disinherited." I shot a look at Drystan, who seemed as puzzled as I was. He shook his head at Gideon. Heartened, I continued. "These lands, if you wish to claim for Faery at all, belong to my family, the Seelie Court, my aunt's blood, not Unseelie."

Gideon rose from his bow and gave me the smirk that ate Texas. "Exactly, my dear cousin, exactly." With a flourish, he threw a hand out to one of the women in his entourage. "I would like to introduce my bride." As she stepped out from behind one of the taller men, I gasped. She was blond, fair of skin, with clear gray-blue eyes. Her beauty, had it been in the sky, would outshine the moon and many of the stars. She stood tall and proud, her grace surrounding her like an ermine cloak . . . and she was very, very pregnant.

"May I present Aoife ferch Angharad, the Seelie queen's daughter and heir."

In the stunned silence that followed Gideon's announcement, another, smaller woman, her hair dark as mine, eyes as gray, stepped forward. She carried herself with dignity and grace, her pointed face blank of all expression. She moved from behind Gideon and Aoife, tilted her dainty chin upward, and stared me straight in the eyes. As her face, blank of any readable expression, registered, I sank into my chair and began trembling.

"Mother?"

Her face still as the lake in the doldrums of summer, she handed me a rolled parchment. "We claim the right of Challenge."

I leaned back into my chair as the words sank in. Adam stood, frozen in place. Gideon, his wife, and my own mother were officially claiming the right to challenge us for our land.

They'd just declared war.

Desire is stronger after dark...
Bestselling Urban Fantasy from Pocket Books!

Bad to the Bone
JERI SMITH-READY
Rock 'n' Roll will never die. Just like vampires.

Master of None
SONYA BATEMAN
Nobody ever dreamed of a genie like this...

Spider's Bite
An Elemental Assassin Book
JENNIFER ESTEP.
Her love life is killer.

Necking
CHRIS SALVATORE
Dating a Vampire is going to be the death of her.
